Night's
Rose

Night's Rose

ANNALIESE EVANS

TOR®

paranormal romance

A TOM DOHERTY ASSOCIATES BOOK
NEW YORK

This is a work of fiction. All the characters, organizations, and events portrayed in this novel are products of the author's imagination or are used fictitiously.

NIGHT'S ROSE

Copyright © 2009 by Annaliese Evans

A Tor Book
Published by Tom Doherty Associates, LLC
175 Fifth Avenue
New York, NY 10010

www.tor-forge.com

Tor® is a registered trademark of Tom Doherty Associates, LLC.

ISBN-13: 978-0-7653-6166-0
ISBN-10: 0-7653-6166-3

First Edition: April 2009

Printed in the United States of America

0 9 8 7 6 5 4 3 2 1

This one is for the boys.

For Mike, my sweet, sexy, wonderful husband. What would I do without you?

For my two little princes, Riley and Logan. Riley, what a clever, sensitive, crazy little man you're growing to be. I couldn't be prouder and still love you more every day. Logan, I can't wait to meet you, buddy. If you're half as cute as your 3-D ultrasound pictures or half as feisty as my abused innards insist, you're bound to be a heartbreaker.

And for Bill, the best father a girl could have hoped for. I miss you every day, Dad.

ACKNOWLEDGMENTS

Thanks so much to all the people who have helped this book be born. To my husband, our two girls and our two boys for their unfailing support. I love you all so much and couldn't ask for a more wonderful family. To my mom and my former in-laws for helping me find the time to write, and never doubting that I could do this. To my critique partner, Stacia Kane, the best friend I've never met face-to-face. To my agent, Caren Johnson, who is always there no matter the hour. To Heather Osborn and all the people at Tor for believing in this project. And to Anna J. Evans, without whom this book just wouldn't be.

In the meanwhile, all the faeries of the day and night gave their gifts to the infant princess. The old faerie's turn came next. With a head shaking more with spite than age, she said that the princess should have her hand pierced with a spindle and sleep as dead for one hundred years. The terrible gift made the company tremble, and all fell a-crying.

— THE SLEEPING BEAUTY,
CHARLES PERRAULT

Once upon a time there was a princess who slept eighty years away, and awoke to find none she had known among the living and her body violated while she walked the gray mists of enchantment. This is not her story. This is my story. I am the one called Briar Rose, the woman of many thorns.

—ROSEMARIE EDENBERG

Night's
Rose

CHAPTER ONE

February 6, 1750
Westinghouse Manor
Bedfordshire, England

"Comtesse de Fournier? Is that you, my lady?" The voice held not the slightest edge of fear, confirming Rose's suspicions. Sir Walter Pithwater knew little of the history of his people. Tonight, that shameful gap in his education would hasten his journey to the grave.

Rose crept slowly through the garden's maze, grateful the hedges had yet to reach their full height. Pithwater was clearly visible above the top of the shrubbery, his bald head gleaming in the moonlight, while her own figure remained concealed. True, she was barely five feet and two in her heeled slippers—but even Lord Drummand, the host of the country party and a man close to six feet, would be largely concealed. The people of the tribe were simply unusually tall, and Sir Walter was no exception.

It was one of the clues that had alerted her to the ogre's true nature, in addition to his monstrous appetite. A late-night venture down to the earl's kitchens confirmed her worst fears. The cook needed little prying to confess she worried the baronet would eat her employers out of house and home, forcing them to end their party early and disgrace themselves in front of many influential friends and members of Society.

The woman should have been more concerned about the ravenous guest eating her out of chambermaids and stable boys. Two of the household staff had gone missing in the past week. Rose doubted their bodies would ever be found. Ogres were unique among supernatural predators in that they ate the entirety of their victims—bones and all.

"Comtesse? Is that your delicate step I hear?" Pithwater called again, a suggestive lilt in his tone. "Come out, come out, my little rosebud."

Rose grimaced beneath the black hood concealing her powdered blond curls from the light of the moon. She had been christened Rosemarie, and allowed a select few to call her Rose, but had *never* been pleased with ridiculous pet names. Especially when they sprung from the mouth of a repulsive goat like Pithwater.

Still, she had no one but herself to blame.

She had led the man to believe she was penniless and in need of a protector, lest she follow in the footsteps of other impoverished women of standing who lived their lives in the shadows of polite society as courtesans. Nothing had been said outright, all communicated in hushed intimations as such things usually were, but Pithwater had taken the bait.

He'd invited her to the garden maze tonight for what she gathered was a trial of sorts, to see if she would please him as a mistress. The reward for his pleasure would be her own cottage near Marylebone Gardens and an allowance he had named generous, but which they both knew to be hundreds of pounds short of a livable sum. Not that the allowance was of any real consequence.

Rose knew what her fate would truly be—a few months in his bed and an eternity in his stomach. Ogres could never retain a human lover for long, no matter how fetching they found them. Their appetite for flesh always outweighed their desire for carnal pleasure.

"I see . . . You wish to play the fox and the rabbit, eh?" She heard Pithwater move through the maze, closer to her position. "But who will be the fox and who the rabbit?"

There was a question she would most happily answer. "I shall be the fox, Sir Walter."

"So it *is* you, my lady." The arousal was clear in his voice. Revulsion served to steady Rose's hand as she threw back her hood and reached between her shoulders for the handle of her blade. The sheath ran the length of her spine and under a dancing partner's hands felt like nothing more dangerous than the bones of her stays. "I would think a dear little thing like you would prefer to leave the foxing to those with more natural aptitude for the art."

"Shame, sir. 'Tis hardly noble to insult a lady's aptitude." Rose maintained an edge of coyness in her tone while increasing her volume, guiding Pithwater to her location.

The handle of her blade thickened and grew longer in her grasp, a result of the faerie magic that had created it. Rose braced herself for the killing blow, knowing she would need a clean cut if she hoped to fell him in one stroke. Unfortunately, there hadn't been time to change out of her evening gown after the formal dinner. As a result, she wouldn't be as sure on her feet.

In recent years, she had made a habit of dressing as a young boy on the evenings she hunted the members of the tribe. It was easier to move freely in male clothing. So much easier, in fact, she began to suspect feminine fashion a plot to keep females docile and submissive.

After all, how could one think on matters of country, estate, or Society, let alone debate them, when one could barely draw a breath unencumbered?

Of course, she *did* love the frock she was wearing, a pale blue and gray sateen with a pearl inlaid stomacher that had cost nearly as much as the "generous" yearly allowance she would have as Pithwater's mistress. It made her hope the man's blood wouldn't spray too madly. Ogre bloodstains were nearly impossible to remove.

"My dearest rosebud, I do not doubt your aptitude in the slightest. If that were the case, I most certainly would not have initiated such a . . ." Pithwater rounded the corner of the hedge, emerging not five feet from where she stood. His eyes, still sunken in his skull despite the human flesh he had consumed, widened at the sight of the sword in her hand. "My lady?"

"Your people call me Briar Rose. She of many thorns."

Rose closed the distance between them in seconds. Before the light of recognition in Sir Pithwater's eyes could translate into action, she had sliced him in half, a feat made easier by the fact that her raised arms were nearly level with his waist.

With a great wail, the baronet fell to the ground. His head and torso flew backward, arms still flailing mightily, while his hips and legs tipped forward, spraying blood and gore like a font.

"Blast," Rose cursed as the thick, black sludge splashed her dress and cape. She should have known better. He had fed on human flesh too recently to have a sluggish heartbeat.

Now blood coated not only her dress, but her gloves, cloak, and face as well. She swiped at her cheek, trying not to gag at the stench. Pithwater had been of the tribe; she had not been mistaken in that. His essence reeked of bile and rot.

But then, she had never been wrong, never drawn her sword to find out too late the creature she hunted was anything other than an abomination. That fact gave her comfort on nights when the violence of her work threatened to undo her. This, however, was not one of those nights. Other than the spray, Pithwater had been delightfully easy prey. Almost too easy. It left her with an "unfinished" feeling about the entire business.

Apparently, she wasn't the only one.

"Truly, Rose, could you have not let the man run a bit? Given him a few moments to plead for his wretched life? *Something*?" Gareth Barrows slunk from the darkness with a sigh, his footsteps as silent as the shadows themselves. "This was hardly worth the time it took to travel from the city."

"This isn't a game, Mr. Barrows. I make the kill to

accomplish the task, not for the sport of the matter." Rose sheathed her blade, her voice more sour than it might have been if she *hadn't* presently been covered in ogre blood. She had been attempting to be patient with her latest protégé, a vampire of nearly two hundred years who nevertheless seemed to have no more sense than a child.

He had volunteered his time to aid in controlling the ogre population of Great Britain, a far from magnanimous act as the exploding numbers of the tribe negatively affected his own hunting grounds. Still, volunteer or no, he could have brought more dedication to his training. In the fortnight since they had been introduced by her liaison among the Fey de la Nuit, he had failed to show for four of his seven assignments. He seemed to think a charming smile at their next meeting was sufficient apology for the time she wasted sending him endless communiqués, and that there was little he could learn about killing he hadn't mastered in his years as a creature of the night.

Irritatingly, the rascal was usually correct on the last account.

"I see you've neglected to bring a weapon, yet again. Must I remind you, Mr. Barrows, that supernatural strength and a pair of sharp teeth will not—"

"Not another lecture on the reasons I shouldn't play with my food, dearest. I don't think I could bear that particular discussion again after such a dreary night," he sighed, smoothing a hand over the dark brown hair tied at the nape of his neck.

Rose had never seen him without a wig before and some foolish part of her wished the moonlight were brighter, for she suspected he looked quite fine. In over a hundred years of working with breathtaking vampires, she had never allowed a professional relationship to become anything more, but that didn't mean she couldn't enjoy a pleasant view.

"I couldn't care less what you do with your food, sir, only with the ogres who will be your prey," Rose said, blushing a bit in spite of herself. "Remember, Mr. Barrows, never—"

"Ingest the blood of an ogre. I understood that directive the first twelve times. As if I would be foolish enough to sink my teeth into anything so rancid." His green eyes shone like a cat's, catching unseen light and flaring in the darkness. He moved closer and Rose did her best to appear unaffected. Gareth was not certain of her origins, and she meant to keep it that way. "In addition, I'm fairly certain strength alone *will* be sufficient. I've killed many a mortal scoundrel with nothing more than my bare hands."

"But did you rip their body in two, top cleanly separated from the bottom?" she asked, refusing to retreat when he moved so close she could feel the heat of his body. He had fed, and very recently if the flush in his cheeks was any clue.

"No, I've never ripped anyone asunder." His hands moved to her waist. Rose managed—just barely—not to flinch at the contact. "But I imagine I could accomplish the business without the aid of a weapon."

His large hands encircled her waist and squeezed none too gently. Rose sucked in a surprised breath, more from the unexpected heat curling low in her belly than from any real fear. Of course, Gareth had no idea she was simply a mortal, though gifted by the Fey de la Nuit. He might assume she could take more damage than was safe.

"Please," she said, not trusting herself to look him in the eye a moment longer. It had been far too long since she'd had a companion of any sort, but especially *that* sort, and her body was aching to betray her.

"Please what, Rose?" His warm breath puffed against the top of her head and she fought the desire to lift her face and find the source of that breath with her mouth. "You are a beautiful woman, you must know that. But for all your beauty you act as if—"

"Wait," Rose whispered, turning to search the shadows. She was certain she had heard a sound, but now all was quiet. She tried to pull away, but Gareth held her fast.

"I won't wait. I'm dying of curiosity. We all are. They've taken bets at my club—"

"Down!" Rose threw her weight to the right, but her strength was not sufficient to move them both out of danger. The ogre diving toward them caught Gareth's cloak in his hands, and took the vampire to the ground.

"Damnation!" Rose scrambled to her feet, throwing off her cape as she reached for her blade. But before she could grasp the handle, she was hit from behind and went tumbling back to the earth.

"Such coarse language," a homely, black-haired female of the tribe hissed as Rose closed her hands around the ogress's throat. She lacked the strength to choke the other woman, but she at least hoped to keep the creature's teeth from her flesh. "But you aren't truly a comtesse at all, are you, *Briar Rose*?"

She lunged forward with a snarl just as Rose relaxed her arms and shifted to the right. The ogress howled as her face connected with the muddy earth and Rose—via pure force of will and with no help from her blasted hoops and heavy skirts—rolled atop her. Rose was reaching for her blade a second time when a hand fisted in her hair and pulled her backward.

She screamed as she was dragged several feet, cursing her aversion to wigs. If she had worn one this evening she might have freed herself without having hair pulled out by the root. Still, better no hair than no flesh.

Rose dug her hands into the dirt and jerked her neck forward, crying out as a fistful of blond locks remained behind in her would-be captor's hands.

"Behind you, Rose!" She was scrambling to her feet yet again, but at Gareth's shout rolled back to the ground, only daring to stand when she had put several feet between herself and the scuffle taking place at the center of the maze.

"Dear God," she breathed as she finally managed to free her blade. Now that she had a clear look at what she and Gareth were pitted against, she wondered if one blade would be enough.

The first three ogres had been joined by two more, and from the sounds echoing through the night air, they would soon be welcoming even more company. There was no longer any doubt. Pithwater—whether he'd been aware of it or not—had been bait, a lure to get Rose to the maze, far from the house where the humans slept and even farther from the dark faeries who would have come to her aid in any parish in

England. After nearly a hundred years the ogres had grown bold, or else she had grown careless.

Whichever the case, she would soon see if she would walk free of this dark garden, or if Lord and Lady Drummand would be missing more than one guest come morning.

"Presumably they will be more troubled by my absence than that of the chambermaid or stable boy," Rose muttered before she raised her sword and threw herself into the fray.

CHAPTER TWO

Thick, black blood spattered onto Rose's face as she hacked at the ogres who had the poor judgment to advance toward her. Her sword became a blur, her arms burning with exertion as she dipped and swung, managing to slice most of the creatures in two.

Some, however, were only maimed. She could see them limping away, screaming as they fled, dragging arms or legs they would be able to reattach given time and the opportunity to feed upon human flesh.

"Damn you to the gates of hell!" One of the tribe howled the battle cry as he ran toward her, his sword gripped tightly and a look of hatred twisting his gaunt features.

"Not today, sir," Rose gasped, leaping into the air to avoid his clumsy jab and slicing his head from his body. Upon landing, another slice caught him at his waist, ensuring he wouldn't be returning to battle another day.

She had learned the futility of defending her actions to members of the tribe long ago. No matter how many humans they ate, or the number of their own children they ground up to feed to larger, stronger young, they would never see themselves as anything other than innocent victims persecuted by a pale, blond woman with a faerie sword.

Perhaps they were correct in their assumption. Perhaps one day she would pass from her mortal life and journey down to the fires of hell. But one thing was for certain: she would dispatch many of their kind to the flames before her.

"Curse you! Let the dark one take you." The woman who had led the attack spat in Rose's direction as she scooped the fallen man's head from the ground with her remaining arm.

There were tears in her eyes as she scuttled away into the depths of the maze, telling Rose the man must have been kin. If she wanted his head for a death ceremony, he was not merely a fallen comrade. Ogres could only produce children with humans—and usually consumed their spouses not long after the birth of their babes—but they were fiercely loyal to their ogre family and believed passionately in their right to a proper tribe burial.

Rose had caught more than one ogre by holding a loved one's head in her quarters as a lure. A revolting tactic, but an undeniably effective one.

"Darkness take the Briar Rose!"

"Death comes for the scourge of the tribe!"

Other curses filled the air as more ogres rushed forward, taking up the battle where their fallen or injured brothers and sisters had left off.

"I didn't realize ogres were particularly pious."
Gareth appeared at Rose's side, reaching down to
the tops of his leather boots and pulling out two
thin faerie blades that immediately began to grow
in size.

So he hadn't arrived unarmed after all. Interesting.

"Stay as you are!" Rose jabbed her sword into
the heart of the ogre looming behind Gareth even as
he spun on his heel, cutting the creature in half at the
knee. Upon regaining his balance, the vampire lunged
forward, striking the fallen ogre at the waist, ensuring
his death.

"I've done you a favor, sir. That waistcoat was
hideous," Gareth said, spitting a wealth of black rot
onto the ground beside the body.

"Gareth, you didn't feed—"

"Simply gnawed upon the lady a bit, as I was unable to reach my weaponry." He growled at an ogre
who rushed forward—a look that transformed his
usually pleasant expression into something feral—
and swung his swords with a swiftness that made the
blades sing through the air.

"Don't swallow," Rose said, grunting as she sliced
through a stubborn bit of bone. "It is toxic, even to
vampires. It will—"

"Dispense with the pleasantries when you're trying to kill things, Rose."

"I was simply trying to—" Rose hacked and
sliced, wincing as more blood sprayed into her eyes.
"—ascertain you didn't—" She and Gareth ran forward, catching two ogres in midflight, slipping on the
oily mire coating the ground. "—do something fatally
stupid—" Back to back, the pair spun in a circle,

swords raised, on the lookout for more attackers. "—before I had the chance to warn you properly."

Rose stood absolutely still, straining to hear from which direction the tribe would attack next. But the maze was quiet, nothing but the sound of her harshly indrawn breaths filling the night air.

"Fatally stupid? Rather than *ordinarily* stupid, I suppose?" The rumble of Gareth's laughter vibrated against her back, bringing a smile to her lips.

"They are your words, Mr. Barrows, not mine." Rose laughed, then gasped as he spun about, trapping her in the circle of his arms. Their swords clanged together with a bright metallic sound as he bent to whisper in her ear.

"Not Mr. Barrows again. I finally had you calling me Gareth."

"Let me go, sir. There are—"

"Sir? Now I merit no more than a '*sir*'?"

"Gareth, we are in the midst of—"

"We're in the midst of nothing. They are gone, fleeing posthaste. I can hear the pitter-patter of their little feet scampering away from the fearsome Briar Rose." His breath was hot on her neck, but strangely it sent a shiver through her, and her pulse raced even faster. "That's what they called you, was it not?"

First the battle and now a wall of muscular vampire pressed against her. Rose wasn't sure her heart could bear the strain. The rest of her body certainly couldn't. Her breasts had already begun to ache and her back arched against her will.

Weakness, thy name is Rose.

The devil claim her, but dispatching members of

the tribe always put her in the mind to get out of her clothes for reasons that had little to do with the stink of ogre blood.

"I've never seen you move so," Gareth said, his breath rushing from between his teeth as he pushed his hips forward, letting her know battle had a similar effect on him as well.

"No?" She circled her hips, just once, rubbing the hard length of him.

Thankfully, she had forgone an extra petticoat due to the unusually warm weather, as she had secretly wondered if the vampire's confidence in his effect upon the female population was due to more than his mesmerizing powers. Now she knew Gareth had every reason to preen, assuming he could properly utilize that long, thick length.

"Not that, sweet. Though I dare say I've never seen you move like *that* either."

Transferring both swords to one hand, Gareth smoothed his fingers up the front of her body until his warm palm rested on her ribs, just beneath her breasts. Her nipples pulled into tight points and her chest tingled with awareness. Goddess help her, but she desperately wanted to feel Gareth's hand there, to feel the warmth of his touch as he slid his hand beneath her gown. She wanted nothing between their bare flesh, nothing but—

"Release me, sir," Rose said, fighting the desire thrumming through her veins.

It wasn't safe to toy with Gareth, no matter how cordial and mannerly he usually appeared. She had seen him bare his teeth during battle, seen the snarl that revealed the vicious creature lurking beneath the foppish veneer. The man behind her was as much a predator of man as any ogre.

Only the fact that his particular hunger need not be fed with skin and bone, and that his victims remained among the living, allowed him to be hunter rather than prey. The Fey de la Nuit sought to destroy all supernatural beings that reduced the number of mortal souls walking the earth. They fed upon the sins of man. A decline in mortal flesh meant a decline in mortal souls and a possible food shortage for the Fey.

It all came down to filling bellies, no matter how proud each supernatural might be of his magical gifts. They were no better off than humans in that manner, just as vulnerable to thirst and hunger, and just as fearful of possible famine.

"You moved so quickly even my eyes had difficulty following the path of your sword." He murmured the words against her neck and Rose let her eyes close. The electricity of that touch nearly undid her. If she hadn't known the vampire's mouth had been full of ogre blood not ten minutes past, she would have spun in his arms and claimed his lips . . . and perhaps more. "What are you, sweet Rose? You are not a black faerie. Any fool could see that by looking at you. But you aren't a Seelie sidhe either, for I have seen you feed as a mortal would."

On the word "feed," his hand slid down over her belly and then farther, until he paused directly over her sex. If some magic could have spirited petticoat and dress away, his fingers would have been resting on the curls that hid where she was already slick with wanting. Her body hadn't responded to a man in such a fashion in . . . longer than she cared to remember, and even the *thought* of his hand between her legs was enough to make her head fall back against his chest with a soft moan.

"You are not a vampire, for I know you have hunted when the sun is at its hottest and needed no time to restore yourself." The hilts of his swords brushed ever so casually against her bodice. She gasped as the metal played across one swollen tip and then the other and an answering rush of heat further dampened her sex.

Her entire body vibrated with desire even as her heart pounded with fear—not of Gareth, but of herself. What was she becoming that it had come to this, that she had lost the strength of spirit to fight a vampire's seduction?

"Release me." Rose pulled away, but he tugged her back against him just as quickly.

"I *will* release you, Lady Rose." He nuzzled his nose into what remained of her elaborately styled curls in a manner surprisingly tender—at least when contrasted with the iron-strong arms encircling her.

She was his prisoner and a part of her found the knowledge exhilarating. After all, if she was a captive, she couldn't be faulted if things went too far.

"Simply tell me how a woman who smells—" He inhaled and his breath came out on a moan, as if her scent were an aphrodisiac he could not possibly resist. "—feels—" His swords clattered to the ground and the arm encircling her waist tightened as his other hand moved to cup her breast, drawing a hungry sound from Rose's throat against her will. "—and most likely tastes like a mortal can move the way you do, and I will release you."

"That is your only question?" she asked, shamelessly arching into the hand that cupped her breast.

"Of course not, but that much would satisfy me. For now." The bastard slipped his hand into her bodice and captured the erect bud of one breast in his fingers. He pinched the aching flesh until her sex pulsed with hunger and her breath came in rapid gasps. "Tell me, sweet, or I may have to steal a taste of that blood I hear racing beneath your lovely skin, just to ascertain—"

His words broke off in a groan as Rose slammed her head into his nose—hard. Gareth's arms loosened in surprise and she spun free. In seconds her sword was at his throat.

Vampires. They always had to ruin a perfectly decent seduction with talk of blood.

"You will steal nothing, and I will give nothing. Contrary to what the ladies you meet in Covent Garden might tell you, not all women relish the idea of assuaging your bloody thirst."

"I must agree with the tribeswoman who attacked you," his said, a smile clear in his voice though she couldn't see his mouth behind the hands clasped over his wounded nose. "That is not fitting speech for a comtesse, not to mention highly unfashionable language for a young lady to use in mixed company."

So he was back to being the good-humored, foppish Mr. Barrows. Only now she knew better than to believe his performance. It was a pity, really. It had been so much easier to resist the draw of those wicked green eyes before she'd felt the strength in his arms, or seen him fight with a ferocity that made her ache for a more intimate acquaintance.

"You have known many comtesses?" she asked,

lowering her sword, sensing the threat from Gareth had passed . . . at least for now.

"A great many. Though I'm not sure, as a good Englishman, I should admit to consorting with the like. You Frenchwomen are—"

"I am not French. I merely inherited French property and title," Rose corrected, sheathing her weapon and searching for her cape on the ground.

The center of the maze was filled with various ogre parts and thick, black blood. Even the light of the moon could not aid her in locating the discarded garment. Probably just as well. Her lady's maid had served her well in their time together. She couldn't imagine asking poor Marta to clean fabric practically bathed in gore.

"A personal detail at last!" Gareth crowed, swiping his arm across his face, smearing red on his white sleeve. Rose had bloodied his nose, a realization that made her feel oddly guilty. For all his faults, the man was relentlessly affable, a fact that softened her tone when she next spoke.

"I am not averse to sharing personal details, Mr. Barrows. But you must win the right to such information, not simply demand it." She ignored the heat in his eyes as she lifted her skirts and leaned over to pluck an ornamental flower from the top of her slipper.

"Are you telling me I must woo you, Rose?" he asked, the hint of amusement in his voice making her bristle.

"No, sir, I am simply stating that no lady in her right mind would bare her soul to a man who hadn't taken the time to earn her trust." She pulled at the top of the flower, revealing the secret compartment holding the black powder the Fey de la Nuit provided for help with the cleanup of the . . . fruits of her labor. "She most certainly wouldn't do so simply because the gentleman had made a bet at his club."

"The wager had nothing to do with *what* you are, Rose," Gareth said, moving out of her path as she scattered powder over the bodies that had been living, breathing ogres not so many minutes past. There was a time when the sight of wide-open eyes and rapidly stiffening flesh had troubled her, but Rose thought she had put that behind her long ago. Perhaps it was the sheer quantity of slain ogres that made bile rise in her throat and her hands tremble as she paced about the courtyard.

"Only a handful of vampires belong to White's Young Club. The rest are human, at least that I know of. Wouldn't do to start talking faeries and ogres with your average earl or duke, now would it?"

"I doubt you have many dukes in the Young Club. I've heard all about the exploits at that den of iniquity you call a chocolate house, Mr. Barrows." Rose paused at the edge of the bodies and traced runes of flame in the air.

The center of the maze flared yellow and orange as the ogres began to burn. She turned her back on the vision. The sight of burning flesh gave her little satisfaction this night. The powder would ensure not so much as a scrap of ash remained behind to give mortals a clue as to what had occurred. There was no need to stay and watch the incineration.

"My club is the oldest, not to mention the finest, in the city." Gareth followed Rose out of the maze, looking offended. "The list of men—nobles among them,

I'll have you know—who are waiting for membership is longer than both of my arms put together."

Men.

"My apologies, Mr. Barrows." Rose sighed, feeling weary, wondering how on earth she was going to make it up to her room in her current blood-smeared state.

And even if that were accomplished, how would she go about having Marta warm the water for a bath without alerting the servants and arousing the curiosity of the household at large? Noblewomen didn't call for baths in the middle of the night unless they'd been about activities that caused quite a bit of scandalous physical exertion. No doubt ogre slaying was scandalous and physical, but she doubted that would be the conclusion drawn in the minds of her hosts.

"No need for apologies, my lady. I should apologize," Mr. Barrows said, catching her arm and turning her to face him. "The wager was ridiculous and I was insensitive to mention it, even in jest. Can you possibly forgive me?"

"How can I forgive you when I have no knowledge of the wager of which you speak?"

"Since you arrived last autumn, there has been . . . speculation, sweet."

"Speculation? Please, Mr. Barrows, make yourself plain." She couldn't be bothered playing guessing games with a vampire, especially one who insisted on calling her by a term of endearment he hadn't won the right to use. If she didn't know for a fact Mr. Barrows called half the *ton* his "sweet," she would have been sincerely troubled by the word. She had neither the time nor the temperament to be anyone's beloved.

"You are a comely young woman, as I am sure you are aware," he said, winking in that rakish way she knew caused most women to swoon at his feet. "The very picture of your grandmother, so the older gentlemen say. But your aspect and manner are so severe, and you seem genuinely disinterested in any of our eligible bachelors. You hardly danced at all at the Astonburys' Christmas ball, and—"

"Are you saying people suspect the truth?" Rose asked, sincerely concerned with Gareth's gossip, for once.

It had been over fifty years since she'd last hunted in England. She had deliberately avoided the British Isles for fear of questions being raised. A comtesse who never aged would become a person of interest, and Rose did her best to avoid that fate.

She had been pretending to be her own granddaughter since returning to England at the request of the Fey de la Nuit. The ogre population on the island had grown so large she could no longer afford to stay away. There were other ogre executioners in the world, but none who had her unique talents. She had been gifted by the Fey de la Nuit both at her birth and later, upon her flight from the ogre who would have become her husband.

No other mortal could claim the same. Black faeries could only grant a boon at a baby's cradle, or in exchange for a mother's greatest sacrifice, the passing of her babes into the service of their dark court.

"Of course not, that would require entirely too much imagination," Gareth said, the laughter in his voice interrupting the black thoughts threatening her mind. "Many have simply noticed your lack of interest in the opposite sex. I believe the ladies presume you think yourself above courting solid, English men and are fairly glad of it. But the men . . ."

"Gareth, the sun will rise in a few hours. I have to make my way to my chambers and remove the stink of ogre from my person before then. If you aren't going to come to the—"

"Some of the men thought you might prefer puss."

"Pardon me?"

"That you might prefer the company of other ladies."

"I very largely do, but what does that—"

"In the *bedroom,* sweet." He had the grace to blush as he said it.

"Oh. Well . . . I simply . . . Really, I . . ." Just when she'd been certain nothing could shock her. "You must have fed recently, sir. I can't say I have ever seen a vampire blush," Rose finally stammered, turning on her heel and stomping back toward the house.

"I won't say a word, Rose. I swear it," he called after her. "Your secret is safe with me."

"What secret?" Rose mumbled beneath her breath, barely stifling a scream as Gareth suddenly appeared in front of her. And he had insisted *she* moved quickly.

"That you are as hot-blooded as any shepherdess I've chased through a field at dusk," he said, fixing her with a look that was not in the least bit humorous.

"Gareth, please."

"Please, what? Anything you desire. You have only to ask." He took her hand and wiped the black blood from her glove with his own sleeve before bringing it to his lips for a soft kiss. Ridiculous as he was, Rose still had to fight a shiver of reaction. He was simply that tempting . . . or she was simply that desperate for contact with the opposite sex.

"The tribe has never dared attack me in such numbers before. I must leave for London first thing in the morning. Ambrose will want to hear of this right away."

Her liaison among the Fey de la Nuit would probably prefer to hear about the attack immediately, but she had no way to contact him while isolated in the country—which the ogres had no doubt known. Black faeries were forced to live in densely populated areas due to their need to feed on mortal sin. There might be a contact in the nearest village who could send a message to Ambrose, but she wouldn't have time to get there and back before dawn. Besides, it wasn't safe to travel at night with so many ogres still running loose across the countryside.

"You will leave for London tomorrow then?" Gareth asked, a curious light in his eyes.

Damnation. Would she never learn to think before speaking? "Yes, I will, and no, you may *not* stow away under my carriage."

"But, Rose, you have a secret compartment designed for—"

"For transporting ogre heads, weapons, bloody clothes, and the like in a concealed fashion. Not for housing sleeping vampires." She lowered her voice as they approached the servants' entrance to the manor. "I can't afford to be distracted with worry that some curious mortal will open the compartment and find you sleeping inside. Humans have more imagination than you think, at least enough to determine how to kill a sleeping vampire."

"Dearest lady, my heart is touched by your concern for my well-being," he said, stopping at the top of the stairs.

"You *have* no heart, sir." Rose continued down to the door leading to the kitchen. There she would find the servant stair, and she hoped make her way to her chambers unnoticed.

"Untrue, Rose. I have a heart, and from this moment forward it beats only for you."

With her hand on the doorknob, Rose turned to glance at the ridiculous creature and felt her breath catch in spite of herself. He did look lovely, bathed in the moonlight, his bright eyes shining down at her, emotion mixing with that familiar wry grin. The emotion resembled sincere affection. But she was not so easily deceived.

Vampires were excellent actors—it was part of what made them such accomplished hunters. Their ability to mimic human emotion made them far more dangerous than any ogre. An ogre might consume your flesh, but a member of the tribe could never break your heart.

"Good night, sir. Goddess speed your journey to London." Rose turned and entered the manor before the vampire's smile recovered from the blessing she had given him.

Crosses, holy water, and the invocation of the name of the Christian god or the Mother of them all had no detrimental effect upon vampires she had met in her long life. But they did tend to react dramatically to reminders they were out of favor with the higher power. Vampires turned to ash and blew away upon their death, not allowing even the barbaric burial sacraments practiced by ogres. Most considered it a sign that they were bound for hellfire.

For her part, Rose wasn't certain, but the opinion was useful at times like these, when she had to make certain Gareth didn't think there could ever be more than friendship between them. She was Briar Rose, the woman of many thorns. She had earned the nickname and intended to continue earning it until her work on earth was done.

Still, even after she had made her way safely to her quarters and was immersed in tepid water—thanks to Marta's preparation of a scalding hot bath a few hours before—she was possessed by a strange melancholy.

"You'll catch a chill if you don't get out soon, my lady." Marta's soft voice wasn't much louder than the hiss of the logs burning in the fireplace.

"Please, call me Rose when we are alone." Rose sighed, knowing even as she made the request it was futile. Marta was determined to conform to her role as a lady's maid and chaperone at all times, lest she act inappropriately when humans were about.

"No, I mustn't," she said, her pale cheeks flushing pink. "Now please, let me help you into your robe. The water grows too cold for human flesh."

And she would know. Marta had once been the guardian sprite of a small river in France and still maintained a strong connection to water. When the banks of her home ran dry, she had gone into the service of the Fey de la Nuit rather than slowly fade away into the Summerland. She was gentle, fearful of humans and just about everything else.

When Rose had first made her acquaintance, the sprite had barely been able to make eye contact, even with her mistress. But by the time she and Ambrose returned from journeying in the east, Marta had developed the ability to chat quietly with Rose when they were alone.

They had begun to build a friendship, which was a lovely thing. Rose hadn't had a female friend in far too long. Or a male friend for that matter, especially one who made her laugh.

Damn him.

For all his faults, Gareth was the closest thing to a kindred spirit she'd met in a very, very long time. He reminded her of the headstrong girl she'd once been. And after tonight, she knew he could make her want, awaken a desire she hadn't felt in ages. He was intriguing, her Mr. Barrows.

Rose didn't realize she'd muttered his name aloud until Marta spoke.

"Will the gentleman be accompanying us on the morrow?" Marta asked, enveloping Rose in a dressing gown as she stepped from the bath.

"No, he will not."

"Oh, what a shame." Marta settled Rose by the fire and turned her attention to soaking her mistress's bloodstained dress in the dirty bathwater. "He is an entertaining travel companion and such a fine-looking man."

"He is a vampire, Marta," Rose said, shocked to hear her shy companion even speaking of the opposite sex, let alone commenting on one's appearance. "He's not a *man* at all."

"Of course, my lady. You wouldn't want to forget that. Such a thing might lead to actually *enjoying* the gentleman's company."

"Sarcasm? How shocking," Rose said, laughing in spite of herself.

Marta joined her laughter. "I am becoming more human every day, it seems."

And I becoming less. The thought was just what Rose needed for her smile to fade, and her melancholy to degenerate into gloom.

CHAPTER THREE

February 8, 1750
London, England

"I would hardly call this a punctual report, Comtesse."
Ambrose Minuit did not turn from the window as
Rose entered his office. The full moon looked lovely
shining down upon the city streets, but she knew that
wasn't what had captured the dark faerie's attention
so profoundly. He was frustrated, and treating her to
a view of his back was a deliberate snub.

Not that she couldn't appreciate the view. Ambrose
was nothing if not a stunning example of a man—over
six feet tall with the muscles of a warrior and raven
hair that hung in soft waves down to the center of his
back—but his rudeness immediately set her on edge.
If he refused to turn to greet a lady, even a mere mortal such as herself, she was in for more trouble than
she had assumed.

"My apologies, Ambrose. Marta and I made our
way back to London as swiftly as possible in light of

the circumstances." She moved to sit in the small wooden chair in front of Ambrose's desk.

On most occasions, he would have had a pair of cushioned chairs arranged near the fire before her arrival. He must truly be angry if he was punishing her with discomfort. For a man who claimed she was a curse upon his immortal life, Ambrose was usually very accommodating of her every need. He had anticipated those needs so often, in fact, that she had assumed he would do so on this occasion. Therefore, she hadn't bothered sending a communiqué when she and Marta were detained at Lord Drummand's estate for another evening.

"I was forced to hear of your attack from the vampire. The creature took great pleasure in that, I can assure you," Ambrose said, turning to stare down at Rose, wrinkling his nose in obvious distaste when he saw her boy's clothes.

No matter that dressing as a boy had saved her life more than once, the faerie preferred her to be dressed in a gown.

"He also insinuated that perhaps another episode of violence had detained you in Bedfordshire."

Ambrose's dark gray eyes were even stormier than usual, and Rose had to fight the urge to glance away. She had known the faerie over a hundred years and he had been at her side during some of her darkest moments, but his anger still had the power to frighten her . . . just a bit. No matter how many times he had carried her half dead from the scene of a particularly nasty battle and tended her wounds with utmost gentleness, she had never forgotten the evening she first made his acquaintance. He had nearly killed her then, and she couldn't help but wonder if at times he wished he had finished what he started.

Times like this, for example.

"Sir Pithwater's disappearance caused far more of a disturbance than I had predicted. After the chambermaid's head was found in Lord Drummand's grotto—"

"The vampire said the missing maid and stable hand were victims of the ogre's hunger."

"That was what I suspected at the time. I still believe Pithwater or another of the tribe killed them, but for some reason they left the maid's head behind. It was found early yesterday morning, even as Marta and I were preparing to depart for London. After the discovery, we could hardly continue as planned."

"It would have brought suspicion upon you both." He pressed his lips together and sat down behind his desk.

"Precisely." Rose nodded. They weren't cozy before the fire, but having Ambrose seated already helped soothe her nerves. "The entire country party was interviewed that afternoon by the local authorities. By the time Marta and I were questioned, it was quite late in the—"

"You were interrogated?" His eyes met hers again, but this time they were filled with concern.

Rose resisted the urge to sigh. The man had no trouble intimidating her, but could be quite a bear if he felt any other had been granted the privilege. It might have warmed her heart if she thought his urge to defend her stemmed from concern for her welfare.

Instead, Rose suspected it was a case of jealousy. Ambrose wished to keep the business of her intimidation all to himself.

"I was merely questioned. No one witnessed me leaving my chambers that night. I made quite a show of being as horrified and sickened as the other ladies present, and spent most of the day on a settee with smelling salts held beneath my nose. The noblemen present were kept quite busy comforting the lot of us."

"Were any of the men suspected? A murderous member of the nobility would be quite a scandal. I wouldn't want your name associated with—"

"No, I heard the gentlemen discussing the matter. The constable suspects either the stable boy or perhaps Sir Pithwater of the murder since both have mysteriously disappeared."

"And will most likely never be found," Ambrose concluded with a nod.

"Pithwater, for certain."

"So the matter will be forgotten within a fortnight?"

"The Season will soon begin in earnest. After that, country matters of all kinds will be forgotten," Rose assured him, hoping he didn't think it necessary for her to move once again.

She hadn't relished the idea of returning to Britain when the elders of the Fey de la Nuit had demanded it, but now that she was here, she couldn't deny she was enjoying herself. The ogres—apart from the attack two nights' past—had been delightfully easy prey when compared with those inhabiting other parts of the globe. And the parties, customs, and general non-sense of Society were entertaining her far more than she had suspected.

Of course, she had spent the largest part of the past fifty years in isolation, slaying ogres across the Ottoman Empire, disguised as anything from a young male slave to a member of a nobleman's harem. Even when she became adept at speaking the language, she'd been an outcast, never staying in one place for long, unable to use her identity as the Comtesse de Fournier until time had passed.

The press of humanity in London, the endless parties, and the scrutiny of Society that had once troubled her were a most welcome change. Not to mention the ability to wear the latest fashions and be clean and well fed on a daily basis. She had endured her share of hunger, filth, and hardship in recent decades and the respite from the like was appreciated.

"You shall remain in the city. Not that we truly have any choice. The past weeks have heralded a surge in the tribe population on the British Isles unlike anything I have ever seen. My sources in Scotland report an influx from the north, and in London the streets are fairly swarming with the creatures."

"Are they refugees from France or the Netherlands? Have other executioners been driving them from their—"

"No. The executioners on the Continent have been living quite the life of leisure. Fey de la Nuit in Paris and Madrid have sent their people on retreat as the tribe numbers in those cities have fallen far below average," he said, shuffling papers on his desk with a pinched look on his face. For a man who resembled nothing so much as a warrior of old, Ambrose did an excellent impression of a vexed London merchant.

"Retreat?" Rose replied, arching her brow.

"Comtesse, it is you who insists on slaving away in your chosen profession. Am I to force you to the country against your will?" He smiled at her then, but for once she did not smile back. Ambrose's smiles were a thing of beauty. Women had swooned at the sight for hundreds of years and Rose wasn't immune, but tonight she wasn't of the mind to be so easily charmed.

"You would force me into many other things I would rather avoid."

"Such as?"

"Such as the tour of the east." she reminded him. "It was time for me to return to Myrdrean before we set out on that mission, let alone our present assignment."

"Myrdrean will still be there when your obligations to the Fey de la Nuit have been fulfilled," Ambrose said, his stormy expression returning. "It is a place accursed. I cannot fathom your urge to return there."

Rose sighed. Nothing could bring out the peevish side of Ambrose quite so quickly as any mention of her returning to her homeland. She knew that, yet some perverse part of her insisted on raising the subject again and again, though the thought of venturing to the place of her birth filled her with dread.

But perhaps that was why she insisted on confronting Ambrose with the matter. If she were forbidden to return home by another, she wouldn't be forced to contend with her own cowardice.

"And I hardly enjoy seducing men out of property," Rose added, changing the subject. "I saw Lord Hastings's grandson at the Christmas Ball and he was quite devastated to learn I was the descendant of the woman his grandfather had gifted with the Berkeley Square lot fifty-two years ago."

"You truly didn't enjoy the business in the slightest?" Ambrose rose from his chair and circled around the desk. "I thought you adored seducing mortal men."

"Lord Hastings was nearly seventy and had the most horrid breath I can personally recall. At least the most horrid of anything still living."

"That's right, I do believe I remember something about that." A wave of his hand sent the dying fire roaring to life and caused two well-padded chairs to appear on the thick carpet before the flames.

There was a time Rose believed Ambrose could materialize objects from the air, but now she knew better. The chairs had been there from the moment she walked in the door. He'd simply had them cloaked with an invisibility spell. The Fey were powerful magical beings, but not nearly as powerful as they would have the rest of the world believe. They couldn't make something from nothing.

"I suppose now you'd welcome such an assignment," he continued, settling into the larger chair with a weary sigh. "Assuming the nobleman in question resembled Lord Shenley."

"Lord Shenley?"

"The vampire."

"I beg your pardon?" Rose asked, still confused.

"Don't beg *my* pardon. I could care less what mischief you and the creature find to occupy yourselves when you aren't about your duties. You are in my employ, Comtesse, I hardly have the right to dictate how you spend your recreational hours." His words were casual, but the look in Ambrose's eyes was not. "Though I do recall you expressing distaste for supernaturals in the bedroom."

"The distaste remains, no matter what Mr. Barrows might have—"

"Mr. Barrows is *Lord* Shenley, evidently. He's an earl of ancient title, though not any great property. His father is still living, but remains in hiding until the time comes to once again take his turn at playing the Lord. Barrows disclosed this at our last meeting when I questioned his motives for seducing you."

"He did not seduce me," Rose said, her cheeks flaming. She'd thought herself above being embarrassed by such things. Apparently not. "That's ridiculous."

"It is common practice for vampires to add to their personal wealth by seducing gullible mortals," he continued as if he hadn't heard her. "But Lord Shenley is possessed of quite a fortune in his own right."

His smug look told Rose the two men had talked at length about what Gareth *was* after. She blushed even more deeply, but met Ambrose's eyes. "Lovely. I don't happen to be after his riches either. I assume you will allow me to continue his tutelage. He is an excellent swordsman and a good man to have at one's side if the tribe is organizing into larger fighting groups."

"Rosemarie," Ambrose said softly. "You hardly need stoop to bedding vampires."

"I did not bed the vampire." She sighed with exasperation. "Not that it is any of—"

"You are a beautiful woman, more breathtaking than any—"

"Faerie magic, Ambrose," Rose said, her chest tight for reasons she couldn't explain. "I was gifted in the cradle with this beauty by a member of your own race. It is no work of mine."

Ambrose stared deep into her eyes for a moment, and in that instant Rose thought she saw something more than Fey snobbery in his heart. Perhaps he had other reasons for wanting her to stay out of the vampire's bed.

"No matter." He turned a disinterested face to the fire, banishing the mad idea that her liaison might desire more from her than a professional relationship.

Of course, there had been a time when Rose had secretly wished for nothing more, in those early days when she had been so desperately alone and filled with grief. What she would have given to fall into Ambrose's arms then. But he hadn't given the slightest sign. He hadn't given *any* sign, even decades later when they had worked in closer quarters than many lovers.

You must have imagined it, Rose.

But she couldn't forget the way Ambrose had looked at her, or that he had used her given name. He only ever called her Rosemarie when she was near death, being pulled back to the land of the living by a mixture of his magic and her own stubbornness. It seemed to her the Fey de la Nuit who had gifted her with eternal youth and longevity would have also thought to make her a bit more indestructible than the average mortal. But then, the black faeries did have a rather wicked sense of humor.

"The tribe may very well be organizing for some scheme or another," Ambrose said, with an impatient motion for her to sit. "They have always kept to their smaller family groups, but the hordes I saw scavenging the food stalls at Covent Garden were most assuredly not related. They've traveled here for a reason that, as yet, remains unclear. The head that was left behind, however, may be a clue."

"The chambermaid's head?" Rose settled into the chair, eager to move onto more pertinent topics. Between the erotic interlude with Gareth and the uncomfortable moment with her liaison, she was beginning to think she was emitting an aura that revealed how desperate she was for a break in her long celibacy. "Do you think it was deliberately left behind?"

"Perhaps."

"One of the females who attacked Mr. B— Lord Shenley fled with the head of what I suspect was her brother. But that is not unusual," Rose said, managing not to jump in surprise as another wave of Ambrose's hand revealed a small table holding two glasses filled with liqueur. She eagerly reached for the closest. Faery mead was the sweetest on earth, and it wasn't often that Ambrose offered to share the contents of his extensive cellar.

"True, but I have never heard of them leaving a human head behind. They consider the brain the most delectable portion of the human animal." Ambrose plucked his glass from the table and gave it a thoughtful swirl. "They also believe that is where the highest concentration of vital energy is located."

"Perhaps they were interrupted during the meal?" Rose swirled her own glass, and inhaled, not bothered by Ambrose's casual talk of the "human animal."

Humans were indeed very much like animals, but animals he himself depended upon for sustenance. He relied upon humanity as much as any other supernatural. At least humans could choose to shun the flesh—or energy—of lower creatures and still survive.

Of course, Rose knew she would find it difficult to do so. She adored a hot meat pie on a cold day.

"Doubtful. You've seen how quickly they can feed," Ambrose said.

"True." Ogres had hinged jaws and rows of hidden teeth that allowed them to completely devour a human in mere minutes. "And the head could easily be carried if the creature was fleeing discovery. Why not carry it away rather than secret it in the grotto?"

"Precisely. The placement of the skull almost persuades me the ogres are about some sort of magic."

"Magic?" Rose paused with her glass halfway to her lips, shocked. Ogres spurned magic as vehemently as faeries embraced it. Legends told how their ancient ancestors were destroyed by attempts to work spells. The working of even rudimentary magic was forbidden upon punishment of death.

Not that the threat was truly necessary. Most ogres feared magic even more than the executioners of the Fey de la Nuit.

"Human sacrifice has great power in black magic. A human head draws even more profound power than human blood. It can serve as an ingredient in a spell or as a conduit of dark power. Even mortals sense that on some level. Why else would the heads of criminals and enemies of the crown be set upon pikes at London Bridge?"

Rose shivered. For such a civilized nation, the English certainly clung to their share of barbaric practices. "So perhaps the ogre was saving the head for work in a spell of some sort?"

"I'll have to consult with a colleague in Hibernia who has greater knowledge of such things, but that is my thought. First they gather in large numbers to increase their presence here on the isles, then they use human sacrifice to lend that presence supernatural weight." Ambrose sipped his mead closing his eyes as he savored the feel of it within his mouth.

Rose's mouth watered, but she sat her glass back on the table, needing to keep her mind clear for a few more moments. "A supernatural weight? I don't understand."

"Their sheer numbers could be used in dozens of different spells—a spell of protection, prophecy, destiny, summoning, destruction, resurrection. The addition of human sacrifice will lend that power a certain import. If they are appealing to ancient gods, or to ancient magic, they need more than mere numbers to have their spell taken seriously."

"The ogres who attacked me mentioned the dark one and hell several times. I've never heard any of the tribe invoke the name of God or Satan before. Do you suppose that could be significant? That they could be using the heads to draw power from the demon realms?" The thought was frightening.

Rose didn't want to imagine the evil a bunch of bumbling ogres could unwittingly unleash upon the mortal world. Whatever their intentions, there were none who could control demon power but demons themselves. The evil creatures would use the ogres to liberate themselves from Hades and then do exactly as they wished once they were free.

"Possibly, though ogres have long attended services both in London and in the country. It isn't safe to appear to be a disbeliever in England. It could simply be that they have begun to believe in the religions of man." Ambrose set down his empty glass and stretched his long legs before the fire. Rose couldn't help but notice how his breeches hugged every inch of his muscled flesh. "They live more among humans than any other supernatural race. In time that will have consequences."

"Lay down with dogs, get up with fleas?" Rose asked, shaking her head. This was Ambrose, the man who considered mortals only a bit more tolerable than mongrels. She must truly be in a sorry state if she was ogling him.

You'd be better off with the vampire. At least he doesn't find the entire human race repulsive.

Rose smiled and sipped her wine, practically moaning her appreciation as the nectar flowed down her throat.

"Something of the sort." Ambrose laughed, a soft rumble that pulsed against her skin and spun through her head. She forced herself to wait to take another drink. Faerie mead was potent, and she was hesitant to relax her guard around Ambrose tonight. Not with the strange tension still in the air. "Of course, there are at least a few among them who remember their very unique history. They identified you as the Briar Rose, correct?"

"They did, but that's nothing unusual. There are always a few among them who—"

"Not in England. None suspected you as the scourge when you last hunted these streets. You haven't been seen on the Continent for nearly a century. The tribe members inhabiting the East have always clung to superstition. I wasn't surprised to see them identify you when we roamed the Ottoman Empire, but—"

"English ogres are too practical to believe a faerie story come to life." It made sense. Tales of the Briar Rose were told to frighten young ogres. Very few actually believed them. "Sir Pithwater did not suspect me. Even my introduction as the Comtesse de Fournier produced not the slightest spark of recognition. I do not believe he was part of the plan."

"Perhaps not knowingly, but he must have communicated the time and place of your rendezvous."

"Or been sent there by someone else, as bait." Rose met Ambrose's gaze and for a moment felt a heat surge through her veins that had nothing to do with the liqueur. Flustered more than she wished to admit, she set her mead back upon the table.

Ambrose eyed her glass and smiled. "Finish your drink, Comtesse. I am feeling generous tonight and will grant you another thumb or two."

"If I didn't know better, Master Minuit, I would think you were trying to ensure my intoxication." Rose nevertheless took another sip, part of her wanting to play with the fire that flared between them.

"I don't believe I've ever seen you intoxicated by anything, Rosemarie."

Rose caught his eyes over the rim of her glass. He'd said it a second time, her full name, and the look in his eye said it was no slip of the tongue. Even the way he'd said "anything" left no doubt in her mind that Ambrose was thinking of things other than liquor that could make a heart beat faster, make a head spin, make flesh burn until it itched to be free of all restraints.

Goddess, why now? Why, after all these years was this strangeness coming between them? Was it simply because she'd allowed a vampire to touch her? Could it be Ambrose had restrained himself these many years, refrained from attempts at seduction because of her professed distaste for any but a mortal in her bed? It seemed insane to even *contemplate* such a thing, but . . .

"Ambrose—"

Rose wasn't allowed to continue her line of questioning, which was probably for the best. She'd been prepared to make a fool of herself in front of a man who was not only her liaison, but her protector, her employer, and the only being in the world who had aided her in staying alive.

What wasn't for the best, was the manner in which they were interrupted.

"On your guard!" Ambrose lunged toward her, knocking her from her chair just before something flaming—something that very much resembled a human head set ablaze—soared past where she had been seated. With a curse, Ambrose withdrew his sword from a hidden sheath in his boot, and was up and running toward the window before she had even rolled to a stop.

Rose drew her sword while still on the ground, determined to have it free sooner rather than later, then sprung to her feet, grateful for the ease of movement allowed by her breeches. If she'd been wearing one of the gowns Ambrose preferred, she never would have managed to reach the other side of the room in time to keep an ogre larger than any she had ever seen from pulling her dark faerie right out the window.

CHAPTER FOUR

The creature howled as Rose brought her sword down on its massive wrist, slicing its hand from the enormous arm shoved through the window. Ambrose shrugged the still spasming appendage from his body and summoned his sword with a word. The blade flew to him from where it lay on the floor some feet away, knocked from his grasp by the creature presently waving a bloody stump of an arm back and forth, spraying them both with thick, black ogre blood.

Gads, but the stench was worse than any Rose had encountered. She had to fight the urge to vomit as she lifted her sword and stabbed the creature again, triggering a wail from the beast and another font of blood from the wound she had inflicted.

"Come, this way," Ambrose yelled from across the room where he was busy snuffing out the flaming head with his overcoat. He motioned for her to follow him to the door to his office. "We must get outdoors if we—"

"Wait!" Rose ran toward the window as the injured ogre tugged its arm free of the hole it had made. She and Ambrose would never reach the street in time if they took the stairs. If its legs were as large as the rest of him, the ogre would outdistance them in seconds.

Throwing caution to the wind, Rose ran even faster, flinging herself out the window. Her legs and arms churned, frantically seeking purchase as she flew through the air.

"Aufh!" She grunted as she collided with the ogre's back. Desperately she clung to the beast, somehow managing to retain her hold on her sword in the process.

She had thought to dangle from the creature's shirt until she could find a way to wound it sufficiently to stop its progress, but soon realized it wasn't a shirt the ogre was wearing at all. It was a pelt, a coat of hair that covered the entirety of its back.

Great Goddess, but the matted hair reeked more powerfully than anything she could remember smelling in her long life. The stench of death and rot was dizzying, a blow that wounded her far more than the hand that sought to bat her from her perch. Thankfully, she had landed near the center of the giant's shoulders and was proving difficult for him to reach. It bought her time to shift positions and bring her sword—its blade shrunk to the size of a dagger— down into the ogre's flesh.

The creature howled as she sank the blade deep and then spun in a sudden circle. Rose clung to the hilt of her weapon, but her feet flew out behind her, making bruising contact with what felt like brick. She cried out and pulled her knees into her chest, wincing against the dull pain throbbing through her right ankle. Luckily, she hadn't sustained a break—she'd had enough shattered bones to know the difference between a fracture and a bruise—but she might not be so lucky next time.

She had to find a way to cease the ogre's spinning before he flung her from him like a rat at the dogfights.

Below her, Rose heard Ambrose chanting in ancient Fey and felt a sudden blast of heat on her skin. He'd set flame to the street ahead of the creature, forcing it to flee in the other direction. And flee it did, running at a speed that had Rose bouncing against its back, quickly losing what breath she managed to draw into her body. But mercifully no screams sounded from the pavement, only thunderous footsteps.

Despite his taste for the finer things in life, Ambrose had his offices in Southwark, in an area largely composed of factories and sweatshops. The businesses were closed for the night and thus far it seemed the entire encounter with the giant had gone unobserved. But then, the black faerie's preference for privacy motivated his decision to inhabit a part of the city filled with the poor and downtrodden by day and the rats by night. He might need the sins of humans to feed, but the man didn't wish to spend any more time among mortals than was absolutely necessary.

"Lean to your right!" Ambrose shouted. Rose flexed her muscles, using her grip on her sword to leverage herself to one side seconds before an arrow whistled through the air, landing with a hearty thunk exactly where her head had been a moment before.

She cursed briefly, but then moved one hand to

grasp the thick shaft of the arrow. There was no sense in wasting time considering the repercussions of disobedience. She had learned to obey Ambrose's orders during the heat of battle without question for many reasons, but the tendency for the man to act in just such a manner was certainly the most persuasive.

Rose groaned as she tugged her blade free of the ogre's flesh. The wound made a moist, sucking sound, emitting a burst of foul blood and an odor that made gorge rise in her throat. She slammed the blade home again a few inches below her first strike as more arrows rained down around her, but the ogre barely flinched in reaction.

He was running quickly now, making swift progress toward the River Thames. Ambrose followed close behind. Rose wondered how he was managing it, but a glance over her shoulder revealed he'd unfurled his giant wings, forced to fly in order to keep up with the beast's progress. She had never seen him reveal himself so completely in such a populous area, and was troubled that Ambrose judged this chase of sufficient import to risk being discovered or potentially enslaved.

Faeries of both the light and dark courts were vulnerable to capture when their wings were bared. If a mortal knew the correct words and could lay hands on those luminous instruments of flight, the faerie would be forced to grant their every desire until their death. It was not a small thing to risk.

But then, the streets were still remarkably empty. Disturbingly empty, actually, making Rose wonder if the beast she fought had consumed a few dozen humans before crashing through Ambrose's window.

After all, the head he hurled through the glass must have come from somewhere . . .

"Release your hold, Rosemarie. I will catch you," Ambrose called, his wings carrying him closer. "You must—"

"Not without my sword." Rose turned her full attention to pulling her weapon from the creature's flesh, but it was stuck even more securely than before.

"You're near the water!"

"A moment more!" She tugged until she feared her arm would be wrenched from her body, straining to free her weapon. The sword had been with her since the day she committed herself to the Fey cause, to *her* cause. To lose it would be to lose a part of herself.

"Now! Rosemarie, that is an order! There are—"

"Nearly . . . have . . . it. There!" Rose let herself fly backward, weapon in hand, trusting Ambrose would be as good as his word.

"Foolish woman." He grunted as she landed heavily in his arms, then lowered them both to the ground, his wings vanishing within seconds. Just as quickly, he set Rose on her feet and turned her around. "Now run back to my quarters. Lock yourself in the pantry and—"

"Hide in the pantry? Surely you—"

"You may choose your hiding place, then. Just make sure to—"

"Wait." Rose looked back toward the river to make sure her eyes hadn't deceived her. "Dear Goddess, Ambrose. What is this?"

"I don't know, but it doesn't bode well for the

mortals or the Fey. Of that I am certain." His lips pressed tightly together as he forced Rose behind him, though not before she saw what danger awaited.

The entire riverbank was alive with ogres kneeling in the mud and the muck, chanting softly in voices that would seem nothing more than a whisper on the wind if you didn't know the origin of the sound. They swayed slowly back and forth, oblivious to all save their dark purpose. Even the giant, who crashed through their ranks crushing those unfortunate enough to be in his path as he surged into the Thames, did not produce a stir.

Rose watched a faint red glow skitter across the surface of the water as the ogre waded into the river, but the light quickly faded, leaving his large head a black silhouette they watched sink slowly below the waves.

"The full moon. I should have . . ." Ambrose cursed in ancient Fey, exchanging his bow for his sword before reaching down to seize Rose's hand. "Come, let us make haste to—"

"There she stands. The scourge still lives!" Rose spun about, her heart sinking as she realized it was a tribeswoman who spoke and that the lady in question wasn't alone.

At least two dozen other ogres surrounded her.

"We must have her blood. Spill her blood," another shouted, the fervor behind the call sending a shiver across Rose's skin.

What would they do if the ogres before them and the hundreds gathered near the river attacked simultaneously? Ambrose's wings could carry him to safety, but with her added weight, he could not hope to escape. At least one of them would likely die this night, and if Rose knew her friend, probably two. He would not leave her to fight alone, no matter that she was simply one executioner among hundreds. The contract they had forged over a hundred years past meant something to the black faerie, but the friendship they had forged every night since meant even more to Rose.

"Ambrose, if we can't win this fight, you must leave me." She gripped her sword as it flared to its full length, grateful she'd managed to free the weapon from the giant's flesh. Without it, she'd have no chance against the ogres advancing down the darkened street.

"Nonsense, Rosemarie." He risked a quick look over his shoulder. "The others are still intent upon the magic they work at the river's edge. We will dispatch these without difficulty."

"Brothers! Sisters! The scourge's blood has not been spilled! The sacrifice is not complete," another female ogre screamed.

If Rose wasn't mistaken, it was the same woman who had fled Lord Drummand's maze with her kinsman's head two nights past. Rose cursed, wishing she had pursued and slain the ogress when she'd had the opportunity. If she had thought the tribe capable of this degree of organization, there was no doubt she would have made certain of the other woman's death. But she had never seen anything like this, never even heard rumors of an ogre gathering of this size.

"Brothers. Sisters. Come to our aid. Slay the Briar Rose, free our people from the scourge!" The ogre's voice echoed sharply off the brick buildings, carrying easily down to the water's edge where others of her kind began to take note of the disturbance. "The sacrifice has yet to be made!"

"You were saying, Ambrose?" Rose asked, glancing quickly between the ogres in front of them and the ogres stumbling drunkenly toward them from behind. They were trapped by immense factory buildings on either side. There was nowhere to run. They would have to fight their way through and hope they dispatched the few dozen before them before the hundreds approaching from behind overwhelmed their position.

"We've faced worse."

"Have we? I do not recall it," Rose said. "I know you can suffer more damage than I, but if they bleed you sufficiently—"

"I will not leave you." For a bittersweet moment, Rose wished she had been given more time with the man, this stranger she had assumed she knew so well. But there was no more time for reflection.

Ambrose raised his sword and charged. Rose followed, banishing all doubt from her heart as she swung her blade and spilled ogre blood for a second time this eve.

"Die, scourge!" Before Rose had freed her blade from the belly of the first ogre, the tribeswoman she had encountered two nights past ran at her, sword raised. Rose deflected the blow with a kick to the ogress's hands, silently thanking the goddess for her long stay in the East. It was there she had learned the ways to fight with feet and hands, to make her body as deadly a weapon as her blade.

The ogress hissed and dropped her weapon, seeming not to notice what had struck her. The gift of grace bestowed on Rose at her birth had been intended to make her the most accomplished dancer at a royal ball. Instead, over time, it had allowed her to become as smooth and swift a fighter as any vampire warrior.

Speaking of vampires . . .

"Behind you, Rose," a familiar voice shouted. Rose met Gareth's eyes before spinning just in time to duck the sweep of an ogre's blade. He was ancient and frail, but his sluggish blow could still have led to her death.

Rose quickly dispatched both him and the female pressing in behind by spinning on her heel, pulling the weight of her sword in a circle of death. Thick blood sprayed, hot and wet, as she leapt over the still twitching remains and into battle with the next tribesman in line. Two more fell easily under her sword before she was seized by the arm. Rose shifted the position of her weapon, preparing to drive it sideways into her captor's flesh.

"Stop! It's the vampire," Ambrose shouted from some yards away. Rose turned to see it was indeed Gareth, looking surprisingly unconcerned for his life considering how close he had come to a mortal wound. Even vampires, with their extraordinary powers of regeneration, would have a difficult time surviving a blow severing their top from their bottom.

"Hurry! Aid awaits at the bridge," Ambrose called.

"Good evening, Rose." Gareth squeezed her elbow gently and smiled as if they were meeting at the Vauxhall pleasure garden, not the filthy streets of Southwark. "Delightful to see you again. I do believe you're looking even more lovely than usual. Those trousers do reveal every—"

"Run, Gareth," Rose ordered with a frustrated sigh before turning to dash after Ambrose. "And never touch me during battle if you wish to live."

"Is that a threat, sweet?"

"It is truth," she replied, picking up her pace as they cleared the last of the slain bodies littering the ground.

"You sound unhappy with me, Rose."

"Now is not the time, sir."

"I see. I don't know what tales that faerie of yours has told you, but I swear on my dear mother's grave I didn't say a word regarding our interlude in Lord Drummand's garden." Gareth easily kept pace with Rose as she ran for all she was worth. The ogres advancing from the water's edge appeared to have shaken off their daze and were quickly closing the distance between them. Each time she risked a glance over her shoulder, their long, thin legs had carried them disturbingly closer. "It's as if he read my mind. Not unusual if we had fed from each other, but I'll have you know I don't go in for the taste of rooster, not even for—"

"Please, Gareth."

"Attend me. I wouldn't want you to think for a moment that—"

"This isn't the time. Run!"

"I can run and converse at the same time, dearest."

"Well, I can't," Rose panted, surging forward as her muscles ached, scowling at his laughter. She could usually appreciate the fact that he retained his sense of humor in the midst of a crisis, but there was nothing laughable about the present situation.

They were still several miles from the bridge

where whatever help Ambrose had summoned was waiting. If he'd managed to contact some of London's other Fey telepathically, they might be able to sense their position and meet them halfway. But if Ambrose had called upon the other creatures sworn into his service, they would not be so lucky.

Trolls were fierce fighters, but not known for their imaginative thinking. If Ambrose had summoned them to the bridge, they would await at the bridge, though it was hoped they would have the sense to journey to the Surrey side. Since the houses built on the Southwark portion of London Bridge had burned twenty-five years ago, the Surrey end of the causeway was usually deserted at night. The gate would be closed and locked until morning, no toll man on duty, and little chance human ears would hear the immortal scuffle taking place. Not that mortal discovery seemed to be a problem at present.

The road to the river had been silent as the grave and even the tenements they ran past were dark and oddly quiet. This was the witching hour, that time when it seemed all humanity abandoned the waking world, but the dark shadows between the buildings always cloaked a few stubborn souls still about their wicked business. And even in the dead of night the cries of hungry children and their gin-addled parents could usually be heard up and down these streets.

Whatever spell the ogres had been about, Rose suspected it had affected the mortal population. It was hauntingly quiet, as if they were running through a country field in winter, not the largest city in the world. There was not a single sign of life.

"Not even a rat or a dog," Rose muttered to herself,

the strange absence of *anything* living sending a chill down her spine.

But if there had been an enchantment cast to keep the mortals quiet and sleeping, why hadn't it affected her as well? The faerie and the vampire's immunity she could understand, but she was mortal still and should have succumbed. It was odd, and made her wonder—

"Faster, Rose. They're getting closer." The humor vanished from Gareth's voice as he placed a hand at her back and urged her forward.

Rose forced the muscles in her legs to work harder, but she knew she couldn't continue for much longer. No matter that she was gifted with superior grace and more speed than the average human woman, she was still only a bit over five feet tall. She had to take two steps for every one of Gareth's and at least three for each of the ogres' loping strides.

It seemed *someone* on the night of her second gifting by the Fey would have foreseen the potential problems her short stature would present with regard to battling ogres and granted her a few extra inches. But perhaps the faeries found it amusing that the scourge of the tribe was not much taller than the dwarves kept for amusement at court.

"Let me carry you," the vampire demanded, reaching for her.

Rose slapped his hand away, not bothering to waste breath forming a reply. Gareth could run a bit faster, but not if he were bearing her weight. She would simply have to maintain her present speed until they reached the bridge. There was no other—

"Release me, sir!" Rose gasped as Gareth's arm wrapped around her waist and lifted her off the ground, holding her at his side as if she weighed no more than a sack of flour.

Her arms and legs dangled and her sword shrank to dagger size as if sensing it must or be dragged through the filthy street. Rose attempted to protest again, but couldn't manage to draw breath with her stomach jostling against the iron band of Gareth's arm. By the time she discovered how to do so, it was no longer sensible to insist she be placed on the ground.

Gareth was moving incredibly fast, closing the distance between them and Ambrose with ease. That speed, combined with his incredible strength, left no doubt in Rose's mind that Gareth had deceived her in more ways than one. Not only had he neglected to tell her he was of noble lineage, he had also lied about his number of years among the undead. No vampire of a mere two hundred years could overcome a faerie with such ease.

Even hanging upside down and bouncing like a child on her first pony, Rose could read the surprise on Ambrose's face as Gareth passed him by. It wasn't anything the average person would have noticed, but in their years together Rose had grown attuned to the smallest signs of emotion from the faerie. Small signs were all the Fey de la Nuit tended to give. They were a stoic lot, not nearly as gay as their Seelie cousins.

"Here we are then," Gareth said, setting Rose on the ground. She righted herself quickly and immediately regretted it as black spots danced in front of her eyes. "Easy there, Comtesse." The vampire laughed, wrapping his arms around her when she swayed and pulling her close. "You mustn't swoon. Think of the effect such a thing would have on your reputation."

"I have never swooned in my life." Rose pulled away with a hard look as the dizziness passed.

There was no time to discuss the matter, but she hoped he read her distrust clearly. In her profession, deception on the part of supernatural beings was not something she could afford to tolerate if she hoped to remain among the living.

"Not ever? How very sad. Every woman should have been made to swoon at least once in her life." There was a smile on his face, but the carefree tone was strained. Perhaps he sensed her anger, or perhaps the approaching horde was beginning to worry even him.

"Follow me, and get to the rear of the ranks, Comtesse. They are after your blood in particular this night," Ambrose said as he ran past.

Rose followed, grateful to see a great number of trolls had come to their aid. The short, square creatures with their massive hands and wide mouths full of sharp teeth stood ten deep and at least thirty across at the base of the bridge. The causeway behind them was dark and deserted and the gateway to the bridge locked, but Rose caught sight of two mortal youths running down the street toward St. Olave's Parish. They were painfully thin and dressed in not much more than rags and did not stop to look over their shoulder as they fled.

Orphans avoiding the workhouse, no doubt. Whatever they had seen, it hardly mattered. No one would give the tales of poor children any merit. In fact,

Rose was rather glad to see *some* sign of life on the strangely deserted streets.

She wondered if the trolls had encountered any humans in their journey here, but had no way of asking them. The creatures didn't speak any language she had been able to discern, but communicated with a series of grunting noises and hand signals. Rose suspected Ambrose knew how to speak "troll," such as it were, but would never stoop to the indignity of grunting, even in the name of communication. He was able to call them in some manner, however, and their presence was most welcome.

They were not as deadly as other Fey might have been, but were more likely to put their lives on the line for Ambrose and therefore Rose herself. Ambrose's magic allowed the trolls to continue living among humans with one of his most powerful illusion spells which made the trolls appear as another native animal to the eyes of man.

In the East, Rose had seen their kind disguised as monkeys or cattle. But in urban areas such as London, they most often took on the appearance of vermin. These trolls would appear to be giant rats to the few brave mortals who ventured down into the sewers where they lived. The creatures were grateful for the freedom from persecution their disguises provided, and most eager to ensure Ambrose remained pleased with them.

"To the rear, Comtesse," Ambrose repeated as Rose came to stand beside him at the front of the makeshift army.

"Fewer of the Fearsome will die if my sword is at the front," Rose said, nodding to the leader of the trolls, an ancient, gnarled man of about three and half feet tall.

His leathery face stretched into what she guessed was an expression of pleasure, though it was difficult to read a smile among the many lines crossing his face. Not many honored the trolls with their chosen name, but her motives were hardly noble in calling them the Fearsome. She was counting on them for aid in defending her life. It was in her best interests if they were feeling every bit as deadly as the name implied.

"The Fearsome understand sacrifices must be made." Ambrose's displeasure with her was clear in his tone though his face was calm as he nodded his thanks to the Fearsome's leader.

"Allow Rose to stay. She fights as well as any man, and should choose her own position," Gareth offered from where he stood on Ambrose's other side, his twin swords raised to meet the ogres now no more than one hundred feet away.

"Your opinion is not needed, vampire." Ambrose practically barked the last word, making it clear that simply naming Gareth's nature was the gravest insult he could impart.

Faeries and vampires had loathed each other for centuries. That hatred always came to the surface sooner or later, no matter how they pretended to be pleased with their cooperation in matters such as controlling the ogre population.

"They have called for your sacrifice on the night of a full moon, Comtesse," Ambrose continued in his most caustic tone. "I care not for your life, but for what havoc your death could wreak on our world. I would prefer not to discover what the tribe will accomplish if your blood is spilled."

"Very well, then." Rose tried not to let hurt cloud her senses as she turned and threaded through the trolls to the back of the ranks. Ambrose didn't truly mean what he'd said. He was simply making a point in the cruelest way possible, as was his practice.

"Charming, Ambrose. You must fare well with the fairer sex," she heard Gareth murmur as she walked away.

Rose thought Ambrose might have growled in response, but couldn't be sure. Seconds later, the tribe descended in full force.

Soon the cacophony of battle filled the streets. Rose could hear nothing but the clanging of metal and the fierce pulse of blood pounding through her ears. She waited impatiently for the ogres to fight their way through to where she stood behind the last of the trolls, sword fairly humming with the need to dispatch more of the tribe.

The anticipation of battle was so much worse than the actual deed—another reason she preferred to be at the front of the fray. She would much rather be defending herself on all sides than shifting from foot to foot, watching those in front of her spill blood, or worse, have their own blood spilled.

Rose was so focused on the battle before her that she didn't think to turn to look over her shoulder. The road leading onto the bridge had been deserted mere seconds before and no creature, mortal or supernatural, would be able to force his way through the locked gate. The trolls themselves were damp and smelled foul, signaling they had crawled from the river and sewers, not crossed into Surrey by bridge.

She had no reason to suspect an attack from behind, though she supposed a part of her mind had been aware of the potential danger, because when two sets of rail-thin arms closed around her, knocking her sword from her hand, she suspected the identity of her attackers immediately.

CHAPTER FIVE

"We've got her! W-w-we've got her," one of the ogre children stammered into her hair.

"Hold her tight," the second ordered and Rose's breath whooshed from her lungs as the first readily obeyed.

Sucking in a desperate breath, Rose began to struggle, kicking mightily, determined to free herself though she was loathe to hurt the children behind her. Both boys were nearly as tall as she, but they couldn't be more than nine or ten years old.

The ogres had apparently brought their young to fight with them. Rose knew she shouldn't be surprised. They thought nothing of grinding up the bones of weaker children to make a paste they fed to the stronger. Why shouldn't they put their offspring in mortal danger?

"Ambrose!" She yelled the faerie's name, but he

did not turn. Neither did Gareth nor any of the trolls notice as she was pulled backward toward the gate.

"Free me now and I will let you live," Rose ordered, still struggling though she was as yet unwilling to use her full strength—or the dagger stored in her boot—upon them.

They were children, as innocent in this conflict as any faerie or human child. They were too young to have fed on mortals, and were victims of the foolish decisions of their parents. The part of her that longed to be a mother, that remembered holding two soft, sweet babes in her arms for a few precious hours, simply could not risk killing children if it wasn't absolutely necessary.

Though she knew it to be a fool's hope, Rose still clung to the belief that some ogres grew to adulthood without becoming rapists and murderers. That was why she never killed without at least the strong suspicion an ogre had slain a mortal. She held fast to the dream that someday her work would be unnecessary, that the tribe would learn to feed their hunger with other than mortal flesh and to mate among humans without resorting to forced encounters.

It was a hope that might be the death of her.

"Get her blood, hurry!" The sharp edge of a blade swung from behind Rose's back, cutting a searing trail across her throat.

Thankfully it was the weaker boy who had made the move. If it had been the stronger, the force might have been great enough to slit her throat in earnest, not merely slice the skin deeply enough for blood to pour, hot and wet, down the front of her shirt. Through the white-hot pain, Rose turned her head and bit down on the boy's wrist until she felt bone crunch beneath her teeth.

"Mother!" The boy howled and released her, allowing enough freedom of movement for Rose to pull one arm forward and thrust a sharp elbow into the ribs of the child behind her. He grunted in pain and loosened his hold as she spun free, reaching for the dagger in her boot.

"Drop your weapons," she said, turning on them with dagger raised. In her eyes, they were innocent children no longer, they had made sure of that.

She would disarm them if she could, and kill them if she must. She should have tried her best to kill them from the first. Her weakness for the young had allowed two rail-thin, untrained boys to get closer to killing her than dozens of their armed elders could have dreamed.

It seemed the pair read the predatory look in her eyes, for they turned and ran, scrambling over each other in their haste, though the smaller one still clung to the dagger coated with her blood. If he had dropped the weapon, Rose would have let them go, no matter how she cursed herself for her weakness. But their refusal gave her no choice but to pursue.

She raced after them, down the entryway to the bridge and onto the street, pressing her fingers to the wound at her throat with one hand and clutching her dagger with the other. She didn't waste time turning to fetch her sword, simply darted after the boys as they cut into a darkened alleyway that descended toward the river.

Rose heard them calling out to each other, but couldn't make out their words. She was getting dizzier by the moment, her pulse thudding in her ears. She fairly stumbled over piles of trash and filth, gagging as the sickeningly sweet smell of death wafted past her nose.

Something rotted there on the slick stones, but it was too dark to see if the corpse was human or animal. Rose thanked the heavens for that small blessing. If she'd been forced to gaze upon a putrid, bloated corpse, she doubted she could have continued after the boys. It was one thing to slay an enemy in the heat of battle, but quite another to be confronted with what that living being became once her sword had finished with him.

"Into the water," one of the boys panted.

"No, I don't think it will—"

"She's at our heels, there isn't time. Go!" There was a large splash and then a smaller one as one boy pushed the other into the Thames and followed after.

"Damnation," Rose cursed. She couldn't pursue them into the water. She was becoming too weak to swim and dared not risk letting the diseased water touch the wound at her neck. The Thames was not only London's water source but a sewer as well, and faerie healing techniques had taught her the evils of allowing filth into an open wound.

Rose turned back, hurrying down the alleyway toward the sounds of fighting. She was hardly fit to join the battle, but could at least rescue her sword from the ground and find a safe position to wait for the victors to be decided. If the trolls, Ambrose, and Gareth defeated the ogres, they would tend her wounds when they were able. If the ogres were victorious, it wouldn't matter that she was bleeding to death. The tribe would simply finish the job and be done with it.

As Rose emerged onto the street, the world began to spin before her eyes Her head felt strangely light and yet so heavy it was nearly impossible to hold herself upright. She was still bleeding freely, and a glance down at the front of her once cream-colored linen shirt revealed it to be crimson and black where human blood and ogre had mixed together. The garment clung to her skin, outlining the scraps of fabric she used to bind her breasts. The quantity of her own blood that had made its way from her body was disturbing, making her breath speed and her vision blur as the street tilted on its axis and a shudder ran through the stones at her feet.

"Ambrose," Rose whispered as she fell to her knees, praying he would somehow hear her plea and come to her aid.

He was in battle with two ogres, but only a few dozen of the tribe remained. The rest had either fled or lay dying on the street. The trolls would be triumphant, but Rose feared she would not live to celebrate the victory. She needed faerie magic to close her wound before she lost any more blood.

Another shudder shook the earth, and Rose's hands fell to the ground. She would have assumed the shaking was merely the product of her own infirmity, but this time she saw several of the ogres stumble as well. Even Ambrose tottered on his feet. Only the trolls, being closer to the trembling earth, seemed completely steady. They took advantage of that fact to rip asunder several of the tribe.

Gareth, however, was nowhere to be seen, and Rose wondered if he was among the fallen. There were several trolls lying still on the stones, but she couldn't spot the vampire. He could also have aided her in closing the wound, though trusting a vampire to mend a rift in the skin without tasting blood wasn't wise.

Still, she couldn't afford to wait and would have gladly gone into Gareth's arms. At this point, it hardly mattered. If she delayed much longer, she would no longer possess sufficient blood to fuel her heart and would die regardless.

"Dear Goddess," she mumbled as the earth shook hard enough to knock stones loose from the surrounding buildings. Bricks and mortar crashed down and the bridge itself groaned in its moorings. The world seemed to be coming to an end, but still the remaining ogres and trolls battled on.

Rose slid to the ground, lying flat on her stomach in the filthy street. She knew the dirt under her cheek was as much animal dung as earth, but she couldn't help herself. Between the lightness of her head and the strange tremors, it was impossible to remain on hands and knees. And she was so desperately tired.

She would simply lie still for a few moments and close her eyes. Surely a bit of sleep wouldn't do any harm. It certainly seemed like a delicious idea—to rest.

Yes. Rest. She would . . . just . . . close her eyes for a . . . bit . . . and . . .

WHEN ROSE AWOKE, the first sensation she registered was a bone-deep chill. It was as if ice had been poured into her very marrow and no amount of shaking or shivering could persuade it to thaw. Upon attempting to open her eyes, she found her lashes to be in a similar state, frozen shut, blinding her as surely as any mask.

Rosemarie . . . awaken, my daughter.

"Mother?" Rose's voice rose sharply as she moved her hands to her eyes, clawing at the ice crystals binding her lashes together.

Her mother had been dead for over a hundred years. If Rose could hear her voice, then she feared she would never truly awaken. She must have passed over the veil, into the world of the spirit, of the ghosts she had glimpsed in her travels through the realms of the supernatural.

There are many veils, dearest, barriers meant to keep the truth concealed. But you will know all if you but have the courage to seek what has been lost.

"All was lost, Mother. All. Our country, our legacy, our people." Hot tears leaked from behind Rose's closed lids, melting the ice that clung to her lashes.

Still, she was afraid to open her eyes, afraid her mother would appear as she had the last time Rose had dared set foot in her native land. The image of those she loved as rotten corpses seated upon crumbling thrones was burned into her mind like a brand. The sight had scarred her, damaged her, and set her upon a course more violent than she would have dreamt possible as a girl.

Look to me and know the truth at last, Rosemarie.

God help her, but she couldn't. She was afraid, so desperately afraid. More fearful than she was of an ogre's many teeth, or of the blades of a hundred enemies.

Do not fear me, my lady. For I am to be your salvation.

Her mother's voice had changed. Now it sounded as if it were a man who whispered into her mind. It was a familiar voice, but one she could not place until he spoke again.

And your husband, as well. If you will have me.

Rose's eyes flew open, but she was screaming even before she met the gaze of the ogre at the end of the bed. Suddenly her flesh was no longer cold, but scalding hot, shining with perspiration from the great effort of bearing the twin sons he had sired upon her in her enchanted sleep.

She was tied to her childhood bed, just as she had been that night long ago, when the pain of childbirth had awakened her from her rest twenty years early, causing the spell that bound her to become a curse. Agony ripped through her body like a knife as the ogre Benoit de Fournier reached between her legs, pulling the afterbirth from her body and drawing it inside his eagerly awaiting mouth.

Rose's stomach began to convulse as she watched him feed, and she barely managed to shift her head to the side before it emptied onto the soiled sheets.

Come away from those dark places, sweet. Yet another voice called to her, one she recognized as Gareth's. She had never been so happy to hear the vampire's voice. *Hear me and come away.*

"Yes, please God," she begged, sobbing as she wiped a shaking hand across her mouth. Before she could marvel at the fact that she was free to move, the scene before her transformed once more.

Now she found herself in a snug parlor before a roaring fire, seated on a padded armchair covered in elaborate silk tapestry. The material was the most extraordinary pale rose color, highlighted with threads of green as bright as new grass. Across from her sat Gareth, looking every inch the lord.

He wore a heavily embroidered coat of red with an overblown lace jabot at his neck nearly the same shade of pink as the chair upon which he sat. And, if she weren't mistaken, the vampire had painted his already pale face with white makeup and rouged his cheeks with two bright spots of color.

Renowned fop or no, she had never seen the man looking so ridiculous. Despite the horror of a moment before, it was nearly enough to make her laugh.

"It is you who have dressed me this way, madame," Gareth said, sniffing as he looked down at his coat. "The space we occupy is within your own mind, and therefore I cannot be held accountable for my ensemble."

"Within my mind?" Rose asked, digging her hands into the padded arms of her chair. It certainly felt real enough, and she had never before experienced anything so tangible in a dream.

"But if you really wish to see me in pink, I'm certain my tailor could oblige. Anything to please the lady." He winked at her, a rakish smile on his lips. "So long as your dressing me thus is not a judgment upon my virility."

"Really, sir, I wouldn't waste time pondering such—"

"Of course you would, but we shan't waste precious seconds arguing the point," Gareth said, his expression growing serious. "There isn't time, I'm afraid."

"What do you mean? I don't—"

"You must make a decision, Rose. I will do all I can to ensure your survival, but the tribe will come for you again before the next full moon." He leaned forward, gripping her hands in his. "You must be ready, prepared to face your enemies, both those in plain sight and those in shadow."

"I am always prepared, sir," Rose said, finding it oddly difficult to swallow as she gazed into Gareth's deep green eyes. "I am not the one who always forgets to bring along the proper weaponry—"

"There isn't time. I speak to you here because it is no longer safe to talk in the world above. But believe me, there are those who wish your death who have not a drop of ogre blood in their veins," he said, his expression tense, as though he too felt the fear that whispered across her skin.

The sight so unnerved her that she didn't think to pull away when he leaned closer and pressed his lips to hers. The kiss was soft, almost sweet, but had much the same effect as his passionate caresses a few nights previous. Rose was instantly aching for another, far less chaste meeting of their mouths, and felt her hands begin to tremble.

"You must seek out the truth," he whispered against her lips before pulling away. "It will be your greatest weapon."

"What truth?" Rose asked, though a part of her

instinctively knew the truth of which he spoke. It was the truth that lay in the past, in Myrdrean, in the places in her mind she feared to go.

"You know the—" A woman's moan echoed through the parlor, drowning out Gareth's words as it cast the room in darkness.

"Time has run out." The vampire released her hands with obvious reluctance.

"Wait, I . . ." Rose shivered as the darkness grew thicker, though she was no longer cold. She was quite warm, in fact. So warm that she began to grow drowsy despite the anxious beating of her heart.

"I would do naught to harm you, Rose." Gareth's voice grew more distant with each passing moment. "Remember that, and trust I do what is best."

Trust. It was no small gift to give, especially for a woman who trusted no one.

Yet you trust him, *blindly. The one who . . .*

Rose suspected the "him" in question was Ambrose, but the rest of the vampire's words were swallowed by the darkness. She was wondering what Gareth had to gain by inspiring mistrust in her liaison and oldest friend when the chair beneath her disappeared.

Then she was falling, without a sound, without a scream. Falling into a black pit so deep she wasn't certain she would ever find her way free of it.

CHAPTER SIX

The second time Rose awoke she felt quite well in body, though vexed in spirit. Something was troubling her, addling her thoughts. A bad dream, perhaps?

But she couldn't be bothered to remember the dream, not when she was feeling so wonderfully warm and content. No, not merely warm—hot. Her skin was burning, but the last thing she wanted was to cool it. She wanted to stay hot, wanted to luxuriate in the sensations racing through her body, stimulating every nerve ending, tightening her nipples and making her sex ache deliciously.

It was as if a thousand fingers were tracing over her flesh all at once, finding every little place where she yearned to be touched and applying the perfect, teasing pressure. Desire flooded her body, transporting her to a realm of pure feeling.

She couldn't remember ever, *ever*, feeling so alive. She tried to murmur her approval for whatever force held her in thrall, but her words came out as nothing more than a gurgle. There was something wrong with her throat, but she couldn't for the life of her remember—

The boy with the knife.

"Lie still, Rose. We've nearly finished." The voice sounded as warm and wonderful as she felt, and caressed her skin with the same teasing touch as those fingers. She could feel his breath puff softly across her lips. His face was close. His mouth was close. If she could just lift her head the slightest bit, she would feel that mouth on hers. Just a few inches more and—

"Shhh. Don't move. Quiet for a bit longer." Rose felt his arms tighten around her. For the first time she became aware of a strong arm cradling her head and shoulders, distinct from the fingers of sensation caressing the rest of her skin. "That's it, darling."

Darling?

The word cut through the sensuous fog. Why couldn't she remember who cared for her enough to call her his darling? She should remember. She should know. But there was no one. No one in the hundred years since her second gifting, no one in the eighty years she had slept, no one in the eighteen years before that when she'd been young and foolish enough to dream of a nobleman who would one day be her husband.

How she'd longed for a happy marriage and many children. She'd even begged her father to find someone young and fit, someone who was as pleasing to behold as . . . as the vampire holding her in his arms.

Gareth's face swam into focus through her slitted eyes. The dream and his warnings returned to her in a rush, making her heart race. She tried to sit up, to put some distance between them, but he held her fast. There was nothing but kindness, even tenderness in his gaze, but for some reason she was frightened, so frightened she struggled, fighting the safe, warm haze that threatened to consume her.

"Do not fight me, sweet. You'll hurt—"

"No." She forced out the word despite the agony slicing through her. She could feel the source of her unusual warmth now and she wanted no part of it. Blood no longer flowed out of the wound at her throat, but something hot and thick was flowing *in*.

"Very well then." Gareth glared down at her as if she were a naughty child. "But we aren't finished yet."

"Yes . . . we . . . are." Rose barely managed to spit out the words, so intense was the pain.

"As you wish, my lady." His jaw tight was tight as he brought his wrist to his mouth and ran his tongue along the deep wound to seal it. "Hopefully what I have done thus far will be sufficient to save your life."

Save her life. Then she hadn't been mistaken. He'd given her an infusion of his own blood. Tears sprung into her eyes. She didn't want to become a vampire, couldn't imagine being anything more bloodthirsty than she already was. She couldn't bear it, wouldn't—

"Don't weep, Rose. Come now, it isn't as bad as all that. In fact, it can be quite lovely if you'll allow it." He smiled, a wicked twist of his lips, and lowered his head to her throat.

"Oh Goddess," she moaned as she arched into his mouth against her will. The feel of his tongue teasing along the wound was disturbing, but that didn't make it any less enjoyable.

Enjoyable. It was a pale word to describe the eroticism of his mouth on her skin, the way her heart raced and her body felt shot full of lightning. She moaned and lifted her hands to his unbound hair, threading her fingers through the soft locks, pulling that kissing, licking mouth closer as his body moved over hers. She was dimly aware of his weight settling between her legs, pressing her into something soft and fragrant smelling, but it was difficult to concentrate on anything but the sensual fire coursing through her every cell.

They were in a bed; that much penetrated her fractured consciousness. She saw the deep blue canopy behind Gareth's head and heard the crackle of a fire burning somewhere nearby. It wasn't that fire that warmed her, however. Her heat came from within, from the foreign blood pulsing through her veins, scalding away her mortality.

The change would begin soon, no doubt.

She'd had the unfortunate experience of observing the transformation from mortal to vampire before, had seen a young woman claw at her flesh as her humanity was stripped away, leaving her a ravenous beast unable to control her lust for blood. Ambrose had been forced to kill the woman before she attacked an army camped nearby. She'd had no maker there to help her through the insanity of a newly born vampire's hunger.

Rose assumed she would have Gareth, but was that any comfort? To be bound to a man she didn't trust as surely as a newborn babe to its mother, too helpless to make her way on her own for decades, perhaps more?

To be dependent on him to aid her in navigating a new world and a new way of life—or rather death—she never would have chosen for herself?

"You should have let me die," she murmured, tears pricking behind her closed eyes despite the fact that she still pressed Gareth close, her hands wandering from his silken hair down his broad back, clawing into the muscled flesh. The very *bare* muscled flesh. He was unclothed, and if her senses didn't deceive her she was . . .

As naked as the day you were born.

Goddess help her, but the knowledge caused a spark of delight to pierce through her sorrow, and her body to send forth a rush of heat hotter than the blood pulsing through her veins.

"I didn't drink from you, Rose. You will not be transformed." He mumbled the words against her throat, but she couldn't seem to make sense of them, not when his palms smoothed up her ribs to tease the bottom of her breasts.

Rose moaned and arched closer to his large hands, wanting more than that gentle touch. She wanted him to knead her swollen, aching flesh in his hands, wanted his fingers to pinch and tease, wanted him to capture each point with his teeth and bite until she screamed.

It had been so long since she'd been in bed with a man, since she'd felt the sensual comfort of another's skin hot against her own. She was already half mad with desire, and he hadn't done more than seal her wound and lay gentle hands on her skin. Still, she was ready for so much more, ready to feel his cock shoving between her legs, to coat his shaft with slick heat as she lifted her hips, pulling him deeper, mating fast and furious until they both lost themselves in pleasure.

"Did you hear me? Do you understand?" he asked as she spread her legs wide and ground into his taut abdomen. His face was level with her breasts, and she was torn between wanting to pull those lips up for a kiss—thereby pulling something more useful between her legs—and postponing that pleasure until he closed his full lips around the pink nipple that strained toward him.

"Rose, look at me," he demanded, hands moving to cup her face, forcing her to stare deep into his hypnotic green eyes. Rose felt herself falling into their depths before she could even think to fight, felt herself spinning into Gareth, into his power, into his control. And she wasn't scared or concerned. She was . . . free. Free to succumb to everything she'd wanted since the moment she laid eyes on him.

"Make love to me," she demanded, her voice husky and thick. She sounded drunk even to her own ears, and felt more intoxicated than she'd ever been on faerie wine, but she didn't care. She wanted Gareth, wanted to feed him, fuck him, to crawl inside his skin and become a part of his very essence.

"Dear Rose, you are more mortal than I thought." He laughed softly, but it was a strained sound and the force with which his mouth descended upon hers was far from controlled.

Rose hummed her pleasure against his lips as he kissed her hard enough for her mouth to feel bruised and sore and deliciously, wickedly alive. His tongue swept through her mouth, and she tasted everything that had been forbidden. He was that last sip of wine she had never allowed herself to drink, the pull of the opium pipe in dark Eastern places, the freedom of bedding a man without holding her heart at a distance.

"You intoxicate me." His voice was harsh and his breath came fast, puffing against her lips in a way that made Rose squirm beneath him, restless to get back to more intimate business. "Wait, Rose. I want—"

"I do not wish to wait," she said, lifting into him in a shameless imitation of how she would move after he had thrust himself inside her.

"Damnation, you *will*. Pull yourself free."

"I don't want to be free, I want to be *yours*." At that moment, she believed the words with all of her heart, all of her soul.

A part of her understood she had fallen into Gareth's thrall and that this desperate devotion wasn't real, but the rest of her couldn't be bothered with such nonsense. She had never felt so safe, so cared for, so . . . loved, as she did staring up into those green eyes. It might very well be illusion, but she was certain she would rather labor under that sweet lie forever than live another day in her empty world before.

"Take me, please. I beg you to—"

He groaned and gave in to the pull of her frantic hands at his shoulders. He met her lips again, but only for a second. Then he was gone, kissing down the column of her throat, across the hollow where her pulse beat fiercely, and down to those wanton breasts that puckered into diamond points, desperate for his attention.

"Gareth." She called out his name in a prayer of thanksgiving as he flicked his tongue across her tightened tip. Sharp tugs of desire tightened her womb, bringing her close to the edge as he opened his mouth and took her breast inside, sucking her deep into his wet heat, pulling hard enough for the pleasure to sting into delicious pain.

Rose shifted restlessly beneath him, legs churning against the soft sheets and the rougher flesh of his thighs. The purely masculine feel of that rock hard, furred skin against hers was almost as breathtaking as the mouth teasing back and forth between her breasts. She was quickly losing her mind with want, tossing her head back and forth, tugging at Gareth's thick arms, silently pleading for him to push that part of him she'd yet to see or feel into where she burned with need.

"Please, please," she moaned, wiggling her hips beneath him. Her skin was hot and sticky, but his was cool and unbelievably hard. The contrast drove her lust even higher. *"Please!"*

"Please?" He pulled away from her breasts and pushed the swells together, staring down at the flushed skin with a heated look that left no doubt how lovely he found the sight. "Please what, darling?" He lifted his eyes to meet hers and slowly, deliberately flicked his tongue out over one dark, passion-flushed nipple.

Rose gasped and arched beneath him, that final touch nearly bringing her over, causing the wet heat between her thighs to become a veritable flood. "Make love to me," she pleaded, being called his "darling" no longer disturbing her in the slightest. In fact, it felt perfect. Desire knotted low and tight in her body, and something that felt like her heart squeezed inside her chest. She needed him, needed him so desperately that she began to beg. "I'll do anything you wish, swear any oath you name. But I beg you, just love me. I need—"

"Rose, please." He surged over her, silencing her with a kiss as his hand smoothed up the inside of her thigh. "You aren't making it easy to be honorable."

"Yes, oh God, Gareth, *yes*." She spread her legs even further, offering him complete access to where she practically wept with need for him.

His breath hissed through his teeth as his fingers played through where she was swollen and slick. He was surprisingly gentle in his explorations, teasing through her folds, brushing ever so softly over where she throbbed, but it was still nearly enough to take her the rest of the way. She trembled and shook under his touch, so close, so terribly close. But she needed more, needed to feel him swelling inside her as they both claimed their pleasure.

"I want to feel you." Rose hummed the words into his mouth, slipping them in between kisses, her hands busy in the hair that hung around her face, a silken curtain that kept out the world and all its harsh realities.

"You *are* feeling me, Rose." He circled her nub forcefully, illustrating his point by drawing more cream from her body.

"Not that. I want—" She reached down, trying to find something hard and hot to fill her, but he pushed her away, shifting until his arousal was firmly out of her reach.

"I want you, sweet. Have no doubt of that," he said, wringing another cry from her throat as two thick fingers shoved inside her channel. "I want you desperately."

"Then take me. Please!" Rose bucked into him, forcing his penetration deeper. He could never be close enough, she could never take him deep enough, and fingers could never fill her in the way she needed. She wanted his body tunneling into hers, couldn't understand why he so stubbornly withheld that satisfaction.

"Then *take* me, Gareth," she repeated, clawing at his shoulders until she scratched trails into his skin, her words ending in a sob. "I will go mad if I don't feel you inside me."

"Rose, you will not—"

"*Fuck* me, Gareth." He paused, mouth open. "Fuck me," she repeated, feeling marvelously wicked as his eyes darkened in response to her coarse language.

She had never spoken thus to a man, not in all her years. But as soon as the words escaped her lips, she couldn't imagine why she had restrained herself. A purely feminine power swept through her, sharpening her desire to a knifepoint. "Fuck me. I want your cock inside my—"

"You test me, Rose," Gareth said, his jaw clenched so tightly muscles twitched beneath the skin. "I gave my oath and will not be forsworn."

She whispered against his lips, dizzy with the excitement of playing with this unique brand of fire. "Fuck me. Please, fu—"

Her words were interrupted by the hot press of his mouth. He kissed her until her head spun, until stars danced behind her closed eyes and she feared she would faint from the pleasure of it. And all the while his hand worked between her legs, delving in and out of her wet heat, driving her passion higher and higher until she trembled and shook beneath him.

She had never felt like this, never in all her life. Even without the penetration she craved, she was connected to Gareth, body and soul, as near to him as she had ever been to anyone. The pleasure coursing through her was more than physical. She was completely exposed. Safe, yet vulnerable in a way that would have frightened her if she'd been in her right mind.

But perhaps she *was* in her right mind, in a way she had never dared to be before.

"Trust me, sweet. I would never hurt you. Never," Gareth whispered against her lips, his breath coming fast. "Remember that when you come to your senses."

The words seemed to infer something more, but there wasn't time to grasp what that something might be before the tension building with her reached its breaking point.

Rose screamed Gareth's name as she came, clawing fingers down his back as her womb clenched with a pleasure so fierce she feared her body could not contain it. Wave after wave of ecstasy swept along her skin, until her very fingertips burned and the entirety of her being was given over to pure wanton bliss.

"Rosemarie." Gareth cried out against her lips, a tortured sound that caused Rose's eyes to fly open.

The vampire hovered above her, the deep green of his eyes nearly eclipsed by the black pupils, lending him an otherworldly appearance that caused a different kind of shiver to work through her. She had a split second to realize where she'd seen that look before, and then he struck, fangs flashing as he lifted her to him with one arm. The movement was so swift, so unexpected, that her head snapped back, baring her newly healed throat to his attack.

Rose didn't tense for the blow, couldn't manage it with the waves of pleasure coursing through her body, flowing from her sex to every inch of her flesh. A part of her even thrilled to feel his arm pinning her to him as his other hand fisted in her hair, holding her captive to his thirst.

She felt his breath on her neck, the barest scrape of his bared teeth, but the anticipated pain didn't come.

"Gareth?" She had barely whispered the word when he went limp, dropping her to the bed and falling heavily next to her. "Gareth?" she asked again, turning to look where he lay no more than a few inches away. She wondered at the strange slackness of his features, worrying for a moment that she might have somehow killed the man before he drew in a breath and let it out with a hearty snore.

He was asleep. Gareth had fallen asleep before taking the opportunity to feed upon her. For a vampire, that was . . . incredibly insulting.

"Would you have preferred he be allowed to sup

CHAPTER SEVEN

February 15, 1750
Vauxhall Pleasure Gardens
London, England

"Comtesse de Fournier! My lady." Lord Pommerel doffed his hat and bowed deeply.

"Lord Pommerel, good day." Rose curtsied, doing her best to conceal her frustration at being forced to exchange pleasantries with yet another member of polite Society. If she had known the gardens would be so crowded she would have donned her boy's disguise before walking abroad.

"Lady Pommerel and I were most distressed to be cheated of the pleasure of your company at Lord Drummand's country party. Our eldest daughter was ailing, however, and deemed unfit for travel."

Oh dear God, not the party again. Rose had obviously underestimated the excitement caused by the discovery of the servant's head. "Indeed, your absence was felt by all assembled, my lord."

"Doubtful, my lady," he said, following the words with a bark of laughter. "His lordship invites the most fashionable of the distinguished members of Society. A country party at Westinghouse is always certain to be a delight, which was why we were so very shocked to hear of the most foul dispatch of a lovely young girl in the earl's employ."

Lady Pommerel's eyes bulged from their sockets with curiosity as her husband finished his speech. She leaned closer to Rose, lifting the edge of her heavily powdered wig away from her ear so as to be certain not to miss a word of the gossip.

Marta, who had been walking a bit behind, quietly moved back a few more paces. Rose could practically feel the anxiety radiating from her companion at being so near the nosy mortals and suspected Marta wished she had stayed behind with the other servants. But Rose had insisted on paying the shilling for the sprite's admission. Not only was it wise to have a chaperone in attendance even during the daylight hours, but Marta's presence was imperative to her present mission.

Besides, it was comforting to have a female companion nearby. Rose had felt in desperate need of a little feminine guidance in the past few days, though she had refrained from mentioning her discomfiture to the sprite. Marta was still distressed by Rose's near death and hardly needed to be bothered by matters as ridiculous as her mistress's romantic entanglements.

"Yes, the entire affair was horrid and shocking." Rose pushed away thoughts of the men in her life and affected a troubled expression as she lifted her face to the fading midwinter sun.

The Vauxhall Gardens were doing a phenomenal business considering the season. February was hardly a month for Society to mingle outside the ballroom, but temperatures had been quite mild. It felt more like springtime than the dead of winter, and the whole of London was out enjoying the weather.

Rose would have been enjoying it as well if she hadn't suspected the warmth to be a result of an ogre pact made with lesser demons. Just as she would have enjoyed walking in the pleasure garden if she weren't looking for signs of blood magic while being detained by curious members of the peerage.

Despite the "earthquake" last week, the murder at Lord Drummand's was still at the forefront of *ton* gossip. Though they would pretend to be appalled were she to confide the details of the event, Rose knew each lord and lady who stopped to chat was practically aquiver for further details about the unfortunate chambermaid.

"Is it true the young woman's head was found in the grotto? And that the authorities have put a price on a nobleman's life?" Lord Pommerel asked, jolted into speech by the pinch his wife administered to his arm.

"My lord, I do not wish to distress Lady Pommerel with such garish details," Rose demurred, lowering her eyelashes to conceal her frustration.

Society and its trappings were quickly losing their appeal. There was much to be done before the next full moon, when the ogres would once more be able to attempt whatever black spell they'd been about by the Thames. She had to put a stop to the tribe's scheme before it was too late. She'd already wasted three days lying half dead in Ambrose's guest room, and another two recovering strength at her own home. It was driving her mad to waste even a single second in idle conversation.

"Come now, dear, I shan't swoon." Lady Pommerel finally spoke for herself, laying a white glove on Rose's arm as she leaned down to capture her gaze. The lady was quite tall for an Englishwoman, but far too round to be of the tribe. Even if a tribeswoman fed on human flesh every day for years, Rose doubted an ogress could ever reach such . . . epic proportions. "I've been beside myself with worry. You must tell us if there is truly a murderer loose among us."

"The poor girl clearly met with foul play, my lady. But as to who might be responsible, I can't say I have heard one way or the other." Feigning great delicacy, Rose unfurled her fan and weakly fluttered it in front of her face. "Now, if you'll excuse me, I fear I must seek out some quiet corner. I was injured during the earthquake, and have been out of sorts ever since."

"Of course, you poor dear. I slept as the dead through the entirety of the event, but was still most unsettled upon waking." Lady Pommerel tutted as Rose gripped the arm Marta slid beneath hers and made her halting progress down the South Walk. She'd assumed she would be less vulnerable to the perils of polite chatter here than on the Grand Walk, but Vauxhall was swarming with people of every shape, size, and rank.

Not to mention several ogres—though none who seemed to recognize Rose—a few faeries, and one or two vampires old enough to walk in the fading light before the sun had fully set.

"Are you unwell, my lady? I could fetch the carriage—"

"I am feeling quite fine. I simply grow weary of polite conversation."

"You should consider a move to the stage," Marta

whispered as they limped slowly past a vampire luring a buxom young wench onto one of the more secluded trails. The lamps had yet to be lit, and under the trees it looked as if night had already fallen. "You could certainly teach the ladies at Drury Lane a thing or two regarding verisimilitude."

"Thank you," Rose said, thinking how those same words would have been spoken in high jest by Ambrose or Gareth. She missed both men far more than she would have thought possible.

Once Rose had crawled from her bed in Ambrose's guest quarters, she had gone to seek him in his study. He'd informed her that he'd given Gareth permission to provide her with an infusion. She had been hovering near death for days and Ambrose's magic could do nothing for her. He had finally allowed Gareth to come to her aid provided he not drink of her blood.

Not trusting him more than any other vampire, however, Ambrose had put a sleeping spell upon him, one that would activate the moment Gareth attempted to sink his fangs into her flesh. Ambrose had also gone a step further, remaining outside the door, using his telepathic skills to oversee the situation. It was something he wouldn't think of doing under usual circumstances, being respectful of the sanctity of the mind.

He had made an exception that evening, to protect her. It was that decision that had cost them their friendship. She had read his disappointment and revulsion from the moment she approached him in his study.

She'd been wearing nothing but a silk wrap and knew she must have looked the picture of a wanton who all too easily succumbed to a vampire's charms.

She had managed to free herself from her spellbound state, but a part of her wanted to believe the passion she'd felt was more than a trick of vampire glamour.

Unfortunately, Rose had been too weak to shield her thoughts from Ambrose. But even if she had, she doubted it would have made a difference. Ambrose had read her mind as she opened herself to Gareth, succumbing to him in a way she never had before with any man, mortal or supernatural.

Whether Ambrose hated her for that weakness, or for allowing a vampire to touch her, or for simply being vulnerable to temptation in a way even she herself had not wished to admit, she couldn't say. But it was certain he loathed her, he'd made that clear. She couldn't even imagine that his reaction was one of jealousy. He was too calm and direct to be mistaken for a man who had ever harbored tender feelings for her.

Even in the midst of these dangerous circumstances, he refused to communicate in person. He sent messengers, or spoke with Marta via the enchanted pool in Rose's garden. When she needed his wisdom, guidance, and friendship the most, he had abandoned her. He'd sent troll guards to protect her home and communiqués Rose knew were meant to aid her in thwarting the ogres before they came for her a second time. But those deeds seemed hollow without the chance to look into his dark eyes or to hear the rumble of his voice as they sat by his fire and worked through the mystery together.

Still, with the help of his research, she'd come to the conclusion that the bloodied blade the boy carried into the Thames had completed some aspect of the spell, causing the quaking of the earth. Even without Ambrose's aid in understanding water spells, it was clear that plunging a blade covered in her blood into the Thames had a disastrous effect.

But either there hadn't been enough of her blood, or words had to be spoken when blood met water, or something else entirely, because the business of the tribe had not been completed. Agitated ogres still swarmed London, though most did not recognize Rose. Only the few survivors who had attacked her in the country garden seemed to know her true identity, and she suspected only those few knew the nature of the bargain they had made with whatever black force hovered around the Thames.

But those few were enough. They would rally the others and come for her blood again. Of that she had no doubt. The dark power demanded it. Whether it be demonic or worse, Rose knew the force was evil, and that the ogres had no clue what they risked in order to wipe one woman from the face of the earth.

"Why not simply hire someone to kill me? A mercenary, perhaps," Rose wondered aloud, bringing her gloved hand to her mouth and nibbling the seam at her thumb. "I'm only a woman, and easily killed when compared to other supernatural creatures."

"You are not just a woman to them, you are a legend." Marta sighed softly as three children walked by with their nursemaid.

The sprite adored children. Rose knew she lamented that she would never have any of her own. She had never spoken of it, but sorrow was clear in every line of her relatively plain face. Just as her rare smiles transformed Marta into something lovely, her pain aged her, making her look every one of her years despite her eternally youthful visage.

"Perhaps you should leave, Marta. It seems anyone close to me is in danger. You could seek other employment," Rose said, feeling strangely maudlin. Everyone else had all but deserted her, why not send Marta on her way as well? Rose would rather her friend be safe than perish due to mere association with her mistress.

"My lady, you are not yourself. You must not succumb to such weak thinking."

"Weak or realistic?" Rose sighed. The sun was setting, deep and red, behind the decorative archways of the South Walk. For a moment it was easy to believe she and Marta truly roamed the ancient ruins the structures had been designed to emulate.

"We are all bound together in this matter," Marta said with surprising firmness. "Neither you nor I will ever be free of the Fey de la Nuit. A contract with them is signed in blood. Just as Master Minuit can not desert your cause, we can never—"

"But Ambrose has deserted me! Not once have we been in such discord."

"The black faerie is a fool, but I had thought better of you, my lady." Marta's words were harder than any she had ever spoken, and shocked Rose into stopping in the middle of the path. "You can ill afford to allow such emotions to affect your mind. I have seen the danger that lies down that road."

"What danger?" Rose asked.

"I . . ." Marta paused, dropping her eyes to her hands. Something was troubling her. The merry Marta who had teased her at the country party had not appeared since the night of Rose's attack. Rose had assumed concern for her was the cause of the sprite's distress, but perhaps something else was amiss.

"Tell me, friend. I swear I will listen—"

"It is nothing. Forgive me."

Rose put a gentle hand on the Marta's elbow. "No, it is you who must forgive *me*." The other woman was hurting, and Rose cursed herself for failing to notice. She was a poor friend to be so consumed by her own troubles that she neglected to notice others.

"There is nothing to forgive, my lady." Marta moved away, as if uncomfortable with Rose's touch. "I am merely concerned because we passed two ogres near the Gothic temple, yet you didn't seem to note their presence."

Rose turned, scanning their surroundings.

"They've gone, but never before would you have let such a thing escape you."

"You're right. I have been . . . distracted." Rose gritted her teeth, furious with herself for letting emotions interfere with her work.

She had served as an executioner to the Fey de la Nuit longer than any other, not merely because of her faerie gifts, but because she kept her head. To let sadness over losing Ambrose's regard, or worry over the disappearance of Gareth affect her performance was foolish in the extreme.

Ambrose might loathe her, but he was aiding her in this investigation and was still her liaison. And Gareth wasn't dead; Rose knew that for certain. Ambrose would never risk the political repercussions that would result from killing an older, well-established vampire.

Besides, this wasn't the first time Gareth had disappeared without word. It was only her own foolishness that insisted she should have heard from him. To him, the intimacies they'd shared were likely of no consequence at all. She was a fool for harboring a naïve hope that he might attempt to woo her as he had threatened.

"I am sorry, Marta. I—"

"No, please don't, my lady. I am simply concerned for you. It isn't only the ogres you must fear," Marta said. Rose shivered, knowing the chill had little to do with the falling temperatures now that twilight drew near. "The messages in the waters have been most disturbing."

"But you've been unable to decipher anything more specific?" Rose asked, gesturing for Marta to join her on a nearby bench.

It would be best to wait for full darkness before continuing their search. In the daylight, they'd had little success locating signs of blood magic. At night, it would be easier.

Black magic produced an aura resembling a bruise, dull green and brown light that would be easier to spot without the competing glare of the sun. Rose wasn't adept at marking the phenomenon, but Marta could read such energies as well as the enchanted properties of water.

"No, the language in the water is not one I've heard before. In fact, it is hardly speech at all. It is more primitive than words, more like . . ."

"Like what?" Rose prodded when Marta fell silent. Marta had only had the power of speech for a short time. Often she resorted to telepathy without realizing she'd ceased to speak aloud.

"Marta, are you well?" Rose asked again, her heart leaping as Marta's wide, brown eyes grew cloudy, fixed upon some distant horror. "Marta—"

"The wails are like the creaking of the floors when the banshee walks. Like the groaning of the trees as a storm blows in." As if summoned by her words, a swift wind rushed down the walk, threatening to lift their hats from their heads. "The old one . . . she is awake . . . I fear there's been a terrible mistake . . ."

Rose pressed one hand atop her straw bonnet and the other around Marta's thin arm. Even through her gloves and the thick wool of Marta's dress, Rose could feel how cold the sprite's skin had become. Marta was behaving just as she did when transported by visions, but there wasn't a drop of water in view. Rose had never seen a vision overtake her companion against her will, and was frightened.

"Marta, come back to me. Close your eyes and think on the present." But Marta didn't seem to hear. Her eyes remained glazed, as if she had been mesmerized by a creature of the night.

The thought made Rose turn her eyes in the direction of her companion's, searching the darkness under the trees. At first she saw nothing, but slowly, as the last rosy glow of sunset faded away, Rose glimpsed a hint of swirling green light just above one of the drainage ditches that emptied into the Thames. Her throat went tight and it became nearly impossible to breathe until she forced her eyes back to the ground.

"Dear Goddess," Rose whispered, the feel of the Great Mother's name on her lips offering comfort.

It was what they had come searching for, but a part of her hadn't truly expected to find it. The aura indicated that blood magic had occured in that very spot.

"Marta, look at me," Rose demanded as loudly as she dared with people still strolling nearby. Dusk was giving way to night, but there was a concert planned for later in the evening. Rose had heard many of the nobility speak of staying for the entertainment before heading off to various dinner parties.

Though a part of her was soothed by the knowledge that others were near, she suddenly wondered what would happen if she and Ambrose were wrong.

What if the ogres did not wait for the next full moon before attempting their spell a second time? What if they threw their people's laws to the wind and attacked during hours when mortals would be out in force?

Communiqués from Ambrose had warned that the blood sacrifices likely ran up and down the length of the Thames and throughout the English countryside. The location of the chambermaid's head was no accident. It had been deliberately placed in the grotto due to its proximity to a tiny stream. A stream that became a tributary of the Thames as it flowed south.

The ogres were using water as a conduit for their spell. The blood sacrifices were like hundreds of hearts that would pump black power into the water when the time was right, turning it deadly. There had been scores of injuries reported after the quake on the eighth of February, many of which could not be attributed to the shaking of the earth. Dozens of dead bodies with no apparent injuries—among them two youths Rose guessed were the young ogres who had attacked her—had been found on the banks of the Thames, dead from causes unclear to the authorities.

Ambrose suspected any who had been in contact with the water while the spell was active had fallen prey to the black magic. But what might happen to those standing in the path of the aura? Rose could only guess, since the first spell had been cast at night and seemed to have a component to it that kept all mortals—except her—abed.

Ambrose hadn't offered any explanation as to why Rose hadn't also succumbed to the deep sleep. He merely sent a note stating "perhaps you have spent too much time abed to succumb so easily." He had been referring to her enchanted rest, something he hadn't mentioned since the night she had been granted faerie aid. That he would mention it now, knowing how the memory of her enchantment haunted her, told Rose the truth depths of his loathing.

"No . . . no . . . never," Marta moaned. "It was not our . . . no!"

"Marta, we must quit this place." Rose stood and hauled the other woman to her feet though the sprite was stiff as a board and twice as cumbersome. Rose grunted as Marta leaned heavily against her, but she forced them both forward as best she could manage.

Marta hadn't mentioned anything about the dark auras having the ability to trouble her mind. Rose would rather abandon their quest than have her companion remain in thrall to some nameless darkness.

As they began to walk away, however, footsteps sounded from behind. The steps were fast and hard, as if the person they belonged to was in pursuit. Some instinct deep within Rose screamed for her to run, to flee the garden as though her life depended upon the swiftness of her escape. She urged Marta to a faster pace, her heart pounding in her throat, wondering if they would be ensnared by whatever evil had trailed them to Vauxhall.

CHAPTER EIGHT

"Comtesse, what an unexpected pleasure." The speed with which the man moved to block their passage left no doubt he wished to engage her attention. The tightness of his tone, however, made her suspect this meeting was neither unexpected nor a pleasure.

Rose ground to a halt, inwardly fuming. She didn't know whether to be relieved it wasn't an ogre who pursued them, or frustrated that it was *this* man. Gareth. Whom she could not rip asunder, no matter how greatly she wished it.

Rip him asunder, indeed. You'd prefer to rip that cumbersome greatcoat from his broad shoulders. Even now your pulse races.

Blast it all. The voice of reason was apparently on holiday, giving the voice of temptation free rein.

"Lord Shenley." Rose curtsied as propriety demanded, but could feel a scowl furrow her brows. No matter how much a glance from those flashing green eyes affected her, she must remember the gentleman before her was a scoundrel. "How delightful to see you, my lord."

"Yes, of course." An arrogant scoundrel, no less. "But you'll have to pardon me—"

"No, you must pardon me. My companion isn't well, and we are—"

"Listen to me." Gareth gripped her upper arm in a manner that anyone watching would judge far too familiar. "I will not allow you to spend another moment in that wretch's company."

"You dare to insult a friend when you—"

"*Friend* indeed. The lady is a snake," he said, his grip tightening until she winced.

"You forget yourself, sir," Rose said, wrenching free from his grasp.

"Forgive me. But I must insist—"

"And *I* must insist that you remove yourself before I'm forced to call a constable." The gardens had their share of constabulary to combat the thieves out to pick noblemen's pockets and those who would force themselves upon an unwilling lady.

"Spare me the theatrics, Rose." Gareth's eyes grew darker, as they did during battle or . . . other instances when passions ran high.

Dear God, woman. Keep your head about you and your thoughts far from the boudoir.

"I would be happy to spare you my company altogether," Rose said, tilting her nose into the air. "Good day, my lord."

"Rosemarie Edenberg!" he roared, drawing the attention of a lamplighter not ten feet away. "Obey me this instant."

"No," Rose whispered, staring straight in his magnetic eyes, making it clear that she was no longer subject to his will. He had made a fool of her once. She would be damned if she would afford him the opportunity to do so again.

"Please," he said, tone more controlled. "Do not allow petty anger to impede—"

And outraged laugh burst from her lips. "You flatter yourself, sir. Petty anger, indeed!" The nerve of the man.

Gareth's eyes rolled. "Women. You are kindred spirits, one and all. Though I had presumed you to be above such behavior."

She barely resisted the urge to pull her sword and cut his heart out on the spot.

"You have already cut me to the core with your distrust. Why not take my heart as well?" Rose lips parted in surprise as she realized Gareth had read her unspoken thoughts. "Now come with me immediately, or I will be forced—"

"Someone help me! Please, I—"

"Very well, my lady."

"My lord!" Rose gasped as Gareth pulled her from Marta's side with one hand and picked the sprite up and returned her to the bench with the other. Marta remained where she was placed, obviously still stricken by the vision that had overwhelmed her.

Rose hadn't truly intended to create a scene, but now she feared she might have no choice but to summon the authorities. Gareth was behaving like a madman. Such a show of strength was bound to draw attention. Surely he hadn't managed to avoid exposure as a vampire by behaving in such a reckless fashion.

"How else is a man to conduct himself in the face of such pigheadedness?" He seized her arm and bustled Rose toward a narrow path leading from the main walk. She stumbled not once, but twice, and her hat flew from her head in a sudden gust of wind, but still he didn't stop.

"My hat! Gareth, I—"

"Damn your hat!"

"Damn *you,* sir!"

"Consider it done. I am a vampire, after all, my most vexing lady."

"Vexing? *You,* sir, are the one who makes a habit of vanishing for days without word. You are the one who—" With no small degree of effort, Rose pulled her mind away from her many grievances, not the least of which was the blood he had placed in her veins, which was no doubt giving him the power to read her private thoughts.

"Forgive me," he said, anger clear in his tone. "I should swing from the gallows for daring to save your life."

Rose felt her anger fade as she was forced to admit the man was right. "Please, Gareth, stop. Let's discuss this in a reasonable fashion. I cannot leave Marta alone. She is in a vulnerable state. She isn't well and—"

"Of course she isn't well. She's looked into the eye of her own dark magic. Any witch out of their first decade would know better. I assume this is Marta's first time dabbling in the black arts."

Gareth guided her deeper under the cover of the trees, away from the center of the pleasure garden where the concert would begin any moment. Perhaps he planned to wait until the orchestra began to play before wringing her neck, reducing the risk of discovery if she were to make some sort of noise.

"Rose," he said, her name a soft accusation. He pinned her with a wounded look. "You don't truly believe I plan to hurt you?"

Rose stared into his eyes as she remembered how he had spoken those same words in her dream, when he had seemed a faithful ally to her cause. Damn, but she was softening toward this man in a way she never had before. It might very well be the death of her, but she knew it was not Gareth's hand that would deal the killing blow. "No, I do not believe you would hurt me. But you distract me, my lord, as you must realize if you can truly read my thoughts."

"You distract me as well, Rose. You have no idea how greatly." He pulled her closer, until she could feel the warmth of his body against her front. "You look simply ravishing in this brown silk, by the by."

Rose sighed. She was hopeless where this man was concerned. He had forced her to abandon her companion and still a part of her longed to drag him further into the shadows, to show him other ways they might distract themselves.

"I find that thought more delightful than I should considering your low opinion of me, sweet," he said. "And I wish for your sake I was mistaken about Marta. But black magic clings to her as thick as it did the ogres who attacked us in the country."

"Would you please stop reading my thoughts?"

"My blood flows in your veins," he said, an intimate timbre to his voice that made her tingle with awareness. "I will always be able to hear your thoughts within a certain proximity. If you would allow me a small drink, it would be the same for you." He cupped her cheek before trailing his fingers slowly down the column of her throat. "Wouldn't you relish such a chance? You would finally be able to prove, beyond a shadow of a doubt, I am the wicked scoundrel you assume."

"I might also be transformed." Rose stepped away, putting distance between them.

Not only was his touch disarming, but his smell was no longer something she could note without being affected. He had always smelled of evergreens and sea air—a strange mix for a vampire, but pleasing all the same. Now, however, she was aware of the subtler smell of his skin, of the soap he used upon his hair, of the distinct Gareth scent that had clung to her body for days, driving her half mad with the desire to bed the man again.

"Only half mad?" he asked, a sparkle in his eye. "Then my mission has yet to be accomplished."

"What mission is that, my lord?"

"To be the first to make you swoon, sweet." He drew closer, leaning down until his lips were mere inches from hers. "Next time, you will be well, and I will have no reason to exercise restraint."

"You are most cocksure, my lord."

"You have no idea, my lady." He winked and Rose could not help but laugh.

"You are a rake."

"One of my finest attributes, in my humble opinion."

"Speaking of your opinion," Rose said, sobering as she was reminded of the reason for their interlude beneath the trees. "I scarcely understand how your opinion should cause me to turn my back on a woman I consider a friend. Who, unlike you, has never lied to me."

"Lied? Colored the truth, perhaps, but when have I—ah, the business about my age. I'll have you know, I haven't reached my two hundredth year. I will swear it on—"

"Very well," she said, strangely disposed to believe him. "But what do you know of magic other than your own personal glamour, which most would not consider true magic at all?"

"Touché. An excellent question, and an answer at the same time."

"I beg your pardon?" Rose looked behind them, disturbed by the fact that she could no longer see the bench where Marta sat. A scoundre might see her in her present state and decide to spirit her away.

"I am sworn to secrecy or I would tell you all."

"Of course." Rose didn't even attempt to keep the frustration from her voice. "Now if you'll excuse me, I—"

"I will not excuse you. Trust me, Rose, I beg of you. I know something of magic. Enough to know that Marta has performed a blood sacrifice, or she would not be so affected by the sight of that aura. We have looked upon it, yet we are not transfixed."

"We are not seers. That is her nature, Gareth. She is a water sprite, she reads the waters, communicates with the realms beyond—"

"She has done so for years and never been so affected. The lady has turned to the dark arts. You must trust me in this for now. The truth is no longer safely spoken here in the world above." His words were so similar to those he had spoken in her dream that Rose wondered if perhaps it hadn't been a dream at all.

"To sleep, perchance to dream—aye, there's the rub," he whispered.

"And in that sleep of death, what dreams may come?"

Gareth nodded. "The lady knows her Shakespeare . . . among other things."

So it was true, he had been inside her mind. He had tried to warn her then, just as he did now. And yet Rose could not believe that Marta would harm her deliberately.

Could she have been deceived, tricked into aiding those who wished her ill? The sprite had not lived long in the mortal world, having spent most of her long life isolated in the French countryside, and might easily fall prey to wicked machinations.

"Could she have been deceived?" Rose asked.

"There is a sacrifice involved, my lady. One doesn't *accidentally* slaughter a warm-blooded creature, smear their blood over a power point in the earth, and speak the necessary words to—"

"Very well. There is no need to for sarcasm."

"Oh, but there is always need for sarcasm. It is one of the most pleasant diversions available to members of polite Society." He had the nerve to grin then, as if they hadn't been discussing the betrayal of her closest female friend.

"Forgive me, but I have difficulty finding anything pleasant about the present situation," Rose said, turning on her heel and making quick time back to the main walk.

"Rose, stop. You cannot—"

"I can and I will, Gareth." Rose spun to face him once more, making certain he read the determination in her visage as well as in her tone. "Whatever Marta may or may not have done, I will see her safely home. From there, I will call for aid in sorting through this matter, an expert on magic perhaps or—"

"Such as Master Minuit?" he sneered, real anger wiping all humor from his features. "That might prove difficult, my lady, when the blackguard refuses to receive your calls."

Rose didn't even want to know how Gareth knew of the rift between her and Ambrose. It seemed the entirety of London was better appraised of her plight than she was.

"I will find an ally," Rose said, turning back to the path with a sigh of frustration, "one who will know whether she is guilty of deliberately—"

"Of course it was deliberate! Dear Goddess, woman." Gareth caught her by the elbow, but she shrugged him off.

"Lower your voice, my lord," Rose hissed, a warning in her eyes. "I prefer that my name stay *out* of the mouths of gossips."

"Too late for that, Comtesse. Sir Pithwater made sure your name will be on the end of every gossiping tongue in the city."

She stopped dead, no doubt exactly what Gareth had intended. He was a master manipulator, there was no question of that, but he sounded utterly serious.

"Go on," Rose said, not bothering to turn. She could just make out the top of Marta's hat from where she stood, and it eased her mind to know her companion was still relatively safe.

"Pithwater did not perish that night in the garden. Hell, not only *isn't* he dead, he's been gadding about all over London." Rose heard Gareth approach, stopping only when the warmth of his body caressed her from behind. For a split second she was transported back to Lord Drummand's garden, to the first time he had touched her.

"How is that possible? I cleaved him in two. We both saw him burn."

"I cannot say, but for all he's been through the man looks remarkably well."

"Truly?" Rose breathed deeply and closed her eyes for a moment, forcing away the sizzle of arousal she always felt when Gareth was near. Pithwater alive? How could it possibly be? Not one ogre she had cleaved with her sword had ever survived. Not even when she had been unable to incinerate the two halves of the corpse.

"I would never lie to you, Rose."

"No, you simply withhold the truth," she said, a hint of bitterness in her tone.

"Not this truth," he said, having the decency not to dissemble further. "I've seen him twice with my own eyes. And Ambrose confirmed his presence at the shops on Oxford Street this very afternoon. The ogre lives, and apparently needs a great deal of pepper and tobacco judging by his purchases."

"This is most extraordinary."

"Indeed. And what is even more extraordinary is that the baronet tells the tale of an illicit meeting between himself and the Comtesse de Fournier." Gareth moved his hands to her waist, and for once her instinct wasn't to flinch away from the unexpected contact, but to melt into him instead.

She forced herself to twist away from his touch. She couldn't afford to let her mind be affected by the strange hold the vampire had upon her. "Surely no one believes such idle gossip?"

"There are always a few who are eager to believe the most fantastic lies. But no, I doubt any who hear the tale will believe it. How could a homely, old, and not greatly moneyed man like Sir Pithwater hope to succeed where so many of our handsome, wealthy young men have failed?"

"Do you believe he seeks to draw me out?"

"I haven't the slightest, but he didn't recognize me when we passed each other yesterday. Of course, he might not have glimpsed me lurking in the darkness behind you that night in the garden."

"Likely not, he wasn't anticipating another man joining us," Rose said, a part of her mind still unwilling to believe Pithwater lived. "And you're certain it was he?"

"Yes. And he gave a rather in-depth description of your lovely body if Ambrose is to be believed. Are you sure you didn't bed the man, Rose? He had a very clear recollection of that delicate little scar near the upper part of your arm."

"The scar is the result of an ogre bite, and is a matter of tribe history. If he'd done his research—"

"Easy, love."

"I am not your love, or your darling, or your sweet, *Lord Shenley*," she chided a bit more sourly than she had intended, "and I would appreciate it if you would remember that fact in the future."

"Please, I was only speaking in jest. No one in their right mind would believe you lay with such a man." He moved a bit closer, and once again Rose moved away, turning her attention back to where Marta sat to hide the blush that stained her cheeks. The man got to her far too easily. "More likely to believe you and Marta are ruffling each other's muffs than—"

"Your language in front of a lady leaves much to be desired, my lord."

"You are indeed a lady, Rose, but I supposed after our evening together you would not object to a little familiarity." Something in his words hurt her as much as Ambrose's desertion. Never in her life had she felt like such a common strumpet.

"If you mean to wound me, Lord Shenley, then you've succeeded," Rose said, before she had the sense to think better of it. "Now may we please return to—"

"Wound you, Rose?" He grabbed hold of her and made her turn to face him, though she fought him as best she was able in her ridiculous frock.

Marta had insisted she don the exaggerated hoops that were so in vogue. Therefore Rose now had obscenely large swells of wire balanced on either side of her hips and the most uncomfortable arrangement of skirts beneath her once lovely and simple brown silk. She looked a fool, and what's worse, she'd be in dire straits if forced to combat an ogre. She hadn't thought it was likely as she had planned to stay among mortals, but now . . .

Now, nothing was certain.

"Release me."

"I will not. I would never intentionally wound you. Do you not know as much by now? Can you not feel how very right it would be between us?" Rose brought her palms up to shove against his chest, but as soon as her traitorous fingers were in contact with his woolen coat she couldn't seem to bring herself to push him away. Instead, she found her hands working the buttons that held the garment closed, then parting the fabric so that she might feel his linen shirt beneath her hands.

"I feel what all women feel when seduced by a vampire," she said, shivering at how firm he felt beneath his clothes, remembering the hot press of his skin against her own.

"Horse shit."

Her lips parted. She was a woman who killed for a living, yet she was shocked that a man would swear at her? The irony was not lost on her, but at the moment she could find no humor in it. "Gareth, really—"

"You were under my power, Rose, but not as others have been. You were not overcome, just intoxicated enough to allow yourself the freedom to do as you pleased." He leaned closer and she felt his breath hot on her forehead. Rose kept her chin to her chest. She would *not* look him in the face—she couldn't or he would know how much that night had meant to her. "Will you not admit that you desired me? That you desire me still?"

His hands smoothed down her back, urging her closer, until her hips tilted forward of their own accord. Rose bit her lip as she felt the hot pulse of his arousal, low and tight against her stomach. Even through her skirts she could feel the strength of his need. Not for the first time, she damned the man for being the perfect height for her. If he were taller his shaft might hit her elsewhere, at a greater distance from where her sex ached, taking up a hungry pulse of its own.

"If I were taller, my cock might press right between your breasts," he said, making her nipples bead tightly. "Would you allow me to do such a thing? To press your lovely breasts together, and fuck the valley between—"

"You'd have to be very tall indeed for your cock to find its way between my breasts, my lord." Her voice was cold and dismissive, a feat managed only because he'd invaded her thoughts again, the bastard. It was nearly enough to make her offer him her throat, simply to be able to show him how unpleasant it was to have one's mind invaded against one's will.

"Truly? I would take just the tiniest little taste. On my honor. Then—"

"Damn you!" Rose hauled back and kicked him as hard as she was able. He was unprepared and she managed a direct hit to his shin. When he winced, she shoved her hands against his chest hard enough to knock him flat.

Rose smiled at the sight he made—sprawled on

the ground, mouth open, as if he'd never had the unique experience of being denied by a female. The expression stayed on her lips until she turned and saw the empty bench.

Marta was gone.

CHAPTER NINE

February 20, 1750
Covent Garden Theatre
Bow Street, London

"Dear Gods, the man doesn't need stuffing. I can't say as I've ever seen the role of Falstaff played without it." Gareth whispered, but the words still carried farther than Rose would have preferred. "The very boards quake in terror as he treads upon them."

"Keep your peace, sir," Rose admonished behind her fan.

"Please, it isn't as if anyone could hear me in this din. I can scarcely hear the actors speak their lines."

And he was right. The stalls below their box were filled with chatty gentlemen and the common folk in the one-shilling gallery were amusing themselves by drunkenly calling out the responses to the familiar lines of the play. Add to that the cries of the wenches selling beer and other refreshments and she doubted King George himself, who was seated right upon the boards, could hear the play, let alone anyone else eavesdrop on the whispered words of one man.

Still, she was loathe to draw more attention to their section of the theatre than they had attracted already. Society was abuzz about the courtship of Comtesse de Fournier by the most eligible Earl of Shenley. She'd heard there were even "wed or bed" wagers at White's Young Club, as the men took sides on which option the notorious rake would be forced to choose in order to satisfy his obvious desire.

Desire. It was a beast she fought nightly as Gareth bedded down not twenty feet from her own chamber, but as yet she had managed to be the victor. Black dreams of her mother's spirit reaching out to her from the grave kept her in a suitably morbid frame of mind and helped her focus remain on the danger at hand rather than on the rascal in her guest quarters.

Still, Rose suspected it was only a matter of time before she succumbed, especially considering Gareth had been so unexpectedly respectful since coming to her home. His deference was eroding her resistance far more than his forward behavior ever had.

Of course, Society knew nothing of their new living arrangements. If *that* bit of news were made public, they would be drawing far more than whispers and stares. It would be the scandal of the Season. Rose would be utterly ruined, and all talk of Lord Drummand's decapitated chambermaid would be pushed from the minds of the *ton* gossips once and for all.

It was nearly all the temptation she needed to ruin her own good name. Dear Goddess, but she was weary of fielding inquiries about the blasted murder.

Gareth continued his discourse, clearly having no intention of keeping his peace. "He's alarmingly obese, Rose. It's hardly a secret. *The Gazetteer* reported two mornings past that three of the Falstaff costumes had to be stitched together to cover the man's arse. Still, I am not at all certain the seams will hold through the second act. I fear I may need to be held to ease my frazzled nerves."

Gareth made to lay his head in her lap, and Rose found herself stifling an unexpected giggle as she pushed him away.

At times during the past five days, she had doubted she would ever be capable of amusement again, but Gareth continued to prove her wrong. He drove her to distraction, but he also made her laugh, surely more than Shakespeare had ever done.

From the guffaws sounding freely around them, however, the rest of London found the actor playing the comic Falstaff the absolute pinnacle of hilarity. Perhaps, not being English, she was lacking that ineffable quality that gave the islanders their queer senses of humor.

"Oh my, there he goes," Gareth remarked as Falstaff exited the stage at a waddle among much cheering from the stalls. "I wonder if they have a wheelbarrow to dump him in once he gets offstage. Surely the man isn't able to move very quickly from stage right to stage left."

"Perhaps. Though who would they find to push the wheelbarrow?" Rose asked, unable to resist playing along. "Surely there are not so many among the company capable of such a great—"

"Silence yourselves, or I shall surely run mad." Ambrose's grumpy pronouncement banished the smile from Rose's lips. Her liaison had appeared on her doorstep the evening after Marta's disappearance, but she wasn't as glad of his presence as she had assumed she would be that afternoon in the garden.

Rather than honoring their dinner party obligations five nights' past, she and Gareth had adjourned directly to Rose's home in Berkeley Square from Vauxhall. It wasn't a difficult decision as they'd lost their appetites after a little digging near the aura that produced a rotted skull buried beneath the vortex.

Rose had managed not to lose her luncheon at the sight, but had allowed Gareth to finished exhuming the head and wrap it in his cloak. Thankfully, the vortex had disappeared as soon as the skull was removed making Rose hopeful that Marta had been freed from its power.

But two hours later, after a thorough search of the gardens and surrounding areas, there was still no sign of the sprite. The hour had been growing late, so she and Gareth had thought it best to adjourn to Rose's home, assuming Marta would return there if she were able. Marta hadn't appeared, but Ambrose had, having grown concerned after being unable to contact Marta via the enchanted waters.

Rose would have been pleased at his return if his company the past five days hadn't been as close to torture as anything she had ever known. She had never seen him so grumpy. His temper flared at the slightest offense, and he and Gareth were at each other's throats whenever they found themselves in the same room. Thank the Goddess Gareth slept until noon or she never would have had a moment's peace since both men refused to leave her side until the mysteries of Marta, the miraculously resurrected Pithwater, and the plans of the tribe were resolved.

Ambrose was deeply troubled that the woman he had entrusted with Rose's safekeeping had possibly betrayed them both and as a result was making certain everyone around him suffered. Rose, however, was far more concerned with the well-being of Marta herself. She still couldn't believe that her friend had willingly betrayed her. She suspected foul play, and prayed she would wake to find Marta back in her bed, ready to explain whatever had kept her away for so long.

But tomorrow would mark the sixth morning since her disappearance, and Rose was beginning to lose hope they would ever find her alive and well.

"Ambrose, the character is comical. It is common for patrons to laugh when observing his antics," Gareth said. "Perhaps you should attempt to play along. Surely you've got a girlish giggle somewhere inside that great bulk of yours."

"If you refuse to shut your mouth, I shall shut it for you, vampire," Ambrose whispered, though Rose could tell he would have preferred to growl. Growling, however, wasn't customary among female chaperones—no matter how vehemently they were defending their charge's honor.

Since Marta had disappeared, Rose had been in need of a female companion if she were to frequent Society's entertainments. Despite her advanced age, she still resembled a young woman of no more than eighteen. Being such an age and not a widow, she was expected to be accompanied by a chaperone, especially while in the company of a young, eligible earl. Rather than risk trusting another female, Ambrose had used one of his illusion spells to make himself the very image of Marta.

Or at least Rose assumed he had. Passersby certainly hadn't looked twice when he and Rose were out and about and the female population was decidedly less interested than was the norm when such a striking man walked in their midst. Gareth and Rose had been forced to take Ambrose's word on the effectiveness of his illusion, however, as he made certain both of them saw him as his true self.

Vanity, thy name is faerie.

Or more likely he simply didn't wish Gareth to forget who was the larger, stronger, and more powerful of the pair. The two fighting cocks had been in a constant state of fluffed feathers and bared beaks since they had taken up residence in her home. Rose almost wished they would have at each other, if only to give her some peace from the threat of impending combat.

"Tut-tut. Such language, Ambrose." Gareth turned his smile to Rose and leaned closer. "I go to see a lady about an orange, would you like one as well, dearest?"

"No, thank you. I shall wait for the interval," she said, managing a small smile for him before he disappeared.

Dearest indeed. She had no doubt that Gareth felt some sort of affection for her. There was no other explanation for how dedicated he had been to her care and protection. But she doubted his feelings were as strong as he feigned whenever Ambrose was present.

Gareth had a knack for knowing exactly how to agitate that was simply uncanny. She'd never have thought Ambrose would be disturbed by another man showing her affection, but Rose could practically feel the anger roiling from the faerie whenever Gareth called her his "dear" or "darling."

"Wipe the smile from your face, Rose. You look a simpleton." Ambrose's harsh tone banished her smile as effectively as his insults. "If you insist on acting like a love-struck fool, you'll only draw more attention to yourself at precisely the moment when discretion is imperative."

"I am hardly behaving like a love-struck fool," Rose said, nearing the limit of her tolerance for the man, old friend or no. He was the one who was behaving ridiculously, and for no reason she could discern, save that he disliked Gareth.

It certainly had nothing to do with jealousy. Ambrose bedded down in the servants' quarters as far away from her rooms as possible and hadn't offered her so much as a smile or a kind word in five days, even when Gareth was nowhere to be found.

"You simper like a schoolgirl every time that vampire so much as—"

"His name is Gareth."

"And now you rush to his defense. Goddess, Rosemarie, I hope you haven't fallen under the spell of that despicable creature," he said, his use of her given name causing a strange ache in her chest. He'd been using it more and more of late, the unusual intimacy increasing in direct proportion to his unusual pique.

"That 'creature' has come to my aid more than you have in recent times, sir. You practically abandoned me last week. Why should I not expect you to do so again? At least Gareth has shown himself dedicated—"

"Dedicated? You little fool. You are merely a pawn, a bit of entertainment to be had while he—" Ambrose pressed his lips together, as if he had said something he hadn't meant to. It wasn't the first time he'd implied Gareth had a hidden agenda, but Rose was ready for it to be the last.

"Ambrose Minuit, either tell me what you are alluding to or keep your peace. I've already been betrayed by my companion and deserted by my liaison. I don't appreciate suspecting another friend of misdeeds."

"A friend?" he repeated, his contempt clear.

"Yes. A *friend*." Rose could not deny that Gareth had endeared himself to her. It was more than shared laughter or mutual attraction. He had begun to earn her trust, to make her reconsider depending solely upon Ambrose's guidance. A part of Rose ached for another confidante, someone with whom she could share her troubles and doubts.

"Very well. But I object to the charge of desertion." His sniff conveyed he thought her a ridiculous woman, prone to hysterics. "I am here at this outlandish diversion so that the investigation might move forward with utmost haste."

It was rumored that Pithwater would be attending tonight's performance—at least the man at the stage door admitted to selling his footman a ticket—but they had yet to spot him. In fact, after making such a great show of himself five days past, Pithwater had been absent from Society. He hadn't attended his club, the gardens, the theater, or even been seen entering or exiting his own home. Ambrose had trolls on constant watch, but they had seen neither hide nor hair nor bald head of the ogre in five long days.

Rose couldn't help but feel that his disappearance and Marta's were somehow connected. Could he have been the one to spirit her away from that bench in Vauxhall? Had he been following them, waiting for the chance to abduct her companion? If so, why? Even her abundant imagination couldn't seem to find a way to connect Marta with Pithwater, no matter how hard she tried.

"And I've been by your side for nearly a week's time, abandoning the comforts of my home in order to keep constant—"

"But where were you after I was injured in battle? Why would you not come to deliver the news of your investigations in person?" Rose felt her pulse speed as she finally allowed herself to ask the questions that had been tormenting her since Ambrose had arrived on her doorstep.

At first she had been so grateful to see him she hadn't dared press him. Then his temper had made certain everyone in the household gave him a wide berth. But now Rose was intent upon answers. Ambrose had been a bear regardless of how delicately she stepped, and she had grown weary of humoring the man.

"I was unavoidably detained," he said, shifting his eyes back to the stage, suddenly feigning intense interest in the "outlandish" play.

"Horse shit." A thrill shot through her at Ambrose's shocked expression. "You have never lied to me before. Why now?"

"The Fey cannot lie. You know that as well as I."
Ambrose searched her face as if she had become a
stranger—a highly unpleasant stranger—but she refused to retreat.

She was tired of cowering in the face of his temper,
of feeling she'd lost his approval. He was the one who
had given Gareth leave to donate his blood. How *dare*
he insist on punishing her for succumbing to a temptation even some of the Fey had fallen prey to? The
seductive glamour of a vampire was wickedly difficult to resist, no matter that the faeries insisted it was
merely a form of supernatural charisma.

"Once again I must say horse shit." Rose kept her
face impassive as she watched Ambrose's lip curl
with disapproval. "The Fey can not break a *promise,*
but I have never heard any law forbidding lying."

"Your language is even more deplorable than usual."

"Do not attempt to change the subject." She returned his hard stare, for once not at all cowed. True,
he had nearly killed her when she'd been a terrified
young girl, lost in the forest with two newborn babes.
If he attempted to harm her now, however, she was
certain events would proceed quite differently. Most
likely he would prevail, but she would give the man a
hell of a fight before she perished under his blade.

Not that she truly thought Ambrose would attempt
such a thing. He would never challenge her directly.
Fighting a woman, a mortal woman no less, was a con-
cept the faerie would find laughable, no matter how
many ogres she had dispatched from the earth.

"Feeling fierce this evening, are we, Comtesse?"
The threat in his voice did little to shake her resolve.

"Perhaps." She had noticed herself becoming less

fearful of many things since the night of her vampire blood infusion. But whether such bravery was part and parcel of having vampiric blood or a side effect of feeling her mother's spirit so near of late, she couldn't say. "While we are on the subject of truth telling, there are several things that have been plaguing my mind."

"People are beginning to stare. Perhaps we should continue this—"

"Let them," she said softly. "It will merely appear I am dressing down a servant, will it not? At the moment you are not so fearsome to human eyes."

"I am not so fearsome to you either, it seems." The look in his eyes was almost . . . triumphant. He was definitely pleased, though she could not fathom why.

"Why did you keep your distance in the days after the battle before Marta was lost? Why do you loathe Gareth so, when it was you who accepted his offer to aid our cause?"

He met her eyes for a long, assessing moment before he nodded, seemingly satisfied with whatever he read there. "I truly was unavoidably detained. I was called back to Paris, if you must know. I then traveled to Hibernia to consult with my source directly rather than through the waters or other magical means. He is an ancient and at times more a part of the earth than separate from it. I assumed he would answer my inquiries more freely if I were to arrive at his home with the proper offerings."

Ambrose turned to watch as the curtain rose on act two, but continued to speak though his eyes were fixed on the stage. "As for the reason I loathe Lord Shenley, it is a private matter. But I will say this, if I had known his true identity when he approached with his *kind* offer to aid our cause, he would have received a very different answer."

"But now that you've made a pact, you cannot send him away," Rose observed, knowing better than to press Ambrose on his "private" reasons. Better to move on to other matters while he was in a communicative frame of mind. "What are his ulterior motives, then? What does he want, and how in the world would he use me as a pawn?"

"How do men usually use women?" He leveled her with a heated look that sent a prickle of awareness skittering across her skin. There hadn't been sexual tension between them since the evening in his study, but now there was no denying that Ambrose was looking at her as a man would look at a woman.

"I am not sharing his bed." She hid her flustered expression with a flutter of her fan. "Not that it is any of your affair."

"No it is not my *affair,* nor will it ever be," he said, his emphasis on the word "affair" giving it a scandalous connotation she hadn't intended. "No matter how Gareth might attempt to force my hand." Ambrose's eyes moved down to her lips, and then to her décolletage, an almost pained expression on his face, as if he were viewing something he had long coveted, but knew to be beyond his reach.

"You believe he is simply trying to inspire jealousy?" The words rushed from her mouth before she could think better of them. A gasp followed as Ambrose lifted his eyes to hers. The hunger, the need swirling in those gray depths took her breath away. There was heat there, but it wasn't merely a sexual hunger.

Ambrose ached for more than her body. He ached for her regard, it was hauntingly clear, etched in every tense inch of his vulnerable visage.

"Why did you . . . I never . . ." Rose's voice broke as emotion tightened her throat.

He had obviously concealed his feelings from her, but how in the world had she concealed her yearning from herself? She was near tears, her heart light and heavy all at the same time. It was as if her most secret wish was coming true, a desire so private her heart hadn't dared to let her mind know of it.

She had always respected Ambrose, longed for his guidance, and ached for his companionship. Yet it came as a surprise that she loved him. Such a complete and utter shock she lost the power of speech for several moments.

"Rosemarie? I would hear your thoughts." His expression was guarded, but he no longer hid his emotions. The cat was out of the bag, a fact of which they were both painfully aware.

"Why, in all the years of—When there has been so much between us—" She broke off for a second time and sucked in a deep breath. "Why now, Ambrose? Why wait until now?"

"A hundred years is not so long for the Fey."

"It is very long for a mortal. You had to know that. You had to know how I felt, how desperately I ached for you in those first years." Rose closed her eyes and fanned her face. She'd buried that old desire so completely that to have it suddenly aired was shocking.

"You were young and had suffered horribly due to a curse laid upon you by my own kind. You were not strong enough to choose me. You would have welcomed any pair of strong arms around you—"

"Do not dare tell me what I wanted. If I were that weak, I would have married the man who had ruined me while I slept. Benoit offered me marriage and I had no one in the world to turn to. I knew not what he was then," Rose said, the words pouring from her like a torrent. "I knew only that he was as vile a man as I had ever met, and no riches or title would make up for the misery of being forced to share his bed, to watch my sons raised to be as cold and wicked as their sire—"

"You must quiet yourself," Ambrose warned, covering the hands she had fisted in her lap. At some point her fan had fallen to the floor, but she hadn't noticed, so consumed by memories of that night, the night neither she nor Ambrose had spoken of in decades.

Rose forced herself to relax. There was something bothering her as much as those old memories. Uneasiness warred with the unexpected intimacy of Ambrose's hand on hers. They had never touched this way before, never touched at all if it wasn't unavoidable during the heat of battle. He had never simply held her hand, never run his fingers softly across her palm, his skin hot enough for her to feel through her glove.

Never. Such an absolute, and the key to her concern. "Why now?" she asked again, pulling away from his teasing touch, knowing she would think more clearly without it.

"I have explained to you, I—"

"No, Ambrose," she said, narrowing her eyes and

assessing the man next to her. "You explained to me why *not* then. You did not explain why *now*."

He was silent, his expression giving nothing away, but Rose could see he searched for an answer even as she fought to unravel the truth. "You just confessed there will never be anything between us, no matter how Gareth works to inspire your jealousy. So why declare your feelings if you do not plan to act upon them?"

"There are times when even I lose control."

"I have never noticed that to be true. At least not in this fashion, not . . ." Dear Goddess, the truth was so close she could feel it struggling to escape even as something within her tried to force the revelation back into the depths of her mind.

"You've gone pale. Let us adjourn—"

Rose pressed her hands over her ears, blocking out his voice, blocking out everything but the growing suspicion bubbling beneath the surface. She could feel the horrible certainty rising, rising, until there was no choice but to speak the words aloud.

"You know what spell the tribe seeks to cast. You've known it from the start." A sob escaped her throat at the knowledge she read in his expression.

"Not from the start."

Rose struggled to breathe, unable to believe he had betrayed her trust so deeply. But it suddenly made sense why she had discovered no new clues in the past five days. Ambrose had been working to keep her from discovering the truth, engaging her in fruitless trips to the opera and the theater while, all around her, the ogres' plot grew toward fruition.

"Pithwater won't be attending the theater tonight, will he?"

"No. He was last seen three day ago at a chocolate house in the company of a young female of the tribe," he confessed, not an ounce of remorse in his tone. "My sources seem to think he has left London under rather odd circumstances, as he took no coach and not even his servants know where the man has gone."

"So you have deliberately misled me. You know what danger threatens, but still you waste precious time—"

"That isn't true, Rosemarie. You don't understand."

"I understand perfectly. You have deceived me, and when I drew close to discovering that deception, you would have distracted me from my course with your admission of *love*." She laughed, but it wasn't a mirthful sound.

"It is not at all what you think, I—Where are you going?" He reached for her arm, but she flung him away, his touch causing a wave of sickness to wash over her entire being.

"Away from you, sir. You are no longer welcome in my home, Master Minuit."

"You are acting a fool. You are in great danger, far greater than you know."

"So you will tell me then? Share with me the secrets you have kept close?" Rose hesitated at the entrance to the box, hand upon the velvet curtain. This was the last chance for any shred of faith to be preserved.

"I cannot. I have sworn an oath." His tone was sincere, but she was far past the point of being appeased by such words.

"You are a dissembler, and as false a friend as any I have known. It is finished between us. I no longer wish your aid, your magic, or your—"

"Fey gifts can not be returned, and I don't give a damn what—"

"That much is clear. You don't give a damn for anyone or anything but your Fey machinations. I will have no more of you." Rose felt eyes upon them, but couldn't bring herself to care that others were more interested in their drama than the one being played out upon the stage. Her world was crumbling, and concern for propriety was the furthest thing from her mind.

"We have a contract, Rosemarie," Ambrose warned, his eyes flashing, as if his passions were inflamed by their argument.

But he was a black faerie, and they relished human rage and grief nearly as much as their sin. Bastards.

"Go to hell, Ambrose," she said, flinging open the curtain. "And take your wretched contract with you."

CHAPTER TEN

Rose raced down the curved staircase toward the lobby before she could reflect upon the foolishness of her actions. Breaking a contract with the Fey de la Nuit was a death sentence. But it seemed she was marked for death in any event. Better killed by faerie sword than by ogres out for her blood. At least the sword would accomplish the task without unleashing untold evil upon the world.

Unless that was what the faeries wanted.

Ambrose knew what spell was at work, and if she were to believe his earlier words, he had been to Paris to report his findings to the high council of the Fey de la Nuit. Yet they hadn't ordered him to put an end to the business. They couldn't have. Perhaps he had ventured to Hibernia in search of answers, or perhaps he'd known the nature of the magic from the beginning. Either way, it was clear to her that his "investigation" had merely been a device to keep her occupied until . . .

"Until the next full moon," she whispered, her heart thudding in her chest as she stopped at the foot of the stairs, searching for Gareth across the crowded room.

He was awaiting his chance to purchase an orange from a girl with painted cheeks who looked as if she would sell more than fruit if given enough incentive. At least he hadn't lied about that, though she suspected him to be as steeped in deception as his counterpart in the booth above.

Their rivalry was the one bit of truth in the web of lies in which she presently found herself. But as to the source of their mutual loathing, she couldn't say. She knew it was nothing as simple as lust for a woman. Or even love.

Love. The word made gorge rise in her throat. She had been an utter fool, and the shame of it made her skin go cold despite the heat of the theater. Secretly in love with one man and lusting after the other. She was no better than the foolish heroines in romantic novels, and just as likely to meet a ruinous end.

Gareth turned, and for a moment Rose feared he had read her thoughts, though she was still quite far away. But the smile that stretched across his face banished the worry, and she did her best to clear her mind as he crossed the room. She thought about his eyes, and how they seemed to mesmerize every lady present even when he wasn't exerting his power.

"There you are, sweet. I was wondering when you would tire—" Gareth broke off, the smile fading from his lips. "What's the matter, love?"

Apparently she had neglected to conceal her emotions from her face as well as from her thoughts. Rose forced a smile while focusing her mind on the colors of the bunting used to decorate the lobby, the smell of the mutton pies being sold by the man a few feet away, and the salty tang of sweat and spilled ale that lurked beneath the scent.

"I am simply a bit indisposed. I will take the carriage and return home."

"And I will go with you," he said. "I care not for the theater without a kindred spirit with which to share the—"

"Ambrose wishes to speak with you." Rose avoided Gareth's curious stare, concentrating on counting the number of men lined up to purchase an orange from the buxom wench. "He did not tell me what it is about. I believe he would divulge some secret to your ears only."

"Truly?" He caught her eye, and Rose noted suspicion in his green gaze. "What could Ambrose possibly share with a vile creature of the night that he would not share with you, dear Rose?"

"An excellent question." She smiled, hoping to compensate for the sarcasm that had crept into her tone. "I assume you will share that news when you have it?"

"Of course, I will always share with you, sweet." A hint of the suggestive made its way into his voice as he brushed his lips across the back of her hand and bid her farewell with a wink. "Until later."

Rose nodded, thinking bland thoughts until Gareth was out of sight.

Then she made haste to call for a hackney cab,

though she didn't know where she would have it take her. Her home was no longer safe. Her cook, chambermaid, footmen, and driver were all under Ambrose's control in one manner or another. Her cook, Erin, was a half-Brownie, half-Fey foundling who had sought sanctuary in the human world to avoid an unwanted marriage. Her chambermaid, Dara, was a tree spirit from an ancient grove that had been desecrated by the Romans over a thousand years before, and the footmen and driver were half-faerie, half-elven men who looked human enough to pass in society, but whose mixed birth caused them to be shunned by both the Fey and the Elvish tribes.

The faeries considered them good enough to work for her, but not good enough to be taught the magic of the Fey, while the elves simply feared faeries too greatly to risk inviting half-breeds into their midst. Thankfully, their Elvish heritage imparted a sense of humor that kept the snubs of either clan from cutting too deeply.

Phillip, Samuel, and Lucas were quickly becoming friends as well as servants, and Rose knew it would be the same with Erin and Dara if they were given time to form a closer acquaintance. But for now they would not dare take her side against Ambrose, or deny him entrance to her home simply because she demanded it. She would be forced to seek out alternative lodgings, and quickly. It was growing late and a lady of rank could hardly board at a common rooming house. Not to mention that Ambrose and Gareth would soon be in pursuit.

Whatever the two of them were about, they seemed to want her to remain safe and well. At least for the moment. There was no other explanation for their protectiveness.

"To Southwark, please," she told the driver before settling back in the dingy seat of the cab. There was only one place she could think to go. Ambrose would look there sooner or later, but in the meantime she would have some time to think, to plan, and, she hoped, to uncover clues that might aid her understanding of her present situation.

What better to place to seek information than Ambrose's own home? Certainly he would find her if she tarried too long, but she should be safe for a few hours while she assembled a disguise that would allow her to walk the streets of London undiscovered.

Assuming, of course, that no ogres trailed her or lay in wait for her to return to Ambrose's offices—the site of their last attack.

It was a chance she had to take. Ambrose had been caught off guard by the giant ogre and the gathering of the tribe by the water of the Thames. But in the time between when she had lost consciousness on High Street and awoken in bed with Gareth, something had changed. She needed to know what had transpired between the two men to transform a fairly straightforward distaste for each other into outright contention, laced with shades of complicity.

Was the talk of portals and power and human sacrifice truly significant, or was the theory that the ogres sought help from the demon realms simply a ruse? It might very well be that Ambrose had merely allowed her to continue that line of thought in order to keep her from learning whatever it was he—and Gareth, it seemed—didn't want her to know.

Her life and the lives of many innocent people were in jeopardy. It was time for her to take the reins and responsibility for her own future. For nearly a hundred years, she had depended upon Ambrose to guide her. Before that, she had depended upon her parents, and on royal advisors who had done their best to keep her safe from a faerie's curse.

There was no safety to be had, for none can flee their fate. The spinning wheel still found its way within the castle walls, you still reached out to—

"To touch that which I had been kept ignorant of." Rose spoke the words aloud, helping push away her weak thoughts.

Long ago, her parents had been so fearful of a faerie's curse that they had destroyed every spinning wheel in the country and ordered all cloth be made from regions to the north and south. From the day of Rose's birth, all mention of spinning wheels and spindles had been strictly forbidden. She had been kept ignorant of the devices and the curse itself, only learning too late what it was she shouldn't have touched and why.

She would not allow the same to happen a second time. She would unearth the truth, even if she had to move mountains and giant ogres to accomplish the deed. The strength of her determination was matched only by the strength of the aching in her chest as she grieved the loss of the men who had meant more to her than any in her long, lonely life.

ROSE PAID THE cab and made her way through the winding roads leading to Ambrose's home. This evening the streets were busy with all manner of traffic, making the journey very different than the one nearly a fortnight past. From doorways whores called to men on their way home from the docks while harried young mothers screamed for damp-nosed children to get themselves abed. The smell of gin and sweat and dozens of pots boiling with supper filled the air as Rose hurried on her way, conscious of the attention she drew in her elaborate gown and powdered wig.

Arriving at Ambrose's home, she found the front door locked and the mechanism too complicated for her to open with no more than a hairpin. The servant's door, however, proved far more compliant. Within a few minutes she was slipping inside the kitchen and shutting the door behind her.

Rose crept quietly across the floor, straining to hear any sound other than the settling of the old building. Ambrose had mentioned sending his staff to his country estate out of concern for their safety, but Rose wouldn't breathe easier until she saw for herself that the home was empty.

Lighting a lamp, she made her way upstairs. The first and second floors were dark and silent. She passed the third floor where Ambrose's private rooms were located, and went directly to the fourth, relieved to find the servants' bedrooms dark and abandoned. After pilfering a pair of breeches and shirt from Ambrose's valet, she removed her wig and changed as hurriedly as possible. Thankfully, she had grown adept at struggling in and out of her stays without the help of a lady's maid.

The valet's clothes were large, but the ill fit would

help hide her curves as she had nothing to bind her chest. She found a coat and hat hanging in the servant's closet and carried them with her.

Leaving her gown spread out on the valet's narrow bed, Rose hurried down to the third floor and into Ambrose's study. All was quiet there as well, but for the sound of the wind whistling through the boards covering the broken window.

Ambrose's desk still sat in the same place as before, though now there was no view of the city streets for him to gaze upon when he turned in his chair. Rose crept slowly to the desk, feeling oddly guilty as she opened drawers and rifled through paperwork. She had never dared to invade his privacy before, and it felt wrong. No matter that he had lied to her, deceived her, and could possibly be conspiring with the Fey to sacrifice her to the tribe, she still winced with shame as she broke open the locked drawer at the lower right hand side of the desk.

Because you still don't believe he's turned against you, just as you don't want to believe the truth about Marta. You are a trusting fool, so eager for friendship that—

"Give me peace," Rose muttered as she lifted what appeared to be account ledgers from the drawer.

She *didn't* want to believe Ambrose had turned against her, that much was true. But he *had* deceived her, of that there was no doubt, though the reasons why remained a mystery. She found it hard to believe the Fey truly wanted her to end her long life as a sacrificial lamb, even if for some reason their goals and the tribe's had suddenly become one and the same.

Thinking logically, it didn't make sense. Despite

Ambrose's strange behavior, she couldn't see that the Fey had anything to gain from her death. She had been an executioner for so long, working slavishly to wipe the tribe from the earth, succeeding where so many others had failed. Very few executioners returned from a tour of the Ottoman Empire, especially females.

Rose was more committed to their cause than any other she had known, for it was *her* cause as well. As much as she loathed the black faerie who had cursed her in her cradle, it was the same faerie magic that had come to her rescue when she had awoken from the curse, and she was suitably grateful for it.

A shiver worked through her body as images of that horrible night once again shot through her mind. Since the eve of her near death, those memories had been closer to the surface than ever. Nearly every night now she dreamt of awakening in agony, seeing her swollen, distended stomach, and below, her ankles lashed to the lower posts of her bed. Between her legs sat the ogre Benoit de Fournier, his eyes glued to her sex as his issue prepared to be born.

He had been surprised to see her wake, but not displeased. He had been seeking a wife, he'd told her, even as she howled and fought to be set free of the bed, free of her body, free from the nightmare of—

Rose's hands shook as she felt around the bottom of the drawer, seeking the latch that would open the false bottom she knew to be hidden there.

She didn't wish to think of that night. Even a hundred years later. But she knew she must. She'd been running from those memories for far too long. Her insistence on shoving the horror to the furthest reaches of her mind was a form of weakness, and had kept her from returning to her homeland for decades.

She couldn't afford weakness. No longer could she blindly follow the orders of the Fey de la Nuit, no matter that her passion for protecting mortals from ogres was as fervent as it had ever been. She had been a fool to place such faith in the black faeries. They fed upon wickedness, and in those odd times when the world was not as evil as was the norm, they did their best to incite mortals to sin.

She had been so desperate for companionship she had turned a blind eye to acts her heart believed were wrong. For all her coldness in battle, for all her strong words and defiance, she was weak. And it was only becoming worse. She had all but bedded a vampire, and nearly let him into her heart. She had dared hope—

"I would be flattered, I think, if your despair was not so thick I could taste it."

Rose spun to see Gareth at the door to the study. He had disposed of his wig, and his hair flowed loose and wild around his face. She remembered the feel of those silken locks trailing through her fingers, brushing against her bare skin, and shivered as much from desire as from fear. For he was fearsome looking tonight, the expression on his face as angry as she had ever seen.

"I am not angry with you, but at the cruel workings of your mind." He crossed the room, each step a sensuous dance that made her ache to run to him, to bury her face and her troubles in his broad chest. But he was not to be trusted any more than the man whose house she had invaded.

The thought was all the encouragement Rose's heart needed to beat even faster.

"Where is Ambrose? Did he accompany you—"

"I haven't a clue. I didn't return to the box, but followed you from the theater. I lost sight of the coach as it crossed the bridge, but had a decent notion where I might find you." He slowed, as if sensing how trapped Rose felt as he advanced upon her. "Every soul craves companionship, Rose. To have a trusting heart is a wondrous gift, especially taking into account the horrors you have witnessed and endured. Where, might I ask, is the weakness in that?"

"Leave me and my mind in peace."

"I will leave your mind in peace when it is a safe place for you to be left alone in." He brought his fist down onto the back of one of the chairs before the fire.

"I would ask again that you leave," Rose said, her voice breaking. Her mind and heart had already been ravished by the events of the evening. She knew she wasn't prepared to fight the manipulations of a vampire.

"Manipulations?" Gareth slammed his hand into the chair again, this time hard enough to split the back in two.

"Ambrose will have your head for abusing his furnishings," Rose warned.

"*Damn* his furnishings. I would never manipulate you. I've only ever wished your happiness. And happiness craves companionship and friends in whom you can place your trust."

"My *trust*?" Rose asked, pulling the false bottom out of the drawer, determined to go about her business, no matter how flustered she felt. "What does a vampire know of trust?"

"Simply because a man feeds on blood—or sin for that matter—it does not follow that he is unworthy of trust." He paced back and forth with the natural grace of a predator. A predator. *That* was his true nature, and what she had to remember when—

"Do you not eat the flesh of lower creatures? Is that not predatory? True, you do not slay the beasts yourself, but they are slain for your pleasure nonetheless. I do not kill my food, I—"

"Your *food* is not a simple animal in the field that has no clear sense of life, death, or destiny. Your food is a human being who has been stripped of free will by your magic."

"Oh, but it isn't *real* magic, Rose," he said, his tone ripe with sarcasm. "It appears, for all your time with the black faeries, you have yet to learn how to insult a vampire with—"

"Please, Gareth." A sigh escaped her lips as she set the false bottom on the desk and did her best to pry the latch open with Ambrose's letter opener. "I haven't the time to argue—"

"Speaking of free will, how many sheep did you ask permission of before you had your cook hack them apart for mutton pie?"

"This is ridiculous. We could go round and round this argument and never— Ow!" Rose cursed as the lock on the false bottom of the drawer suddenly flew open, causing the letter opener to jam into her thumb.

The wound was bleeding, so she wasn't surprised when she looked up and saw Gareth standing no more than a foot away.

"I am a vampire, as you are so quick to remind me." He caught her eye, then reached slowly for her hand. "Now, why don't you let me heal that for you?"

"I suppose that would qualify as a taste, wouldn't it?" Rose asked, watching her hand float toward him as if no longer under her control. Surely such a small quantity of her blood couldn't bring about the change, and it would be so intriguing to hear Gareth's thoughts. Then she would finally know if he was friend or foe.

"Right, there is that . . ." Gareth stepped away with effort, putting her offering just out of his reach. "I can fetch some ointment and a bandage from below stairs. The cook has a—"

"No, it won't be necessary," she said, sticking her thumb in her mouth and sucking away the salty, metallic taste of her own blood.

"You can't know how it pains me to see that. It's almost like watching you touch your . . ." Gareth's words faded away as his eyes locked on her closed lips. "I would love to watch you bring yourself pleasure, Rose. Someday, when all of this—"

"You forfeit the opportunity to taste my blood because you feared what I would learn from your thoughts, my lord." Tears stung at the back of her eyes as she opened the secret compartment and searched inside. "I doubt I will ever allow you any liberties with my person if you are so very untrustworthy."

It was ironic, really. The man who insisted she should trust was the one revealing himself to be unworthy of her faith.

"I am not unworthy. There are simply too many secrets—"

"Keep your peace. If I hear one more word of secrets I swear I shall—"

"What? Break into Ambrose's home and rob him for the answers you seek? I doubt you'll find anything, by the way. Ambrose is not so foolish as to leave evidence lying about."

Rose ignored him, pressing her lips together as she tried to make sense of the objects she pulled from the drawer. There was a perfectly round black stone that she knew to be part of the spell the faeries of the black court used to pass over into their realm. There were several small books filled with yellowing paper she suspected were Ambrose's spell records, though the words were protected by an invisibility spell, so it was difficult to know for certain. Besides those obviously important articles, she found a large key and an identical smaller key with an *M* engraved upon them, and a few irregularly shaped shards of glass.

"Bloody hell," she cursed, kicking the desk hard enough to wince. She'd forgotten she was in her stocking feet, hoping to find her boy's boots in the guest room she'd used when staying with Ambrose. The valet's shoes were far too large, even if she had stuffed the toes with rags.

"Ambrose loathes it when you curse, you know."

"I've been acquainted with the man for a hundred years, Gareth. I am aware of his likes and dislikes." She sat down heavily in Ambrose's chair, brooding as she realized the futility of her search. If Ambrose had secret writings, he would have them spelled to be invisible to all but himself, or written in a language only he and other black faeries would be able to decipher.

"Well then, I assume you are also aware that he adores it when you curse. That it makes him think of all the naughty things he'd like to do with that pretty little mouth of yours." Rose's eyes flew to where Gareth leaned against the bookshelves, pondering a tear in one of his gloves.

"Is that the nature of your discussions with Ambrose when you aren't bickering?" she asked, both angry and strangely curious at the same time.

"You aren't curious, you are aroused. I can smell it from across the room." His eyes flicked to hers, the heat in those green depths taking her breath away. "I am overcome with jealousy that the mere mention of that blackguard can make you so."

"I—"

"But still, I adore the scent of you. I would drown in it, bury myself between your legs and never come up for air if you allowed it."

"I did not think vampires required air."

"I also adore how you are so utterly serious when you jest." His smile was sad, which made Rose's heart ache for reasons she couldn't understand. "To answer your question, Ambrose and I do not talk at all. I have simply learned how to eavesdrop on a few of his unprotected thoughts."

"Truly?" she asked, surprised. She'd never known any but the Fey to be able to breach the walls Ambrose built around his thoughts, and at times she knew many of his own kind had difficulty doing so.

"Truly. Though it wouldn't have been possible had he not plucked thoughts of you from my mind during our second meeting. He has built quite a wall of defenses, nearly as strong as yours, dear Rose."

"I beg your pardon?"

"Do you want the answers you came looking for this night?" he asked, his voice not much more than a whisper.

"Of course."

"Then I suggest you follow your instincts."

It took very little thought to guess at his meaning. "The truth will be my greatest weapon?" she asked, quoting his words from her dream vision.

"Confront those demons that haunt you. The living may be sworn to silence, but not the dead. At least not yet."

"I don't have time to decipher—"

"Truer words have never been spoken. But I cannot guide you further. Pithwater died that night because he lacked the proper knowledge of his tribe, his people. Do not allow the same to happen to you, sweet." He paused, eyes roaming over her as if he would memorize every inch. "I do not think I could bear it."

"But now I am to believe Pithwater *didn't* die," she said, refusing to acknowledge the complicated emotions that surfaced whenever Gareth looked at her that way.

"Exactly." He smiled and blew her a kiss from across the room. "Now hurry, Ambrose is coming and I doubt he'll be happy to see you've brought his secret faerie playthings out—"

Rose raced to shove all of the objects into the hidden compartment and place it back in the drawer. By the time she'd gathered the ledgers and placed them on top, the vampire had gone, and she made haste to do the same.

If she left London now, she could reach Dover by

morning and cross the channel to France by nightfall. From Calais she could seek alternative transport of the supernatural variety. With a bit of luck, she could be in Myrdrean within five days, six at most.

For all of her planning and determination, however, the thought of returning home still filled her with dread.

CHAPTER ELEVEN

February 25, 1750
The Kingdom of Myrdrean

"No missus, I won't. Can't pay me enough to take you in there." The young man driving the hay cart shivered, and turned away from the sight of the castle on the hill.

Rose couldn't say that she blamed him.

Since they left Austria the road had been utterly abandoned. Even the dark forest that lined it was eerily still, as if the usual creatures of the woods were too frightened to risk habitation.

Still, the road was positively cheery when compared to what lay ahead.

The turrets she remembered standing tall and strong were crumbling, and the wall that once surrounded castle and village had been overtaken by the forest. The last of the evening light dripped scarlet tears on the horizon, and carrion crows circled above, as though lingering to pick at the rotted remains of her people.

Gorge rose in her throat and for a moment Rose wanted to tell the boy to turn around, to flee this place as quickly as his old mules were able, though she knew she would find no rot within the palace walls.

Her family, the members of court, and the villagers would have crumbled long ago, their skeletons bleached in the hot sun of over a hundred summers until the bones became brittle and blew away. When she had returned from her executioner training in the Fey realms—the passing of four years in earthly time—the bodies had already been not much more than bones and leathered skin.

She had returned to Myrdrean determined to awaken her people, but it had been too late. Instead of an enchanted castle, she had walked into a land of death. The worst of it, of course, was the sight that awaited her in the great hall. Three skeletons sat upon their thrones—her father, mother, and younger brother—all decked out in their finest clothes, the ones they had worn to celebrate her eighteenth birthday.

What Rose hadn't known the night she was spirited from the castle by the ogre was that the enchantment of her people would not continue without her sleeping body lying in her bed. She had awoken twenty years early, and whether it was intentional faerie evil or that the curse wasn't able to function in the wake of her absence, the entirety of her kin and blameless subjects had perished that very night.

Upon discovering the tragedy, Rose had wept on the stone floor of the great hall for God only knew how long before fleeing the place. Ambrose had waited for her on the road, as though he knew what she would find and hadn't wanted to be privy to her despair. Even after such a short acquaintance, he realized she preferred to weep alone if she wept at all.

Her eyes had been dry, however, when she'd asked him to take her to Benoit de Fournier, to allow her to test her newly learned slaying skills on the creature who had transformed her enchantment into a true nightmare. Rose had killed Benoit, his brother, his two sisters, and even his old mother in her bed, hacked at them with all the despair and rage filling her body. But it still hadn't been enough.

Would it ever be enough? No matter how many of the tribe she killed, no matter how she told herself—

"Missus? I said I can't—"

"You will wait here, then?" Rose pulled her mind back to the present.

Her driver, a young man from the village of Horn, hadn't wanted to drive her across the border into Myrdrean in the first place. Enough gold in his palm, however, and he'd consented. It was nearing the end of winter and his family was unable to pay the high prices for bread, meat, and potatoes at the market in Rosenburg. In the end, the emptiness of the younger children's bellies had convinced the eldest to transport her.

Their plight touched a place in Rose's heart. She intended to leave them enough gold to keep hunger at bay for years . . . assuming the boy looking at her with wide eyes didn't leave her to walk the ten miles back to the village.

"I will return before morning, I assure you," she added when the silence stretched on.

"But missus, I didn't bring anything for sleeping. The night grows colder and—"

"Bury yourself in the straw. That should keep you warm enough," she said, motioning to the back of the wagon with one gloved hand.

It was indeed cold, a shock after the unusually warm London weather and a reminder of what was at stake. The lesser demons must have been granted access to a higher level of hell by whatever magic the tribe had worked. It was the only thing Rose could think of that would explain the unusual weather on the British Isles. The creatures still remained beneath the earth, however—if they were allowed to surface through whatever portal the tribe sought to open, England would be no more. The whole of the planet would be plunged into a state of hell-like heat from which few would emerge unscathed.

Even the Fey, who could seek refuge in their alternate realms, would still be damned. If humanity were destroyed they would perish soon after from a shortage of sin—or joy if the faerie was of the Seelie court. It was another of the dozens of reasons that convinced Rose the Fey didn't want the ogres to succeed in their plan. There had to be another reason for their silence, for the secrecy of Ambrose and Gareth.

She hoped that secret would be found within the crumbling walls of the castle before her.

"I'll wait until dawn, missus. Then I'll head back to Horn," the boy said, the clench of his jaw convincing Rose he truly would wait for her return. "The cows will need milking and the younger ones will have use of me by then."

"Fair enough. Thank you, sir."

"It's Jack, missus. Just Jack." He blushed a shade of red as bright as his chilled fingers and turned his blue eyes away from hers.

"Thank you, Jack," she said softly, resisting the urge to reach out and ruffle his dark brown curls. He was a good boy, but she doubted he would take the gesture kindly from someone who appeared near his own age.

Rose pulled her gray woolen cape tightly around her shoulders, but allowed the hood to slip from her head. She didn't want her vision to be obscured in case anything unexpected awaited her on the trail. There hadn't been any sign of the tribe since leaving Dover—where she had been forced to dispose of a female with her dagger after watching the ogress consume a young man working in the belly of the ship— but the last leg of her journey inspired a healthy dose of caution.

Her former kingdom was a no-man's-land, a blighted, cursed place too feared for surrounding nations to take over. She had no idea what she might find behind the castle walls, and was glad she had risked returning to her London home to fetch her faerie sword. She had a feeling she might have need of it.

"Be careful, missus, they say the dead speak there and the sound is enough to drive a man mad." The boy's concern was clear as he handed her one of the lamps and kept the other for himself and the mules, which did not seem at all pleased to be hitched to one of the black forest's trees.

"Good thing I'm not a man then, eh?" Rose smiled

at him with more confidence than she truly possessed. The last time she had entered this keep, she'd had Ambrose at her back. Now she went alone, seeking answers she had a feeling the dead would do their best to keep.

AN HOUR LATER, Rose stood in the first courtyard, a wide expanse of stones as haunted and forlorn as the houses she had passed on her way to the castle. It was the place she'd watched the falconers train their birds, where she'd taken her little brother to run when he was too young to keep still, and where a traveling theater troupe had performed on the afternoon of her eighteenth birthday.

It was the troupe's costume mistress who had the spinning wheel.

Rose had felt compelled to return to the courtyard hours after the performance, to investigate the lives of the actors. That in itself wasn't strange. She'd been possessed of a curious mind and a mischievous spirit from the time she was a young girl, and was a bit tipsy on the Rhine wine her parents had imported for the birthday celebration. She didn't question the urge to spy on the troupe, only the strange compulsion to follow the sound of one singing woman, an ancient crone who sang mournful ballads of love lost as she spun wool into thread.

Perhaps it was the theme of her songs that lured Rose, for she was to learn the identity of her future husband that very night. She had been betrothed once before, but the arrangements between her father and the groom's sire had soured. Afterward, she'd spent two more years in Myrdrean, secretly grateful to have more time to run wild and free through the woods, to hunt with her brother and chat quietly with her mother after dinner. Her body had been as curious to know a man's touch as any other young woman's, but she'd loved her family and her kingdom so dearly a part of her had been unwilling to leave.

"But not so unwilling as to spend a hundred years asleep," Rose whispered, certain something in the shadows heard her voice.

The castle of her youth was haunted, by spirits once human and by other forces as well. She'd seen a number of souls as she'd passed through what remained of the village, hazy specters whose sadness she could feel when they brushed against her. If she'd been un-schooled in the supernatural, she surely *would* have run mad just as her young driver feared.

The others she felt watching her progress might do the job yet.

Rose suspected they were wraiths, but couldn't say for sure as she had only briefly glimpsed streaks of green and gold darting through the rubble. Wraiths were known to feed on the misery of lost souls, and there were an abundance of tormented spirits here, enough to nourish a host of the creatures. They seemed content to hide from the living for now, but she wondered if they would grow more aggressive when the witching hour grew near.

"It'd be wise to leave long before then." Rose turned from the tattered wagon, still set with the scene the ac-tors had performed nearly two hundred years ago.

Even in her soft boots, her footsteps echoed eerily across the yard as she made her way to the entrance of the castle proper. The colonnade, which had once connected the ancient section of her family's home to the newer chambers farther down the mountain, ran alongside her. At the corners of her vision she saw more streaks of green and gold dash between the pillars, but did her best to ignore them, though she assumed they could sense her fear. They could feed on the terror of the living, as well as the despair of the departed.

Rose grasped the handle of her sword and pulled it free. Immediately she felt calmer, and her fear abated a bit as she watched the blade grow long and thick in her hand.

She concentrated on counting her footsteps, on observing the different vines that twisted through the stones of the court. She didn't think about the wraiths, didn't let her eyes be drawn to the scattered bones in various stages of disintegration. She simply held her lantern high and pressed forward, grateful for the light of the moon, which aided in picking her way across the rubble.

Inside, nature had begun the process of reclaiming the keep. Smashed windows had allowed the outside elements in, lending a musty smell to every room. The wind had overturned furniture and tables, scattering the floor with broken glass. And as she crept through the room where her mother had once received people from the village in search of her aid in settling disputes, Rose spied the head of a tiny bear among the smashed crystal and china.

She swallowed, tearing her eyes away from the piece and the memories it inspired. How she had loved to sit by her mother as she took her calls, playing with the animal figurines Marionette had collected when she was a girl. The bear had been a favorite.

"Keep your mind in the present." Rose felt the press of despair in her chest, and fought the sudden urge to run to the throne room, to look once more upon the remains of her dear ones. Perhaps she could find some way to gather the bones and give the royal family the burial they deserved. Perhaps she could . . .

"I haven't come to bury the past, but to unearth it," Rose reminded herself.

She hadn't come to rip open old wounds either, which was the only thing to be accomplished by viewing those corpses still upon their thrones. If there truly was a heaven or a Summerland, she was certain her family's souls had found their way there.

Rose had thought about Gareth's advice all the way from London, and decided the royal library would be the first place she'd investigate. History could be concealed, but never rewritten. Somewhere in those thousands of volumes her father had collected, there had to be a history of her family. A true history of the Edenbergs, not the version they had told her as a girl. She needed the darker story, the one that wasn't colored over in shades of pastel so as not to frighten the children.

She needed all the information she could lay her hands upon. Her life and the lives of others depended upon it—she became more and more certain of that fact the farther she walked into the castle. There was still black magic at work, some darkness that haunted the Edenbergs. She would bring the past to light and see if Gareth spoke truly, if the revelations to be found here would be a weapon to use in preserving her life.

Then perhaps, after she foiled the ogres in London, there would be time to return to Myrdrean, to build a new future for her family besides this legacy of horror.

Turning a corner, Rose passed a mirror that had somehow withstood damage, but turned away from her reflection. She could not bear to look upon herself. She was simply another ghost here.

Finally, she arrived at the library door, a massive barrier nearly twice her height, plated in heavy gold and ornamented with elaborate etchings of the mythical animals of Myrdrean's black woods. It looked like the entrance to a treasure room, not a library, a fact that revealed much about her late father. He'd never been happier than when surrounded by his books, and had valued knowledge far more than gold.

She tugged at the handle, first lightly, and then with more force. Finally, she laid her sword and lantern on the ground and leveraged one foot on the wall. The hinges were tight with disuse, but after several minutes the great door finally swayed outward with a groan. A puff of stale air was released from inside, oddly warm against Rose's face as she gathered her lamp and sword and made her way inside.

"Goddess." Her whisper echoed through the room, which appeared exactly as it always had, but for the layers of dust coating the furnishings. There were no windows here, nothing to let in wind or rain. Her father's collection was miraculously intact.

Rose sat her lamp on the great table at the center of the room and set to work, passing by the sections she knew to be written in Greek or Latin. She doubted her family's history would reside on those shelves. The Edenberg origins were in Austria and Germany, though Rose's mother had come from France to marry Rose's father when she was barely fifteen.

"It was Mother who knew about the faeries." A memory—sudden as a flash of sunlight on water—raced through Rose's mind. Her mother, whispering of the Fey who had visited her with great gifts and great sorrow in her own cradle. She'd warned that nothing wondrous came without a price, and that patience would be rewarded.

Rose hadn't understood then, but perhaps her mother had been trying to prepare her for the long sleep that was to come. Rose's father was the one who had forbidden all talk of magic and curses and spinning wheels.

That truth of the curse had been made clear to her on the eve of her eighteenth birthday, as she was lifted from the spinning wheel by an enchanted wind. The wind had whispered all the secrets of her birth and promised a new beginning if she would be a good girl and go to sleep, just rest her eyes for a hundred years until the time was ripe for an even greater gift.

"For a greater gift . . ." The words came to her again, echoing through the halls as her limp form floated past her courtiers and her family. In her mind's eye, Rose watched them succumb to enchantment, and once more felt the safety of the wind that embraced her.

Her hands trembled as she reached for the first book in a row of unmarked volumes. It was as if a window in her mind had flown open and all manner of forgotten things were spilling into her.

How could she have forgotten the wind? That promise? Even given the horror surrounding her waking, she should have remembered that she was—

Never to pass the castle walls, or doom the Edenberg keep befalls. Her heart beat fast in her throat, and Rose knew her eyes were wide with the horror of her realization. Her legs buckled and she fell to her knees, the heavy volume she'd retrieved falling to the stone floor with a thud.

She had *known*. She had been warned not to leave, but she hadn't fought him.

When Benoit had settled the two babes in his carriage and then helped her inside, she had gone meekly. True, she'd been awake less than a day and her body was still torn and bleeding. She'd been out of her mind with the shock of what had happened while she slept and upon seeing her family trapped in enchantment, but she should have *remembered*. She should have fled Benoit sooner, should have returned and begged whatever force had enchanted her to put her to sleep once more, to spare her family and her kingdom.

There are so many things you should have done. What of the babes? Sold into service to the black court, raised as slaves to the Fey, never to know the comforts of humanity, never to know—

"Silence," Rose said to the cruel voice of her conscience. "Better slaves than raised to be killers and rapists. Or perhaps never raised at all if stronger ogre children required the nourishment of their bones."

You could have taken them with you, bartered with the black faeries for your lives and raised them in the proper way.

"I could not. I barely escaped with my own life. Ambrose came at me—"

And you begged for your own salvation, unconcerned with the bundles you carried into the cold night. You wanted them to freeze to death there on the ground, to be rid of the offspring of the man who raped you—

"Quiet. Quiet!" Tears flowed from her eyes, but she did not weep. It was as if her body had frozen there on the ground, incapable of sobs. The only movement was a strange plucking sensation near her mouth. Only when she tasted blood did Rose realize she had torn the flesh at her lips with her nails.

Where had her gloves gone? She didn't know. There was so much she didn't know.

You've only ever been concerned with one thing, Rose, your own selfish desires.

"I've served the Fey, I've aided humanity by hunting the tribe for nearly a hundred years. Surely that proves I've served others, that I've—"

You have done as you wished, thriving on each kill like a sin-eater. But you are not of the Fey, there is no excuse for your love of death but your own black heart.

"No, I loved them. I loved them." Rose whimpered against the painful words, curling into a ball on the floor, not knowing if she spoke of her family or the babes or both. "I loved them all."

What know you of love? You are the woman of

*many thorns. Your rose is poisonous to all who dare
look upon you.*

She wasn't sure how long she would have lain there
weeping if her eyes hadn't landed on the open book
before her. Her mother's handwriting leapt out at her
from the page, a tender caress that banished the fog of
despair for a moment, allowing her to see with eyes
unclouded by pain.

"Get out! Leave me be, you wicked things!" Rose
shooed at the green and gold blurs surrounding her,
as if scattering flies from a plate of food, shuddering
to realize she had nearly been their meal. "Go back
to the ghosts and feed well, for the woman of many
thorns comes next for you."

Rose grabbed her sword and surged to her feet,
chasing the wraiths until they vanished through the
walls. She stood at the door, panting for breath, waiting for them to return, sword raised as if the weapon
could do damage to incorporeal creatures.

"Despair. They feed on despair, Rose, not fear." She
found the realization oddly comforting. She could not
help the fear that pulsed through her veins, but she had
never been one to despair.

To despair was to turn one's back on hope, and to
turn your back on hope was to wish for death. She
had never wished for death, not even now, after realizing the role she had played in her loved ones' destruction.

She had awoken to the agony of childbirth, a pain
she knew to be far more dreadful than any battle
wound. At least battle wounds did not last for twelve
hours without relief—one tended to pass out from

blood loss after an hour, maybe two at the most. Her mind had hardly had time to absorb the shock of such pain before she'd been bustled out of bed by a man nearly twice her size who reminded her of the grim reaper himself. She'd been out of her mind with terror and exhaustion. She could forgive that younger self.

She *must* forgive. Letting the knowledge destroy her would serve no purpose.

Rose retrieved the book she had dropped, moving it and its companion volumes to the large wooden table near her lamp. They were her mother's memoirs, she could tell that much, but she didn't know which volumes pertained to her personal mysteries. She thought to read a bit of each and try her best to discern which she should carry with her back to where Jack waited. She never dreamed the first few chapters of the very first book would reveal so much.

But it was no accident that she had reached for that volume. It had fairly glowed up there in the highest corner, beckoning for her to take it down. Here in this room, she felt much as she had in her dreams of late, connected to the past, to her legacy, and most especially to . . .

"Mother?" Rose knew the name did not fall on deaf ears. Her mother was here. Her spirit had been near since she stepped through the gates, as close to her as her own skin.

"I'm sorry, Mother. I am so sorry," she sobbed, more tears spilling down her cheeks. She wrapped her arms around herself and squeezed, grateful for the love that surrounded her.

Her mother didn't blame her for what had happened. Rose could feel it in the way her spirit moved within her. She wasn't a ghost, she was truly a part of her, a drop of water in the ocean that was Rose. She was the part that had given Rose strength in the darkest moments of her life.

She had been with Rose before this night, living within her daughter since the day she left Myrdrean.

The memoirs told her the why of it, but her spirit was the way.

"Thank you," Rose murmured, unable to believe she'd been blind to so much for so long.

Not blind, my sweet girl, simply unwilling to see. It is all right, your time comes and you will be ready. I love you, daughter of my heart. Go, and do well.

"Oh, Maman," Rose whispered the name she had called her mother as a child. The words in her head were too precious to be believed. It was her mother's voice, faint but there, and it meant more to her than she knew how to express.

Her mother did not speak again, but a sudden wind whipped through the library, stirring the leaves of the book, causing a piece of parchment to fall from its pages. It was a betrothal agreement, signed by Rose's parents and the mother of the man who was to have been her husband.

The picture was complete, and Rose struck dumb, unable to utter a sound even in thanks.

So she said nothing, merely took the book and parchment, her sword and the lantern, and ran as fast as her legs would carry her out of the castle and down

press the gold she'd wrapped in her handkerchief into his hands before she stepped down from the cart.

"Unfortunately I do, Jack. All too well." Rose hugged her book close to her chest, then turned back. "I left my bags with the magistrate, and will depart on the next boat upriver. Thank you again for your aid."

The boy nodded, saying nothing as he tucked the handkerchief into the pocket of his threadbare coat. Before the journey to Myrdrean, he had warned Rose that boats leaving Horn were few and far between, but she suspected a part of him knew she wouldn't be taking just *any* boat. A woman who walked free of the Edenburg castle with her mind still whole was obviously consorting with the supernatural.

Thankfully Jack was a gentle soul, or she might have found herself fleeing Horn amid charges of witchcraft. Rose doubted that confessing river naiads, not witches, had made possible her swift passage from the port of Calais to the small village in Austria would make much of a difference to a terrified mob.

"Gee, gee!" Jack called to the mules. Their hoof-beats were the only thing breaking the silence as Rose crossed the cobblestones to Ambrose, rage building within her until she practically buzzed with it.

"Rosemarie, I swear to you—" His words cut off abruptly as her hand whipped out and slapped him across the face, seemingly of its own accord.

She hadn't consciously intended to strike him, but couldn't deny that it felt good. So good, in fact, that she struck him again, and then a third time for good measure. The sharp cracking sounds rung in her ears and a low, mad laugh escaped her lips, but it didn't frighten her. She wasn't insane. She was saner now than she had been in a hundred years.

"I deserved that. But if you strike me again, I will defend myself." Ambrose's long hair was pulled into a queue at the back of his neck, bringing the sharp angles of his face into harsh relief. His skin was unusually pale and his dark eyes rimmed in red, as if he had recently wept.

"Have you been crying, Ambrose, crying to see the end of your deception?"

"The Fey never weep," he said.

"And yet another lie spills from your lips. You have deceived me. For a hundred years and more," Rose whispered, her hand itching to be back at his face, to drive him to fight back.

But a scuffle would serve no purpose. This wasn't something that could be banished with fists or sword. A part of her insisted even talking was in vain, but she couldn't keep the words from spilling from her lips. "You had to know it would come to this someday."

"I knew when you were strong enough to know the truth you would come hunting for it. But I didn't expect it would be like this, I didn't—"

"It hardly matters. I shouldn't have had to hunt for the truth, it should have come from your own lips, *husband*." The word was filled with so much scorn Ambrose actually flinched in response.

"I am not your husband."

"No, but you would have been. Yours was the name my parents would have told me that night, after my birthday dinner, wasn't it? Or is there another A. Minuit of the night tribe whom I have yet to meet?"

"There is no other." His jaw clenched and a muscle there leapt, but he gave no other sign that he was affected by her words. It made her hand itch once more, but Rose managed to keep her violence contained in words.

"Truth at last. It was so kind of your mother to amend her curse in exchange for the hand of a half Fey princess in marriage."

"Quarter Fey. Your mother was half Fey, her father my mother's fourth cousin on—"

"I care not for a lesson in lineage, Ambrose. The legacy of my mother's family is clearly outlined at the front of this volume. I am more concerned with other revelations." Rose stared at him, not at all disturbed by the cold look on his face. He was hurting, furious with both her and himself. She could feel the emotions rolling from him as clearly as the cold wind on her face. "The curse was initially for death once my finger was upon the spindle. Your mother would have killed me to have her revenge."

"Marionette de Feu Vert was far from an innocent, she—"

"My mother was fifteen when she came to this land to marry my father, not much more than a girl."

"There is wickedness even in the young."

"My mother was not wicked! She was an angel, a sweet spirit of the utmost—"

"Your judgment is clouded by grief. You can not possibly understand what—"

"I understand more than you realize, Master Minuit." Rose reined in her temper with no small degree of effort, her entire body trembling with the need to rip the hard look from his face with her clawed hands. She lowered her voice to a whisper, knowing they risked waking the entire town if they continued to rage at each other. "Your mother did not tell mine of the prophecy foretelling my family's deaths. It was a trap from the beginning, not the mercy my parents were so grateful for."

"The prophecies of our people are not hidden. Marionette could have demanded access to the scrolls at any time."

"So it's her fault that she trusted the solemn vow of another Fey?"

"How many times have you mocked the tribe for their ignorance of their own history?" he asked, his whisper harsh and his cheeks flushing red. "Ignorance is not valid cause for mercy. Your parents were fools to enter into a solemn pact with anyone, especially a Fey de la Nuit, without examining every last element of the agreement."

Rose stared at him, her mind growing calm. He would never admit to any wrong. He was incapable of repentance, just like any other Fey. It was useless to speak, but there was still one thing she had to know. "Did you ever intend to honor the agreement? Did you intend to wake me from that bed you spirited me away to? It was you. Don't deny it. I remember it all, the feel of your arms around me and your voice in my ear, telling me of the great blessings to be had at the end of my hundred years of sleep."

"The prophecy clearly stated—"

"Damn the prophecy. You throw my words back to me, but what of your own? How many times have you decried the mystic riddles your people cling to so blindly? How many times have you sworn that a Fey prophecy is not worth the parchment it is written on, they so often prove false—"

"Yes, Rosemarie! *Yes,* I hoped the prophecy would prove wrong. Is that what you wish to hear? That I pined for you to be my bride, that I wished for nothing more?" He shouted the words, and this time Rose was the one who flinched.

"I wish to hear the *truth,* Ambrose. *That* is what I wish to hear," she said, fighting the sudden stinging of her eyes. She would not cry again, especially not in front of this man.

"Yes," he said, quietly now, his gaze falling to the stones at his feet. "I hoped—no, I didn't merely hope, I was *certain* the prophecy would prove false. My mother was blinded by jealousy. Your mother was . . . She attracted too much attention. Her father sent her away from the court and then betrothed her to a human man to save her life, as he knew any so favored was at risk. There are those who would have killed to keep a half-breed from sitting on the Seelie throne and Fey de la Nuit like my mother who would have done the same to keep her from gaining power within the dark court. On the day of her wedding to a mortal man, she forfeited her right to live among the faeries. That should have been the end of it."

"Should have been, but it wasn't," Rose said softly.

"Not long after her marriage, your mother invited every one of her Fey cousins to bless you in your cradle. Everyone except my mother. It was a deliberate slight, and against Fey law. Mother had the right to seek retribution with a curse upon the babe."

"The babe?"

"Upon you," he amended. "She cursed you to prick

your finger upon the spindle of a spinning wheel and fall down dead on the eve of your eighteenth birthday."

"But why did she later alter the curse? Why not have me die in truth? Would that not be the better revenge?"

"She didn't want revenge, Rosemarie, she wanted your mother dead. Marionette was doing her best to amend Fey law, to convince the high council and her father to allow faeries with human mates to continue to legally reside in both the Fey and mortal worlds. If she'd succeeded, she would have continued to amass power and supporters my mother coveted for her own purposes. But Mother couldn't work toward Marionette's death outright, she had to deceive her into arranging the circumstances for her destruction of her own free will."

"So, some years later, after forcing my mother to plead for my life—"

"And abandon her efforts to alter Fey law."

"Of course. Your mother relented, arranging for the curse to be amended to one hundred years of sleep, rather than death, in exchange for a betrothal between the two houses."

"There is royal blood on both sides," Ambrose said. "The marriage would have been a powerful one should the Fey de la Nuit ever abolish the council and return to monarchy rule."

"But your mother insisted a one-hundred-year delay was necessary for her son to grow into his adulthood, despite the fact that you were fully matured."

"Marionette was not aware of that fact, or of the prophecy declaring a quarter-blood daughter of the

Fey would roam the world for hundreds of years as the scourge of the tribe, seeking retribution for the deaths of her kin."

"You were aware." The words were accusing, no matter that her tone remained even.

"I expected you would sleep the hundred years and we would marry, Rosemarie. I'd never seen a prophecy fulfilled. Perhaps I was a fool, but I believed my mother's vindictiveness would do nothing more than cause a nation to sleep, giving time for her temper to cool."

"You truly thought we would marry? You would have honored the betrothal?"

"I would have married you, gladly. I'd watched you since you were a girl of sixteen. I adored you, your fire, your beauty, your love for those you claimed as your own. I would have been . . . honored to be your husband." His eyes were still on the stones, but Rose could hear the thickness of genuine sorrow in his voice. He truly felt despair over this matter, but it wasn't merely for a marriage lost. There was something else, something that hovered at the back of her mind, struggling to break through as the first rays of the sun broke onto the square.

"The prophecy also says the scourge will slay her betrothed," she said, the missing piece of the puzzle falling into place. There was a reason her mother had drawn her attention to the book with the prophecy written on the very first page.

It was a warning for the future.

"You killed Benoit, did you not?"

"He was not my betrothed," Rose said softly, stepping away from him and quietly drawing her sword.

"No," he whispered, not moving a muscle, his eyes still fixed to the ground. He appeared defeated, as if he would accept death if she were to deal it.

"That's why you nearly killed me that first night, when I ran from Benoit's carriage into the woods." It wasn't a question, a fact Ambrose recognized. His silence, however, was answer enough to send a sharp pain through her heart. "Why did you stay your hand? Why did you aid me instead of saving your own life?"

"There is a penalty among the Fey for interfering with a prophecy."

"Not death."

"No."

"Then why? Why, Ambrose?" Rose pushed him, a part of her knowing the answer she sought would only bring more torment, but unable to stop herself, to keep her mind from hunting for the truth with the same ruthlessness she had hunted the tribe.

"I couldn't do it. I couldn't look into your face, your spirit so damaged by the pain I'd caused you and do you any further harm."

"The pain *you* caused? It was your mother's doing, Ambrose. You never—"

He lifted his stormy eyes to hers, all the walls that had been built to hide the truth stripped away. Rose's breath caught at his beauty. He looked younger, softer, yet at the same time every one of his five hundred years.

"I cared for you then, Rosemarie. In the years since I have come to love you. My punishment is complete, I assure you."

"No," she said, shaking her head, fighting the realization that threatened to level her where she stood.

"I kept watch over you in the enchanted waters. Every day that you slept," he said, forcing the truth on her with his soft words.

"You let him in." A choked, wounded sound echoed through the courtyard, and only when she tried to draw breath again did Rose realize the cry was her own. "You let the ogre in. You could have stopped him, could have—"

Her knees buckled and she fell to the ground, the horror of it all washing over her, a cold wave that chilled her very soul. Her liaison, her friend, her *protector,* the man she had secretly loved and held in tender regard even when she knew there could never be anything but friendship between them, had betrayed her more completely than she had dreamt possible.

"You—I can't—" She felt strangled by the words and the tears pressing hot against the backs of her eyes, demanding exit from her body but blocked by the shock that fisted in her chest. Rose fought for control, forcing away every emotion, bringing herself to the place in her mind where she lived during battle, that cold, heartless void where all that mattered was the continued beating of her heart.

Finally, she lifted dry eyes to Ambrose, watching his face closely as she spoke. "Did you watch, Ambrose? Did you watch him strip my sleeping body bare and take my maidenhead?"

"Rose." Her name was a quiet plea for mercy, a mercy she couldn't find in her heart.

"How long was he there?" His guilty silence threatened to smother them both. "Answer me! How many times did he fuck me before he got me with child? How many times—"

"I will not continue this. What's past is past." He turned away, striding across the square toward the road that led to the river.

Rose followed, her sword still drawn, though she knew she wouldn't be able to fight while she held her mother's book in her arms. The volume was large and thick, and seemed to grow heavier with every step she took from Edenburg castle. Still, she forced her feet to fly across the stones, to catch up with Ambrose despite his longer stride.

"The past is *not* past. That past destroyed my family. That past kept my brother from ever growing into manhood. That past—"

"I will not argue this point with you, Rosemarie. Your parents' choices were to blame. That is the end of it."

"It is not the end of it. It is your *inaction* of which I speak. That inaction killed my family and determined the entire course of my future," Rose said, breath coming faster as Ambrose broke into a run in his quest to be rid of her. "Not only mine, but two innocent children born of your sin."

"My sin? *Mine?*" His face grew stormy with anger, though he didn't turn to face her, only ran faster toward the smell of the water.

Damn him, he would soon outdistance her. On impulse she whipped her leg into his path, sending them both tumbling to the ground. Her shoulder hit the tightly packed earth hard enough to make her wince. She dropped her sword and the book as she rolled, coming to a stop not two feet from where Ambrose knelt. Even when caught off guard, the man fell in such a manner that he landed upright, not sprawled across the ground.

"Yes, *your* sin," she said, struggling to her knees. "Benoit was going about the business of the tribe, acting as ogres have for centuries. You were the one who knew what he was, and what he would do. You were my betrothed, the man charged with watching over me as I slept."

"I was charged with nothing. I *chose* to watch."

"Precisely. You chose to watch. To *watch,* like a coward." Rose reached out to cup his chin, urging his eyes up to meet hers. "The night I awoke from my enchantment was as close as I have ever come to living a nightmare, even in a hundred years of bloodshed. Handing my children over to become slaves to the Fey has haunted me every day since."

"You have lived well, Rosemarie." Ambrose's eyes, looking more human than she had ever seen them, bore into hers. "You're wealthier than you ever would have been, even as ruler of your country. Your life span has been greatly extended, you—"

"But at what price? Ambrose, dear Goddess, you—"

"You've seen the world, known magic and mystery no other mortal can claim. I've heard you laugh, I've watched you dance, I've seen you enjoy pleasure as well as pain."

"Are you *blind*?" Rose asked, shaking her head as she realized what had happened.

He'd not only lied to her, he'd worked very hard to convince himself that what he had done was for the best. Self-deception was usually a human trait. The Fey, especially the Fey de la Nuit, did not feel guilt or shame the way humans did, and therefore rarely had the need to tell themselves lies.

"There are scars on my heart that I doubt will ever heal. I've lived as a shadow of myself, driven by the need for revenge and the greater need to run from my own shame." The truth spilled from Rose's lips, and miraculously, she felt the heaviness in her chest begin to ease. "I've never loved a man and I've never dared to love a child because of those that I gave away. I've never even had the strength to ask you what became of them, to know—"

"The babes have grown well, and are no slaves," he said softly, the words bringing tears to her eyes despite her vow to refrain from weeping. Rose pressed her hands to her lips, as if she could hold the emotions at bay. "They are tall, like members of the tribe, but as fair of face and hair as their mother. They work for the council in Paris. One as a steward for a Fey elder, and one as a soldier in the high council's guard. The boys are well liked and paid a good wage for their labor."

Ambrose smoothed a gentle hand over her hair, tied back in a long braid in keeping with her peasant clothes. He brought the braid over her shoulder and absently ran his hand up and down the blond plait. The affection in his eyes, in his touch, banished the last of her anger, bringing grief to live in its place. She would never forget what he had done.

Forgive . . . perhaps, but never forget.

Ambrose knew that, had known it for a hundred years. That was why he'd never touched her. He'd known she would seek the truth out eventually and would feel even more betrayed if he'd taken her to his bed. Refusing to act on his desires had been his way of doing penance for his actions, she supposed.

"Are they happy?" Rose pulled away from his touch, and came to her feet, but her eyes remained on the ground. She couldn't bear to look at his face anymore. The conflicting emotions within her were too strong.

"Benedict married a half-breed of Seelie and Elvish descent. He and his bride are quite content. Thomas hasn't chosen a wife, but there are many who would have him. He is . . . not as steady as his brother, but is a good man. He will likely sign up to fight some war with the Fey army, serve a tour or two, and return to Paris with his youthful fire tempered."

"Do they ever ask about their parents?"

"No. They know they are foundlings. I have never told another the origins of their birth."

"The histories of the tribe tell the story. If they wished to know the truth, it wouldn't be hard to discover." Rose closed her eyes, cursing her stupidity. "I should have killed Benoit that very night and let him take the secret of the twins to his grave."

"It would have been for naught. Benoit sent word of the birth to his mother. The messenger left not long after the twins were delivered." His voice was tight, as if he were loathe to mention that night once more. Still, Rose appreciated his honesty. After a hundred years of secrets, it was a pleasant change.

Slowly, she bent to retrieve her sword from the ground and sheathed it once more. "I will journey back to London. When I return home, I wish to have every

last Fey prophecy in my study. I have less than a fortnight to thwart the plans of the tribe, and I'm certain
my education is sadly lacking."

She would definitely benefit from further research
of the prophecy that had doomed her people. And there
was little doubt in her mind that another prophecy must
be at work at the present. The talk of secrets, the swear-
ing of Ambrose and Gareth to silence, it suddenly all
made sense.

The Fey prophecies were respected by every supernatural being. No one would dare say a word, even
to alert her to danger, if that would in any way interfere with what had been foretold. Gareth had obviously realized as much. She should have been able to
reach the same conclusion without traveling halfway
around the world.

But she was glad she had come. For the first time
in a century, her mind was clear of guilt and shame.
Gareth had been correct on that account, as well. The
truth had set her on the path to properly arming herself for the coming fight.

She would have to thank him, assuming he could
answer a few questions. There were still more mysteries to be uncovered, such as how a vampire came
to be so intimately acquainted with Fey prophecy.

"I will send word to Paris of your request," Ambrose said, nodding his approval.

Rose held her mother's book close to her chest,
knowing there was still much she must learn. She
turned back to where Ambrose stood, an ease in his
posture she had never seen before. No matter how
much he had dreaded this day, it was clear a weight
had been removed from his broad shoulders.

She wished she could be glad for him, but couldn't manage it. Not now, perhaps not ever. The fact remained that he had cursed her family and her life as surely as his mother had. That knowledge would always be between them. Which made her wonder . . .

"Why did you say those things to me in Covent Garden, Ambrose? Why, after all the years we spent together?"

"I sensed you were close to the truth. The time of your great testing is at hand, and you have risen to the challenge with your usual strength." He paused, his eyes caressing her face in a way she would have gladly killed for not too long ago.

Rose's throat grew tight and she dropped her gaze back to the ground, realizing she grieved the love lost between them nearly as deeply as she grieved the loss of her family. Right or wrong, he had been her companion and friend for a hundred years, and time had forged a bond as strong as blood.

"And there was the vampire, of course. That you allowed him into your affections showed your heart was growing stronger as well."

"Stronger?"

"The wounds you carried—they sapped your strength. That you'd come to care for someone, especially a vampire. It gave me some small hope . . ." His words halted, swept away by a chill wind that whipped down the road.

"I am sorry, dear friend," Rose said, knowing the words were some of the truest, and most painful, she had ever spoken. "I doubt my heart will ever be *that* strong."

Rose walked past him, veering off the road toward

the river, to the deep pool where the naiads had agreed to meet her shortly after sunrise.

"Turn away from the vampire, as well, Rosemarie," Ambrose called after her in warning. "He is not what he seems."

"I am beginning to think hidden motives are the only things I should take for granted," she whispered under her breath, knowing he would hear. Ambrose had been inside her mind from the moment she stepped from the mule cart. She'd felt his invasion in a way she never had before, as if a previously undiscovered muscle had begun to function after a lifetime of rest.

It's the Fey part of you. Your mother's spirit finally left the earthly plane, allowing the gifts of her Fey lineage to be visited upon her daughter.

"Thank you," Rose said, still not knowing how to mentally carry on her end of the conversation. "Have you been in my thoughts always, then? When I assumed you had such great respect for the sanctity of the mind?"

No. Only this morning. I had to know . . . to be certain . . . Rosemarie, please, I—

Rose broke into a run, fleeing Ambrose's words. She dashed through the reeds to the water's edge, wondering if she'd ever be certain of anything again.

CHAPTER THIRTEEN

February 28, 1750
Davington Hill
Faversham, England

She didn't dare waste time with the ferry, though the naiads weren't pleased to extend their journey over two long days. They were even less pleased to travel through the dangerous, kraken-inhabited sea from Calais to Dover, and then up to Faversham creek.

But Rose offered them the one thing the water folk couldn't refuse—her hair.

"Let me do it," the shorter naiad cried before they had even made it to the darkened shore near Davington Hill.

"I shall make the harvest, 'twas I who shook on the deal," replied the taller, elder female.

No sooner had the two spit her upon the bank, but long, cold fingers were tugging Rose's locks free of their plait.

"Do not take more than the agreed-upon amount. I must still function in the human world, and hair is a necessity." Rose forced herself not to shiver at the feel of slime-covered skin pawing through her waist-length hair. The naiads had done her a great service. She couldn't allow her revulsion to show, no matter that the two ladies circling her with excitement were hideous to behold.

If only the men they enchanted knew what lay beneath their seductive illusions, they would run in horror rather than be lured into the water for eternity.

"You don't have need of much. I've seen the wigs you gentry wear," the shorter said, spitting chunks of raw fish on Rose's clothes as she spoke.

Both of the women had caught and consumed a wide variety of sea creatures during the journey. Rose had closed her eyes and feigned sleep after a time, knowing she would never enjoy a finely baked filet again if she continued to watch the naiads feast on raw marine life—scales, innards, bones, and all.

"Made of real hair some of them are. You hardly have need of your own if you can be buying such as that," scolded the elder, leaning down to survey the curled tendrils that framed Rose's face. The creature's bulbous eyes were easily three times the size of Rose's and covered with a transparent eyelid that protected the sensitive orbs when the naiad was submerged. The cataract-like film was disturbing to say the least, and it was only with effort that Rose refrained from dropping her gaze. "You said we would be having enough for two, scourge. Don't think we won't be demanding our due."

"Certainly worked hard enough for it, didn't we now?" The shorter one sidled closer to her sister, treating Rose to a whiff of her repellent breath.

"You only need thirteen strands apiece for the

illusion spell. I'll happily give you twice that amount, but no more." Despite the foul odor accompanying the frustrated sighs of the women, Rose managed a smile.

Knowledge was indeed priceless. Her knowledge of naiad magic allowed her to keep all of her hair save a small chunk at the base of her neck—though the ladies did their best to make the harvesting of those strands as painful as possible by way of retribution. Rose prayed her knowledge of the Fey would prove just as advantageous as she made her way up the steep slope leading to Davington Hill.

She might have been remiss in her study of prophecy, but she knew more Fey secrets than any other mortal. She knew the places where it was easiest to travel between the two realms. She knew where the Seelie went on holiday and where the Fey de la Nuit celebrated the longest night of the year. She knew where a faerie went to meet with others of its kind, and where they would hide things they didn't want to be found.

The abandoned mansion on top of Davington Hill had long been used as a combination supernatural inn and dumping ground. Faeries came here to break their journey between Europe and Britain, and hid here when Fey politics left them temporarily out of favor. The catacombs of the mansion were also a favorite place for disposing of unwanted items. Dead bodies, the remnants of illegal spells, a half-breed child the Fey were unwilling to claim—all had been found at Davington at one time or another.

Tonight, Rose was hoping to find an ogre, or at least a part-ogre. Pithwater couldn't be pure tribe or he would have perished that night in Lord Drummand's garden. But he couldn't be pure anything else or he wouldn't have the taste for human flesh evidenced by his black blood. Whatever he was, she suspected she would find him here if he still lived. The ogres might have convinced him to draw Rose out that evening in the country, but she smelled a faerie's influence behind his reappearance in the city, and subsequent disappearance shortly thereafter.

Certain faeries could easily wipe clean the mind of an ogre and replace actual events with alternate memories. That would certainly explain why Pithwater appeared to have no recollection of that night in the garden.

His fear and shock that evening had been all too real. If he recalled being cleaved in two, he would have fled Britain and never whispered the name Briar Rose in his privy, let alone attempted to sully her name and reputation among the *ton*.

No, it was a faerie trying to draw her out . . . for reasons she could not yet fathom.

Perhaps the Fey in question would benefit from her death and wished to facilitate her capture. Despite Ambrose's insistence that none dared interfere with prophecy, faeries had done so before and would continue to do so as long as they had free will. If caught, punishment was a century or two in a Fey de la Nuit torture chamber, but the rewards for shaping the future could be tempting enough for bolder Fey to take that risk.

The fact remained that someone had removed Pithwater from London not long after his reemergence. Someone who wished to assure her ignorance.

Pithwater held secrets in his mind, no matter how deeply buried, and Rose meant to have them. She *had* to have them, or she entered London as ill prepared as when she'd left.

A barn owl hooted overhead and Rose shivered despite the unusually warm temperature. The closer she came to the top of the hill, the heavier her feet became, making her glad she had stashed her mother's book in a hollow log at the bottom of the hill.

Since leaving Myrdrean, it had grown so heavy as to be nearly impossible to hold for more than a few minutes at a time. It was faerie enchantment at work, she had no doubt, but she hadn't the time to work at undoing it. She had to press forward, no matter how great the burden she bore, or how the ruins ahead unnerved her.

She was as safe on the hill as any human on supernatural ground, but there was still a chance she walked into a trap. Whoever had plucked Pithwater from the garden in Bedfordshire might have hidden him here, knowing she would come looking. Even if a friend had removed Pithwater from London, her enemy might seek him here as well if the motivation was sufficient.

Rose wouldn't be able to read the prophecies until she returned to London and therefore couldn't guess what role a half-breed ogre might play in the story of her life—or death, as some would have it. But it would be a waste of time to travel to London and then return to Faversham by carriage. The full moon was a week away and there was much to be done, not to mention that Pithwater could have vanished by then if there truly were others looking for him.

"Or he might be dead already, and all this a supreme waste of time," she muttered. "As well as an unnecessary risk."

Despite her best efforts, fear took root in her heart. She didn't belong here.

By the time she set foot at the edge of the neglected gardens, it was if her very soul was begging her to turn and flee.

Twisted shrubbery that had at one time resembled architectural structures littered the yard, disturbed by overgrown weeds or mounds of shattered statuary. This had been a family home, just as Edenburg castle had been hers. She wondered what could have driven the mortal occupants from their lush, palatial surroundings, and began to suspect the faeries of more treachery.

How easy would it be for them to "encourage" a human to abandon a place they found desirable? How simple to appropriate lands "haunted" by black spirits?

A flutter of white at a shattered window reminded her that actual haunts frequented this place—restless spirits who remained to torment any who spent the night in the former mansion. She'd also heard tales of "little people" making camp in the catacombs, drawn by the promise of half-Fey young. Leprechauns delighted in consuming the flesh of children, but faerie children were considered a particular delicacy. Rose had slaughtered her share of the wee creatures in the years she'd lived in Britain. She'd heard they'd fled back to Ireland for a time, but wouldn't be surprised to learn they'd returned in the years since.

She would kill as many of the wicked little buggers

as she could if they crossed her path tonight. And she *would* encounter them if they had returned, for the catacombs were where she was bound. Hidden among the burial rooms below the ruins were holding cells that could contain any supernatural creature. If Pithwater was being kept here against his will, it was there she would find him.

Rose drew her sword as she circled to the back of the mansion, where the woods pressed in against the crumbling structure. There the secret entrance to the catacombs was concealed within an old human well.

Or at least it had been upon the occasion of her last visit to Davington Hill . . .

"This is no time to hesitate," she chided herself once she stood at the edge of the stones, staring down into the fathomless black of the enchanted well.

Faerie magic would spirit any who leapt from the well's edge down into the catacombs. She'd been just as uncertain the first time she'd jumped, but had landed safely. Of course, the Fey had been known to make changes in their spells occasionally. They might have removed the portal spell from the well and transferred it elsewhere. She could be leaping to her death—

"Oh, God's blood. Jump, woman." She jumped, her sword pressed tightly to her chest.

THREE HOURS LATER, a part of Rose wished she *had* plummeted to her death. The catacombs reeked of decay and rot even more fiercely than they had fifty years prior. Some of the Fey had been busy of late. Scores of corpses, mostly human, littered the catacombs, in every state of decomposition imaginable.

Some had been killed only a few days before, and still retained their flesh, though their organs threatened to explode through their skin at any moment.

Thankfully, the dim light afforded by her enchanted blade allowed for only the most superficial inspection of the corpses, but her nose suffered enough torment for all five of her senses combined. She would have to report what she'd found here to Ambrose. Her own distrust aside, the faeries needed to know they had a killer among them, one a bit too free with their death magic. They enlisted executioners to keep ogres from decimating the human population and wouldn't be pleased to learn one of their own had taken to killing humans at an alarming rate.

The only positive part of the experience was that she'd yet to encounter any leprechauns. She supposed not even those beastly little creatures could contend with the horrid smell.

Rose cursed as she turned a corner and pressed deeper into the maze. Just one more hour of searching, and then she promised herself she would allow her sword to seek the sun. She could feel the impending dawn. The newly discovered Seelie part of her was attuned to light or lack thereof, and when the sun was shining she felt her supernatural strength grow significantly.

Down in this endless dark, however, she felt alarmingly mortal. She wanted out—badly—but wouldn't allow herself to flee until she had explored every inch of the catacombs. Surely she'd seen the worst of their horrors by now.

No sooner had the thought crossed her mind then

a feral hiss sounded from the blackness ahead. Rose moved forward slowly, her sword held aloft for protection as well as light, but stopped dead when the inhabitant of the cell was illuminated.

"Goddess." She had descended into the catacombs looking for Pithwater, but hadn't truly expected to find him. Yet there he was, which meant the odds were better than good that a faerie was involved in some way.

But it had to be a particularly vicious member of the Fey, one with an overdeveloped capacity for cruelty. Even knowing what Ambrose had allowed to happen while she slept, she could not believe even he would do such a thing.

Whoever had placed Pithwater behind the bars of the cell to starve to death had obviously intended his death to be long and painful, and his suffering to be great. Whether it was friend or foe, she couldn't say, but he was most certainly without a shred of compassion.

The creature that had once been Pithwater hissed and flung his body, teeth first, against the bars. Not much more than skin and bones, he bounced off the enchanted iron with little effect. The pitiful wretch fell to the floor, but was immediately back on his feet, his hunger having pushed him to a place beyond reason. He was no longer even remotely human in appearance, an animated skeleton with grotesquely sunken eyes that glowed with the fever of madness.

A madness born of being eaten alive by his own insatiable hunger.

Pithwater flung himself against the bars again and again as Rose wondered how best to slay him. There would be no investigation of his thoughts now. It was too late for that. Even if she were to drag one of the decomposing bodies over and allow him to feed, she feared it would do nothing to return his mind. She had seen a similar look in feral vampires' eyes before.

There were particularly vicious vampires who turned humans and then chained them away under the earth, not allowing them to feed for the first month after their transformation. The vampires of the Eastern world called them blood beasts, and used them much as humans used dogs, to guard the boundaries of their property. The unfortunate creatures were not capable of rational thought, condemned to prowl the earth as mindless killers until someone put them out of their misery.

"Agh . . . ahhh!" Pithwater grunted and hissed, now on his knees reaching a skeletal arm through the bars toward Rose. A place on his forehead began to bleed from the force with which he pressed his face into the iron in his lust to reach her, to reach food.

She stepped back on pure instinct.

Despite the fact that he was contained by a faerie prison, she hesitated to move closer. Pithwater's jaw had dropped nearly to the center of his chest, revealing a dozen rows of sharp teeth. Deep in his throat, multiple tongues churned, straining toward Rose with a life of their own. A shudder ran through her, and she imagined how a field mouse must feel staring into the open mouth of a snake.

If only she knew what he was besides part ogre. She'd cleaved him in two and set fire to the remains and somehow he'd risen from the ashes. It seemed foolish to get close enough to slice at him with her sword. She could take off his arm and his head, and then he *should* be incapable of harming her when she entered the cell and moved in to sever his top from his bottom. But what good would that do if he managed to pull himself together again?

She supposed she could bury his body parts in various locations, but for all she knew he was capable of regeneration. In that case, at best she would have freed an enemy, at worst a mindless killing machine that would wreak havoc on the small parish of Faversham.

"Think, Rose," she demanded of herself, closing her eyes for a second to block out the sight of Pithwater and then opening them just as quickly. Seeing him was horrid, but hearing him and *not* seeing him was even worse.

She stared at the wall above him instead, desperately trying to figure out what type of creature would be invulnerable to fire. Vampires were excessively susceptible to flame, so he couldn't be part vampire. Faeries of both varieties, Seelie and Fey de la Nuit, could also be destroyed by flame, but the temperatures had to be higher and more sustained. Still, she'd used Fey fire powder on Pithwater, so that should have accomplished the deed.

He was too tall to have troll, pixie, or leprechaun in his heritage, and all of them were vulnerable to flame in some fashion.

As she pondered, Pithwater growled and moaned, saliva spilling from his mouth like water. Rose felt her jaw tighten. She was past the point of compassion for the creature who had been locked away to starve to death. She simply wanted to silence him, or flee this place as fast as she was able.

"No." She couldn't leave and risk that someone else would happen this way and set Pithwater free. She chewed on her lip, forcing herself to think. *What else?* What could this creature possibly be?

She raced through the remaining list of supernaturals. It couldn't be naiads, nor sirens, nor satyrs, nor hellhounds—

"Not hellhounds, but what of something else from hell?" Even as she muttered the words a part of her wished she could force the realization back. She'd never killed a demon, never even set eyes on one of the beasts, and yet they frightened her more than any known enemy.

A demon would be invulnerable to flame. And a demon would be strong enough to overcome an ogress and force itself upon her. If Pithwater were truly half demon, there was nothing she could do to destroy him, at least not with her present arsenal. She would need an ancient blessed weapon or the aid of the undefiled Amiantos coven, though only the Goddess herself knew where to find them. The witches had fled Athens hundreds of years ago and had only rarely been seen in modern times.

Her mouth grew dry as she realized that Pithwater was close to indestructible. That was the truly frightening thing about demons—not how dangerous they were, but how blasted durable. If the lesser demons were ever freed from hell they wouldn't overcome the world quickly. It would take several weeks, maybe even longer, until humans and supernaturals grew weary of fighting and became victims of their own exhaustion. If you were too tired to fight back, even the weakest of creatures could kill you.

And demons were not weak, as Pithwater proved when he began to bend what she'd assumed were unbendable bars.

For a split second Rose considered running, but forced herself to stand her ground. She could dispatch Pithwater in the same manner she had the first time, though she imagined he might be more difficult to disable in his present state.

"Not if he doesn't have a head. Goddess, Rose, now is *not* the time to turn into a simpering ninny." She closed the distance to the bars in a few steps and sliced off Pithwater's arm to avoid his clawlike hand. Then she thrust the tip of her sword through his eye, shocking him into closing his mouth before she slipped the sword between the bars and decapitated him with one swift stroke.

What was left of the man fell to the ground, writhing in apparent agony. Thankfully, however, the cell was silent as he no longer possessed a mouth with which to scream. Well, he was possessed of one, it simply wasn't attached to the rest of him.

Rose traced the runes of liberation over the charm near the door. The bars groaned as they slid open, but she refused to acknowledge the shiver the sound sent prickling across her skin. It was time to stop dwelling on what she didn't know and take advantage of what she did. She'd walked away from Pithwater once, she would do so again.

This time, there was no splash of black blood when she severed the twitching body on the floor. He hadn't fed in so long that his blood resembled thick sludge rather than anything liquid. Even when she kicked the top of him far away from the bottom, there was relatively little mess left behind.

Rose stood for a moment observing the segments, but neither moved an inch. Perhaps she was wrong and Pithwater *wasn't* capable of resurrecting himself, perhaps he'd required the aid of whatever faerie had brought him to London. Just to be safe, however, she plucked his head from the ground. She'd bring the trophy home and keep it somewhere safe, ready to be pulled out for display should Pithwater once again miraculously reappear.

For the first time since she descended into the blackness of the catacombs, Rose felt relatively un-afraid . . . until she exited the cell and came face to face with the creature responsible for the mass of dead bodies littering the catacombs. She should have suspected, but she'd assumed she would have heard if Fey grounds had been overtaken by a creature with a penchant for rotted flesh.

But then she hadn't been privy to the latest Fey news for quite some time.

"Damnation," she cursed, chucking Pithwater's head at the creature before she turned and ran as fast as her legs could carry her.

Anything else she might have stood and fought, but not this beast. Her best bet for survival was to seek the sun where the creature could not follow. Wyrms could shoot fire from their mouths as well as any of their dragon brothers, but thankfully they possessed neither legs nor wings. Even Rose, with her pathetically short legs, did a decent job of evading capture . . . until she turned a corner and saw another Wyrm blocking her exit.

She doubled back, nearly tripping over her own feet in her haste to find an alternate route. She managed, just barely, to slip down another tunnel before flames erupted at her heels. An enraged shriek followed the burst of heat, and she assumed Wyrm number one had been singed by Wyrm number two. She hoped the incident would buy her enough time to find an alternate path to the exit.

Rose raced down the tunnels, willing her sword to seek the light. It hummed and warmed in her hand, subtly urging her to veer right and then left. Her breath rasped in and out of her throat and she felt every hour of sleep she had missed in the past few days. She wasn't in peak fighting or fleeing form and it would only be by the Goddess's grace that she escaped this hellish place.

"Gods and goddesses help me," Rose half sobbed, scarcely believing she had the gall to think she deserved such a gift.

Still, there was no harm in sending out a prayer, especially when the portal came in sight . . . along with one of the Wyrms. It was squirming forward to block her avenue of escape, proving the creatures weren't nearly as brainless as Rose's studies had led her to believe. She'd have to share that news with Ambrose when she returned to London—*if* she returned to London.

With a wild cry she thrust her sword forward and muttered the Fey prayer to the Goddess of all, begging her to guide her weapon, to protect her in this, her greatest moment of peril. For a moment, no sound was heard but the panting of her breath and the hiss of the Wyrm drawing ever closer. But then Rose's very cells seemed to shudder and quake.

Her heart raced and her flesh began to burn, but her mind alerted her to the possibility of something more, a gift of her Fey heritage she could claim as her own. In that moment she discovered another previously unused muscle and flexed it with all her might.

Fey wings sprouted from her back seconds later, miraculously spiriting themselves through her clothes and lifting her feet from the floor. The wings were small, a pale gray rather than the vibrant colors of the Seelie court or the metallic black of the dark faeries. But to Rose, they were the most beautiful things she had ever seen.

She churned her newfound saviors with all her strength, reaching the portal only seconds before the Wyrm. She hit the magical causeway moving faster than she ever had before, and was whisked to the safety of the outside world, though not before the Wyrm shot one last burst of flame at her retreating form.

Rose was on fire when she emerged into the gray light of day. Thankfully, a light rain misted from the sky. With a cry, she fell to the ground and rolled, the damp grass snuffing out the tendrils that licked at her wings and hair.

"Only two minutes old and already damaged." She turned to survey the burnt edges of her wings and laughed until she feared she might never stop.

Then she began to weep for the millionth time in a few short days.

This had been a trap, of that much she was certain, but that wasn't why she wept. She really couldn't say why the tears refused to cease spilling from her eyes. So she sat there in the rain, cold mist mingling with her salty tears, so forlorn a sight that not even the spirits tapping at the windows of the mansion dared interfere with her sorrow.

CHAPTER FOURTEEN

March 2, 1750
London, England

> *A blood man of the night will betray the Fey, and the*
> *scourge shall be no more.*
> *The blood of the maid will burn, banishing hellfire back*
> *to the depths.*
> *The son will rise again, but no sooner rise than fall.*
> *When the clock strikes four, order is restored,*
> *though humankind runs like the rabbit from the fox.*

The words swam before Rose's eyes. Each carefully etched letter seemed to blur and run, becoming skittering insects that dashed to the edges of the page, eager to throw themselves to the floor.

"It's too late to run. I've caught you at last," Rose whispered, bringing the tip of her letter opener down in a swift, stabbing motion, pinning the faerie scroll to the wood desk beneath.

A soft exclamation from across the room made her lift her head and reach for her sword.

"My lady, you must sleep. I fear for your health if you stay much longer at your work." Dara, the chambermaid, stood in the doorway to Rose's study, staring at her with round, frightened eyes, looking seconds away from fleeing.

Her entire staff had given her a wide berth since she'd returned home early that morning, dressed in peasant clothes, her hair in a wild tangle, and drenched to the skin from the rainy trip back to London as an outside passenger on an express coach. Though she'd had the fare for an inside seat—and thankfully discovered how to pull her wings within her body so as not to alert the humans to her true nature—her bedraggled appearance demanded she sit separate from the tidy people snuggled together within the carriage.

Not that she'd minded. The fresh air and cool rain had kept her focused on the task ahead.

"The task that is now beginning," she whispered, narrowing her gaze on the paper she'd skewered.

She was certain she had the correct prophecy, and now the real work began. Somehow she had to discern what the blasted thing meant and arm herself against it before the next full moon. Or before her enemies made another move against her—whichever came first.

The first line seemed fairly self-explanatory, but it brought into doubt the one man she'd hoped she could trust. Gareth was certainly a "blood man of the night," the only blood man in her inner circle and one who'd already aroused the distrust of at least one of the Fey. Ambrose certainly seemed to feel betrayed by the vampire, though Rose still couldn't pinpoint the source of his animosity. If only she had pressed him for more information when she had the chance. Now it was too late.

Ambrose had attached a simple note to the crate of prophecies delivered to her home less than a day after their meeting in Austria. The missive explained that he would be in Paris for at least a fortnight, and therefore unable to aid her any further.

Rose had been furious, until a conversation with her footmen led her to the truth behind Ambrose's disappearance. The three men were half Fey, and therefore privy to the latest faerie scandals bandied about the supernatural London community during Rose's absence.

According to the most recent whispers, Ambrose's part in the ogre battle on the riverbank had been the reason for his first trip to Paris. Some members of the council had wanted him imprisoned on the grounds of prophecy interference for daring to defend his executioner's life. But because it was his home that was attacked, he was released with a warning after he'd convinced the powers that be he was simply looking after his own interests.

Still, he'd been watched closely and chastised for moving into her home even though he hadn't spoken a word to her of the prophecy. Sending her the Fey scrolls two days past, however, had vanquished the last of the high council's patience. Ambrose was being held in the council prison, expected to be charged with treason.

No matter how they had parted, Rose owed him his freedom. She had to prove the prophecy false, for his sake as much as for her own.

". . . you don't wish to be disturbed, my lady," Dara said, the rising panic in her voice drawing Rose's attention once more.

Dear lord, she must truly look a sight if she was terrifying the woman while seated calmly behind her desk. Perhaps it was the sword that inspired concern. Until that moment, Rose hadn't realized she'd kept her weapon out, or that she'd been using the shrunken blade to stab the desk as she thought. The magnificent cherry wood would never be the same. Still, she would count herself lucky if a ruined furnishing or two was the highest price she paid for her unwitting involvement in faerie prophecy.

"Pardon me, Dara," Rose said, forcing what she hoped was a reassuring smile as she sheathed her weapon. "I'm afraid I wasn't listening."

"You're exhausted, my lady. I shouldn't have disturbed you." Dara curtsied and began backing out the door. "I'll tell the gentleman to call another time. Perhaps tomorrow morning, after you've had some rest."

"I do not require rest, I require another pot of tea." Rose pushed back her chair, ignoring the dizziness in her head and the hollow feeling in her limbs as she paced around the side of her desk.

She'd lost track of how long she'd been awake. She suspected it'd been nearly three days, but wouldn't place a wager on it.

Dear Goddess, but she was weary. Perhaps a short nap wouldn't be amiss.

"Who is the gentleman?" She sagged into one of the two chairs before the fire, her mind returning once more to the lines of the prophecy. "If he's human, you may ask him to return tomorrow."

Or perhaps not return at all. She was weary of trying to maintain her place in human society while being beset on all sides by supernatural danger. It was enough to kill the last vestiges of her humor.

"And if he isn't human, he might simply take it upon himself to seek the lady of the house without waiting for permission." Gareth, as dashing as ever in a deep blue waistcoat and collarless frock coat, brushed past the chambermaid, who made no move to block his path. "Rose, you're looking . . ."

"Ravishing as usual?" she asked, firming up her mental shields.

Not only did the newly discovered Fey part of her allow her to hear some of the unspoken thoughts of others, it allowed her to maintain a certain measure of mental privacy. She hoped the shields would hold against the vampire.

"Sadly, no. I cannot tell a lie," Gareth said, taking her hand and feathering his lips across her skin. She shivered in spite of herself, her suspicion not cooling her lust for this man a single degree. She couldn't deny it was good to see him again. His presence thawed something within her that had felt frozen since her return to England. "You look absolutely awful. That dress is an eyesore. It should be burned immediately and . . . is that mud in your hair?"

The horror on Gareth's face would have made her laugh at any other time. Even now it was enough to inspire a smile. "I don't dare waste time indulging my vanity."

"You might wish to reconsider, Rose. I believe you're frightening the servants. That dear little chambermaid's nerves are shot."

"My nerves are not in the best condition either."

"The journey to Myrdrean was a trying one." Gareth's eyes were filled with compassion as he eased into the chair across from hers. Sitting in front of the fire with him reminded Rose of her vision, the night he had done his best to warn her of danger.

Why would he do such a thing if he wished her ill? Could his sincere attempts to help her be the betrayal of which the prophecy spoke? If so, how could that betrayal lead to her death?

Blast, but there were so many questions and so few places to look for answers.

"It was the journey home that nearly proved fatal." Rose informed Gareth of her discovery in the catacombs at Davington Hill, watching his face closely as she retold the tale. He didn't seem surprised to hear that Pithwater had been left in a cell to die. "I believe he was deliberately placed there by one who knew I would journey to Faversham to seek him out."

"A faerie then," Gareth mused, fingertips drumming lightly against his lips. It was a gesture he often employed while thinking, and it never failed to turn Rose's thoughts to how delightful those full lips felt against hers. "I wouldn't be shocked to hear one of them is behind the ogre business, but still . . . to meddle so is dangerous."

"Indeed it is," Rose said. "Even if they seek my death, it is still interference with prophecy. Events must be allowed to unfold as fate would dictate, or so I've been led to understand."

"That is my understanding as well." Gareth leaned forward to capture her hands in his. "I knew you would find your way to the truth. I hope you don't find this condescending, but I'm quite proud of you."

Rose blushed and pulled her hands away, not at all certain how to respond to the affection in his tone. "Yes, well. You were right. Discovering the prophecies surrounding my own enchantment certainly set me upon the right path," Rose said. "Though it did make me wonder why you pretended not to know my pedigree. You knew I was part Fey all along."

"But *you* did not. At first I thought perhaps my own curiosity might arouse yours, but then realized you would need a more forceful urging toward the truth."

"Hmm, of course," Rose said, not bothering to conceal her doubt. "It also made me wonder how a vampire came to be so intimately acquainted with Fey lore."

"Any supernatural out of his first decade knows the faeries are quite obsessed with their fortune-telling and punish any who interfere with their prophecies." Gareth's contempt for the Fey was clear in his tone.

"Punish," Rose echoed. "I don't feel the word quite conveys the dangers inherent in crossing the Fey. A century of torture is the minimum sentence."

"They are a most unreasonable lot."

"And a most dangerous one." She pinned him with an assessing look. "Which makes me wonder why you would risk such punishment to aid a near stranger."

"First, you are no stranger to me, love. Second, I gave no aid. I fear your long journey must have addled your thoughts." His eyes warned her to keep her peace, but she didn't heed him.

"I believe you did aid me, Gareth. And I believe you want something from me in return, though I cannot fathom at present what that something might be."

"I want nothing but your happiness, crave nothing but—"

"You stand to benefit from the information I have learned," she said, rising to pace in front of the fire. "But how could my discovery of my past positively influence your future? That is what my weary brain can't seem to unravel."

"You *are* weary. Your thoughts are muddled from lack of sleep." Gareth was the picture of innocence as he rose from his chair. Still, he didn't deny her assertion, making her even warier.

What did he want from her? More important, why did a part of her desperately hope that whatever he desired, it would be something she could afford to give? Preferably something other than her life.

"Do you wish me dead, Gareth?" she asked, the words catching in her throat, betraying the fear that lurked far closer to the surface than she wished to admit.

"Never." He closed the distance between them in two long strides and brought a gloved hand up to cup her cheek with a tenderness that threatened to undo her. "I would die before I'd do you harm. If you believe nothing else, please believe that."

His green eyes were as serious as she had ever seen them, his jaw clenched with the force of his passion. For a moment she glimpsed the feral creature behind the civilized veneer, but wasn't afraid. It was concern for her that had brought the beast from its lair.

Rose's breath caught as he leaned close, so close she could feel the warmth of his body, smell a hint of tobacco and mint. She tried to focus on those tangible details, to keep her thoughts from straying to how desperately she wanted him to kiss her, to hold her in his arms and assure her the future was not so very bleak. But if he kissed her now, Rose feared her fragile control would shatter and she would fall to pieces again.

Gareth pulled away, as if he sensed her anxiety. "Let me escort you to your chambers, and I'll make certain you rest comfortably."

"I told you that night in Ambrose's study," Rose said, standing firm despite imagining all the ways Gareth could find to make her "comfortable." "I'll allow you no further liberties with my person—"

"You filthy-minded lass. I meant to see you tucked safely abed, nothing more." He turned away, affecting a wounded expression. "Truly, Rose, the direction of your thoughts is quite shocking. Let us adjourn—"

"We shall adjourn nowhere until you—"

Gareth opened the door, ignoring her. "I'll have the little chambermaid heat water for a bath. Oh chambermaid! Ho, where are you, sweet? Come out, come out, your mistress has need of you!"

"I do *not* have need of her," Rose said, barely resisting the urge to stamp her foot in frustration. "I do not require a bath. I require the truth."

"And the truth is that you require a bath," Gareth said, ringing the bell to summon Dara from beneath the stairs. "Your dress begins to reek like the sheep who gave its wool to make it."

Rose sighed, a small smile tugging at her lips despite herself. "You're the first man of my acquaintance to tell me that I smelled."

"I'll always tell you the truth, sweet. Even when it isn't easy to bear."

"If that's true then why won't you—" Her words were interrupted by a scream echoing through the house, followed by a great crash and an ungodly wail. Seconds later Dara rushed down the hall, her face as white as the apron she wrung in her hands.

"What is it?" Rose asked, already drawing her weapon, prepared to fight whatever devil had dared invade her home.

"It's Marta, my lady. She's returned, but she's . . . Never have I . . ." Dara swooned before she could finish her sentence, but thanks to Gareth's quick reflexes, was eased to the ground gently.

Rose jumped over her prone form, unable to spare any time for a person who'd faint before a drop of her blood had been shed.

SEVERAL HOURS LATER, Rose found herself alone in her chamber with Gareth, but she no longer had the slightest desire to lose herself in his arms.

Blind trust was a luxury she couldn't afford, no matter how fiercely a part of her wished to think well of the man who lounged on her bed, looking very much at ease.

"Finally, you've returned. I feared I might be forced to pry you from that witch's side with brute force," he said, rolling to sit at the edge of the bed, staring at her with obvious desire. "I cannot believe that you've taken her in without a second thought."

"She can do me no harm in her present state. Besides, I won't believe Marta's a witch until the proof is in my hands." Rose turned toward her dressing table, doing her best to firm up her mental shields while she removed the few pins that remained in her hair. She was exhausted and afraid, but it was imperative she keep her secrets, at least until she achieved her last goal of the evening.

A goal that would involve quite a bit of control and end with one very angry vampire, but she could see no other way to discover what she must know. Marta's appearance had raised questions she must have answered before she put her trust in the man watching her from across the room.

"You realize that your decision has left me no choice but to remain here with you to ensure your safety." Gareth's voice had taken on the purring quality that usually sent shivers across her skin. "I'd never forgive myself if I were to leave and you suffered cruel treatment at the hands of that bedraggled wretch. So I will abandon the comforts of home to keep watch upon you while you sleep."

"You are indeed noble to make such a sacrifice," Rose said, ignoring his second insult to Marta. The poor woman *was* in a wretched state.

Her eyes rolled around in her head like a madwoman and her skin burned with a fever that would have singed the flesh from a mortal's bones. The Elvish doctor Rose summoned had been unable to cool the sprite, even after submerging her in icy water for nearly half an hour.

Aside from her maddened state, Rose was distressed by the thoughts she'd overheard while reaching toward Marta's mind. The woman was tormented by dark visions, memories of being used savagely by an unknown man. A man with long, thin fangs, who tore at her flesh like a beast while he abused her.

Rose shuddered at the memory and pressed trembling fingers to her temples.

"The bathwater is still warm," Gareth said, his voice void of erotic suggestion. "I'll go down to the kitchen and fetch you something to tempt your appetite while you bathe."

The bed frame groaned as it gave up his weight and Rose heard the soft pad of his steps as he crossed to the door. He had sensed her inner turmoil and was no longer trying to seduce her. He'd never sought to lure her to him when she was in a weakened state of mind.

"Wait a moment." Rose's hands trembled as she worked the buttons of her dress, but her voice was strong and firm. She had one goal left for this evening and it would not be accomplished by allowing Gareth to play the part of the chivalrous friend. She required his lust, not his friendship, if she were to gain the knowledge she sought. "I fear I am wearier than I knew. I'm not certain I have the strength left to lift my sponge, let alone manage the washing of my hair."

"You do have quite a bit of hair," Gareth said, watching her fingers with undisguised interest. "Should I ask the maid to—"

"No." She shrugged off her dress, letting it puddle at her feet.

"No?" His eyes flashed as they had that night in the garden, as if they were capable of emitting light, not simply reflecting it. His tongue darted out to dampen his lips, the gesture oddly sweet and vulnerable.

"No." Slowly, she untied the ribbon at the front of her corset, and began pulling the satin length through the eyelets, one by one.

Her heart raced and her nipples drew tight beneath her chemise, her body responding to the heat that always flared between them, no matter what her rational mind had to say about it. By the time she had divested herself of her corset, she was aching to be touched and her thighs were damp with the evidence of her need.

And it *was* need, not merely want. She *needed* to feel his hands upon her, his lips pressing against her skin—needed it so badly it would be hell to deny herself.

"Please do not deny yourself, sweet," Gareth said, his tone low and rough as he closed this distance between them with measured steps. "Deny me if you must, but never yourself."

Rose had only a moment to reinforce her mental shields before Gareth's large hands were at her hips, bunching the fabric of her chemise in his fists. "Gareth, I—"

"I assume you are not so modest as to wear your chemise in the bath?" His lips pressed lightly to her forehead, a chaste kiss that was completely at odds with the way he pulled her chemise up and over her head seconds later.

Rose's breath rushed from between her lips and her nipples tightened even further in the cool air. A tremor swept through her as Gareth's gaze roved over her exposed flesh, the need etched upon his features humbling to behold. Never had a man looked at her with such haunting want. Not even Ambrose. Goddess help her, but it made her desire that much more difficult to control.

His hands shook slightly as he brushed a lock of hair behind her ear. "I don't see how one can get properly clean wearing clothes in the bath."

"I imagine it would be difficult," Rose said, her lips buzzing with the need to press against his. It took all her strength to keep from twining her arms around his neck and pulling his mouth down to meet hers.

Gareth's eyes were dark with passion, but he made no move to touch her other than soft fingertips playing at the delicate flesh just behind her ear. Even that small intimacy was enough to make her skin burn and her sex ache.

Gareth smiled as he took her hand and led her toward the bath.

Rose laughed, a breathy sound that turned into a sigh of pleasure as she stepped inside and sat down. The water was the perfect temperature and scented with the rose oil she kept on her dressing table. Dara never bothered adding scent, so she could only assume Gareth was responsible for the fragrance that surrounded her. For some reason, the thought of him preparing a bath for her made her heart ache. Such a small thing, but it revealed a side of him she hadn't known existed.

And what else don't you know about the man? You can ill afford surprises.

"Thank you," Rose said, reaching for the sponge in a bid to regain control.

"Close your eyes. Rest. I'll make certain you don't

fall asleep and drown." Gareth plucked the sponge from her hand and set it beside the soap, then dipped a pitcher into the water, filling it to the brim.

"It would be rather difficult to drown in a hip bath," Rose said, closing her eyes as Gareth poured water over her head, dampening her hair.

"Perhaps you should keep your lips closed as well, you contrary girl." Seconds later, soapy hands were working through her hair, adding the smell of lavender to the rose.

At first Rose found it difficult to breathe, let alone rest, but soon the feel of Gareth's strong hands working through her hair, kneading over her neck and shoulders, lulled her. She was trapped somewhere between relaxation and excitement, her entire body humming with awareness of the man beside her. She'd been bathed by servants for much of her life, but never had she been so conscious of the way soap slid across her damp skin. Never had the feel of another's fingers working between her toes made her tremble.

By the time he was finished with her feet and calves, Rose felt as if she might very well be at risk of drowning. Not in water, but in pure sensation. Then he went to work on her arms, scrubbing each finger with firm strokes she felt across every inch of her aroused flesh, making the neglected portions practically scream with the need to be bathed just as thoroughly.

And then, finally, his hands dared to cross between arm and torso, smoothing across her breasts, capturing her nipples and soaping them until delicious sparks of need shot between her legs. Rose moaned and arched into his touch, all thoughts of denying him vanishing in the wake of the desire awakened by his wicked fingers.

"Rosemarie, kiss me." He whispered into the shell of her ear with such longing she couldn't refuse. Keeping her eyes closed, she turned her head, capturing his lips at the same moment as his soapy hands slid beneath the surface of the water.

She moaned into Gareth's mouth as his hands played between her legs, all pretense of washing her body vanishing as he explored where she was slick with wanting. He drove his fingers inside her until she ached for something thicker to take their place, until she squirmed and reached desperate hands up to cup his face and pull him closer.

Her tongue pushed between his lips, tasting, devouring as he moved his fingers to the sensitive bud guarding her entrance. Rose thought to demand he claim her properly, but he brought his other hand to her breast. He pinched a nipple tightly between finger and thumb even as he circled her nub with a firm, insistent pressure, bringing her over the edge before she could prepare herself.

"Gareth!" She called out his name, sobbing as wave after wave of pleasure swept across her skin, banishing the aches and pains of the past few days, yet awakening a new pain in her heart.

Even as she climaxed, her fingers digging into the muscle of Gareth's arm and her body consumed by the fires of passion, Rose knew she had made a serious error. She should never have allowed him to pleasure her, to further weaken the defenses around her heart—not when she had to continue with the plan she had conceived while sitting beside Marta earlier.

The plan that would make use of the restraints she'd had installed on her bedroom wall sixty years before, in order to keep a young ogre alive while waiting for his kinsmen to seek him out.

"Now it's your turn," Rose mumbled against Gareth's lips, forcing herself to return her attention to the true task at hand before she lost her resolve.

"No. I'm not finished with you yet." His fingers slipped between her legs again. "You haven't been thoroughly bathed. I'm certain there are several places I've missed—"

"The water grows cold," Rose said, rising from the bath before Gareth could argue the point. "And I grow hungry."

"Then I shall fetch you something from the kitchen," he said, watching with disappointment as she shrugged into her dressing gown without bothering to dry her skin. For a moment she could nearly hear his thoughts, feel how agonizing it would be to leave without being allowed to touch her.

"But I do not hunger for food," she said, pushing lightly at his mind, only to find his thoughts locked firmly against her.

"No?"

"No." She closed the distance between them, running her hands up and down his chest before beginning to work open the buttons of his linen shirt. He had removed his waistcoat before sprawling across her bed, so she need only dispose of shirt and pants before she would have him as bare as the day he was born.

"Then what do you . . . *Goddess*, Rose." Gareth moaned as she untied the string fastening his drawers and tugged them down to the floor, revealing the large shaft straining between his legs. Once again his control slipped and she was aware of how he ached to feel her hands upon him.

But when she reached toward his arousal, he caught her wrist. "Why the rush, sweet?"

"I told you, I'm hungry," she said, slipping her tongue out to dampen her lips. "And eager to give you the kind of pleasure I have received. But if you would rather I not take you in my mouth—"

"Oh, I *would* rather." Gareth was out of his shoes in a trice and then took her hand, tugging her toward the bed. "Heaven forbid I make a lady wait when she is eager to dine."

"But wait, my lord. I do not make a habit of eating in bed." Rose slipped her hand from his and moved to the curtains covering the far wall. "I find it difficult to sleep if there are crumbs in the sheets."

"Very well. I am most willing to accommodate you. Where do you prefer to dine?" Gareth asked, amusement and frustration in his tone. "I shall gladly accompany you to the kitchen, though I fear the sight of us in our present state might shatter the last of your maid's fragile nerves."

"There's no need for that. I prefer to sup in private." With a naughty smile, she pulled the curtain aside, revealing the restraints built into the wall.

Gareth's lips parted in shock even as his eyes lit up with a wicked gleam. "*Rosemarie Edenberg,* you naughty thing. You've rendered me quite speechless."

"Then why, my lord, are you still talking?" Rose reached for the nearest cuff and opened it with a teasing wink.

Moments later, she'd captured her willing prey, hand and foot. Unfortunately for her lusty lord, he was a prisoner of war, not of desire.

"I apologize if this proves to be unnecessary," she said, backing away slowly, refusing to gaze upon his nude form lest she be swayed. "But I hope you come to understand that the position in which I find myself means that I cannot risk trusting false friends."

"False friends? When have I proven myself anything but—Where are you going?" Gareth's voice rose to a shout as she scurried toward the door. "*Rosemarie! Come back here at once! I demand you release me—*"

Rose shut the door and hurried to her study, knowing sleep would be impossible. No matter how weary, she would never be able to rest knowing Gareth was strapped to her wall, no doubt planning the punishment he would inflict on her after gaining his freedom.

She would grant him that freedom if he proved innocent of wrongdoing. If, however, he was the fanged monster who had abused Marta so terribly, he would never be free again. She would push a stake through his chest as he hung helpless upon her wall, despite the fact that he had come so close to claiming her own heart.

CHAPTER FIFTEEN

March 3, 1750
London, England

Rose finally fell asleep as the sun was rising, but was awoken several hours later to the sound of voices raised in heated argument. Fearing the worst, she rolled from the chaise in her study and raced toward the disturbance. But instead of an enraged vampire or distraught chambermaid, she found her footmen bickering among themselves as they debated who should tote the bathwater up to Marta's room in the wake of Dara's departure.

The chambermaid had apparently fled when a bouquet of black roses was delivered to the house along with a note promising a slow and painful death to any who helped thwart Rose's destined death. Dara had packed her things immediately and urged the other servants to do the same.

Thankfully, Phillip, Samuel, Lucas, and Erin, the cook, were made of stronger stuff. They remained in her service and swore they would continue to perform their duties as long as Rose was alive.

"We'll not be scared away by a few faeries," Lucas said, a smile on his face though he'd drawn the short straw and would be taking over as chambermaid until a replacement could be found.

He and the others remained relentlessly cheerful, despite the terrifying gifts that continued to be delivered throughout that afternoon. The Fey no longer wished to keep Rose in the dark. Instead, they seemed determined to frighten her into taking her own life with their black bouquets, gift boxes containing goat skulls, and other gruesome tokens.

None of the Fey had expected her to live, let alone to return to London with a new pair of wings and a mind turned toward prophecies. She had been a joke for a hundred years. But no one was laughing anymore—not the high council, which had dispatched warriors to deal with the Wyrm infestation in Faversham; not even Gareth, the man she'd assumed could laugh at anything.

"You've returned for me then. I was beginning to think you'd leave me here to starve to death." Gareth's voice seemed to fill the darkness, a tangible force that enveloped Rose as she made her way into the room late in the afternoon.

"It would take more than a day for you to starve, dearest."

"Dearest? Does that mean all is forgiven?"

"A moment ago you behaved as though there was nothing to forgive." She turned to face him, desire speeding her pulse in spite of herself.

It had pained her to leave him the night before, but she had no choice. A hungry vampire was a weak vampire, one whose thoughts would be far easier to invade. She must find out if Gareth was the one who'd attacked Marta, or the "blood man" who betrayed the Fey. Or perhaps *both*.

"Oh there is *much* to forgive." Gareth's eyes glittered as if he could read her thoughts, though she knew he couldn't. Now that she was rested, her mental shields were quite impenetrable. "We can begin by exchanging places. I'll chain you here and kiss my way across every inch of your—"

"No. I haven't yet fulfilled *my* part of the bargain." Rose untied the belt of her dressing gown and let it fall to her feet, standing before him in nothing but her chemise. She deliberately moved in front of the fire, knowing the light would bring her curves into sharp silhouette.

"Call me mad, Rose, but I'm no longer as interested in having my cock serviced as I am in getting off this damned wall." His tone was amazingly light, but she could feel the tension in his voice.

"I'm not sure your cock would agree." She removed the pins from her hair, freeing it to tumble down to her waist. " 'A blood man of the night will betray the Fey, and the scourge will be no more,' " Rose recited, watching Gareth's reaction closely. " 'The blood of the maid will burn, banishing hellfire back to the—' "

Gareth cursed. "I should've known."

"Should've known what?" She pulled her chemise over her head. She'd learned Gareth's thoughts were more easily read when he was aroused, and she deliberately put the knowledge to use.

"I should've known no good would come of allowing you to paw through those scrolls on your own," he said, though he was wondering how much she knew and what to tell her to keep her from asking a certain question. But what question? "Ambrose should've never allowed it, any more than he should have allowed you to exercise your new Seelie gifts without instruction."

"Ambrose isn't here. He's in prison for daring to help me. What have the Seelie to do with this?" she asked, though she had an inkling.

Her mother's memoirs had revealed her to be of the Seelie court, a princess, no less. How it had amused the Fey de la Nuit to see a royal—even a quarter royal—of the golden court earn her living slaying ogres for them. But once Rose had signed the contract that dark night, she became their creature. No Seelie could approach her. Not even her grandfather, the king of the golden Fey, could come to her aid.

He'd recently appeared in her dreams, however, expressing his pleasure that her mother's spirit had finally passed into the Summerland, and vowing to champion her cause—as soon as the conditions were favorable.

Favorable. Rose assumed that to mean as soon as she found a way to thwart her fate and free herself from her contract with the black faeries. Ambrose had told no one of her vow to break with the Fey de la Nuit, and she was not so foolish as to repeat it, not when her death would be so wonderfully convenient for them.

Only after she was free, however, would King Stephen de Feu Vert be willing to meet his mostly human granddaughter. She expected nothing from the Seelie until then, and not much after. A three-quarters human woman was tainted by mortality, a fact far less forgivable than having killed hundreds of ogres for the Fey de la Nuit. Her humanity alone made her an undesirable relation, and she suspected she would have remained unacknowledged by her kin if she weren't fourth in line for the throne.

As if they would allow her to ascend even if the heirs before her were to simultaneously drop dead. She'd be assassinated first, a fact that made her wish for the long and healthy life of her uncles and cousin . . . assuming she survived the next week.

"I always saw the Seelie in you, Rose," Gareth said. "No true human possesses hair like spun corn silk. And your eyes are an unearthly shade of blue."

"What have you to fear from the Seelie?" she pressed.

"Give a group of fanatics the power to summon the light of the sun even in the darkest night, and you'd be surprised to what lengths we sun-fearing creatures will go to appease them." Gareth's eyes trailed down over her bare breasts, down to the tuft of golden hair between her legs. "I once heard of a Seelie duchess who could summon rays of sunlight from her quim. Killed a great many vampires before the treaties were in place, or so I've been told."

"Gareth," she said, his name a warning.

"Not the worst way to meet your death, I suppose." He licked his lips and a knot of desire twisted low in her belly. "Tell me, sweet, would you shoot sunlight from your cunny if I were to lower my head between your legs, feast on all that sweet—"

"Please." Her breath grew even faster. She was

already half mad with the need to press her body against his and feel the bliss of his skin upon hers. She'd ached for the comfort of his arms throughout the long night, no matter that her body had found release by his hand. In the midst of so much betrayal and secrecy, it seemed there was no one she could trust, but how she wanted to trust him. Which made his reluctance to speak all the more maddening.

Ambrose had been right. She *had* softened toward Gareth.

"I would never make you beg. Never." His eyes were serious, and she felt the silent plea with every cell in her body. "You can trust me—"

"Tell me what it is you don't want me to know. What is it? I know you're hiding something, I can feel the lies simmering beneath every word you—"

"Damnation, Rose!" He roared her name with enough force to make her flinch. His hot breath stirred the air around her face, and his green eyes gleamed with anger. The time for polite conversation had ended. "A faerie prophecy is at work. I've already shared more than I should—you know that. I *must* keep my secrets. I don't respect their prophecies, but I—"

"I know you're not Fey and you don't respect their prophecies so why—"

"No, I don't respect their prophecies any more than you or Ambrose." His eyes didn't meet hers as he spoke, and Rose knew she was on the verge of enlightenment. Something in his words carried a depth of meaning that went beyond the obvious. "But I've no choice but to honor their customs. To ignore them is to court death, and I don't wish to die. Even for you."

"To court torture, you mean."

"Some say the Fey kill those they claim they will torture. You've heard the same, don't deny it."

Rose didn't answer, and instead ruminated on what she knew of Gareth. Ambrose had warned that Gareth was not what he seemed. Had she been wrong to assume he was accusing Gareth of deception?

"You aren't Fey, you don't . . . You are part faerie as well!" she said, the realization suddenly so clear. That was why Ambrose had allowed Gareth's blood donation the night she lay near death. He knew only a full-blooded vampire could create another of his kind.

"Clever. Now let's put an end to this nonsense," Gareth said, as if that were the end of it. "Cut me loose and I'll punish you with a spanking upon your naughty—"

"Not just yet." She stepped back a few steps, her mind racing. "I'm curious. You did your best to inflame Ambrose, to force him into revealing his feelings. Why?"

"I did no such thing, I simply—"

"Of course you did." Rose waved away his protest as she began to pace the floor. "You knew he was my betrothed, and knew I would never forgive him for keeping such a secret. Did you simply want Ambrose to suffer sooner rather than later? Or did you have something to gain from my discovery?"

"Perhaps I thought you'd kill him and rid us both of the inconvenience."

"You know better," she said, keeping her eyes on him, watching his mind work as he decided what to share. "If you truly care for me, Gareth, you must stop prevaricating."

"I adore you, Rose," he said with a frustrated sigh. "And I will gladly fight by your side for a hundred years or more. Set me free, and let's talk about—"

"And now you're urging me to set you free before you tell me what you've done. So it must be something I won't care for. Am I correct?"

He stared into her eyes, a grudging respect mingling with what seemed to be genuine anxiety. She had never seen him anxious, and it made her nervous as well. Goddess, what had Gareth done? And would she be able to trust him once she found out?

"Ambrose also warned—"

"And you would heed his words? Even after all you have learned of him?" Gareth's voice was thick with emotion.

"What do you know of that?" She met his eyes, and knew then that her mind had not been as tightly shut as she'd hoped.

"A bit, but if I'd known before your return that he allowed that creature to violate you as you slept, I'd have challenged him to pistols at dawn."

Rose's throat grew tight, and her mind clouded by the emotions that were so close to the surface of late. "There's no need. What's past is past."

"No. That wretched past still taints your present. And I would gladly kill him for that."

"Don't," she said, a soft warning. "I don't want your pity."

"I'm not offering you pity." Gareth strained against his bonds, bringing his face nearer to her own. "I'd have offered you comfort if you would have allowed it. Instead, I offered you control. I'd hoped it would help banish that lost look from your eyes."

"I'm hardly lost. I know the truth and—"

"Don't lie to yourself, Rose. Lie to me if you must, but not to yourself." His eyes began to change, becoming fathomless depths that lured her to him. "I am yours to command, to do with what you will. If it will heal some part of you to torture me, then go ahead."

"I didn't secure you to the wall to heal myself," she stammered, her lips buzzing with the need to brush against his. "And I'm hardly a proponent of torture."

He smiled, but it wasn't the sarcastic grin she had grown accustomed to. No, it was a look of such tenderness that she felt her heart threaten to burst from her chest. She realized in that moment that he'd known she planned to leave him chained to the wall all along.

"No," he said, stopping her as she turned to fetch the keys to free him.

"A moment ago you insisted upon your freedom."

"A moment ago we were playing a different game. You needed me to push you."

"Oh, I did, did I? And what do I need now, if you're so attuned to my every whim?" she asked, furious with herself.

She'd allowed herself to be manipulated by grief and rage. She should never have trapped Gareth, no matter her reasons. She wasn't strong enough to force his secrets from him and she couldn't trust herself to resist the temptation he offered. The clear mind she had found so briefly in Horn was once again clouded.

"You need to rid yourself of some of that pain locked within you."

"And how do you suggest I manage that?" Rose

fisted her hands at her sides until her fingernails dug into her skin. For some reason, the pinching helped ease the ache within her heart, made her feel more in control.

"What better way to gain control of yourself than to take control of another?" He leaned against the wall, visibly relaxing even as his cock began to thicken. "Take control of me, Rose. Hurt me if you like, mark me, whatever you need to purge yourself—"

"I don't want to hurt you." Her voice broke as she realized what she *did* desire.

"No?" His eyes darkened, as if he had read her wicked thoughts.

"No." It was a whisper, and her eyes fell to the floor, confusion and excitement warring within her. What was wrong with her? How could she long to be chained to that wall, at Gareth's mercy?

"Because you're wiser than you know, Rose. To willfully submit is a sign of great inner strength."

"Remove yourself from my thoughts," she ordered, anger flaring.

"I will not. I'll invade your thoughts anytime I choose and you'll learn to enjoy it. To crave the touch of my mind." This forceful side of Gareth was one she hadn't seen before, at least not completely. Whether she enjoyed his words or not, her traitorous body still clenched in response to his tone.

"Tread carefully, Gareth, or I *will* leave you there another night. Do not doubt me."

"And do not doubt my ability to exact retribution for holding me captive against my will."

Rose's mouth dropped open and a shocked gasp escaped her lips. She watched, frozen in place, as Gareth tore his manacled wrists from the wall with less effort than it took to pluck a flower from a garden. He'd been able to free himself all along. Her mind scarcely had time to understand the implications of that fact when he bent and released the fetters on his ankles. He crossed the room before she could even think to turn and run.

"Let go of me," she demanded as his hands captured her wrists, forcing them together. "I'll call for help. My footmen are—"

"They will not come, because you won't call for help."

"Gareth, I swear—"

"In fact, you won't speak unless I give you express permission." He transferred her wrists to one hand, pulling her across the room as he went for the key to the manacles.

"Take your hands off of me, immediately." Rose struggled, tugging at her wrists without effect. His grip was as powerful as iron. "I demand—"

"Silence. You may fight me if you wish, but you'll do so in silence or you'll be punished." He unlocked the first manacle and it fell to the floor with a thud. He released her to open the manacle on his other wrist, but for some reason she didn't run.

She simply stood there, pondering his words, a dark wave of emotion rolling through her mind. It was a mixture of so many feelings she couldn't place each one individually, only knew that as the wave broke upon her she was suddenly set free. She had been unleashed, and like any animal kept in captivity, she lunged for freedom.

As Gareth reached for her, Rose launched herself

at him. She pummeled his chest, hitting him with all the power she could muster. Her breath came fast and small sounds accompanied her efforts, but she did not speak, honoring the command he had given. He didn't speak either, allowing her to strike him for a few moments before he captured her wrists and hauled her toward the bed in the corner of the room.

She fought him with everything in her, kicking and thrashing, lifting herself off the floor in her fury. He didn't make a sound when her feet connected with his shins and they both came away with bruises. He threw her on the bed and when she scrambled off he pulled her back again and again. Finally he tossed her near the headboard and landed heavily upon her, pinning her beneath him.

Rose struggled even more fiercely, scratching at him, trying to bring her knee between his legs. But he was too powerful, too quick. He easily avoided her blow, and spread her legs wide though she fought him with every muscle in her body. Blood ran down his back and his cheek as her nails found his face before he trapped her wrists and pinned them to the pillows above her.

Bucking and thrashing, every muscle in her body tensed with the effort, she fought to free herself, but he was too heavy, too strong, and finally something inside her broke. Rose screamed at him, screamed and screamed until her throat was raw and the screams gave way to tears. After she'd sworn she was done with them, that she would never cry again, that she would never give people who had hurt her, betrayed her, the power to bring her this low.

But the tears were different this time. They

were . . . purging somehow. As she wept, Gareth released her wrists and cupped her face with tender hands. He whispered soft things she couldn't understand as he pulled her into the circle of his arms. The struggle between them had been a struggle against herself. She realized that as she wept and wept, the pain of many years slowly leaving her body as the tears flowed down her face.

She was crying so hard, in fact, that she barely heard the pounding at the door. "Miss Rose? My lady? Are you all right?"

"We heard you scream," another voice added, jiggling the door handle and finding it locked. "Are you—"

"I am fine, I . . . Please, leave me," she said, hoping her tears weren't too obvious in her voice.

"But we don't think—"

"Leave me," she shouted as she turned her tear-streaked face back to Gareth's chest.

"She's fine, boys. I swear I will take good care of her," Gareth said, causing her footmen to retreat. They trusted Lord Shenley, but they feared him as well.

After that, Gareth simply held her. Rose lost track of time, only knew that when she finally lay still it felt like a hundred years had passed. She was limp, exhausted, her head filled with cotton and thorns. But she felt better than she had in decades, connected to her soul in a way she had never known she could be.

"Thank you," she whispered into Gareth's chest, her voice sounding odd and yet strangely familiar. She sounded . . . younger, like the girl she had been so very long ago.

"I told you not to speak unless you wanted a punishment." His tone was as gentle as the arms that slowly turned her onto her back. "Are you ready for your punishment, Rose?"

For a brief moment, Rose saw what looked like the sheen of unshed tears in Gareth's eyes before he lowered his head and began to kiss his way across her bare skin.

"Yes," she whispered as her eyes slid closed. She remained limp, pliant, completely open and vulnerable as the hot, soft flesh of his lips pressed against her.

First her shoulder, then across to the hollow of her throat, trailing soft kisses like bread crumbs through a forest, helping her find her way home. His tongue flicked out, teased her where the pulse beat at the side of her neck. She sighed as a shiver swept over her skin. So perfect. It was so perfect to be touched this way, to be laid bare to the man whose large, warm hands trailed over her belly and down one thigh, stroking her with a reverence that communicated this moment was sacred to him as well.

His kisses moved lower, down her breasts where her nipples were hard as diamonds, hot with the need to be taken inside his mouth, to be pinched between his fingers. But that need didn't create any tension in her body, even when he moved lower, ignoring the tight buds that begged for his kiss. Rose was incapable of doing anything that would mar the freedom she had finally achieved. So she remained quiet, letting his deliberate avoidance fuel her desire, quicken her pulse, and send a rush of wet heat between her legs.

Lower, and lower still, his hands stroking her thighs, opening her wide before he moved between her legs.

She felt his breath, hot and quick, warming the curls shielding her sex, but still she did not move a single muscle, not even to arch her hips toward the mouth she ached to feel kissing her so intimately. Gareth groaned softly, and Rose felt a shudder in the hands that smoothed up her ribs, teasing the skin just beneath her breasts. But he didn't cup the aching fullness in his palms, didn't move his lips or tongue between her legs.

"Do you want me to touch you, Rose?"

"Yes, so very much," she said, the words spilling from her mouth on a sigh of pleasure.

"Then open your eyes." Rose obeyed, looking at the canopy above her and wishing it were a mirror instead. She suddenly longed to look down and see Gareth hovering between her thighs. Imagining the sight was nearly enough to bring her over the edge. "A mirror can certainly be arranged, but for now I would rather feel your eyes on mine."

"That would involve movement, I'm afraid," she sighed.

"You're quite right, please allow me." Rose smiled as he positioned pillows beneath her head and shoulders, propping her up. He smiled back, and her breath caught. She knew tears would have pricked at the back of her eyes if she'd been capable of producing them at this point. "Gareth . . . I . . . Do you—"

"Yes, I do."

"Do what?" she asked, though her heart already beat faster with the knowledge.

"Love you." He bent and tenderly kissed her lips. "But I still expect complete obedience until we leave this bed."

"But not after?" she asked, teasing. A part of her was terrified by Gareth's love, but a part of her felt more lighthearted than she had in a hundred years.

"I'm no fool, Rose." Gareth kissed her again, his sweet kisses enough to make her ache with longing. "As independent as you are, it may take years to mold you into a proper wife."

Rose felt her eyes go wide with shock. "I—"

"Don't argue. In fact, don't speak." His kisses grew more demanding as one hand finally moved to her breast and pinched her nipple between his fingers. "I don't want to hear another sound from these pretty lips unless you're screaming my name."

And why would I be screaming your name? Rose reached out with her mind, testing their ability to communicate, trying to ignore the rush of thoughts inspired by the mention of marriage.

Marriage. As if she had the time to ponder such madness.

There's always time for love. Gareth's fingers swept between her thighs, gathering moisture. He brought the digits to his mouth and suckled them, tasting her passion with such obvious relish Rose nearly forgot her own name, let alone whatever it was they were discussing.

Keep your eyes on me, sweet, and discover why you will be screaming my name.

His thumbs dug into the flesh of her thighs none too gently as he spread her wide, but the bit of pain only made her throb with fiercer need. She watched as he lowered his mouth between her legs, his green eyes holding hers as he slowly, deliberately lapped the center of her sex.

Her breath rushed from her body in a silent whoosh, and it was all she could do not to close her eyes. One sweep of his tongue had nearly overwhelmed her. Fire burned beneath her skin and her pulse thudded in her ears. She'd never felt such desire. It was terrible and beautiful, and possibly more than her body could handle.

Gareth smiled, but the look in his eyes was far from humorous and his fangs had grown long and thin in his mouth. Far from being frightening, the sight aroused her in much the same way it did to watch his cock thicken. Her body let forth another rush of liquid and the plumped petals of her sex swelled even further. It was beginning to feel like a bruised place, so filled with anticipation that pleasure was becoming pain.

I would never cause you pain. Gareth traced her folds with a light teasing pressure, and this time she couldn't help but lift her hips.

"Lie still," he ordered, withdrawing until she forced her body to relax. "Good girl. Remember to keep your eyes open."

She was about to tell him that she wasn't a girl, but a woman dying for him to end this erotic torture, when he set to work in earnest. Soon she forgot the meaning of language, let alone how to use it as she watched him flick his tongue across her swollen clit again and again. He attended to the sensitive nub until her head swam dizzily, then moved back to her entrance, dipping his tongue in and out.

Rose moaned, her breath coming fast, half out of her mind from the discipline required to keep her body still and her eyes on her sweet tormentor. Just when she was certain she couldn't bear it a second longer, he guided her legs up and over his broad shoulders, cupped her buttocks in his strong hands and pulled her tightly to his mouth. He sucked her bud into that wet cavern even as his tongue thrust deep into her core with a relentless rhythm that urged her higher and higher.

"Gareth!" Rose screamed his name just as he'd said she would, as waves of pleasure more intense than anything she had felt in her long life washed over her again and again. The release seemed to emanate from everywhere all at once—her lips, her tightened nipples, her fingertips, her sex. She felt the bliss down to the tips of her toes, and was certain she could know no greater fulfillment when she felt the sharp press of Gareth's teeth against her thigh.

"Yes, Goddess, yes!" Rose pushed her hands down to tangle in his hair, no longer able to control herself.

She pulled him closer, pulsing her hips in time to the rhythm of his sucking. She could feel her blood spilling warm and hot into his mouth. She could feel the pleasure it gave him, how he found his own bliss no matter that his cock still throbbed, stiff and aching between his legs.

Rose heard his thoughts, felt his emotions, became tangled with Gareth in a way she'd never believed possible, as if their very souls had woven together. And for the moment, it wasn't frightening, but perfect. She'd come home, finally returned to herself. It was only right he should share that home, share her life, her heart, everything she could give him unto death.

"My love," he whispered as he withdrew from her

flesh and rose above her, finally pushing his cock into where her body still reverberated with waves of pleasure.

"Yes. Oh, yes." Rose pulled him closer, wrapped her arms and legs around him, and arched her hips. His thickness stretched her inner walls and brought her to the edge again, simply from that one deep thrust, and she knew this wouldn't last as long as they would wish.

He kissed her as he began to work his way in and out of her with a force that made her gasp into his mouth. Gareth thrust his tongue through her parted lips and Rose tasted the flavor of her blood, bright and metallic, but it was far from repulsive. Instead it made her wilder, nearly frantic. She opened herself completely to the invasion of his mouth, moaning as their tongues twined together with reckless desperation.

Yes, my love. I knew it would be this way between us. Gareth's thoughts were accompanied by even more forceful thrusts of his cock.

Rose bucked into him, relishing the sweet pain each time they connected, the tension in her belly coiling tighter and tighter until she cried out, clamping down around him. He joined her then, his back arching as his cock pulsed deep within her.

It was only much later, after they had come together again and Rose was falling asleep for the second time, that she realized Gareth had never answered her questions. Though their mental connection had revealed he couldn't be the man who had hurt Marta, he'd avoided giving her the real reason he'd baited Ambrose . . . the rat.

He was fooling himself, however, if he thought she would be so easily deterred. She would have her answers eventually—once she recovered from the satisfaction that had apparently rendered her mute. As her eyes drifted closed, she vowed to question him again . . . first thing in the morning.

CHAPTER SIXTEEN

March 4, 1750
London, England

When Rose awoke the clock near the fireplace was chiming noon and the fire had died. Gareth sat in the chair in front of the hearth, sipping tea and watching her sleep.

"You awakened early," she noted, stretching, delighting in all the places where she felt sore. She had never greeted the morning with a man and, though it was technically no longer morning, she relished seeing Gareth lounging in his dressing gown. He looked at home in a way that pleased her.

"I don't suppose Ambrose ever told you what became of his mother."

"No, he didn't." She sat up and rubbed her eyes. Though not much sleep had been accomplished, she felt well rested. Still, she would have preferred a bit of tea before they began this particular discussion.

"I have a cup poured. It's still warm," Gareth said, reading her thoughts. Surprisingly, it no longer bothered her. She slid from bed and crossed the room to pluck the saucer from his hands.

"Thank you," she murmured, watching him over the rim of her cup as she sipped, oddly pleased to discover he'd added just the right amount of cream and sugar.

"I took note of your likes and dislikes and have done my best to please." He smiled, an expression filled with masculine satisfaction that made Rose smile as well.

"You have. I won't quarrel with you there, my lord." He looked even more handsome with a hint of dark stubble on his cheeks and his hair loose and wild. She scanned his face, drinking in his beauty as she drank her tea, finding it impossible to keep her eyes off his lips as she remembered all the wonderfully wicked things he had done to her the night before.

"Please, my lady. You must cease looking at me in that fashion, or I'll take you back to bed and never set you free."

Rose smiled into her cup, wondering which aspect of that threat was supposed to spur her into action.

"The part where I refuse to answer your questions until you're my lawfully wedded wife."

"Until? I haven't agreed to be your bride, Lord Shenley." She set her cup down on the small table before him, then turned to fetch her dressing gown from the floor. She took her time doing so, moving slowly as she bent to retrieve the garment, aware of Gareth watching her as she did so.

"You are wicked." He laughed, but it was a tight sound, not the seductive rumble she was becoming accustomed to. Something was wrong, though he was shielding furiously to keep her from discovering what it was for herself. She pushed a little harder, the equivalent of a loud knock on the door of his mind. "There's no need to pry, Rose. I'm prepared to tell all, as soon as you cover yourself and join me by the fire."

"What fire? Should I call one of the—"

Gareth snapped his fingers and flame erupted in the hearth. Rose didn't bother to hide her surprise, knowing he would read it in her thoughts.

"Exactly when did vampires become skilled at calling flame?" she asked while shrugging on her dressing gown and fastening the tie at the waist.

"I told you that I knew something of magic."

"Explain yourself."

"Answer my question first. Did Ambrose ever tell you what became of his mother?" He smiled softly as she took the seat across from him. For the first time in their acquaintance Gareth looked tired.

The anxiety from the night before returned, but her fear didn't return with it. Whatever it was he had to say, Rose knew he wouldn't reveal another betrayal. She'd seen the heart of the man last night, and knew without a doubt he loved her, though she wasn't sure what she'd done to deserve his devotion. Nevertheless, she had faith he would do nothing to damage her trust.

"Of course he didn't." Gareth answered his own question, shaking his head. "He had no idea where she went once she was exiled. Quite a thoughtless son, but then Mother was a bit . . . unbalanced. Hardly the sort to inspire loyalty, even in her offspring."

Rose took a deep swallow of her tea, wondering if this was his rather perverse idea of a joke. She knew he was part Fey, but surely he couldn't mean—

"I *can* mean, I'm afraid," he said with a weary sigh. "My Fey blood comes from Agatha Minuit. Ambrose is my half brother, though he had no knowledge of that until he'd accepted my offer of assistance."

Gareth searched her face, the vulnerable look in his eyes making Rose rush to reassure him.

"Darling, it's all right. None of us can choose our parents." She touched his hand, surprised at how right it felt to call him her darling. She suspected she *was* in love with the man, but wasn't ready to confess to it just yet, not to Gareth and most assuredly not to herself.

"You understand what I've said? And you aren't cross?"

"Well, it's clear why Ambrose loathes you." Ambrose loathed vampires, and being forced to share parentage with one was no doubt enraging to him, but she couldn't comprehend why Gareth was so afraid of her anger. "Other than the fact that your mother destroyed my family and cursed my existence, is there another reason I should find this news disturbing?"

"You wouldn't hate me for that alone?" he asked, his tone cautious, though he captured her hands in his.

"Of course not. We can't be held responsible for the sins of our parents, especially those committed years before our birth."

"It was only a year before my birth," he said, a bit of tension draining from his features, though it was clear something still troubled him. "After Mother signed the betrothal agreement with your parents she got a bit too cocksure."

He dropped Rose's hand and rose to pace before the fire, running his fingers through his unruly hair. "I believe she tried to murder someone—some ancient council member's daughter perhaps. In any event, the Fey de la Nuit banished her and of course the Seelie wouldn't have her after what she'd done to your mother. She was forced to make nice with other supernaturals in order to survive. Enter my father. He was a recently turned vampire, and a member of the nobility. He had a thing for wicked women. The first one made him a blood man and then abandoned him, and then for some bizarre reason he agreed to marry my penniless mother—"

"This prattling isn't like you, Gareth," Rose said, a sinking feeling in her stomach. "What are you hiding?"

"Nothing at all." He smiled, but seconds later the smile faded. "Well, perhaps that's not the complete truth. I'm not *hiding* anything, though this would be less awkward if you'd come round to the truth on your own. I'm sure you'll see what I'm about if you think about faerie law for a—"

"Speak plainly, please. I haven't the time—"

"I'm Ambrose's brother. I'm also his only—"

"Gareth, I swear to you if you don't . . . Oh, no . . . you . . . No." She dismissed the idea as soon as it arose. Gareth couldn't be thinking . . .

But faerie law *did* allow for a younger sibling to make good on a marriage contract if the older was judged unfit. Rose hadn't married Ambrose, and their argument on the road to Horn made it clear he was an unfit candidate, at least in her mind. That meant the contract would fall to Ambrose's next single male relative of marriageable age.

"Ambrose has two brothers," Rose said, her thoughts racing, uncertain what to make of this latest development. "His father took another wife after—"

"But it wasn't his father who pledged the betrothal." Gareth had ceased pacing, and now watched Rose as if she were set to explode at any moment. "It was his mother, so a male child of hers would be first in line. Then, afterward, any male nephews on Mother's side whose parents had not pledged them."

"You're next in line to be my betrothed?" She needed to repeat the words for her mind to comprehend them.

"Yes," Gareth said, with a slight smile.

"And you've been waiting for me to refuse Ambrose so that it would be your turn to honor the contract?"

"Precisely."

"To honor the contract and marry me," she repeated, still battling the sense that this was yet another one of his jokes.

"My mother made no other arrangements for me before her death, and my father . . ." He shrugged and rolled his eyes, making Rose wonder what sort of man his father was if even Gareth found him ridiculous. "Well, let's simply say Father refuses to acknowledge that Fey law is binding to a half vampire, but I think he also—"

"Gareth, stop teasing me."

"Rose, I'm not teasing, I—"

"I'm serious."

"As am I. Seriously discussing the reasons you will be my bride."

"This is madness." She leapt to her feet, searching the floor for her slippers. For some reason she felt that putting on her shoes would bring order back to the world. Unfortunately they were nowhere in sight. Where had she put them?

"Why are you crawling beneath the settee?" Gareth joined her on her hands and knees, though he searched her face, not the shadows beneath the furniture. He reached out to her, but she pulled away, sitting back on her heels in frustration, the quest for her slippers forgotten.

"You could've already married any number of women, human or vampire," she said, trying to force him to see reason. "There was no need for you to honor a faerie prophecy. It's ridiculous, and I—"

"It's ridiculous to wait for a woman I love?" he asked haughtily, simultaneously making her want to laugh and slap him silly. "It's ridiculous to put off marriage to some simpering fool with hardly two decades to her credit so that I might wed a strong, courageous, intelligent, beautiful—"

"We've only known each other two months, Gareth. I can't believe—"

"I knew *of* you, Rose. I'd heard the stories. I knew Ambrose was dying to have you, and that he had forfeited a place on the council because of his singleminded determination to stay with you. Did you never wonder why a five-hundred-year-old Fey de la Nuit with his power was dealing with an executioner? He could have been—"

"So I'm to understand you desired my hand simply because Ambrose wanted me?" she asked, while realizing she'd never even questioned why Ambrose had such a lowly job. He'd simply always been there beside her, to the point that she'd taken him for granted until he was gone, leaving her to fend for herself. "That was why you taunted him, why you made such a great show of calling me your 'dear' and 'darling.' You were rubbing his nose in what you assumed would soon be yours."

"Absolutely not," he protested with a guilty expression. "You misunderstand."

"I think not, my lord." Rose moved to stand beside him before the fire. "You acted out of jealousy and spite, wanting to punish the brother who looked down upon you as a worthless half-breed."

"Not at all—"

"He hadn't even bothered to learn your name, had he? He didn't know that your mother became Lady Shenley after she was cast out."

"He didn't even know she was dead," Gareth said, the pain in his tone abundantly clear. He'd cared for his mother, no matter that she was a conniving monster. "Being kept from the faerie realms finally killed her."

"That angered you. It made you want to punish him, by taking what was his."

"Perhaps there was an element of satisfaction involved initially, but that wasn't my motive. I wanted you, Rose, and I was never happier than the night I saw you begin to care for me. Perhaps I enjoyed the effects our mutual desire had upon my brother, yes. But he deserved more than—"

"So you decided to make him suffer. To punish him."

"Would you rather I hadn't? You'd be forced to marry him if there were no other male relatives to honor the contract. You are Fey, no matter how small a fraction, and they demand the obedience of their own."

"So you were merely being obedient?" Rose asked, refusing to consider the greater implication of his words. He was right, she could still be forced to wed Ambrose if she survived the week. Her anger with her betrothed was not sufficient reason to prove him unfit. Not even the fact that he had allowed Benoit to rape her would be reason enough for Fey who believed any betrayal acceptable in the name of honoring a prophecy.

Marriage to Ambrose was a fate better than death or imprisonment—the penalty for breaking a faerie contract signed in blood. But wouldn't marriage to Gareth be preferable, if she had to marry one or the other? Or was she completely mad to even be considering such a thing?

"I am half Fey. I'm as bound by the contract as Ambrose himself."

"So you don't truly desire me?" She was feeling confused and contrary and strangely inclined to push Gareth to his limits. "You were simply being a good faerie?"

"You're twisting my words to suit your own purposes."

"Just as you twisted my desires to suit yours."

"They didn't require much twisting, my lady." He moved closer, firelight dancing in his eyes. The man could stir lust in her simply by lowering his voice to that rough whisper. "You were mad to bed me from the moment our eyes met. I could hear your heart racing, see the flush in your cheeks."

He captured one of her loose curls in his fingers with obvious fondness, but the accompanying smug look didn't give her the slightest urge to smile.

"Well I'm *not* mad to bed you now!" Rose turned, determined to return to her study and lock the scoundrel out. But suddenly he was in front of her, blocking her path.

"Rose, stop it," he said, his tone soft as he tried to draw her into his arms. She pulled away, but didn't lash out at him as she had the night before, which surprised her.

She was furious. Wasn't she?

Damned if she knew. Who had time to explore her feelings when her entire world had been turned upside down?

"Listen, just for a moment. Then I'll let you go free." Gareth held his hands in the air.

As if she had ever been free. Her entire life had been mapped out by concerned parents, scheming faeries, and Fey prophecy.

"It's true, I haven't known you long," he said, his eyes pleading with her to listen with an open heart. "But I've known your story even longer than you yourself have."

"You and the rest of the Fey world. I don't see how my ignorance is—"

"I thought you were listening. That sounded—"

"Very well." Rose crossed her arms and set her

face in her least encouraging expression. He could talk, but that was all. She would make no promises, especially not of the matrimonial sort.

"I've long known your story, and yet I longed to claim you. My mother made certain I was aware that Fey prophecy states you will kill your betrothed, and yet still I desired you."

"You are brave, my lord," she said in her most fawning tone. "You should receive a medal for your—"

"Silence, Rose. Your cutting little tongue doesn't require exercise at the moment," he snapped, though she saw a brief flash of humor in his eyes. "I meant what I said about your courage and your spirit. I value both highly, as well as your advanced age."

Rose nearly laughed. It was such an odd thing to hear from a man, but she managed to hold her peace. Gareth was attempting to be serious for once, and she *had* promised to listen.

"I rarely meet anyone clever under the age of two hundred, but somehow you've managed to acquire quite a quick wit without losing your sense of humor." He smiled at the portrait over the mantle, one Rose had commissioned when she'd lived in Britain decades before. "And yes, your beauty is also a factor. I won't pretend to be above such considerations."

"My beauty? I hardly think that sufficient reason to—"

"You were blessed from your cradle to be one of the most beautiful women in the world. Though your sour expression at the moment leaves much to be desired, you can't refute what was bestowed upon you."

"Faeries always give such gifts," she said, relaxing in spite of herself. Wise or not, a part of her craved

Gareth's admiration. "They've given a hundred babes the gift of epic beauty. It's hardly reason to—"

"To me you're the most beautiful. If you weren't before, you most certainly are now."

"Really? What's changed?"

"I fell in love with you," he said with such heartfelt simplicity that Rose had no idea how to respond. "I fell in love with you our first night in the East End, watching you kill half a dozen ogres and then turn to lecture me with a prim little look on your face."

"I'm hardly prim," she said, too confused to say anything else.

"Mr. Barrows, I must insist you carry a sword, the sight of your hands stained with ogre essence is simply repulsive," he said, mimicking her voice and mannerisms with such perfection she nearly smiled.

"In those years after you awoke," he continued in his low rumble, "I heard of your adventures and I listened to the Fey de la Nuit mock you behind your back. I never understood the perverse pleasure they took in claiming you for their slave, they—"

"I was hardly a slave. I chose that life, and for many years I relished it."

"Still, every time they sneered, I took satisfaction in knowing they would be proven wrong. You will not fall victim to—"

"How will they be proven wrong? They do their best to force their prophecies into fulfillment, no matter how often they swear to let events occur naturally." The hopelessness of her situation wasn't something she wanted to dwell upon, but it couldn't be denied. She'd be lucky to live through the week, let alone worry about who she'd be forced to marry.

"We'll prove them wrong, Rose," he said, taking her hands and leaning down to catch her eyes, his passion obvious in every word. "We'll prove their prophecies false, prove their laws flawed, prove the Fey aren't—"

"No, Gareth."

"Marry me, Rose. Marry me today."

"You can't go out in the sunlight, how would we find someone to marry us—" She broke off with a slightly strangled laugh, and attempted to tug her hands from Gareth's larger ones. "No, it's impossible. Even if I wanted to marry you, even if you wanted to marry me, I—"

"Of course I want to marry you. In addition to my nobler reasons, you are devilishly attractive. I could stay abed with you for years and never tire of it." He wrapped long arms around her waist, pinning her so tightly to him she was forced to tilt her head back to catch his eyes. "And you're dying to be Lady Shenley, I can see it in your eyes. A woman in love if ever there was one, a woman ready to settle down to hearth and home, to tend a large brood of quarter vampire and whatever percentage Fey children—"

"Gareth, really!" Rose laughed; she couldn't help herself. He always made her laugh, even when it seemed nothing else would.

It was a rare gift he possessed, and it was nearly enough to change her mind.

"Truly, I'm flattered, but I can't draw you into this any further than you are already," she said, her smile vanishing as quickly as it had appeared. "My cause is hopeless. I'm expected to die in less than a week.

There are hundreds out there working their hardest to make sure that happens."

"All the more reason you need a husband by your side, and a thwarted prophecy to your credit." His hands drifted to the tie of her dressing gown and tugged. Before she understood what he was about, he'd parted the fabric and was smoothing his hands down to cup her bare bottom. "Marry me, Rose. I love you. That you can trust. And I will do my best to make certain your next hundred years are infinitely more enjoyable than the last hundred."

"That will be easy to accomplish, my lord," she said.

"When you're my bride, you'll no longer be bound by contracts signed when you were alone." He smiled and she could see how much it would please him to be able to steal her away from the black faeries.

She could have taken offense, but there was little point. The idea pleased her as well. She would be free, no longer an executioner, no longer forced to honor the contract signed in blood one hundred years past. She would, however, be forced to forfeit a measure of independence, as well as her wealth and property, to her husband.

"You can keep your money, Rose. All I want is you." He pressed a soft kiss to her lips that managed to take her breath away. "And I believe, in time, you'll no longer miss your independence. Being dependant upon another for pleasure, companionship, and amusement seems quite agreeable."

Her breath caught at the sincerity in his eyes . . . or perhaps it was the way he kneaded the flesh under his hands, quickly building her desire.

"No, my wanton girl. You shan't have my body again until you are my bride."

"I suspect I could have your body whenever I wish." She ran her hand over the hard length beneath his dressing gown, shivering as she realized she could feel an echo of Gareth's pleasure within her.

They'd shared blood, shared their bodies. She was more connected to him than anyone else in her long life. He knew her and had an instinctive knack for understanding what she needed and providing it with a selflessness that was humbling.

"Not selfless at all. I want you for a variety of self-ish reasons, which I believe I've outlined quite—"

"Very well, let us make the arrangements," she said before she could rethink the decision. She had taken her share of chances with her physical well-being, but never with her heart. It was time to see if she could be brave in a way that didn't require a sword.

"You'll marry me? Today?" he asked, obviously surprised convincing her hadn't required additional hours of persuasion.

"I've killed ogres for a hundred years, I suppose I could rid myself of one vampire husband if the marriage doesn't turn out as I hope," she teased, pulling open his robe and urging it off his shoulders, baring the delicious body of her future husband.

"A death threat and an acceptance in nearly the same breath. I truly am a lucky man." He smiled, and it was wicked and wonderful. Despite the number of things to be done, arrangements to be made, and prophecies to be thwarted, Rose didn't resist as he lifted her in his arms.

Time was of the essence. Once, not long ago, she

would have used that as reason to deny herself pleasure, food, sleep. But now she could see the value in claiming a bit of bliss when it was offered. If this was truly her last week on earth, she would prefer to spend at least part of it in bed, with Gareth.

CHAPTER SEVENTEEN

March 4, 1750
Knebfield House
Shenley, England

She was a married woman.

Rose was certain her thoughts would have revolved around that shocking yet oddly thrilling development if she hadn't soon after received disturbing news from London. Not twenty minutes after the departure of the magistrate, two of her three footmen appeared at the door. The pair were in sorry shape, covered in soot and grime and bearing several wounds.

The news they brought was as disturbing as their appearance.

Rose's Berkeley Square home had been attacked and set aflame. Erin, the cook, was slain as she stood preparing the evening meal, her screams alerting the rest of the house to the invasion. Phillip and Samuel had managed to fend off several ogres and escape outside to free the horses before the fire spread to the carriage house, while Lucas raced upstairs to fetch the unconscious Marta from her bed.

He'd never returned. The brothers had fled before the flames were put out by the human fire brigade, so they couldn't say for certain, but they suspected both Marta and their brother were dead.

"What of the trolls? Were they not there to aid you in defending—"

"The Fearsome were gone, my lady. They took their leave before you adjourned to the country," Phillip said, his usually carefree face lined with worry and his blond hair singed badly on one side. "You left in such haste, I forgot to tell you the pallets in the carriage house where the trolls had been sleeping were gone."

"I believe the Fearsome received orders from the enchanted waters," Samuel added, his dark eyes haunted. "Their leader was near the pool late last eve, before your departure. Perhaps the faerie council forced them to abandon your cause."

"Or perhaps Ambrose seeks to make amends with the Fey de la Nuit by depriving you of armed protection." Gareth's tone was as fierce as Rose had ever heard it. She didn't try to defend Ambrose. She doubted it would do any good, especially considering there was a chance Gareth was correct.

If Ambrose had recalled the Fearsome, Rose couldn't blame him for it. He'd done what he could. She'd simply have to make due with the allies she could presently claim and pray it never came to a battle between herself and the tribe. They certainly had her outnumbered at this point, and no amount of superior fighting skill could compensate for such unfavorable odds.

"Master Minuit may have recalled them, but he

wouldn't alert the tribe of the trolls' departure. He wouldn't endanger Lady Rose." Samuel spoke the thought Rose hadn't allowed to cross her mind.

"I don't believe he would alert the tribe either, Samuel," she said, cutting off Gareth before he could snarl at the footman. "But the ogres may have had someone watching my home, a spy who observed the departure of the trolls. A week ago I was certain they knew not where I lived, but the situation may have changed."

"Its likely someone betrayed you while you were abroad. The shielding spell on your home must have been deactivated. If Ambrose were not imprisoned, I would hold him responsible for that as well," Gareth said, draining his brandy in one smooth swallow.

Ambrose had only ever done harm with inaction, not active betrayal, but Rose refused to argue the point. It was ridiculous to be distracted by the past when the present was so challenging.

"How many of the tribe were present?" she asked, wondering if it had been another massive gathering, or a smaller band such as the one she and Gareth had faced in Lord Drummand's garden.

"Twenty, perhaps thirty," Samuel said. "But they were different than most. They fought well, and didn't stop to . . . to eat Erin."

"I don't believe they're capable of eating one with Brownie heritage." Rose paused, not wanting to speak aloud what they were all thinking. Ogres *could* eat a half elf/half Fey if they could catch him, as well as a former river sprite. Lucas and Marta might never be found.

"Damn the Fey straight into the pits," Gareth said,

pacing angrily around the room. Samuel and Phillip shrank into their chairs, intimidated by his rage.

They were barely sixty years old and had spent their first forty years in the forests. They'd been raised by dryads, a gentle race of woodland nymphs, and were far more innocent of violence than either Gareth or herself.

"Calm yourself, my lord. We are all some part Fey. There's no need to wish our own damnation," Rose said, forcing herself to remain composed, unlike her husband.

Dear God, she had a *husband*. She wondered if there would be time to get used to the knowledge before she met her end.

"I won't. A faerie was watching the waters. The Fey knew you'd returned to London and one of them betrayed you to the tribe. The attack came barely two days after you returned from your travels," Gareth said, drumming his fingers as he thought. "And I wager the ogres would have struck sooner if the trolls weren't nocturnal creatures."

Rose made to interrupt him, but he continued without stopping to draw breath.

"And if I hadn't hidden beneath the carriage to enable our early departure, we would have still been in your home—*undefended* though we didn't yet know it—when the creatures attacked. They would have killed us as we lay abed."

"I am aware of that, Gareth. As I told you, I believe a faerie is responsible for Pithwater's return, and for secreting him away in Faversham where they knew I would seek him out."

"Precisely, so—"

"But it wasn't a faerie who violated Marta's body and mind," Rose said, knowing it was past time she shared what she'd learned. "It was a vampire. I couldn't see his face, but I'm certain he took her blood and used it in some black ritual. Therefore, it would seem the ogres also have the aid of a blood man—"

"You told me nothing of this," Gareth said, pinning her with an accusing look. "I suppose you suspected me, didn't you?"

"Perhaps at first."

"Of all the ridiculous—" He broke off with a foul curse. "I have aided your cause from the very beginning. That you could suspect me—"

"You were keeping secrets, my lord."

"Of course I was keeping secrets," he shouted. "We're all keeping secrets, that doesn't mean I'm guilty of—"

"I know you're not!" Rose shouted to be heard over her raging husband, but lowered her voice when Samuel flinched. "Please, further argument is pointless."

Her footmen were dear, but if they could be frightened by the raised voice of a woman half their size, they could hardly be counted upon as useful allies, no matter that they were still loyal to her cause.

"*I* am loyal to your cause," Gareth said, glowering at her from across the room. "Do I no longer count as one of your friends?"

"Gareth, now is not the time—"

"You're right, now is not the time to humor your husband. Now is the time to tell your husband everything you've kept from him so that he might endeavor to save your life." His eyes were hard and angry, but for some reason they still sent a shock of awareness through her body. Her life was in more peril than ever, but she couldn't help but respond to the word "husband" coming from Gareth's lips.

He *was* her husband, and it was a covenant that spared them concerns for secrecy. Even the Fey couldn't fault a husband and wife for sharing secrets and aiding one another, even in ways that might be punishable by imprisonment for others. Just as a mate couldn't be called to serve witness against his spouse in the high council's court, neither could he be tried for placing the aid of his partner ahead of the concerns of his supernatural order.

"Gareth, are you acquainted with other vampire-faerie half-breeds?" Rose asked, the hint of a plan beginning to form. "Or half-breeds of other sorts with power?"

"At least a dozen or more, and I believe some of them would come to our aid," he said, reading her thoughts before she had the chance to speak them.

"Even against high council orders?"

"Phillip and Samuel are here. I am here," he said, turning to pace the sitting room. "Those of us who are less than purebred have little love for the Fey de la Nuit or the Seelie. Most fear them, and fear can be turned to rage if given the proper fuel."

"And what fuel would that be?" Rose asked, wondering if mixed heritage would be enough to bring half-breeds to the aid of a mostly mortal woman and her Fey/vampire mate.

"Dear Rose, you are a legend." Gareth turned to

smile at her, a warm look she could feel brushing softly against her skin. "You aren't considered mostly mortal by anyone but yourself."

"I am an object of scorn and derision, my lord, I scarcely—"

"To the Fey, perhaps, but to the tribe you are the *scourge*." He crossed the room and grasped her by the shoulders, giving her a shake. "Thousands of ogres, at least one traitor Fey, and a vampire have joined forces to ritualistically murder you. That's hardly the sort of effort one makes for an object of scorn."

"Thank you," she said dryly, earning a smile.

"And it works in our favor," he said, pressing a soft kiss to her forehead before turning to prowl the room once more. "There's not a vampire or half vampire alive who would suffer an ogre to live, let alone murder you simply because the wing-flappers think it would work to their advantage."

"Neither would vampires wish the human race to be destroyed," she reminded him. "The prophecy clearly states that—"

"Damn the prophecy. It says the *maid's* blood must burn. Who's to say you're the maid in question? Going by some meanings of the word, the definition would exclude you entirely. For you are certainly no serving girl or virginal miss. I will attest to the latter myself."

Gareth, please. She chastised him mentally, not wishing to embarrass the footmen further.

"When we discuss in detail all you have kept from me—"

"I have not *kept* anything from you," she insisted, wondering if she would spend the rest of her life bickering with this man, and even more disturbingly, wondering why the idea excited her.

"Don't interrupt me, dearest. Respect the authority of your lord and master." The twinkle in his eye allowed Rose to keep her protest to a roll of her eyes. "When we have our chat, I'll share my theories on how we might twist the prophecy to our benefit, and perhaps gain ourselves even more allies."

"Truly? You think such a thing possible?"

"It is not a given, of course." He poured himself another brandy. "But if we gain only the aid of the half-breed Fey, we will be well matched against the tribe. For all their numbers they're poor fighters and even more poorly organized. Only a few seem to know the real specifics of their mission."

"I noticed the same," Rose said. "I'd wager they're the ones responsible for the magical aspect. The average ogre wouldn't be able to resist the urge to consume a human head long enough to bury it in the ground and perform black magic."

"I agree, those few dozen magically involved and the faerie who aids them are the true enemy," Gareth said.

"And the vampire, as well," Rose added. "I am certain the blood man who abused Marta used her blood to work dark magic."

"Though it remains to be seen if that is related to whatever black rite the ogres are about. It might very well be a different thing altogether."

Rose sighed, and rubbed at her weary eyes. "True. Though a part of me prays they're all working together. One threat is enough to deal with at the moment."

"Indeed, but the threat is not as dire as it would

seem," Gareth said, remarkably cheery now that he'd had another drink. "Nearly all of the ogres can be discounted entirely. They've merely responded to the call to battle, intoxicated by the idea of destroying the scourge and eliminating the executioners for good. But they're sheep, and will lose their direction if we remove the shepherds who guide them."

"So this goes deeper than my own destruction?" Rose crossed to the cabinet and poured herself a drink. She rarely indulged, but the talk of battle made her desire something strong in her cup. "It seems I'm not the only one in possession of information I haven't shared,"

"I didn't have leave to share the findings of my investigation with you at the time, wife."

"Investigation?" she asked, not terribly surprised by the disclosure. "So may I assume your kind offer to train as an ogre-killer had more ulterior motives than originally assumed?"

"Perhaps, but I wasn't at liberty to reveal those prior to our marriage. Just as I'm not at liberty to discuss them in our present company." Gareth nodded to Samuel and Phillip, who were staring at them in confusion. "My apologies, gentlemen."

Gareth pulled one of the ropes Rose had glimpsed throughout the enormous home. It rang a bell in the servant's quarters and in the great kitchen located in the south wing of his estate. He only had a few servants, despite the size of Knebfield, but she imagined it was difficult to find trustworthy help when one could be destroyed by sunlight and slept the majority of the time the servants were awake.

"Being a creature many consider damned isn't

helpful either. Even among the servants of the super-natural community, that can cause its share of prob-lems." Gareth crossed the room with preternatural speed and plucked Rose's glass from her hands just as she began to lift it to her lips.

"Might I have my drink, my lord?"

"I don't think that's a wise idea, dearest," Gareth said, drinking the brandy she'd poured for herself be-fore placing the glass on a shelf too high for her to reach. As if that would stop her from having her drink if she wished. The bottle itself was still there and she was not so ladylike she would refrain from taking a swig—

"Please, madam. Control yourself. I'm merely looking after your best interests. I doubt the wisdom of clouding your wits at this time."

"And what of your wits?" she asked, wondering what other actions her new husband would feel justi-fied in taking for "her best interests" now that they were wed.

"I am largely immune to the effects of spirits un-less I've recently fed, which you know I've not." He shot her a hard look, and Rose fought the childish urge to stick her tongue out at the man.

They'd begun an argument on the road to Kneb-field as to how his eating habits would need to change to keep his new wife happy. He hadn't been pleased with Rose's conditions, and she hadn't been pleased with his insistence that he didn't "dine upon rooster." After having felt the effects of his vampire's kiss for herself, Rose found she didn't relish the idea of an-other woman finding such pleasure in Gareth's arms, no matter that she was a meal and not a lover. The line between the two was far too clouded for blood men, and she preferred to be Gareth's only female donor.

Unfortunately, as a three-quarter mortal she was incapable of providing for his needs on her own. It was probably only the first of many situations they'd wish they had considered further before running off to wed.

"Thinking rationally is overrated when it comes to love," Gareth said, continuing before she could think how to respond to his words, or to the slightly giddy feeling it still gave her to hear him profess his affection. "My secretary will be here in a moment. He'll arrange for messengers to contact the ladies and gentlemen who I believe will be willing to aid our cause."

"You'll have him send a list of names to the study afterward?" Rose asked. "I'd like to view the potential allies so that I might get a feeling for their unique talents."

"To plan our attack?" Gareth asked.

"And to hopefully provide for their protection. We will need to proceed with caution. I don't want anyone harmed. We've already lost members of the Fearsome and Lucas, Erin, and Marta," Rose thought aloud. "That's already far too many casualties to this ogre madness. I don't wish to add any more names to that list."

Every supernatural had unique strengths and weaknesses. The Fey had fewer weaknesses than most, hence their ability to control others and bend them to their will. But even they were not invulnerable. There was a chance a group of half-breeds could fend off any Fey who came to take them into custody if they were prepared. That was assuming, of course, that the Seelie or the Fey de la Nuit sent officials in the first place.

Rose couldn't help but hope that the Fey would be caught off guard by the knowledge that she and Gareth had married and neither of her betrothed had been slain by her hand. One of their prophecies had not concluded as written. There was no arguing the point no matter how creative their logic. That failure might be enough to give them pause, thusly allowing Rose and Gareth's forces time to thwart the ogre plan without interruption. Only a few days remained until the next full moon. Discerning what spell the tribe hoped to unleash and preventing them from achieving their goal was going to be difficult without Fey interference. With it . . . the mission might very well be hopeless.

"Nothing is ever hopeless," Gareth said.

"No, it's not hopeless, my lady. We will send word to the dryads in the north. There are many of our kind there," Phillip said, strength coming into his pale face as he rejoined the conversation. "We aren't trained in battle, but I know my brothers and sisters will be willing to fight. One of our own is dead by faerie treachery. We aren't so gentle that we do not believe in vengeance."

"But Lucas is dead because he was in my employ. I wouldn't ask you to summon your brothers and sisters on my account." Rose was willing to call upon other supernaturals, but the half Elvish/half Fey were already so poorly received.

"No, he was killed because the Fey have no sense of their place in this world," Samuel said with a passion she could not refute. "They are *of* our world, not Gods above it. It's time they remembered that all life is sacred to the Great Mother."

He was right. The time had come to challenge the standing order. That her hardship was a catalyst was merely coincidence. All supernaturals, great and small, were tired of pandering to the Fey. Rose didn't doubt many humans would feel the same if they knew of the liberties the Fey took in appropriating human holdings when it suited their purpose.

"How may I assist you, my lord?" Gareth's secretary had entered the room so silently Rose jumped when his voice suddenly sounded behind her. Andre was a full-blooded vampire, and quite an ancient one if her senses were correct.

Why he was in the employ of a half-breed less than half his age, she had yet to discern. But he seemed quite loyal, and had grown emotional during the witnessing of their marriage vows. He appeared to care for Gareth a great deal, an impression that was solidified by his response once they'd outlined their plan.

"You may depend upon my aid. I'll contact those among the vampire community who won't object to bending the terms of the peace treaty with the Fey for a worthy cause."

"I'm certain you will find several. The council's investigation has yielded disturbing news for the vampire community. Those aware of it are sufficiently enraged that the peace treaty may soon be a thing of the past."

"Quite right, my lord. I'll send out communiqués straight away."

"Thank you, Andre. Would you take Phillip and

Samuel upstairs, as well, and have the housekeeper attend to their comfort?"

"If the young masters will wait on the second landing, I will guide you to your quarters momentarily." Andre motioned for the two men to precede him out of the room and up the winding staircase before turning back to Gareth. "I will also tell the groundsmen to keep watch. If the tribe found the comtesse at her home in London, there is little doubt they will find her here."

"They were also able to locate Ambrose's lodgings," Rose added. "The battle we fought the night of the earthquake began when a giant of the tribe hurled a flaming object through his study window."

"Perhaps because he notified them of where you would be, and when you would be there." Gareth said. "It is terribly convenient that you just happened to be in Southwark at the exact time at which the tribe was organizing for its spell."

"I doubt that was any of Ambrose's doing, Gareth. He could have been killed by the giant if I hadn't come to his aid."

"That hardly assures his innocence."

"And he did call the trolls to join the fight," she said, tiring of Gareth's inability to see any Fey but Ambrose as a suspect. "Without them, the tribe would have achieved its goal. He saved my life, and I don't believe he's capable of—"

"You don't believe him capable of betrayal? Damnation, Rose, what will it take—"

"What sort of flaming object?" Andre interrupted, decidedly less servile now that the men had left the room, making Rose wonder at the nature of his and Gareth's relationship.

"It was a human head," she said. "The ogres are using the heads of human victims in whatever black magic they're about. That much I was able to discern before the Fey began keeping knowledge from me."

"No, Rose, they began to ensure your ignorance as soon as news of our battle made its way to Paris. When you lay near death, Ambrose received word to cease his investigation immediately."

"And to let you to die. My lord has had a price on his head since it became known an infusion of his blood helped you to live." Andre's tone wasn't reproachful, but Rose felt the unspoken accusation nonetheless. "He risked his life every time he escorted you to the opera or the theater."

"That's why you disappeared," she said, turning to Gareth, the pieces falling into place. "And why you came to stay with me."

"I came to stay to watch over you. The fact that your home was protected by complicated secrecy spells was simply a happy coincidence." Gareth shot Andre a look that communicated his displeasure. "And there was a price on my head long before I helped pull you from the edge of death. My enemies among the Fey de la Nuit were aware I'd signed on to aid Ambrose and suspected I was about some slippery business for the vampire council. They haunted my every step, causing me to abandon several of my training missions when I suspected they might be lying in wait."

"Was Ambrose aware of it?"

"I don't believe so. Just as few among the vampire community know of our investigation into the Fey, only a few of the Fey are aware that relations between our people are deteriorating rapidly. Those few would prefer to eliminate the investigators—"

"To send a warning to others who would cross them," she finished his thought, and wished again for a strong drink. "This doesn't bode well. We're both marked for death. They will come for us if we enlist the aid of—"

"They would never dare invade Knebfield. The manor was built to withstand the attack of all supernatural invaders." Andre's imperious tone communicated clearly that *he* somehow took credit for this development. "The only creature we need fear is the devil himself, or his demons. The keep is not defended against the divine. Therefore, I would ask again about the human heads."

Divine. Not the word Rose would have used to refer to demons, but she took Andre's meaning. Before she could explain, however, Gareth spoke.

"The skulls are buried along the river Thames and its tributaries. The vortexes created as a result serve as portals to funnel some sort of black power into the water, possibly from hell, though that hasn't been confirmed. Rose and I unearthed one of the heads at Vauxhall. I found and removed several more while she was abroad, but not enough to do any damage to their power," Gareth said, surprising her once again. "Especially if they continue to slay humans at such a ghastly rate. The thief-takers out of Bow Street have reports of nearly two dozen men and women gone missing from their homes. They have no suspects at the moment, but many of the victims' families believe they were kidnapped."

"You should have communicated these developments—"

"Andre, I owe you much, but I won't hesitate to keep my future information to myself if you presume to tell me what I *should* or shouldn't do—with regard to any aspect of my behavior." A moment of tense silence followed.

Rose practically itched with the need to demand his secrets, but forced herself to keep her peace until they were alone. Andre seemed to be a person Gareth respected and trusted, but the two men were engaged in a power struggle she couldn't begin to understand.

"In any event, I suspect the tribe is seeking to increase its power, to make certain there's no chance of failure at the next full moon," Gareth finally said, rubbing the tops of his eyes with fingers and thumb, as if his head ached. Rose had never heard a vampire complain of a headache, but she expected any man married to her would find his head aching sooner or later.

Gareth smiled at her thoughts, but the grin was short lived.

"No amount of power will ensure success if they don't have the blood of the scourge," Andre said, the way he so casually discussed the taking of her life sending a shiver down Rose's spine. "You would do well to keep her safe and find another from which to feed. If her blood is in your belly, you may soon find it slit open. It's a dangerous marriage you've made, one as likely to result in death as walking out to meet the dawn."

"Thank you, Andre." Gareth smiled, but Rose felt tension surge between the two men. "We'll adjourn to my study and I trust you'll send word once the messengers are on their way."

Gareth claimed Rose's hand and pulled her from the room with a roughness she knew had little to do with her. He was angry with Andre, and she couldn't say she blamed him. She began to suspect the elder vampire's emotion during their vows hadn't been joy to see his master joined in wedlock, but grief to witness the first step toward his utter ruination.

Rose turned to look back over her shoulder, meeting the cold eyes of the ancient vampire. The deference of a servant and the warm concern of a friend were banished from his features. In their place was a look of such contempt she flinched to feel it upon her skin. He smiled a moment later, as if to conceal his hatred, but the damage had already been done.

Somehow, she had made another enemy, even as she sought to find friends. She wouldn't be safe in her husband's home as long as Andre held his position. She felt that truth in her very bones.

"You will be safe. I would kill any who tried to harm you," Gareth said as he urged her up the stairs. "Andre is a complicated man, but he wouldn't dare harm my wife."

Rose didn't respond as she raced up to the landing, ready to have a thick door between Andre and herself.

CHAPTER EIGHTEEN

March 5, 1750
Knebfield House
Shenley, England

Half-breed vampires of all sorts began arriving shortly
before sunset the next day. The half Elvish were first,
followed by the half Fey, both of whom were able to
walk the earth when the sun's rays were not at their
strongest. Later in the evening, more exotic hybrids
joined the impromptu country party. Quarter vampires
with brownie blood, three quarter vampires with a bit
of pixie, even a vampire who claimed a spot of leprechaun heritage several generations past.

The show of support was humbling, although it
proved Rose's theory that a vampire would bed any
female willing to spread her legs.

"For shame, Rose," Gareth said, swatting her bottom with the brush he held. "Why shouldn't it prove
a female vampire will mount anything with a cock-
stand? To place all the blame upon the males of our
species is unfair."

"Forgive me, my lord." Rose smiled. She was infinitely more hopeful than when they'd sought their bed late the evening before.

The guest rooms of Knebfield House were filled to capacity and even more allies were expected to arrive on the morrow. By midnight the next eve, they would be ready to adjourn to London where they would stand against the tribe. Several of those assembled were possessed of homes in town and had graciously offered to quarter them until it was safe for them to inhabit Gareth's Mayfair home.

Or until they were all killed the evening of the full moon, whichever came first.

Once more, Gareth abandoned his work detangling her hair to use the brush upon her hindquarters. This time with enough force to make the bare flesh sting as Rose drew in a swift breath. "Pardon me, husband, but I was under the impression you meant to brush my hair, not paddle my backside."

"And I was under the impression you meant to cease dwelling upon our certain doom," Gareth said as he smoothed the brush softly across the skin he had abused, awakening a tingling sensation in other places. "Our allies are nearly thirty strong, with ten gifted swordsmen included in the number. I fail to see how the tribe will best such a force."

"But what if your informant is wrong?" Rose asked, pulse speeding from a heady cocktail of fear and arousal. "What if the ogre the vampire council captured is ignorant of the plot? How will we discover who aids the tribe? What if the other Fey get word of—"

"What must I do to distract you from your gloomy thoughts?" His fingers smoothed lightly across her skin, tracing the path of her spine until he reached her nape. There, he fisted his hand in her unbound hair, wringing a gasp from Rose. "Perhaps I should continue to put this brush to better use."

Gareth's grip on her hair grew even tighter, holding her in place as he brought the flat of the brush down on her bottom. Once, twice, three times, until a moan burst from her lips. To her surprise, it was not a sound of protest or pain, but an invitation for her husband to continue his rough treatment. Her sex already ached, damp with excitement, her body eager to feel Gareth's cock shoving inside her from behind.

He had hinted at such rough play last evening, after he'd brushed her long hair with more tenderness and care than any lady's maid. But somehow they'd ended up tangled on the rug before the fire before threats of disciplining his new wife could take form.

Apparently tonight, however, Gareth was determined to make good on his promise to show her the many faces of pleasure. Rose was glad of it, eager to explore the depth of the passion between them, to indulge her scandalous and wicked urges before it was too late. Before she went to her grave a woman who had wasted a hundred years guarding her heart.

"That sentiment is the very last straw," Gareth said, his breath coming faster as he picked her up in his arms and tossed her onto the bed. Seconds later he was atop her, his weight pressing her into the soft coverlet, his hands busy at the close of his breeches. "Prepare to be scandalously used by your husband."

Rose sighed in anticipation and wriggled beneath him, urging her husband to move faster by arching her back, presenting herself like an animal in heat.

The freedom to revel in her every carnal desire was so new, so thoroughly intoxicating, that it took several seconds for her to realize the pounding in her ears was someone at their chamber door, not the frantic beating of her own heart.

"Lord Shenley! My lord, you must—" The manservant's shout ended in a strangled yelp. Gareth was off the bed and reaching for his sword moments later.

Rose followed suit, lunging for her abandoned clothes and pulling her faerie blade free, heedless of her state of undress. If she must do battle naked, so be it. She hoped her nudity would prove more of a distraction to her enemies than to herself. She rushed behind Gareth as he made haste to the chamber entrance, and was only steps behind as he threw open the heavy door.

Gareth's oldest and most faithful human servant fell onto the carpet between them, his throat slit from one ear to the other.

"Andre! Our defenses have been breeched!" Gareth roared the words and leapt over the corpse. "Stay here, Rose. Lock the door behind me and—"

"I will not. I'm coming with you."

"You are not," he said, edging out into the hall, searching the passage in both directions. "I forbid you to leave this room wearing naught but a sour expression."

"Then I shall put something on." Rose grabbed her dressing gown and shrugged it on before following Gareth out into the hall. At first, all seemed quiet, but as they drew closer to the main stair, a veritable din of psychic complaint hit with enough force to make Rose sway unsteadily on her feet.

"Are you all right, love?" Gareth's arm came about her waist, holding her tightly to his side while his weapon dangled uselessly from his other hand.

"Gareth, your sword . . . we must—"

"It is too late," he said, the defeat in his voice frightening her more than the angry din of telepathic voices raging louder and louder between her ears.

"What has happened?"

"We are undone."

"No," Rose said, forcing herself to stand on her own feet. "We'll fight. Whatever awaits, we shall—"

"There is no fighting to be done, Rose. We're surrounded." Gareth pulled her toward the stair. "Can you not hear the voices of our guests?"

And suddenly she did hear a voice clearly above the rest, though it was not one of their allies who spoke.

Listen to the scourge, vampire. Come, fight us, and let us be done with this tiresome business. The high council has more pressing business than dealing with upstart half-breeds.

"Gladly, sir, if you did not outnumber us at least two to one." Gareth smiled at the faerie who stood on the landing, a satisfied expression on his sharp, angular face. At the base of the stairs stood their guests, rounded up like sheep in a pen, cornered by immense Fey men armed to the teeth with all manner of weaponry. "Or if you honored supernatural law by fighting with steel and magic, not pistols."

"But what are such odds when you have the scourge by your side?"

"She's no longer yours to claim, faerie," Gareth said through gritted teeth. "You will refer to her as

Lady Shenley, or better yet, you will not refer to her at all."

"Come now, Lord Shenley." The faerie laughed, showing the large black teeth that were the fashion of the dark court in Paris. "If you would defend your lady's honor, I would gladly face you over pistols at dawn."

"Dawn, how charming. We vampires do so adore the sunrise." Gareth bowed, setting his sword upon the floor as he did so. "Let us lay down our weapons, my lady, and throw ourselves upon the mercy of this jester."

"You're a coward, then," the faerie said, tossing his long, brown braid over his shoulder. Rose had time to note he was the least stunning Fey man she'd ever seen, before a more important realization hit her full force.

"The Fey de la Nuit," Rose muttered, the words numbing her lips as she spoke them. "But how could they— We didn't— Blast it all!"

"Eloquent, my lady." The sneer on the faerie's face made it nearly impossible to lay her weapon on the floor next to Gareth's. "But then, I'd heard you excelled at baser activities rather than the fine art of conversation."

"You wretched—"

"You heard correctly, sir," Rose said, laying a hand on Gareth's arm and forcing a smile. "Why bother with an eloquent turn of phrase when 'go to hell' will more than serve my purpose?"

"Not today, *love*." The faerie lingered on the last word, rolling it along his tongue in deliberate insult, attempting to goad her husband into losing his temper.

"But perhaps I will have the honor of sending you there before too long. Though I hope not before I've had the pleasure of slaying your husband whilst you watch."

"I will take my own life before giving you the pleasure," Gareth whispered, his controlled tone far more threatening than any shout.

"Well then, perhaps I'll have to shoot the lady betwixt the wind and the waters whilst *you* watch, my lord. Her liaison swears she's the most delicious piece—"

"No, Gareth!" Rose flung her arms around his neck, pleading with her eyes for him to keep his head. "If you allow him to bait you, there is no hope of rescue."

"I beg your pardon, my lady, but rescue will elude you no matter what course your husband chooses." The Fey laughed. "You'll be abandoned to your fate, and Lord Shenley escorted to Paris if he isn't man enough to die—"

"No, I beg *your* pardon, sir," Rose said, turning back to the contemptible excuse for a high council officer. "You will not deny us an audience with the Seelie king before exercising the orders of the dark court. To do so is to take action far above your station. The high council dares not menace those under the golden king's protection."

"You will find no protection, scourge," the faerie said, though his gray eyes flashed. "You are a lowly half-breed, more mortal than—"

"Take me to my grandfather, sir, and let us settle the matter for certain." Rose stood as straight as she was able, looking down at the man as if she'd been raised a princess of the Fey, not merely a princess of men. "We'll leave immediately, and reach Manor High before dawn."

CHAPTER NINETEEN

March 6, 1750
Manor High
Hertfordshire, England

> *A blood man of the night will betray the Fey, and the*
> *scourge will be no more.*
> *The blood of the maid will burn, banishing hellfire back*
> *to the depths.*
> *The son will rise again, but no sooner rise than fall.*
> *When the clock strikes four, the order is restored,*
> *though humankind runs like the rabbit from the fox.*

"You must see that this leaves the Seelie court in a very awkward position, Rosemarie," her grandfather said, finally lifting his eyes from the parchment he'd been studying for the past twenty minutes.

He was an immense man, larger than any she'd ever seen in the flesh. Not only was he tall and solidly built, but it seemed his very bones were triple the size of even the average Fey male. His head was gigantic, and his large mouth capable of fitting an entire apple inside in one bite.

Rose hadn't been able to keep from staring, no matter that she'd warned herself to be on her best behavior for this picnic with the only person in England who might be willing to aid her cause.

"Your highness, Rose and I understand how this prophecy has been interpreted by the Fey de la Nuit, but we hoped you would see our marriage is hardly a betrayal. We married not only for love, but to honor the dictates of Fey law. After my brother was proven unfit, I was the next in line to fulfill the marriage contract," Gareth said, as charming as ever, despite the fact that he'd been forced to hide in a tent for the majority of the sunny day as he disclosed the findings of the vampire high council's investigation.

He'd decided to share the knowledge he'd revealed to Rose the night before. Considering they were close to being prisoners already, there was little to be lost by exposing the findings of the council and much to be gained. Rose prayed that knowing the vampires had captured an ogre who was in possession of the location of the tribes' organizers would convince her grandfather to help them.

Unfortunately, the rereading of the prophecy was not working in their favor. Rose ran her hand gently through her husband's unbound hair, trying not to panic as she watched her grandfather's face.

Now that the sun was beginning to set, Gareth had joined her grandfather, his various attendants, human servants, and herself on the expansive blanket spread upon the grass. He sprawled next to her, his head in her lap, emulating the men and women nearby who lounged about as if they hadn't a care in the world. And perhaps they didn't. The Seelie were joy-eaters and as such encouraged happiness and gaiety in each other and the humans invited to make their home at Manor High.

"The Fey de la Nuit see this differently, Lord Shenley," her grandfather said, smiling as the women behind him plaited his long red hair into dozens of braids that swung about his face.

Manor High looked like any other nobleman's home from the outside, but that was where the similarities ended. Inside, the world of the Seelie reigned supreme, from furnishings to clothing to hairstyles. She and Gareth were the only two dressed in current human fashions. The rest of the company wore robes that seemed to be spun of pure sunlight, rainwater, or the first bursts of spring bloom. Their garments were stunning, as were the lords and ladies of the Seelie court. They were beauties, every one, though Gareth assured Rose she was still the loveliest woman present.

As if she cared for such nonsense now. Rose had assumed conditions would be favorable now that she was no longer subject to the contract forcing her loyalty and servitude to the black faeries. She hadn't anticipated that the Fey de la Nuit would see her marriage to Gareth as a fulfillment of the first aspect of the prophecy. Honoring a betrothal contract hardly qualified as a "blood man betraying the Fey" in her mind.

She'd hoped the Seelie would be equally inclined to see reason, but the situation looked less than promising.

"Surely the Seelie king isn't forced to bend to the

dictates of the black faeries?" she asked, her tone innocent.

"Of course not." Stephen de Feu Vert plucked another apple from the basket near his hand and consumed it with a few swift movements of his massive jaws. "But the prophecies are those of all the Fey, Rosemarie. We must honor them as we honor the Great Mother, the Goddess herself. To do otherwise is to court disaster."

"Most assuredly," she said, doing her best to keep a sour expression from her face. Why had she come here? This man had allowed his daughter to die and his granddaughter to be raped by an ogre as she slept. She'd been a fool to hope for his aid.

But there hadn't been a choice. It was either make haste to Manor High, or allow the men who had come for her and Gareth to escort them where they would. She hadn't wanted to be in a vulnerable position coming into the Seelie court, let alone dependent on her relatives for her very life, but there had been no other option. She was a dead woman if she climbed back into the black coach that waited outside the Seelie grounds, there was no doubt in her mind.

"Majesty, I would agree, but for the fact that the last prophecy has clearly not come to fruition. My half brother and I are alive. Rose no longer has a *betrothed,* she has a husband," Gareth said, sitting up and reaching for an apple from the king's basket. "A husband who is willing to do anything in his power to keep his bride safe. Her blood will not burn so long as there is breath in my body."

Her grandfather met Gareth's gaze, and she knew

at once that her husband had dropped his relaxed air. She couldn't see his eyes, but she could see the king's. They swirled with bright gold and green, anger and admiration mixing in their depths.

"I also wish for the long life of my newest granddaughter," the faerie king said, his voice holding a warning Gareth didn't heed.

"Then you'll give your leave for our forces to travel to London," he urged. "The black faeries surround my home and trap my guests within. These people came to champion our cause, and will aid in a plan that will end this plot before the full moon."

"A plan that goes against prophecy and carries a prison sentence no doubt."

"Surely it's not a crime to work for my wife's salvation when I believe those who think her death necessary are misguided."

"Who are you, *vampire*, to decide such a grave matter?" her grandfather asked, showing his true Fey colors at last. And she'd been so pleased to see him greet her husband warmly earlier in the day.

"I will not suffer the indignity of—"

"You will suffer if the prophecy decrees it." The king interrupted Gareth, which was probably for the best. Losing his temper with one of the most powerful men in the world wasn't wise, no matter that he was married to his granddaughter.

"Please, Grandfather, husband. We're all dismayed at the course of—"

"I'm not dismayed, I'm enraged. Damn the prophecies of the Fey. You condemn your granddaughter to death if you allow those who brought us here to return Rose forcibly to London." Gareth stood with a rage that was palpable. Several of her grandfather's guards rose as well, but the king raised a hand, stopping them at the edge of the blanket. He was listening, though he certainly wasn't pleased. "She has no home, she has no protection. You might as well slit her throat yourself if you agree to the terms set forth by the Fey de la Nuit. Prophecy or no, to effectively abandon your own kin to death in order to escape censure from the black faerie high council would reflect badly on the Seelie court."

"The reputation of the golden court is hardly of your concern, Lord Shenley." Her grandfather smiled as if amused by the upstart before him. "You are the son of an exile of the black court, are you not?"

"Is that pertinent, sire? Think on this—the black faeries have mocked you for a century, pleased to have one of your kin under their control. Now she is free and you would deliver her into their hands without a fight? It is a weak decision and one your enemies will not soon forget."

Silence fell, thick and heavy, over the yard. Those seated on the blanket held their breath, the lute players ceased their playing, and even the older children leaping hoops in the grass grew silent. Rose saw a human woman bustle toward the children with a large feather, and sweep them toward the doorway of the mansion. Amazingly the young faeries began to float, swooping through the air in response to her movements, quickly carried away from the scene of the crime.

Or future crime. Her grandfather hadn't killed Gareth yet, but judging from the rage purpling his face, it was only a matter of time.

"Grandfather, I thank you for the audience." Rose

stood slowly, not missing the fact that the armed guard had surrounded their picnic.

The sun had set and lightning bugs were moving through the eternal spring night that ruled in the royal yard, but it felt as if all the joy had gone out of the world. She could feel her grandfather's anger like a lead weight tied to her leg, pulling her down into an endless abyss. When the Seelie king was unhappy, none with Seelie blood were immune to the effects. Not even his quarter Fey granddaughter.

"I am grieved we couldn't come to a meeting of the minds," she added, taking the hand Gareth pressed into hers. "But I pray we have the opportunity to meet again under more joyful circumstances."

"You will not beg my forgiveness for the words of your husband?" her grandfather asked, meeting Rose's eyes with a look that increased the oppressive thickness of the air.

"My husband is his own man and a wise one. His words were sincerely spoken, though perhaps stated in a manner not befitting your royal presence." Rose held the king's stare, despite the fear that whispered across her skin. "Additionally, I believe he is correct. We go to our deaths if you order us back to the black carriage. I also believe there are black faeries who will count that as a triumph over the Seelie."

The king's eyes softened. Obviously he found it easier to swallow truth spoken in a soft voice and sweetened with feminine deference. He reached again for the apple basket, and the rest of the company relaxed along with him. The guards remained, however, and Rose knew it would be impossible to escape them.

She was skilled with a sword, but these were no untrained ogres. This was the royal guard of the Seelie king. They were handpicked from among the most talented Fey warriors in the world, and likely had magic that could fell her before she had time to draw her weapon.

Their lives were in her grandfather's hands. Giant, soft, pampered hands that had never known the fear associated with mortality.

"I cannot be seen as actively defying officers sent by the high council of the Fey de la Nuit, Rosemarie. I can remind them of the treaty that forbids their actions at Knebfield, and they will allow your comrades to disperse without harm. I cannot deny them your capture, however. I don't wish to start a war over something the Goddess will decide in a few days time," the king said, his voice soft, as if he were telling a bedtime story to children, not discussing her possible death. Rose's hope had begun to fade when he unexpectedly continued. "But if you were to disappear from Seelie grounds without my knowledge, there are none who could fault me. After all, I am old and have a tendency to forget small details."

"Small details?" Rose held her breath, not daring to hope until she knew what obstacles stood in the way of liberty. For there would be obstacles, of that much she was certain.

"Such as the fact that my little three-quarters mortal granddaughter has wings. I never expected such a thing, and was shocked when she didn't return from a walk through my woods with her new husband. I had no idea she was capable of flying over the wards placed at the back of my property."

"Thank you, Grandfather. Your mercy is great." Rose sank into a deep curtsy.

"Yes, your mercy is great, your majesty," Gareth said, a note of wry humor in his tone Rose didn't understand. "I trust you're aware I was not blessed with the wings of the Fey."

"That, my dear grandson-in-law, is none of my concern." He smiled and it was a fearsome thing. For a creature who fed on joy, he was surprisingly wicked, and it was only with great effort Rose kept the disgust from her face as he turned back to her. "You have a half hour before I discover your escape, Rosemarie. Best wishes to you both. Should the sun rise in your favor on the morning of the waning moon, I trust you will return for a celebration befitting your status as a princess of the Seelie court."

"Thank you, gracious king. We will look forward to that bright morning," she said, hoping he read the promise in her eyes. She *would* live to see the ninth of March, as would her husband, no matter what she had to do to ensure that fact.

Gareth bowed and Rose curtsied and then they ran straight toward the tree line at the back of the great lawn. Faint laughter whispered through the night air behind them, the Seelie returning to merriment now that their tiresome business had been concluded.

"Ghastly people, those relatives of yours." Gareth pulled her into his arms and ran even faster. She didn't argue, knowing he could move more quickly than she, especially considering the ridiculously formal gown she'd donned in anticipation of this meeting.

"Wretched, aren't they? I'd apologize on their behalf, but your mother—"

"Of course, Mother was a horrid bitch." Gareth leapt over a fallen tree and landed without any sign of the effort it must cost him to move in such a fashion while carrying her weight. "Still, you'd expect better from the golden Fey, wouldn't you? I wouldn't be surprised to hear they were taking wagers on whether or not you'll abandon me at the wards."

"I'll not abandon you."

"If they're only able to be flown over, there's no way I'll manage them, and you can't carry me. We may have no choice." She read his determination to send her over the wards without him on his face, though their minds were still closed to each other, a precaution they'd believed necessary on Seelie lands where one could never be sure who might of slip into one's unshielded thoughts.

"But you move with the strength of the Fey, even stronger than Ambrose—"

"No, I move with the strength of an ancient vampire. The Fey aspect of my nature lends me power, but I am a vampire through and through."

"Have you ever thought to experiment? I had no idea I had wings until—"

"I *don't* have them, Rose," he said, sounding irritated as they neared the edge of the wood. The glowing wards stood before them, shining with a golden light. They were at least twenty feet tall, without a single tree nearby to give hope that Gareth might somehow find his way over. Rose scanned the surrounding area for another possible route, feeling desperation threaten to cloud her mind. "Rose, you must go. I'll return to the coach, go with the officers to Paris—"

"You will not. I won't leave you. There must be a way to see us both safely over."

"There is no other way. I have some Fey magic, but nothing that could contend with a barrier like this. Unfurl your wings and go. With any luck you'll be halfway to London by the time they pick up your trail." He kissed her, just a swift press of lips, but she felt it across every inch of her skin. "Find humans of your acquaintance and hide yourself as best you can among them."

"But what of our plan?" she asked, taking his hand as he set her on the ground. "If the ogre captive has disclosed the location, then—"

"Damn the plan. Without aid, it's impossible."

"My grandfather said he would talk to the Fey de la Nuit and remind them that holding our allies captive goes against the treaty."

"It doesn't matter. Without being there at Kneb-field . . ." He trailed off, refusing to meet her eyes, and she knew he was keeping something from her. It was amazing how well they'd come to know each other in such a short time, but she wanted to know even more. More about him, her unlikely husband, who was swiftly becoming someone she didn't want to live without.

"What aren't you telling me?" she asked, bringing her hand to his cheek and willing him to turn his eyes to her. He did, and her breath caught at his beauty. With every day that passed he became more delightful to her eyes, her body, her heart. She didn't want to leave him here. It would be like leaving part of herself behind.

"The council didn't discover our plan without help."
He lifted his fingers to play at her throat. "I am certain
we were betrayed, and by someone close to me."

"Andre," she said, her guess confirmed by Gareth's
betraying flinch. "He wants you rid of me enough to
risk your life?"

"I hadn't thought him capable, but that's my guess."

"I knew he couldn't be trusted," she raged, turning
to kick at a pile of nearby leaves.

"It doesn't matter. You must go. Now."

"It does matter! We were so close. We had allies,
we nearly had a location for the masterminds of the
tribe." She shrugged away the hand he placed on her
shoulder and turned on him. "I tried to warn you,
Gareth."

"Yes, you did, but now isn't the time for an argument."

"I told you," she continued. "I swore I wouldn't
feel safe as long as Andre was employed at Knebfield. But you couldn't even dismiss one servant in
the name of—"

"He's my father, Rose! I can't very well dismiss
my own father." Rose stared at him, finally shocked
beyond words. Gareth ran a frustrated hand through
his hair, and continued in a softer tone. "Father has
been posing as my servant for the past fifteen years,
since he returned from touring the East. He's been
waiting for me to marry so that he might eventually
reclaim Knebfield house as my heir. I thought he'd be
pleased to see me wed, no matter that he didn't ap-
prove of my plan to make good on the Fey betrothal."

"Andre is my *father-in-law*," Rose said, disap-
pointed beyond words. She was beginning to wonder

if she and Gareth would be better off without any family at all.

"I'm sorry, love." He pulled her into his arms and kissed her forehead. "When this nasty business is over, I will insist he treat you fairly. He can have Knebfield house, we'll move somewhere out in the country, away from Society, and spend our time tending sheep and making love."

"What do you know of sheep?" Rose asked, tears pricking the backs of her eyes as she kissed him deeply, communicating everything in her heart.

"Go." His voice was thick as he pushed her away. "Go, and don't do anything foolish. Keep yourself safe. The tribe cannot complete its plan without your sacrifice. Live to see the morning of the ninth of March, and you will save us all."

"Gareth, please, I—"

"There's no way out for me. You are my and Ambrose's best chance for freedom." He stepped back several paces, moving toward the great lawn.

"Wait, I—"

"We've waited too long already. Fly, Rose, as fast as you are able."

He turned and ran back the way they had come, while Rose flexed the unseen muscle that freed her wings from her skin, magically spiriting them through her clothing. She kept her eyes on Gareth's retreating form for as long as possible, a part of her certain it was the last time she would gaze upon him.

She wasn't going to abandon hope of stopping the tribe. Gareth must have known that. Perhaps that's why he stopped and turned, holding her eyes as she rose into the air, up and over the enchanted wall. It was only when she'd landed safely on the other side that he blew her a kiss and turned to run once more. And it was only when she turned to fly away into the twilight that she realized she had never told him that she loved him.

CHAPTER TWENTY

March 7, 1750
3:48 P.M.
London, England

"And that isn't the half of it, my lady," Lady Chissick said, lowering her voice though the nearest carriage was nearly twenty feet ahead. "I have it on good authority that the Earl of Ansely has had her, or rather *him,* in his employ since the scarlet creature left the stage for good last autumn."

The Marchioness of Chissick was in possession of more gossip than any other person Rose had ever met.

Her interest in the doings of absolutely *every* member of the *ton* was tiresome, but was also responsible for Rose's presence in her carriage. Thanks to the burning of her London home and her attendance at the house party where a chambermaid was murdered, Rose was a person of interest to Lady Chissick. Without that, she wouldn't have been intriguing enough for the marchioness to invite her to take the air, let alone stay at her Mayflower home for the duration of the Season.

"Can you believe it? The *scandal,*" she said, turning wide blue eyes to Rose.

The marchioness was the picture of innocence, a slightly round woman in her early thirties whom no one would guess capable of destroying another's reputation looking at her sweet, guileless face. Rose knew of her power, however, and had done her best to keep her behavior beyond reproach, no matter that she had no idea whether or not she would live long enough to be concerned with the condition of her good name.

"It's completely scandalous." Rose widened her eyes and leaned a bit closer, hoping she had convinced Lady Chissick of her interest, at least for a few more moments. It was nearly impossible to keep her mind on the conversation when she knew in a few short hours she would be embarking on the most dangerous mission of her life. Alone, without a single person to champion her cause, and with several hundred enemies actively working toward her death.

Yet someone on the vampire high council had pitied her enough to send an anonymous note sharing the findings of the interrogation of their ogre captive, giving her the address of the mastermind behind the ogre's plot. But that was all the aid he was willing to give. The entire supernatural community—with the exception of the dark faeries she suspected were tailing her every move—was avoiding her like the plague since word of the arrest of Lord Shenley by Fey de la Nuit officers reached London.

Her situation made her thankful for her efforts to maintain the respectability of her mortal identity. Without it, she would truly be without a friend in the world.

". . . and indeed, even more scandalous is that the man is aware his new valet is not a man at all, but a creature of perverse affectations. Lord Ansely finds it amusing to be aided in dressing by a woman, no matter her queer habits." Lady Chissick sighed and turned to look out across the park, no doubt seeking more inspiration for gossip.

It was another unseasonably warm day and half the *ton* was taking the air in Hyde Park, some on horseback and many in carriages, though none so magnificent as Lady Chissick's. Her dark brown phaeton and matching team of four were the envy of the *ton*. Even her footmen complemented her chosen color scheme, the two tall Africans as deeply chocolate as the coach itself.

"What does Lady Ansely think of the matter?" Rose asked, scanning the park.

Since it was daylight, there was no need to worry about vampires, but she knew the Fey de la Nuit were looking for her. It didn't matter that they'd intended to return her to London themselves, they wouldn't be pleased she had taken matters into her own hands. In fact, Rose suspected several among them would kill her if they managed to catch her. Luckily, she had yet to see a single faerie during the carriage ride, nor any of the tribe. But then it was rare for an ogre to rise to a position of any great rank, let alone accumulate the wealth required to maintain a carriage in the city.

"Lady Ansely will surely be beside herself, once she learns of the creature's true identity," Lady Chissick said, her words underscored with mirth. "The last I heard, however, the poor dear was still in the dark. Honestly, I can't believe Lord Ansely would dare. Having an actress in your employ is scandalous in itself, but an actress who dresses as a man and prefers the company of women in the boudoir? Really! It's too desperately wicked to be believed."

"Indeed. How shocking." Rose tutted softly beneath her breath, not daring to say more. Gareth had said several members of Society suspected her herself of preferring the company of women in her bed. Knowing Lady Chissick, that had probably been the point of the entire discourse, to draw from Rose her opinions on relations with members of one's own sex.

"But now, you simply must tell me Comtesse, if there is any truth to a certain piece of news I have heard floating about the *ton*," Lady Chissick said, her tone turning disturbingly conspiratory.

Dear God, no. She *wasn't* going to ask if Rose enjoyed the company of other females in a biblical sense. What would she say? Just the fact that she'd *asked* would be an act of scandal in itself.

"I will most certainly share any knowledge I have," Rose said, demurely. "Though honestly I have had little time for socializing since arriving in London. With the murder at Lord Drummand's, the earthquake, and the burning of my home, I've been quite beside myself."

"Of course, you poor dear! I'm simply thankful I kept my pleated silks from before Arnold was born. They fit you perfectly and with a little updating you'll look gorgeous while waiting for your new clothes to be made. Which reminds me!" Lady Chissick clapped her gloved hands together in delight. "I've set an appointment with my dressmaker, Françoise, for Monday next. His secretary insisted he was booked for a solid month, but once Françoise heard of your dire situation and that you were a personal friend of mine, he agreed to fit you in right away."

"I can't express the depth of my gratitude, Lady Chissick," Rose said, a genuine smile stretching her lips for the first time that day. "I must thank you again for your generosity. I don't know what I would have done without you."

"Oh, pish," Lady Chissick said, though her pleasure in the praise was evident on her flushed cheeks. "You have more friends than you know, Comtesse de Fournier. The quality of London are pleased to have you here, no matter what a few defamers might have to say."

"Oh dear, defamers?" Rose asked, funneling her concern about everything else in her life into her question. If she were truly an eighteen-year-old comtesse, she surely would be as concerned about her reputation as potentially having her blood spilled in a ritualistic sacrifice. "You must tell me what you have heard, Lady Chissick, so that I may put your mind at ease that you have not invited scandal into your home."

"Please! I would never assume the gossip to be true!" She laid a gentle hand on Rose's, as if she hadn't moments ago hinted that she was assuming exactly that. "As an older woman, I simply hate to see younger ladies taken advantage of. If your dear grandmother or mother were alive, I'm certain they would be able to guide you to make a better match than Sir Pithwater."

"Sir Pithwater?" Rose asked, her interest fully captured in truth. "What of the baronet? I have not seen him since the party at Lord Drummand's estate."

"Truly? And he would have had my husband believe you were with him only two night's past. He intimated that you were spared death the evening your home burned to the ground because you were safely ensconced in his own home. The *entire* evening, well past the time when you should have been abed." Her soft gaze sharpened, as if she would read Rose's guilt or innocence in her features.

Rose could only hope her shock at hearing Pithwater was alive and back in London after what she had done to him in the catacombs and being trapped afterward with flesh-eating Wyrms would be read as the surprise of the innocent.

"What a wretched man. I was visiting Lord Shenley in the country with my companion, Marta, that evening," Rose said, judging the best way to divert suspicion from involvement with one man was to mention another. "She took ill, however, and remains at Knebfield house, which of course makes me even more indebted to you, Lady Chissick. If you hadn't opened your home, I do not know what I would have done for a chaperone, as my closest acquaintances remain on the Continent."

"I'm delighted to have the opportunity to present you to Society more properly. That you have appeared at court and been in London since before the holidays, yet still not been properly introduced about the *ton* is inexcusable. Lord Shenley should have seen to it that the necessary introductions were made." She narrowed her eyes again, clearly on the hunt for more interesting news than that of the homely baronet. "But then I suppose the earl was reluctant to share the pleasure of your company."

"He has been most kind," Rose said, trying to affect a girlish blush when in truth the thought of Gareth made her chest ache.

At this very moment, her husband was on his way to Paris to be tortured or perhaps even killed, and she had neglected to share what was in her heart. She vowed she would remedy that situation as soon as possible, no matter how many tribesmen she had to slay to achieve her goal.

"But I must ask," Rose said, turning back to Lady Chissick. "Will Sir Pithwater's falsehoods damage my chances to be well received?"

"I shouldn't think so, dear. Sir Pithwater is not particularly well received among the *ton* himself. The man has been in London scarcely more than half a year. Beforehand he was a bit of a recluse. He owes his membership in White's to the sponsorship of a wealthy peer, not his own fortune or standing."

"Truly? I wonder who would sponsor him?"

"It's seems to be a matter of great secrecy. Most odd, if you ask me."

"Quite odd. Where did the baronet reside prior to his move to London?" Rose asked, not wanting to seem overly interested in the man, but unable to control her curiosity.

"I honestly can't say. He's rather an odd creature." If she only knew the half of it. "He seems very tight-lipped on matters that should be common knowledge, and yet terribly forward when speaking of alleged assignations. I fear your Lord Shenley may be moved to challenge him to pistols at dawn. I've heard the earl has quite a temper, despite his amiable nature."

"He hasn't shown that to be true in my presence." Rose blushed as her mind filled with images of the night she'd chained Gareth to the wall. "Lord Shenley was called to Paris on business. I will miss his companionship, but I'm glad he is away if Pithwater's nonsense would prompt him to risk his safety."

"So true. Men are such rash creatures when defending the honor of their lady."

Rose smiled and stared shyly down at her hands. Judging from Lady Chissick's satisfied sigh, she had performed well enough to provide fresh fodder for gossip.

"We will simply give Sir Pithwater the cut direct if we happen to see him at the ball tonight," Lady Chissick said. "I will inform Lord Chissick we no longer wish to be acquainted with the man."

"That is so good of you, Lady Chissick."

"Please, call me Charlotte."

"And you must call me Rosemarie."

"Never fear, Rosemarie." She smiled and patted Rose's hand, then motioned for the driver to turn down Rotten Row. "Receiving a cut from a man as well respected as my husband will teach the baronet to think before spreading vicious lies."

"Indeed," Rose said, thinking that the sort of cut she would give the man would prove even more satisfying.

She might not be able to benefit directly from the allies she had gathered at Knebfield, but they would prove invaluable to her yet. While there, her blade had been blessed by a vampire who claimed Amiantos witch ancestry and it glowed with new power. The next time she met Pithwater would be the last. Even if the man had demon blood he would perish, and those who aided him in returning from the dead would fall soon after.

March 7, 1750
11:45 P.M.
Grosvenor Square
London, England

The ball was already well under way, and the ballroom of Lord Covington's immense home filled to capacity by the time Rose and Lord and Lady Chissick arrived. Being in no great hurry to arrive, the Chissicks had lingered over their after-dinner port. Then Lady Chissick had ordered her driver to circle the square, so that she might show Rose the exact home once occupied by the first King George's mistress.

She narrated the tour with a lengthy retelling of the lady's long, colorful life and subsequent death at the age of six and seventy. Lord Chissick joined the conversation at that point to interject his opinion on how best to ensure survival into old age. Being near fifty himself and possessed of rather poor health in the winter months, this was a subject dear to the marquis's heart, and deemed worthy of yet another turn about the square as he regaled both Rose and his wife on the benefits of a daily sherry and the liberal use of castor oil to ensure freedom of the bowels.

By the time Rose was finally helped from the carriage by two large Swedish footmen—with hair like corn silk that matched the golden hue of Lord

Chissick's covered landau—she was a mass of nerves. And more than ready to escape the relentlessly cheerful company of her hosts. Feigning attentiveness to their chatter was driving her mad.

Of course, Lord and Lady Chissick were unaware that next door to the Duke of Covington there lived quite . . . unique neighbors. Or that these neighbors were Rose's sole reason for sending word to Lady Chissick of her unfortunate circumstances. There'd been no doubt the Chissicks would be on the guest list for this evening's festivities, and they were of sufficient standing to bring along any number of guests without repercussion. They were Rose's entrée into the ball, and into the best position to thwart the tribe's plot.

Despite the warmth of the evening, Rose shivered as they mounted the outer stair to the impressive Covington home. There was darkness nearby—she felt it whispering across her skin. If she'd needed any additional convincing that she was in the proper place, the almost palpable evil wafting from the mansion next door would have done the job.

Even half an hour later, flushed from the first dance of the evening, she could feel the chill. It wasn't merely ogres inhabiting forty-eight Grosvenor Square. There was something else, something much more powerful housed inside the deceptively lovely building. She'd find out what before the night was through. Whether it was a demon, as she suspected, or an ancient death god, as Gareth thought likely, she must face it. She couldn't simply hide and pray disaster would be averted because her blood remained unspilt.

If her blood were so necessary, she should have

been captured by now, not allowed to roam half the Continent and inhabit her home for more than a day before the tribe sought her out. She'd also been seen in London today, and had caught sight of nearly a dozen ogres once she and Lady Chissick departed Hyde Park. Yet none of them seemed to take notice of her. It didn't make sense.

Even if her freedom could be attributed to clumsiness on the part of the tribe, she couldn't deny that part of her simply *knew* there was more to this plan than ridding the world of one woman, no matter that she was "the scourge" of the tribe. Even if the tribe thought this magic would destroy all Fey executioners, it still didn't seem to be worth the trouble. For the tribe, yes, but not for whatever black force manipulated their actions, or for the unknown faerie and vampire who aided them.

"Are you well, Rosemarie?" Lord Chissick had lapsed into calling Rose by her given name even before they had formally dispensed with titles. The man had two daughters from an earlier marriage, and Rose knew he viewed her with fatherly eyes. He and Lady Chissick had both been unfailingly kind, which had surprised her, what with their power among the *ton*. Rose knew she'd owe them a debt of gratitude if she were to survive the night.

"I'm well, my lord, simply a bit fatigued," she said, joining in the clapping as the quadrille came to an end.

"Shall I secure the next entry for your card, dear?" Lord Chissick asked, only slightly out of breath after nearly half an hour on the dance floor.

"No, thank you. I believe I'll seek out some refreshment. I saw a few young ladies of my acquaintance at the door to the parlor only a few moments ago." Rose curtsied and hurried toward the door as Lord Chissick made his way back to where his wife sat to one side of the room with several of her friends.

Lady Chissick had insisted her husband dance the first dance with Rose, which had given her more time to spread the news of Rose's infatuation with Lord Shenley. Judging by the disgruntled looks of several of the ladies, there would be a day of mourning declared when news of their marriage was made public.

And it will *be made public, because you will not fail in your mission.*

Her resolve strengthened, Rose pressed through the crowded parlor and out into the farther reaches of the mansion. No one seemed to notice her leaving, and she quickly found an abandoned room where she could begin her transformation. Locking the heavy door behind her, she disrobed silently in the dark. Beneath her borrowed gown of pale blue silk, she had hidden black breeches, a man's shirt, and a black coat, cleverly stuffed into the large panniers Lady Chissick had donated for her use.

For the first time, Rose was grateful for the bizarre hoops that made a woman's hips seem at least three times their normal width. They were wonderfully handy for storage.

Rose hid her gown beneath a desk in the far corner of the room, being careful to smooth the silk so it would be in a condition to be worn again in an hour or two. She prayed that was all the time she'd need. If it was merely the core group of ogres, Rose had no doubt she could dispatch them quickly, but there was still their faerie and vampire mentors to reckon with, as well as the unknown element.

"The unknown evil," she whispered to herself, placing a hand against the wall nearest her, able to feel the darkness seeping through stone and plaster. The house next door was truly accursed.

Still, as Rose crept out the servant's entrance and into the street behind the square, she couldn't help but be impressed by the mansion. Even the mews of the home were immaculate and well appointed. She glimpsed no less than twelve stalls, each occupied by a handsome horse. The animals thankfully made no sound as she moved through the shadows, drawing closer to the rear entrance of the mansion. She didn't consider their silence odd, however, until a large hand closed around her mouth.

Rose willed herself not to scream as she was pulled backward into a solid wall of male flesh, but she struggled as fiercely as she was able, kicking and clawing at her captor until he lowered his mouth to her ear.

"Rosemarie, it's Ambrose. Cease kicking me at once," he hissed, his breath warm on the tendrils of hair that had escaped her cap.

She relaxed, relief flooding her body though her mind warned her to use caution. Rationally, she knew she couldn't trust Ambrose—that his presence here might even mean her death, but on an instinctive level she still rejoiced to see him. No matter what had come between them in recent weeks, in her heart she still saw him as the man who had saved her life more times than she could count, who'd stood by her side for nearly one hundred years though the rest of his kind had ridiculed him.

"I've spelled the animals into silence," he continued, his hold loosening as she stopped fighting for freedom. "Can I expect your cooperation as well?"

Rose nodded and drew a deep breath as his hand moved away from her lips. Ambrose took her elbow and pulled her down to crouch beside him in the shadows provided by the stable's roof.

"What are you—"

"No time for questions. You must run from here. The Fey de la Nuit are coming to my aid. They'll be here before the clock strikes two."

"I won't run. I'm here to aid the fight, as long as I can be certain your comrades will not slit my throat." Ambrose turned away from her with a sigh. "Tell me what's happened, Ambrose. How is it you're free? Last word from Paris, you were a captive of your people."

"I should have known better than to think I could deter you," he said, cupping her cheek in his hand. A mad part of her warmed to the touch, no matter that she was another man's wife. She couldn't deny it was good to see him.

"I was released when word came from London that Lord Shenley and his new bride had been taken into the custody of Fey de la Nuit enforcement officers." The look on his face promised bad news. Rose's muscles braced themselves as if for a blow. "I was to aid in recovering you—and Gareth."

"But why? Couldn't the council demand our release and be done with it?"

"They most certainly could, if the officers had been on orders from the high council. The council was most displeased to learn others have been acting in their name, angry enough to risk interfering with the prophecy." Ambrose's eyes met hers, and only a second passed before the truth hit.

"Those men, the Fey who came for us?"

"Half or quarter Fey at best."

"Whatever they were, they're working on behalf of the tribe," she said, cursing herself for being so foolish. She should have known the Fey de la Nuit would not send such brutes to arrest a high-ranking vampire, or the granddaughter of the Seelie king. Which raised the question . . .

"But they took me to see my grandfather. Why would they do such a—"

"I assume they knew they couldn't deny such a request without arousing suspicion. They expected your pleas for mercy to be denied. Yet you managed to escape, I see."

"My grandfather turned a blind eye while I flew over the wards at the back of his estate."

"I heard you'd acquired wings," Ambrose said, the muscle at his jaw tightening. "It was difficult to decide whether that or the tale you'd married my half brother was the more outrageous. But now I learn both accounts are true."

"We were married at Knebfield." Rose ignored the ache in her chest. "There was no way to bring Gareth over the wards, however, so he returned to the carriage. If only I'd thought, I could have found some way to convince my grandfather that—"

"It's too late for such thoughts. We must simply find a way to free him. Information from Gareth's father has led us to believe he is being held here. We suspect the creature who owns it is a Svartalfar, a black elf who's been masquerading as a member of the Fey de la Nuit sympathetic to the vampire cause."

"So Andre sent word to him, the night that he sent the messages seeking others to come to our aid," she said, a part of her grateful that Andre wasn't the traitor she and Gareth had assumed.

Ambrose nodded. "The black elf had Lord Shenley's father and several other members of the vampire nobility convinced he was working to forge a new treaty between the Fey and the vampires. A treaty that would be more favorable to the blood men."

"And the reason for this deception?"

"We aren't certain, but the man was doing his best to bring about a war. The investigations from the vampire council revealed a few of our own who appear to have been abusing their power, but the majority of the 'faeries' cited in their reports are not Fey de la Nuit or Seelie."

"More dark elves? Perhaps using glamour to disguise themselves?"

"Perhaps, though we won't know for certain until we take them into custody. So far, the creatures have evaded capture. Likely because they have gathered here."

"This isn't simply about eliminating the scourge or the Fey executioners, is it?"

"It's doubtful, though I would wager that's the motive that ensured the tribe's cooperation. The black elf has need of their aid, though I cannot guess why."

"And to ensure their aid, he needs my blood."

"Precisely, and exactly the reason you should run from here. To remain is to risk not only death, but the

possibility that you may help bring about the fulfillment of some black rite and destruction we can only
guess the scope of."

"But the tribe hasn't hunted me today, nor has anyone else. I moved freely among human society and
passed several ogres on the street. Surely if they still
required my blood . . ."

Ambrose sighed, a defeated sound that confirmed
the suspicion rising in Rose's mind.

"Gareth fed from me the morning before we left to
see my grandfather. My blood is still within him." As
she said the words, Rose heard Andre's voice echoing
in her ears, warning Gareth that to have her blood in
his belly was as good as a death sentence. She pressed
trembling fingertips to her lips as her stomach threatened to empty itself of the little food she'd managed
to consume during the elaborate dinner with Lord and
Lady Chissick.

"And it will remain there for at least three or four
more days. A vampire of his age and strength wouldn't
need to feed more often," Ambrose said. "They will
bleed him to get what they desire. He may be dead already, Rosemarie. Can you bear to—"

"Let's go. Now. We can't afford to waste another
moment," she said, starting across the lane before
Ambrose stopped her with a hand on her arm.

"Take this." Ambrose placed a black journeying
stone suspended from a thin strip of leather around her
neck. "If it seems you will be captured, trace the runes
of liberation as you clasp the stone in your hand. It will
transport you to the lower villages of the Fey realm.
Even a quarter Fey is enough faerie blood to take you
there, and you may have more than that. Your wings

make me suspect your father had a bit of faerie in his bloodline, as well."

"They are small, gray wings." She tucked the stone into her shirt. "Nothing to boast about."

"I'm sure they are as lovely as the rest of you."

"Please, Ambrose, we must go. I can't bear to think what might be happening to him."

"You love your new husband, then?"

"I do," she said, seeing the hint of pain in Ambrose's eyes, but knowing this wasn't the time to mince words. "I must make certain he lives to know how deeply."

Ambrose nodded and drew his sword. "Then come, but beware the touch of dark elves. Kill them before they can lay a hand on you, or you may be bespelled. Their strongest magic is that which can be communicated from skin to skin or through water."

"That won't be a problem," she whispered as she followed him across the lane, ready to send any creature she found within straight to hell.

CHAPTER TWENTY-ONE

There were a number of pale, malnourished servants in the dark elf's kitchen, a ragtag lot who fled out the back door without resistance.

Rose was glad to see them go, no matter that she was prepared to kill every living thing in the mansion if necessary. It worked in their favor to gain entrance without alerting its occupants of their arrival. Until the other Fey de la Nuit arrived, they would be sorely outnumbered.

"I'll go up the main stair, you take the servant's stair," Ambrose whispered. "The stone will glow if you near any wards."

"I should take the main stair. My sword has been blessed, and will be of use if Pithwater is not the only one with demon blood."

"Demon blood?"

Rose quickly recounted her time in the catacombs and her theory that explained the man's ability to rise from the dead. No sooner had the words passed her lips than their significance became clear.

"The son shall rise again, but no sooner rise than fall," she said, quoting the prophecy. "I'd thought perhaps the word 'son' had been written incorrectly, but do you suppose it could be referring to Pithwater?"

"He's apparently 'risen' several times, but I doubt he's demon born."

"What other possible explanation could there—"

"Dark elves are invulnerable to flame: he might possess that blood. They are unique in that they are sensitive to the sun like bloodmen, but not to the light or power of flame." Ambrose paused and scented the air. "Neither will they be harmed by whatever blessings you've placed on your sword."

"All hope can't be lost," Rose whispered, hearing the faint humming that Ambrose's superior hearing had caught. It was eerily similar to the chanting they'd heard that night down by the Thames.

"There are ways to banish them back to their realm beneath the earth, but that will be impossible if the human heads the tribe gathered are still in place. The dark elves can channel great power into the Thames and—" Ambrose cursed, a light appearing in his eyes, making them glow silver. "I should have seen the truth sooner."

"What is it?" Rose shifted nervously from foot to foot. It was nearly impossible to keep from rushing toward the sound of the chanting, where she hoped she would find Gareth before it was too late. But as with anything supernatural, the laws governing the dark elves could be as valuable a weapon as anything forged from iron or steel.

"The Fey de la Nuit are fools. I'm a fool."

"Please, Ambrose, we don't have much time. Gareth could be—"

"We assumed banishing the scourge was the main thrust of the prophecy. It isn't. You're merely a means of convincing the ogres to use magic."

"How can you be certain?"

"The damned elf means to awaken Alvar, one of the ancient ogres banished thousands of years ago. He's slept for so long no one knew where he was buried, but it must be here, somewhere beneath the River Thames."

"One of the ancient giants?"

"If memory serves, he couldn't be killed. He's a direct descendant of the Mother of us all, and therefore truly immortal," Ambrose said. "Alvar and his twin sister, Illona, were put to sleep long ago, in secret graves far beneath the earth, and a spell worked to ensure they stayed there for all time."

"A spell the black elf found a way of undoing."

"With the aid of Alvar's ogre descendants it might just be possible. The ogres have already had success summoning one of Alvar's sons from whatever corner of the earth the wretch was banished. We saw that much with our own eyes."

"The giant we battled?" Rose asked. "Before the earthquake? Could that not have been Alvar himself?"

"Alvar would be at least fifty times the size." Ambrose cursed again and gripped his sword until his knuckles turned white. "In fact, I imagine the shaking of the earth was no natural phenomenon, but a product of Alvar's struggle to emerge from his prison."

"Goddess," Rose said, not wanting to think about the damage that could be wrought by such a creature. She'd assumed freeing lesser demons into the world would be the absolutely worst thing that could happen, but if the giant was large enough to cause an earthquake merely by moving . . .

"Why now?" she asked, refusing to contemplate such destruction. "Is it simply because the one hundred years I was to fight the tribe are nearly complete?"

"Likely. The black elf required ogre aid, and that would be an excellent way to convince them to join his cause. Even with blood magic involved, a massive ogre presence will be needed to call Alvar from his rest."

"What will happen if the creature is freed tonight?"

"The earth will shake as it did before, but this time it will not cease till the beast is released from its prison. London will likely be destroyed, along with every creature near the river."

"So this black elf has been using the ogres for his own purpose, and doesn't plan to honor his part of whatever agreement they've made."

"Perhaps," Ambrose said, though he didn't look convinced. Or perhaps he was simply distracted by the moans now rising above the faint chanting.

It didn't sound like Gareth, but Rose couldn't be sure. Still, she had to know if she was correct. If she and Ambrose could convince the ogres of the elf's betrayal, perhaps they would terminate their participation before it was too late. Surely not even the tribe would see the destruction of the largest city in Europe and the death of hundreds of their people as justifiable losses.

"Gareth said his investigation led him to believe the ogres think destroying me will put an end to the Fey de la Nuit executioners. They don't think the black faeries would lower themselves to hunt the ogres once their human slaves are gone, and the tribe would thus be free of persecution for a great many years."

"Remember when I told you the Fey cannot lie?" he asked. "The black elves *truly* cannot lie. If the elf promised the ogres your death and the death of all humans who serve the Fey de la Nuit, then he will do his best to deliver it."

"That's why Gareth was captured," Rose said, her hopes falling once more.

"And why, I would wager, the Svartalfar was responsible for the trap in Faversham. Catacombs are his realm, and Wyrms creatures long loyal to the dark elves. He could have demanded they swallow you whole and bring you—"

A louder wail sounded and a shiver ran down Rose's spine. Someone was in great pain. Whether it was Gareth or not, there was no more time to waste.

"I will take the servants' stair," she said, gripping her sword and willing all fear from her heart. Whatever it was they would find in this house, it must be faced, for the sake of every human and supernatural soul in London.

"Do not allow yourself to be taken, Rose," Ambrose called softly after her. "The blood they harvest from Gareth may not be sufficient. On the chance that blood direct from your veins is what's needed to wake Alvar, you must put your safety before all else. Better a few dead than an entire city destroyed."

Rose made her way up the stairs to the first landing without bothering to reply. She knew one of those deaths he spoke of would be her husband's, and she didn't know if she was good enough to put the welfare of the majority before his own dear life. Gareth was the only man, the only person, who'd made her feel completely loved since the day of her enchantment nearly two hundred years before. The bliss of it had made her desperate for more.

More time, more love, and the chance to prove she was deserving of the faith he had placed in her.

I will do everything in my power to save my brother, Rosemarie. I will even give my life if the sacrifice will ensure Gareth's survival. You can trust me to honor that promise. I trust I can be certain of your commitment to serving the greater cause.

I will do my best, Rose replied to Ambrose in her mind, even that bringing an additional ache to her heart.

It was with Gareth she had learned to use her limited telepathic skills. For a man she'd known such a short time, he had become a fixture in her life in a way not even Ambrose could claim. She would not give him up easily, not if any sacrifice on her part could ensure his survival.

At the top of the stairs, the chants grew louder. Rose paused, pressing her ear to the door she suspected led to the hallway of the second floor. The exteriors of the Covington home and this one were very similar. She hoped the interiors would be as well. It would give her an advantage when it came time to flee.

Rose closed her eyes and strained to decipher the sounds filtering through the door. The voices were louder than they'd been in the kitchen, but still possessed a distant quality, a bit of an echo in the quieter moments. The second story of the Covington home housed the ballroom. If the layout of the two homes was the same it would account for the echo.

Ambrose. I believe they're in the ballroom on the second floor.

She waited for a reply, but none came. Perhaps they were too far away from one another already, or perhaps he'd judged it wise to discontinue telepathic conversation. Rose suspected the only person capable of overhearing them was Gareth himself—ogres and elves had no mind-speaking powers she was aware of, but Ambrose was always the cautious sort.

"Unfortunately, I'm not," Rose muttered as she pushed the door open and peeked into the hall. Thankfully, the passage was empty, not a guard in sight.

She slipped through the door and pressed it quietly shut behind her. Now it was clear the chanting was coming from her left. In the Covington home she would have been able to see the door of the parlor. Here there was no parlor, only a pair of immense silver doors she guessed led to a ballroom even larger than the Covingtons'.

The closer she came to those doors, the louder the chanting. Louder also were the occasional wails that soared over the droning tribesmen. Hearing it more plainly, Rose guessed the voice belonged to a woman, though her tone was low and hoarse, as if she had been crying out for quite a long time.

Rose pressed her ear to the door, only to jump

back as a bolt of power shivered across her skin. The stone around her neck grew warm and glowed faintly through the dark fabric of her shirt. The door was warded, and not with any minor magic she could disarm with a few traced runes.

"Damnation," she swore, fighting the urge to slam her fists against the barrier. The panic she had been battling since entering the mansion threatened to consume her. She'd never felt so helpless, knowing the man she loved was in the room before her, probably near death, and she was trapped on the other side with no chance of gaining entry.

"There's *always* a chance." Rose turned and hurried back down the hall, thinking of Gareth's words to her that evening at Knebfield House. He'd sworn nothing was ever hopeless, and seemed to believe it. Gareth had walked the earth a hundred more years than she, and if he still held onto hope there was no excuse for her lack of faith.

She raced back to the servants' stair and up to the fifth floor. All was quiet there, and excessively warm even on this early spring night. The simple servants' rooms she passed contained only a narrow bed with cheap linens and no blankets. The dark elf obviously had little concern for the comforts of those who served him. The men and women she and Ambrose had sent scattering into the night would be better off in workhouses than such a place as this. Though, in truth, blankets didn't seem necessary at the moment.

She fought the urge to toss aside her cap. Indoors, the thing did little to conceal her, but she might find herself fleeing into the night. There, her blond hair would shine like a beacon under the glow of the full moon. She couldn't afford to remove the thing, no matter that sweat already dripped down her face and she hadn't yet made it to the attic.

Ambrose. Ambrose? Are you there?

Rose sought him again as she pulled the cord releasing the ladder leading to the mansion's attic. Once again, silence met her call. She began to worry that he had been captured. Surely the main stairway was more heavily guarded than the servants' stair. Even now, Ambrose might be fighting for his life, or lying wounded and dying, or—

"Don't think on it. It will do no good," she whispered as she emerged into the attic. A few rodents scuttled away as she stepped onto the boards, but even the vermin didn't bother moving too quickly. It was absolutely sweltering within the room, the air too thick to breathe. A wave of dizziness made Rose stumble, and she had no choice but to throw the cap from her head and unbutton her coat as well.

She shrugged it off, revealing the cream shirt she wore beneath as she tossed it onto the floor. There would be no missing her now if she were to run into the night, but there was no help for it. She wouldn't live to flee anywhere if she succumbed to the wretched heat.

There had to be something supernatural at work here to cause the extreme temperature. No matter how warm the weather in London had been of late, it couldn't transform an attic into the seventh level of hell. If she hadn't talked with Ambrose, she'd have been more certain than ever that the ogres had been consorting with demons. There seemed no other explanation for the ungodly heat.

As she neared the center of the attic, Rose dropped to her hands and knees, breathing a bit easier. The air was cooler near the floor. She crept along the dusty boards until she began to hear chanting, fainter than before, but still clear enough to pick out individual voices. With her hands pressed flat, she could feel the tingle of evil she'd sensed from the Covingtons' home, but nothing more. As she'd hoped, the black elf hadn't thought to ward the ceiling of his ballroom against invasion.

Her heart beat faster as she dug her sword into the old wood. Even using an enchanted faerie blade it was relatively slow going through the thick floorboards, but after several minutes, she'd formed a circle wide enough for her hips to fit through. Leaning on her sword, she leveraged the last piece of wood out and onto the floor of the attic. Now there was only the plaster of the ballroom's ceiling remaining, a barrier easily penetrated.

For a mad moment, Rose debated leaping on the plaster and breaking through with the weight of her body, but thought better of it. Even if the falling pieces of the ceiling alerted the people below, surely it was better to have a second or two to view what she was up against before throwing herself into the fray. No matter how eager she was to reach Gareth, her rational mind insisted upon a degree of temperance.

Rose dried her damp hands on the fabric of her shirt and wiped the last of the sweat from her brow. Then, with both hands on the hilt of her sword, she shoved it quickly downward. With only a few strikes, a chunk of the thick ceiling fell away, treating her to a view unlike any she'd ever dreamed.

"Goddess protect me," she breathed, then muttered an extra prayer to the Christian god as she flexed her wings free. Considering the madness of what she would soon be landing in the midst of, she assumed she could use a variety of divine assistance.

Ignoring the voice that insisted she was leaping to her death, Rose jumped, bursting through the remaining plaster. She plummeted downward, using her wings only to break her fall. The moment her feet hit the center of a strange symbol etched on the floor, she drew the attention of every creature in the room—the shocked gazes of hollow-eyed ogres, the onyx glare of a man she could only assume to be the dark elf, and the fiery blaze of a woman with hair of pure flame that rose several feet above her head.

No matter what Ambrose had said, Rose wasn't ruling out demons, not when the floor was littered with tiny red bodies writhing at the feet of the burning woman, a woman who bore a striking resemblance to a friend . . . if she had recently returned from the fires of hell.

CHAPTER TWENTY-TWO

"Well then, isn't this unexpected?" The Svartalfar's voice was as dark as the rest of him, a throaty rumble that spoke of places deep beneath the earth, places where the air was unfit for breathing and anything human would quickly perish.

The elf stood at the far side of the room, near a fireplace twenty feet tall. He was at least eight feet in height and more thickly muscled even than Ambrose, with deep green skin so dark it was nearly black. It shone like the hard covering of an insect, reflecting the light of the fire. His eyes, however, made their own flame, glowing bright red as they peered out behind raven hair that flowed all the way to the floor.

Beside him stood what had once been Marta, though only the Goddess knew what she'd become. She was nude, her pale skin glowing orange and red from the combined light of the roaring fire behind her and the flames that now served as her hair. At her feet writhed dozens of small, dog-sized creatures with the bright pink skin of newborn rats. Rose didn't know what they were, only that they were repulsive in the extreme. Gorge rose in her throat as she watched their bodies churn over and around each other, every so often treating her to a view of their bulbous eyes and wide mouths.

Marta's countenance wasn't any more pleasant to behold. Her once gentle face was filled with an ancient hatred, a fury that burned in the depths of her eyes. The hiss that sounded from her mouth as she met Rose's gaze was nothing short of menacing, inspiring the instinctive urge to back away, though there was nowhere to run.

Rose couldn't believe the gentle sprite still inhabited that body. Something else had taken her over, something not of the earth.

"Your royal highness." The Svartalfar bowed in a courtly fashion. "It's a pleasure to make your acquaintance."

"I am no royal, sir." Rose held her sword aloft, but none of the assembled company advanced. Not the dazed ogres kneeling in a circle around her, nor the armed guards she could see positioned at the top of the steps leading down into the ballroom. "And I assure you, there will be nothing pleasant about our brief acquaintance."

"Oh, you mean to leave so soon?"

"No, sir, I mean to kill you," Rose said, mocking his cordial tone.

"Master, shall we take her?" The voice came from the traitor who had led the invasion of Knebfield House, though now the Fey's eyes were as black as his master's. He and the others on the stairs behind him had no doubt used glamour to conceal the evidence of their Svartalfar blood.

"No, Tempest. I am pleased to take care of our guest. I am Ecanthar, your host this evening, and I'm so pleased you've been able to join us." He smiled a wicked grin that left no doubt he was the source of the evil throbbing through the mansion like poison through the blood. "What is a royal ball, after all, without an eligible princess in attendance?"

"I have not been a princess, eligible or otherwise, for many years," Rose said. "I am Lady Shenley now, though you may call me Rose if you'd like. I extend that privilege to all I mean to kill."

The dark elf laughed. "Yes, that's correct. You married beneath you, so I hear." He moved slowly down the steps in front of the fire, and practically floated across the blindingly white tiles of the ballroom floor. "Such a loss. Royal blood courses through your veins, and yet you've been reduced to a lowly countess."

"I've been a Comtesse of France for many years," Rose said, grateful when he stopped several feet outside the circle. If the ogres were to attack, perhaps she could manage to escape any further conversation with the creature.

But even the mention of the title she'd stolen from Benoit de Fournier aroused no response in the tribesmen and women. They remained slack jawed and unresponsive, making Rose suspect they'd been entranced.

"But the French do things a bit differently, don't they? Passing title along with property, requiring a certain degree of wealth?"

Rose shook her head, unable to believe the man wished to discuss status and rank in the midst of this carnival of terror. The markings on the ground below Rose's feet were demon runes, if she wasn't mistaken, traced in blood. Whatever business he was about, there was more than her death or the raising of an ancient ogre at stake. He was communing with the demon realms. She hadn't been mistaken on that account, no matter what Ambrose had discovered.

"Tell me, have you ever been to the court in Paris? I've heard it is quite a sinful and decadent place, dedicated to the pleasures of the flesh," he said, running his hands down the front of his body. He seemed to take great delight in his touch, if the stirring beneath his skintight breeches was any indication. Rose's skin crawled.

"What are you about, Ecanthar? I don't have time for idle conversation. What have you done with my husband?"

"Your manners are absolutely appalling. Aren't they, dearest?" The creature that had once been Marta howled, the agonized sound Rose had heard before. Far from a wail of pain, however, the cry seemed to be a call for blood to be spilled. *Her* blood. Terror trickled along Rose's spine, following the damp furrows of her own perspiration.

It was burning hot in the room, as if hell itself had been invited to the ball. The air rippled and waved, thick from the heat, and her head swam for a dizzy moment. Rose blinked beads of moisture away from her eyes, took a deep breath, and struggled to remain calm though her stomach cramped with the need to empty itself. Whatever the little beasties at Marta's feet were, they smelled wretched. Each wave of heat from the fireplace carried the stench toward her, until she was hard pressed not to faint.

"I will ask once more," Rose warned. "What have you—"

She screamed as Ecanthar's hands suddenly gripped her shoulders from behind. She'd never seen any but an ancient vampire move with that kind of speed. He was simply before her one instant and behind her the next. She nearly dropped her sword in shock.

"Is he *truly* your husband? Have you consummated the marriage?" He pulled Rose closer, until the full length of her back was pressed against him. "Is your womb ripe with his child?"

"Remove your—"

"Answer me."

"You contemptible—"

"Answer me!" The elf's hands tightened on her shoulders until the pain made her cry out. "I *will* have an answer!"

"Yes . . . but there is no child," Rose said reluctantly. "Now release me." She tried to step away, but he tugged her more tightly to him, until she could feel the thick, hard length of his arousal pressed between her shoulders.

Rose only barely suppressed a hysterical laugh. In her mind she heard Gareth's voice jesting about thrusting between her breasts. This man could truly do the deed, but that would be the only place she could take him. He was obscenely large, and would break her body if he attempted to force himself upon her.

She vowed to cut off the oak limb in question before she allowed that to happen.

"Release me, this instant or I'll—"

"What will you do, little scourge? *What?*" His voice was no longer an excellent imitation of a member of the peerage, but a raw, growling sound that made it difficult to decipher his words.

"I'll—"

"You'll do nothing!" His scream was pure terror, a shout Rose feared would shatter something vital to her frail mortal life.

She shivered against her will, and barely swallowed a small, frightened sound before it made its way past her lips. The ogres surrounding them moaned low in their throats and then slowly, one by one, began to chant once more, as if urged to action by some unseen conductor. The sound filled the great hall, and soon Marta's unearthly wails soared above them, a mournful keening that sent a bolt of pain shooting through Rose's already overheated brain.

Her sword was still in her hand and for a moment she thought to shift her feet to the left and bring it up between the legs of the man behind her. Surely he would no longer be capable of intimidation if bleeding freely from his stick and stones. A part of her took great pleasure in the thought, but for some reason she couldn't force her legs to move. A test of her arms found them to be in the same state.

It was as if her body had turned to stone—not the cool marble of a statue, but the soft liquid of molten rock. Her bones were melting, her skin becoming a fiery prison she would have given much to escape.

"Do not fight me, my sister. You have not the

magic nor skill to free yourself. You're as weak and pitiable as any mortal." Ecanthar's breath was hot and moist against the top of her head. If Rose had been capable, she would have shuddered in disgust, but even that small movement was denied her. "And I'll have you know, your husband was even easier to catch. He walked into my home and shook my hand, foolishly pleased to be spared a trip to Paris."

"What have you done with him? Where is he?" Rose asked, grateful to find her lips still capable of movement.

"His blood is serving its purpose, or rather *your* blood. Lord Shenley fed from none other than your own sweet self for several days. It must be true love indeed." He laughed and Rose wished more than anything she had cut him when she had the chance. "What do you think, sister? Do you think the vampire loved you? Or was he simply looking for a way back into Faerie?"

"Have you killed him?" she asked, her voice thankfully not betraying her despair at the thought.

"How very Fey of you, to answer a question with a question." His hands slid under her shirt until his cold fingers were inches from her breasts. "It reveals the true depths of your ignorance."

"Perhaps I *am* ignorant, but I know the Fey have discovered your treachery. The vampires as well. It's only a matter of time until they arrive—"

"Yes, yes," he said, obviously unimpressed with her threat. "But did you know this? Your dear husband was only a few short months away from certain death." His hands moved even lower, until his fingertips brushed against her nipples.

"Vampires are immortal, Ecanthar." Rose forced herself to ignore the intimate touch, to appear as unaffected as possible. "I've lived among supernaturals for one hundred years. I'm not as ignorant as you might think."

"But you've never *known* a dark elf, have you, sister?"

The way he emphasized "known" made it clear he meant in the biblical sense, so Rose declined to answer. Instead she stared at Marta, trying to understand what she'd become and if the frightening state was catching. Rose certainly felt hot enough for her hair to catch flame any moment. Even the waves of heat from the fireplace were a welcome relief, cool to her burning face. She wasn't long for the world if this torment continued. The fever would consume her.

"Release me, please," Rose finally begged, knowing her knees would have buckled if she weren't frozen in place.

"Yes, begging is good," he said, as the heat abated a bit. "Your husband begged for his life as well, ready to have you take his place if I'd allowed it. Sadly, there was no time to spare."

"You lie."

"You truly haven't known any Svartalfar." He laughed and let his fingers trace across her skin. "I cannot lie, not as your dear husband could. But then, a man nearing death will—"

"He wasn't near death." Her head swam with the effort it took to keep talking, but she forced the words out. Something within her insisted that speaking was imperative, that to abandon the ability would force her even further under the black elf's control.

"Lord Shenley never went to the Otherworld, never walked in the sun of the Fey villages. His mother was an exile, and her son cursed for the sin of having such a parent. Without the infusion of life gained from visiting the faerie lands his mother died, and your husband would have followed on his two-hundredth birthday."

"That isn't true," she said, though a hint of doubt penetrated the fog in her mind.

"Lord Shenley required a faerie connection, ties to one who could take him to the lands beyond and save his wretched life." Ecanthar found the stone beneath Rose's shirt and lifted it slowly to the light. Flame danced across the smooth surface of the obsidian rock. "He thought you were his salvation—though he hadn't told you, had he?"

Rose didn't answer right away. She let her eyes play about the room, searching for a sign of Ambrose or the Fey de la Nuit forces he'd sworn were coming to their aid. If she could keep Ecanthar distracted for just a bit longer, surely they would come to the rescue. They'd circumvent the wards by discovering another way into the ballroom. They had to. She wasn't the only one clever enough to find an alternate entry.

"Tell me, sister, it's all right," the elf cooed, his continued reference to her as his kin turning her already fitful stomach.

"No, he hadn't." Rose spoke slowly, though her thoughts raced with quiet desperation. Where was Ambrose? Where was Gareth? Why was Ecanthar toying with her? What could he possibly have to gain?

"A pity. Honesty should be a matter of course between two who are wed, don't you agree?" He dropped the stone and leaned nearly double to whisper against Rose's cheek, his lips moving on her skin as if it would aid his communication.

Gorge rose in her throat, and she wished she was able to move away. Even if she couldn't fight, if she could simply pull his skin from hers, she knew she would feel infinitely better.

"I've promised the ogres your death, but we might still convince them to see reason," he whispered. "What say you? What sacrifices would you make to ensure your survival?"

"You'll kill us all if you raise your giant from the ground. Have you shared this news with the tribe?" Rose spoke as loudly as she was able, but the ogres didn't seem to hear. Despair threatened once more, but she fought against it, struggled to hold onto the hope of salvation for her husband, no matter what Ecanthar accused him of.

She had seen into Gareth's heart. His care for her was real, his love for her as true a thing as she'd ever felt. The dark elf's story might be correct, but the betrayal he intimated was purely fiction.

"You know of brother Alvar, then. Lovely." He sounded as though he considered the news wonderful. "But he's not the only kin we will welcome here this night. You've already made the acquaintance of my son, the baronet."

He spun Rose slowly in a circle, granting her a brief respite from the heat and stench flowing from the fire. At the other end of the ballroom sat a banquet table she hadn't seen before she leapt into the hall.

The table was laid with a lavish repast, and practically groaned with the weight of the heavy, silver serving dishes sitting upon it. In chairs along the table sat Pithwater and Pithwater and ... Pithwater. Every head that turned to gaze upon her, every pair of lips that stretched in a friendly smile, they were all the baronet. A full dozen of him, who raised their hands in identical greetings and cordial "hellos," as though they were meeting at a Society function.

"Goddess," Rose muttered. She'd never seen anything like it in all her years wandering among the supernaturals.

"Say hello, sister, and drop a curtsy. Mustn't be rude," Ecanthar said, his delight in her shock apparent. His fingers moved lightly on her shoulders and she found herself curtsying against her will.

"He's become a bit of a simpleton since three parts of him were slain, but he is a dear boy," Ecanthar continued in a whisper. "He proved quite useful in your capture."

"You didn't capture me and neither did ... they," Rose said, struggling over what to call a man who seemed to be contained in so many different bodies. "I came here of my own free will, to defend my husband's life."

"Your *husband*. If I hear one more word of your husband I shall scream." Rose flinched as he released her shoulders and fisted a rough hand in her hair. "Perhaps meeting the rest of the family will distract you from your single-minded course."

He dragged her across the room, stopping in front of a female ogre who didn't look familiar. She was prettier than the average tribeswoman, possessed of light mocha skin that glowed warmly in the firelight.

She would have almost been attractive by human standards if her shell had been animated by a soul. But the light of intelligence, reason, and emotion was absent from the eyes she lifted slowly to meet Ecanthar's. Her mouth hung open, revealing the many rows of her teeth.

"Cecilia is my ogre bride," Ecanthar said, sounding proud to make the introduction. "I'd hoped that together we might conceive another giant after I came into possession of seeds from the Great Mother's body. It was, after all, the rape of the Great Mother by a demon that created Alvar, his sister, and all their ogre descendants."

Rose swallowed another surge of bile as Ecanthar resumed caressing her body, certain he must be wrong. The Great Mother had been dead since the earliest days of the earth. No one knew the location of her grave, or even if she'd been a real woman at all, and not simply a way of describing the forces that had given birth to the first supernaturals. But even if she'd been flesh and blood, her body would have long since turned to dust.

"My Cecilia was only too willing to take those seeds within her womb and lay with me in my demon form as we sought to give birth to our new world. Isn't that so, my dear?"

Cecilia made a choking sound low in her throat but didn't move, or show any sign of having heard her "husband." Obviously there was no love for the man in her heart or what was left of her mind. Ecanthar was mad if he assumed the ogre a willing mate. But then, he was clearly out of his mind. Combined with his speed, obvious power, and magical strength, that fact made him the most dangerous creature she had ever confronted.

"Alas, the experiment was unsuccessful. When the birth pains hit her, there was no way for the child to be born. She was far too small. I attempted to open her to facilitate the babe's passage, but it was too late. The boy had already split into pieces." Ecanthar shook his head sadly, but then looked down at Rose with a small smile. "But Pithwater's served my purposes better than I ever thought he could. A son who can walk in the sun and die many times over for his sire is valuable offspring indeed."

"And what of your wife?" Rose asked, closing her eyes against the horror of what he'd done. "She is a broken thing."

"Cecilia is *honored* to be my bride," he growled, forcing Rose to look at him by tugging fiercely at her hair. "She survived through my magic alone. Without it, the damage from our son's birth would have destroyed her. The wounds where I worked my knife were too deep to be survived."

"Your mind is out of order, sir," Rose said, doing her best not to look toward the ceiling. She was certain she had glimpsed movement there, but she couldn't draw attention to the fact. The element of surprise was the best and perhaps *only* weapon against a monster with such speed and strength.

Rose prayed that it was Ambrose she had seen, and that his comrades among the dark faeries were not far behind him.

"No, *your* mind is out of order, dear sister. You are

blinded by your mortal upbringing." Ecanthar smiled. Deep within the onyx of his eyes Rose saw the reflection of her frightened face, as if he'd already swallowed her whole. "But that is something that can be remedied."

His hand gentled in her hair and for a split second Rose felt a wave of desire flood through her. But the passion was tainted with disgust and terror. Even as lust tugged low in her belly, gorge rose in her throat, as if her body would force the alien need out through her mouth.

"You repulse me." She spat at him, full in the face.

For a moment, she feared he would break her. The howl that sounded from his throat was unspeakably angry. Marta mimicked the sound, and Rose joined in a second later as Ecanthar picked her up by her hair and strode across the room toward the fire.

Thankfully, he stopped at the foot of the stair and set Rose back on her feet, shaking her like a dog with a rat in its mouth. She didn't know whether to be relieved or terrified. Death by fire would be unspeakable, but whatever else Ecanthar had planned would most likely be worse.

"You know Marta, my sprite bride. I allowed her to return to you for a time, hoping she would lead me to your hidden home. But sadly, she was unable to aid my cause," Ecanthar growled, his voice still not recovering its human-sounding veneer. "I was forced to contact the trolls through the enchanted waters to find your precise location."

"She's not your bride. You kidnapped her and—"

"She *willingly* gave herself to me in hopes of a child," Ecanthar said and Rose knew in that moment that he was telling the truth. If he'd promised her a child, Marta would have done almost anything, even bed a monster. "And I've granted her wish, as you can see. We have a fine brood and will no doubt breed many more before our years together are through."

One of the creatures squirming about Marta's feet was dislodged from the pile, and rolled to a stop on Ecanthar's boot. He nudged the squirming monster affectionately, urging it toward Rose. "Here, sister, greet the little one."

Rose screamed, a wild sound that came from her very core as the thing lunged at her leg, attempting to sink its small fangs into her flesh. Perhaps it was that terror that finally gave her the strength she needed to move. She kicked at the beast, sending it back to its brothers, and lifted her sword, only to have it plucked from her hands a moment later and hurled across the room.

Ecanthar tugged her close to him once more, and a part of her was grateful for it. He was cool to the touch, a small mercy to skin that felt close to bursting into flame.

"Naughty girl. I will expect better of you with *our* children. A mother must learn to nurture her young," he said, indulgently, as he petted her hair away from her face. "I know our offspring will be extraordinary, no matter which of their parents they favor."

He leaned his face toward hers. For the first time Rose noticed the small fangs in his mouth, and watched them grow longer as his gaze roved over her body. This was the face from Marta's nightmares, the blood man who'd betrayed the Fey. Not a vampire at all.

She wondered if she'd live to share that news,

considering the next line of the prophecy swore the scourge would be no more.

No, you're no longer the scourge. You're free of the contract you—

Ecanthar interrupted the voice in her mind, words that seemed to come from somewhere outside herself, though she was too befuddled to be sure. "Our children will be powerful beyond imagining, creatures unlike anything the world has known. I'm certain of it, sweet sister."

"I am not your sister, and I won't have you," Rose panted, dizzy from the heat. "I won't!"

"But you will, my dear." He moved one large hand down to her ass and cupped her flesh appreciatively. "You'll bear sons well, I believe. Your hips are wide, though you are small. And I will teach you to shift your form, if needed. It is an easier magic than one would think."

"I'll kill myself first." Her voice rose hysterically as she fought against the blackness that teased the edges of her vision. She was close to fainting. If she did, there would be no way to fight him, to keep him from claiming her while she slept, as another had done before him.

The thought made Rose scream, a howl of rage she directed straight into his wretched face.

"Calm yourself. There's no need to fear. You are no river sprite. Your lovely blond locks will not turn to ribbons of flame. It is simply that Svartalfar magic is tied to water and flesh. When Marta and I mated in this form I had no idea the effects would be so . . . severe." He looked over at Marta and smiled with a fondness that chilled Rose as profoundly as his anger had. "Still, she is lovely. A fitting bride for the new world. A queen."

"There will be no new world . . . You'll be . . ." Rose's lashes fluttered and her eyes burned as perspiration flowed down her brow. Her knees bent and she sagged in Ecanthar's arms, only held up by the hands that gripped her bottom and neck.

"When Alvar rises, he'll break the last barrier between the flames of the Svartalfar kingdom and the human world. Ecanthar worked centuries to dig so close to the surface, sold his own people to the lesser demons in exchange for their aid. It would be a shame to waste such sacrifice."

Rose felt hopeless tears begin to stream down her face. Now Ecanthar talked of himself as if he were another being entirely. Such madness couldn't be reasoned with.

"The demon fires are burning, and will bear a smoke that will cover the earth in darkness. In that darkness demons will rule and the black elves and their wives will finally walk above the earth, earning a place of honor among those who survive our endless night."

He lifted Rose in his arms and turned her to face the flames. Behind them, she thought she saw the shadows of men. No . . . of elves. There were more of them, hundreds more, *thousands*.

"They'll be free of the yoke of demon slavery when the magic is done." Ecanthar pressed a soft kiss to her forehead. Rose wasn't strong enough to fight the sick desire that flowed along her skin in response.

"And I'll play the part of their king for as long as it amuses me. Now it's only for you to decide if you will be one of my queens."

"No." Her whisper was so soft, Rose could barely hear it herself.

"Don't worry, sister. *She* will not survive the coming night. The demons will roam the earth, destroying her power forever, and you and I . . ." he pressed another kiss on her cheek, "will finally be free."

Rose's eyes slid closed and she felt her mind soften. She could no longer make sense of the madman's ravings. Perhaps she was dying. Even that seemed preferable to being Ecanthar's bride, to bearing his monstrous children.

"Your blood is falling into the waters of the Thames as we speak. Only the blood of a female of our line could raise our brother, you know. All the blood magic in the world wouldn't have accomplished this great act without you, Rose. And I am grateful. So I give you the chance to become my bride. Join with me and I'll teach you the secrets of the Great Mother's magic, the greatest power the world has ever known."

Rose whimpered in protest, a small sound lost to the roar of the flames.

"Don't answer just yet. Let us have a kiss first." Rose felt his lips on hers, as though one part of her body was submerged in ice while the other was set aflame.

She would have screamed if she were able, but when she opened her mouth his tongue slid inside and the torment increased. She was being burned and frozen at the same time, consumed by a pain stronger than anything she'd ever known. In seconds, her mind shut down, and she sank into the black velvet of unconsciousness, welcoming oblivion with open arms.

CHAPTER TWENTY-THREE

Rose awoke with a gasp, as if surfacing from too long underwater, but didn't possess the strength to open her eyes. Or perhaps she simply felt too wonderful to open her eyes and risk that the bliss vibrating through her was merely a dream. It had to be a dream, there was no other possible explanation. But Goddess . . . what a dream it was.

She was being kissed, but immediately knew it wasn't Ecanthar who claimed her lips. No, the arms cradling her were achingly familiar, as was the smell of this man—cloves and rain and the first herbs of springtime. Surprisingly, however, his kiss was not immediately recognizable.

Not that it mattered. Nothing mattered as long as she could remain lost in him, in the feel of his strong arms holding her tight, in the caress of the lips that demanded her complete submission.

"Open to me," he ordered in a soft whisper and she

did, parting her lips, meeting the expert sweep of his tongue with her own.

Rose moaned and pressed closer, moving her limp arms to wrap around his neck. The fire and ice were gone, replaced by a warmth, a *rightness* she felt in every fiber of her being. Desire rose, a fierce wave that surged to the surface of her skin, a bright celebration of life after feeling so close to death. Her breasts were heavy and full, aching to be touched.

"Yes . . ." she murmured as he pulled her to him, angling his mouth until they couldn't get any closer without crawling inside one another's skin.

She kept her eyes closed and funneled all of her need, all of her passion into the kiss, close to finding release simply from that blissful contact. He groaned in response, and shuddered slightly before he shifted her in his arms, not breaking the contact of their mouths for a moment. Her legs were urged apart and she felt a thick, male thigh between them. Rose straddled him eagerly, rocking on his muscled flesh as the kiss grew feverish, wild.

Her shirt gaped open of its own accord and his hands were suddenly on her breasts. She gasped and squeezed her eyes even more tightly shut as he cupped her heated skin and captured her nipples in his calloused fingers. The tension gathering low in her belly, thick and hot between her thighs, built impossibly further as he manipulated her body with a touch that was pure magic.

A magic she felt surrounding them, shining brighter and brighter until golden lights danced behind her eyes. Her hips moved faster, grinding into him with a shamelessness that spoke of how desperately he made her want, yearn, ache for the pleasure she knew only he could give.

She had never felt anything like this, never felt such pure lust crashing over her body, banishing every thought but getting closer, moving faster, riding his leg, his cock, his hand, whatever this man would use to bring her over the edge. She was wild with it, intoxicated by him, and it wasn't long before she realized the soft, desperate moans that echoed through the glittering light surrounding them were her own.

"Yes, Rosemarie. Yes, love," he mumbled against her mouth as he pinched her nipples with the perfect, nearly painful pressure.

Rose's body obeyed without a second's hesitation, even as her mind finally realized the identity of her dream lover.

"Ambrose!" She called his name as her eyes flew open, meeting his only a few inches away. His features were twisted with passion, his breath coming faster as he watched pleasure claim her.

Rose continued to rock against him, riding her release to the very end, milking every last bit of magic and bliss from the sensual explosion, no matter that a part of her swore she was wicked for doing so. She was a married woman. She loathed Ambrose as much as she loved him, and he had certainly waited long enough to come to her aid in Ecanthar's ballroom.

Ecanthar's ballroom . . . Where was the ballroom?

A swift look revealed she and Ambrose were on a thick rug before a fire, nestled in a small chamber that was at once strange and yet incredibly familiar. There was no sign of Ecanthar, his guards, or the ogres, only two chairs with pale pink upholstery, shot through with threads of bright green and—

"In my *mind,* we're in my mind," Rose said, turning back to Ambrose, her breath catching as she realized their lips were still nearly close enough to touch.

"We are." His silver eyes flashed. "But we must leave now, if you're strong enough to return. Gareth still lives, but—"

"Let's go. Now. There is no—" Before she could finish her thought, the room flooded with a radiance that blinded her, forcing her to squeeze her eyes tight against the glare. As soon as her eyes closed, she experienced the sensation of falling, tumbling through space to land back in her corporeal body with a jarring thud.

Rose's lids flew open, and she gasped, finding no pleasure in her material form, only ribbons of pain that lashed across her skin. She lay on her back, Ambrose above her, a concerned look in his eye and a deep gash down the side of his handsome face. Her fingers reached toward the bloodied flesh at his cheek, but flinched away as the sounds of nearby battle met her ears, shocking her fully back to reality.

"My sword, where is it?" She bolted upright with a groan, ready to fight, though grateful they appeared to be at some distance from the worst of the battle. Her muscles ached, and her joints felt every one of their nearly two hundred years.

"I retrieved it from the floor," Ambrose said, handing her the sword and helping her to her feet. "I'm sorry, Rosemarie. We were detained outside the ballroom. The black elf's forces are greater than we feared and could not be swayed to lay down their arms. I stayed to fight, but I should have sought you out, should never have—"

"Never mind that now, we must help them. The battle isn't won." Rose tried to move around him, the sight of the Fey deep in battle with what remained of Encanthar's guard and the black elf himself banishing her confusion and shame.

"There's no need for shame." Ambrose pulled her back to him, leaning down to catch her eye though his attention remained split between her and the bloodshed. "Ecanthar sought to bind you to him, putting some dark magic to work within you. It had to be removed. Binding you with my own magic was the only way I could—"

"Ambrose, this isn't the time," Rose said, not wanting to think about his words. Bonds of magic between the Fey were as serious as marriage vows among humans, but she couldn't allow her focus to be divided. "We must find Gareth."

"I'll find him. You must transport yourself to the Fey lands. You cannot fight."

"I can fight, and I will. There aren't enough of you, Ambrose, you need my—"

"You owe us nothing, Rose. You're no longer an executioner, your contract with the Fey de la Nuit was rendered null and void by the fulfillment—"

"Damn the contract. You're my friend, and you just saved my life," she said, knowing that had to be the only explanation for falling asleep in Ecanthar's arms and waking up to Ambrose. She wasn't certain what their bond would mean for the future, but it certainly felt better to be filled with golden bubbles than the mind-destroying poison of the black elf's power. "I won't watch you fight and not raise my own sword."

"Rose." He only said her name, but the word held more meaning than she knew what to do with. He reached out and cupped her cheek in his hand, making her heart twist in her chest.

She still loved him as much as she ever had, as much as she always would, no matter that she loved Gareth as well. It was a more complicated love, a painful love, but powerful nonetheless. Ambrose felt the same, she read it clearly in those gray eyes. They were a hopeless pair, but that didn't make the sentiment any less true.

Amazing the perspective to be gained after nearly dying in a monster's arms.

"We must fight," Rose said, her voice stronger than she truly felt.

"Are you certain? Your skin was on fire only a few minutes ago."

"I feel well enough." Rose pressed her lips softly to the palm of his hand before stepping away. "Never fear, I'll seek sanctuary rather than risk falling into Ecanthar's hands again, I assure you of that."

"Then we fight. The clock strikes three, and there's little time to spare." He drew his sword. "Guard yourself well, Rosemarie," he added, before turning to the center of the room.

There Ecanthar and the two remaining members of his guard battled ten of the Fey de la Nuit warriors, men who were all nearly as large as Ambrose and possessed of the same strength and magic. Still, even outmatched, Ecanthar held his ground, wounding first one and then another of the Fey until they pulled back, widening the circle they formed around him. His own wounds bled freely, however, and he no longer moved with the same dizzying speed. If the Fey held strong, they would defeat him and the last of his protectors. It would serve no purpose to join the battle there. She'd simply be in the way, a slow moving quarter Fey.

But in the killing of ogres she could still prove herself useful. She turned, and found them near the banquet table . . . or rather what remained of them. Two Fey warriors fought the remaining ogres, though it looked as if they neared the end of their task. The tribe members who had chanted the elf's spell had been slain, one and all, their blood spilled thick and black across the white tile. No doubt they'd been easy prey in their weakened state.

The many Pithwaters also lay strewn about in pieces. The taller Fey fighter slashed the final two into halves while they sat eating at the table, as oblivious to their fate as insects beneath a gentleman's shoe. Rose was glad that this time there would be no resurrection for Pithwater. Not that there ever had been before.

"Not that there ever had been before," she repeated beneath her breath, certain now that Ambrose was correct. Pithwater wasn't the son who would rise.

It was Alvar the giant, the Great Mother's son, who would be summoned from his rest under the River Thames. Whatever black work Ecanthar had been about here, Rose sensed that the most damning spell was being cast near the water. That was where Gareth would be found. She would stake her life on it.

As Rose ran toward the steps leading out of the

ballroom, she realized she might be doing just that. There was no chance she could free Gareth from hundreds of ogres without aid, but the Fey de la Nuit were otherwise occupied. She was his only hope. She had to at least attempt a rescue, trusting that Ambrose and his warriors would send Ecanthar back to his realm beneath the earth.

She'd nearly reached a set of large, silver doors, ones she hoped would open into the foyer, and from there out to the street, when Marta wailed. Rose cried out and fell to her knees, dropping her sword in her haste to cover her ears. From behind her she heard other cries, and the metallic clanging of steel hitting the floor.

Spinning around, Rose watched as one after another the Fey succumbed to the horrid noise. With their incredibly sensitive hearing, the pain must be even more excruciating. Even with human ears, she was half willing to claw her flesh from her head if it would end the torment.

Marta, no! Marta, please!

Rose begged the sprite with a mental scream, not knowing if Marta was even capable of hearing her, but knowing she had to try. If there was any shred of the gentle soul she had known still within Marta, she wouldn't doom the earth to despair. Marta honored the Goddess, most especially her water aspect. She wouldn't wish to see the rivers polluted by black soot, the oceans and streams laid to waste as hellfire moved over the earth, burning everything in its path, turning the planet into a desert wasteland where water would be the stuff of faerie stories, told to the monstrous babes who—

They are not monstrous. They are my children! Marta's voice, her *true* voice, sounded in Rose's mind. Her shrieking came to a stop, but she didn't turn to look at Rose. She remained by the fire, her eyes staring into the flames as her children continued to writhe at her feet.

In seconds the Fey were back at the fight, pulling Ecanthar off the man he'd leapt upon in their moment of distraction and killing the last of his remaining guards. But Rose kept her attention on Marta, on the connection between their minds. Marta had heard Rose's thoughts, seen the desperate, hopeless future they faced if Ecanthar were to succeed. Perhaps she wasn't unreachable, no matter what control Ecanthar had over her.

I'm sorry, Marta. I know how you've always valued the lives of young ones.

These are not merely young ones. These are mine. *They came from me, born of my pain as I labored, my insides aflame with a fire I begged him to quench.* The haunted quality of her tone made Rose shudder, her heart aching for the poor sprite. *I begged him for death, but he wouldn't deliver it.*

Begged whom, Marta? Rose asked gently, knowing she must tread carefully with her friend. She'd endured unspeakable horror, and Rose wished to cause her no further pain. *Who did you beg for death?*

They are my babes, they feed from my skin, suckle as real babes would, she said, a note of hysteria in her tone. *You shant take them from me, you shant slay them as you slayed the others! He warned me, he told me—*

They are yours, dear friend. I won't harm your

children. I swear it to you. I ask only that you tell me who it was you begged to quench the flames.

Him . . . the man . . . the black elf. Her voice was a whisper now, as if she told a secret she knew she oughtn't. Rose could feel her fear like a physical caress and shivered. She knew that fear, had felt it threatening to overwhelm her from the moment Ecanthar laid hands upon her.

Is he your husband? The black elf? Rose whispered. *Did you choose him, dearest?*

No . . . not my husband. I . . . He promised me a child . . .

And you lay with him, but didn't promise yourself to him, didn't speak vows to bind him to you? Rose prompted, feeling Marta pull away from the connection between them for a moment before she turned her head, making eye contact across the great room.

Even at a distance of some fifty feet, Rose could see the change in her aspect. The flames still rose from her head, but her eyes were softer, almost human looking. Her mind reached out to Rose's once more, the connection washing over her like a wave, stealing her breath with its intensity.

Rose, you truly are here! She sounded like the old Marta, the one who would wake her if she overslept and chide her for not dressing as fashionably as she should. Rose practically wept with relief. It wasn't too late. There was still a chance she could be returned to herself.

Yes, I am. We will free you, Marta. The Fey de la Nuit are fighting the black elf, and they will be victorious. Rose let her eyes slide over to the battle, pleased to see it looked as though her comforting words would prove true. Ecanthar was faltering, and soon the Fey warriors would overcome him. *When he is slain, we will find a way to rid you of his magic.*

His magic? I don't . . . I don't understand. She shook her head in confusion, but that very action seemed to stir awareness within her. Slowly, she reached up to touch her hair and pulled her fingers away with a terrified gasp. *My hair, dear Goddess, what has—*

Don't worry, dearest. He has bespelled you. But you have sworn no vows. Without them he cannot—

No, oh no. No, no, no. The flames on her head grew even higher as she shook her head back and forth and her eyes turned toward her feet. Rose could feel her horror, her shock, and knew in that moment that Ecanthar had prevented her from seeing the true appearance of her children. *Goddess, no. No!*

Marta, it will be all right.

Marta screamed, but it wasn't the unearthly howl of before. It was a woman's scream, a mother's tortured wail.

No, oh Goddess, no. Please, no. Her shoulders shook as sobs racked her thin frame. She didn't want this knowledge, didn't want to see the truth. She didn't want to know she'd given birth to stinking, wretched beasts, creatures who had marked her legs with their fangs as they drew her blood again and again until her flesh was torn and savaged, filled with rot and disease.

But now that she saw clearly, there was no choice but to kill them, to kill herself, to rid the world of such abominations. To force the hellfire that burned within her back where it—

No! Rose screamed as she realized the direction of the Marta's thoughts. *Ambrose can help you, Marta. Please!*

"No!" Rose screamed aloud as Marta tilted back her head, letting the flames move from her hair to her face. The rest of her body was engulfed in seconds.

The howls of her children filled the air as they burned, underscored by the low, deep cry of Marta herself. She was chanting something, ancient words Rose had never heard before and couldn't comprehend through her sobs. So close, Marta had been *so close* to salvation. To see her burn was desperately horrid, a waste of a gentle soul.

The room instantly cooled as Marta turned and leapt into the flames of the fireplace and disappeared. The fire died a swift death and when the smoke cleared only stones could be seen at the back of the hearth. The portal to the underworld had closed.

The blood of the maid had burned, sending hellfire back to its depths.

Rose wept softly, tears rolling down her face even as she struggled to her feet. Marta was gone, but Gareth might yet live. She had to get to the river, to find him before it was too late.

If it wasn't too late already.

"Rosemarie!" She turned to see Ambrose and two other Fey rush up the steps. Ambrose healed the cut on his face and another on his shoulder with a wave of his hand as he closed the distance between them. "Dolar, Cian, and I will come with you. The others will join us when they've completed their work."

Behind him swords swung, though there was no longer any battle to be fought. Now they worked only to sever the limbs and head of Ecanthar. The Fey had been victorious, though not soon enough to save dear Marta. Goddess, Rose would have rushed to join the Fey in chopping at the monster if there was time. If she could have brought him back to life and killed him again, she would have done that as well. He deserved to die a thousand times for what he'd—

"He still lives." Rose jumped as an anguished groan sounded from the pile of bloodied flesh and bone beneath the Fey swords.

"As long as his magic fills the Thames he can't be sent back to the underworld or killed by anything but the light of the sun. They will cut him into pieces and fly them to the roof, securing him there to await the light of day," Ambrose said as he raced up the steps.

"Hopefully we'll have rescued Gareth before then," she said, following the three men out the silver doors. "I would dearly love to watch the hand of death claim that monster."

The two other Fey de la Nuit grunted their approval as they burst out onto the street, taking off at a run toward the River Thames. They were covered in blood, carrying swords, and none of them dressed to blend into human Society, but for once Rose didn't care. Thankfully Ambrose did, and muttered the words of an invisibility spell just before they were spotted by a dozen humans descending the steps of the Covington mansion.

"Now we fly. Can you keep pace, Rosemarie?" Ambrose asked.

"I'll try, but if not, press on without me, I will find you." She flexed her wings free of her clothing as the three men did the same. Her wings were much smaller, but she was a great deal smaller than they.

She might be able to keep up. She knew she would try. No matter what she said, she didn't want to be left behind. Didn't want to have to trust the Fey to do all they could to save her husband. She wanted to be there, to do everything in her power to make certain no one else was lost, not if she could prevent it.

THE WESTMINSTER BRIDGE was not yet open to foot traffic or carriages, having many places where the road was not yet complete, but it was perfect for those with wings. It provided places to touch down if necessary, and a direct shot down to Southwark where they suspected the tribe had congregated once again.

Rose prayed they were right, and that they wouldn't be forced to hunt for the ogres' location. If that was so, they would never make it. Church bells across the city struck the quarter hour as they raced onto the bridge. There was no time left. According to the prophecy, order would be restored when the clock struck four, but Rose sensed that would prove true only if they succeeded in their mission.

If she'd learned nothing else tonight, she now knew firsthand the power of individual actions and choices in fulfilling mystic prophecies. Free will was required to restore the order of the world. She only hoped they would have the chance to exercise that will before it was too late.

They were halfway across the river when the ground began to shake again. Rose had never been more grateful for wings as she watched several of the newly constructed pilings crash into the river. If she'd been standing upon them, she would have been lost. This quaking was far worse than what London had endured a month past. Church bells clanged wildly throughout the city, and screams sounded from a tenement near the river's edge as the entire structure sagged into the ground.

"Faster, the creature rises!" Ambrose's voice channeled the urgency they all felt, urging their wings to swifter movement.

The water below her feet churned and for a brief second, amid the confused fish leaping from the swells, Rose caught a glimpse of a massive finger, covered in silt, rising from the waves. It was no sooner there than gone, but if she'd needed any more persuasion to move quickly, that brief glance would have sufficed. Based on that finger, the creature was larger than she could fathom. It wouldn't be merely the homes and people near the river destroyed, but the whole of London itself. They couldn't allow that to happen. They had to stop the spell while the damage could still be contained.

Ambrose and the other warrior Fey pulled ahead, but Rose was no more than one hundred feet behind as they landed on the shore in the midst of the ogres who knelt in the mud, their eyes glazed with the power of the magic they worked. Their desperate chanting filled the air, louder than before, the sound bursting forth from their widely spread mouths. They looked ready to feed, but for the fact that their eyes were closed and their arms limp at their sides, obviously held in thrall by their own spell.

In the water, not far from the foul-smelling shore,

stood the giant ogre who had attacked her and Ambrose a month ago to the day. He was chanting as well, though in a more primitive language. In his arms he held a figure Rose knew had to be her husband, though Gareth looked smaller than she could have imagined.

Pain knifed through her heart as she saw what they had done to him. By the light of the full moon, she beheld what looked to be giant pins pushed deep into his skin. There were dozens of them, as if the ogres had used him as a witch's poppet. It wasn't clear whether he was alive or dead, but as she watched the ogre giant lift him higher into the air, an offering to the beast that shook the ground beneath them, Rose vowed that every member of the tribe soon would be dead.

White-hot rage blinded her for a moment, and when she came back to herself she was flying through the air, straight for the creature, her sword aimed at his black heart. The blade made contact with a thick, sucking sound. The giant screamed, dropping Gareth and reaching for Rose with his large hands. She didn't hold still long enough to be captured, but flew in a swift circle around the beast, slicing him in two, sending his thick blood shooting like a fountain into the equally dark water of the river.

Battle cries sounded from the shore, but she didn't turn back to join the fight as Ambrose and his comrades set upon the ogre ranks. Instead she dove beneath the waves, desperately seeking a flash of white skin. Deeper and deeper she swam, using her wings to move toward what looked like the barest hint of a man's arm lost in the churning water. Her lungs were near to bursting by the time her hands closed around that cold flesh and surged toward the surface. She couldn't see if she held her love or simply another body lost to the Thames until she broke free of the water, carrying Gareth up into the air, higher than she would have thought she had the strength to manage.

The sight of his dear features, slack and pale, gave her the last burst of power she needed to guide them both to the shore. As soon as they collapsed upon it, free from the water, the desperate shaking of the earth came to a stop . . . though the true chaos had only just begun.

From the buildings near the river, people poured out into the street, screaming, praying to whatever gods they worshipped, dragging along children and treasured belongings. They surged onto the city streets as if they could escape disaster simply by fleeing on foot to only the gods knew where.

None of the humans seemed to take note of the Fey warriors who were dispatching the few remaining ogres who hadn't fled into the night. Neither did they stop to stare at the couple at the river's edge, though the woman sobbed loudly as she pulled large pins from the frighteningly still man's skin.

The woman wept as if her heart were breaking, as if all the light had gone out of the world, while she mumbled nonsensical words about order being restored, though humankind ran as if a rabbit from a fox.

EPILOGUE

As far as earthquakes go . . . we have had a second, much more violent than the first. In the night between Wednesday and Thursday last, the earth had a shivering fit between three and four; I thought somebody was getting from under my bed, but soon found it was a strong earthquake that lasted nearly half a minute, with a violent vibration and great roaring.

I got up and found people running into the streets, but saw no mischief done. There has been some; two old houses flung down, several chimneys, and much earthenware . . . Several people are going out of town, for it has nowhere reached above ten miles from London: they say they are not frightened, but that it is such fine weather, "Lord, one can't help going into the country!"

—The Lord of Strawberry Hill
in a letter to Sir Horace Mann

The tribe has sustained losses unlike anything in our long history. The "great benefactor" has proven to be

the great betrayer. Women and children were killed,
their blood coating the rich tiles of his home and the
streets of London. We fled, those who were able,
barely escaping with our lives. Send aid when you
can. I will await word in the south of Spain.

> —*Letter from Adelfieri of the tribe,*
> *to his mother in Venice, intercepted en route by*
> *enforcers of the Fey de la Nuit*

April 16, 1750
Edenburg Keep
The Kingdom of Myrdrean

In the end, Rose decided against tending sheep in the
country. England was tainted for her, for all of them.
The various intrigues of the faeries and vampires had
taken their toll on the supernatural community and
few were certain how long their truce would hold.
Soon the blood men and the Fey might once again be
at war, putting an end to nearly four decades of peace.
That was, of course, if the black elves didn't find another way to bring hell to the surface of the earth beforehand.

Ecanthar had somehow managed to thwart his in-
evitable death. The Fey de la Nuit had secured his
body to the roof of his home before flying to join the
fight on the banks of the River Thames, but when
they returned several hours later, the pieces had disappeared.

The rest of his people had fled so far beneath the
earth that not even the bravest Fey warriors dared
pursue them. A missive from Ecanthar's true wife,

however, now the queen of the Svartalfar, swore her husband had been slain.

According to her tale, he had been killed before her eyes several months past and she herself imprisoned to prevent her from alerting her people of the assassination. Or from telling the strange tale of the creature who'd shifted skin and bone until he bore the exact visage of her dead husband.

The creature who, if the queen told true, could even now be wandering the earth in search of the woman who'd escaped him and the blood he'd sworn he needed to raise the giant Alvar from his watery grave. If there truly was such a being, one who could assume the shape of any creature, it would be impossible for Rose to elude capture for long.

"We'll kill the monster if he dares come near you again," Gareth said, his voice echoing through the newly repaired rafters of Myrdrean castle.

Despite the painful memories she'd unearthed during the last trip to her country, Rose had longed to return home. For the first time in one hundred years, it was possible. Lord and Lady Shenley had eloped and were on their wedding tour, and Rose was no longer an executioner or tied to the Fey in a way that limited her freedom.

"But don't think about those dark things now," Gareth said, limping carefully across the room, joining Rose at the window where she stood watching the sun set over the black forest of her native land. "I wager a flock of harpies ate the wretch's remains and we'll never hear of him again."

"Should you be out of bed, love?" Rose asked. "You must recover your strength."

"I shall recover more swiftly if I find a way to make myself useful. I came to warn you that Ambrose is sulking in his chambers, refusing to come out to welcome the newest villagers to the keep."

Ah yes, Ambrose. She wasn't tied to the Fey in a way that limited her freedom, as of *yet,* but she was most certainly bound to one faerie in particular.

"He is presently the law in Myrdrean. Did you remind him of that fact?" she asked, looping her arm through her husband's to lend her strength to his.

He was still not recovered from the wounds he had sustained. His powerful stride was marked with a limp and his cheeks were hollowed in a way that made Rose fuss over him at supper.

Rose knew she would never again take for granted his health and well-being. The night she'd thought him lost had been the darkest she'd ever known. In the time since, she'd devoted herself to showing him, every day, just how precious he was to her, and how greatly she valued his love.

With that love in mind, Rose had decided Ecanthar's claims could be investigated at a later date. If Gareth truly did need to visit the Fey lands in order to continue living, she'd arrange for them both to travel there as soon as he was fully recovered. She no longer cared if Gareth had needed to marry her to save his life or not. He needed her love just as desperately as he needed to visit Faerie. Of that she had no doubt. The passion and affection they shared was as real and honest as anything she'd ever known.

"Have I told you how much I love you?" he asked, as if reading her thoughts. Which he probably had.

"And I, you." Rose smiled, eagerly accepting the

soft press of his lips to her cheek. "Now what of Ambrose? Did you at least try to reason with—"

"The man will have none of me, as you know. His delicate feelings are wounded, no matter how the gruff bastard denies it. He craves more than a magical bond." Gareth gave her a meaningful look she did her best to ignore.

Rose's and Ambrose's destinies were as tangled as they had ever been. She was more grateful than she could express that he'd freed her from the control of the black elf. Still, she wondered, if he had to make the choice again, would he still banish the terror from her body with his golden magic?

As things now stood, neither of them could live long without the company of the other. They'd be forced to endure each other's presence for several years as his magic rebuilt its strength and Rose learned how to manage the power she had acquired. Without his guidance, the strength of Fey de la Nuit power was more than she knew what to do with. She was as likely to cause an explosion as a small fire in the hearth.

Which occasionally came in useful. Explosions were handy for blasting holes in the rocky soil. She and Ambrose had put the skill to use as they buried her family during their first few days in Myrdrean. They had labored side by side in the old churchyard as Gareth lay in the darkened library, in a sleep so like death it would have devastated Rose if Ambrose hadn't sworn to her his brother would make a full recovery.

"Rose, dearest, you know you mean more to me than anything in this world, and I wouldn't have you risk your health," Gareth said. "But I urge you to—"

"Shhh, I'll go to him in a moment," she said, interrupting Gareth before he could finish his thought. "For now, let us enjoy the sunset."

The longer they spent in her home country, the surlier Ambrose became. Gareth assumed the only cure for his temper was to find a way to break the magical bond between them so that Ambrose might depart Myrdrean for good. He insisted a severing of the tie must be possible, no matter how vehemently Ambrose denied it, and had sent inquiries to his contacts in England asking for aid in the matter.

The Fey de la Nuit Rose had spoken with during their brief stay in Paris had offered another suggestion for managing two men, but Rose was not ready to experiment with that either. No matter that Fey brothers often shared one woman in the faerie lands, she wasn't a creature of those lands. She was a mostly human woman and the very idea of two lovers—both of them in her bed at once—made her cheeks heat as if she were an untried girl.

She was still becoming accustomed to one man in her life, bed, and heart. She wasn't sure if there was room for two, though Ambrose was as dear to her as he had ever been, and there were nights when she dreamed of his hands running over her skin, making the air thick with golden magic.

But even if she was to suddenly crave what the French Fey called the *ménage à trois,* she doubted her husband would entertain the idea. He and Ambrose had called an uneasy truce, but Gareth was possessive of his wife and not inclined to share. Not that Rose could blame him. She wasn't inclined to share her husband either.

"I'll go fetch him," Gareth said. "Enjoy the sun."

"No, sit. You'll exhaust yourself." Rose urged Gareth toward a chair. "And I think Ambrose will be more easily coaxed from his temper by a member of the fairer sex."

"There's no need. I have managed without your gentle ministrations, Rosemarie." Ambrose's voice came from the entry to the parlor, but it didn't surprise her. She was always aware of him, sensing his presence on a soul-deep level even when her conscious mind was otherwise engaged.

"You've worked miracles today, I see," Ambrose said, walking slowly through the room.

Rose had spent the day in the parlor, arranging the furniture that had arrived from Vienna and carefully pasting together the pieces of her mother's porcelain animals she'd salvaged from the wreckage. She'd saved her mother's parlor for last, knowing she would finally feel their new home complete once this special place was restored. They would greet the latest group of immigrants here tonight, welcoming them to their fledgling city.

"Thank you, I'm quite pleased with it," she said, her concern for the future vanishing for a moment as Ambrose smiled that new smile, the human one, filled with hope.

Gareth was mistaken if he thought surliness consumed Ambrose completely. There were times when he was as happy as he'd ever been. Rose could see it clearly, just as she knew he saw her happiness with Gareth, and was pleased by it in a way that made her feel truly loved.

"You *are* truly loved, Rose. More truly than any

woman in the world." Gareth pressed a soft kiss to her hair as Ambrose came to stand at her other side.

And it was right, just then, to stand between the two dear men in her life and look out onto a land no longer haunted by the past, but filled with possibility for the future. A future Rose vowed she would claim as her own.

TOR
ROMANCE

Believe that love is magic

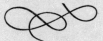

Please join us at the Web site below for more information about this author and other great romance selections, and to sign up for our monthly newsletter!

www.tor-forge.com